Table of

CW01083082

HONOR BOUND
Lady Warrior Saga, Book Three

For Marlona,
Who heard it first

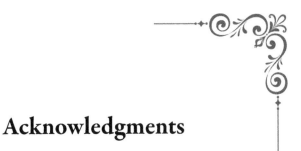

Acknowledgments

You hold in your hands my fifth novel. At this point, I'd like to extend a special thank you to those who have given me their time and expertise, helping me to achieve this milestone. To Sandra Alagona, who fixes everything, to Tamra Riley and Nancy Michael, the best beta readers of all, and to my son, Kevin, who is always willing to walk through a battle with me. To Caragh Artfield for bringing life to my stick figures, and to my husband, Chris, for holding me to high standards. Words cannot express the gratitude I have for the patience, love, and input from all of you. There have been others who have helped so much, including Susan Rathke, Jackie Liddle and Susan Nelson, Marlona Reid and others. Thank you all for all you've done and said. Finally, thank you, Dear Reader, for your continued interest in my stories.

Sherrie Bakelar

August 2023

Into Port

Wood creaked around her. She'd grown accustomed to the shifting, groaning sound and now found it comforting, even though her bunk lay below deck and the waterline. Above her, scuffling footsteps ran back and forth amidships. D'Mique contemplated opening her eyes, but decided against it. She sighed and shifted in the close quarters, relieving the pressure on her shoulder as much as possible without actually rolling out of bed. A member of the merchant ship's crew blew a high whistle to call an end to that morning's hustle. Thumping footsteps continued back and forth above her head. D'Mique opened her eyes and glanced at the wall where a series of tally marks had been carved. One for each day she'd been aboard.

She had a vague memory of the Captain, Dris by name, telling her it was two days to Ebony Bay. *"Wind willing,"* she added to herself with a mirthless smile. Captain Dris had told her this same thing four days after her rescue, and again as they reached Freeport. Another two days and she'd cornered her goblin escort, demanding how much further until Ebony Bay, "wind willing." Chagrined, the goblin, Karok, had admitted that the journey from Freeport to Ebony would take another two cycles. They had lied, but only for her own good. Thinking now, counting her tally marks, she realized it had been for the best. The goblin chiurgeon, true to Karok's word, had worked wonders on D'Mique's wounds. Not as good as an elf, but worth her weight in salt and gold. If D'Mique really had been dropped ashore two days later, the stitches would have torn, her bleeding would have continued, and, she admitted silently—and only to herself—she likely would have died.

There were twenty-three tally marks. She closed her eyes again, listening to the second mate bark orders at the motley crew. Usually, she told them off for slouching about when they should be mending rope, scrubbing the deck, or caring for sails and lines. The commands she gave now brought D'Mique fully awake. It sounded like they were preparing for something big. *"We're here!"* she thought, catching a thrill of excitement in her throat before it could overwhelm her.

She rolled out of bed, slower than she would have liked, but cautious of knocking her head on the wooden beams that crisscrossed the ship inches from her top bunk. She dropped feet-first the last few inches to the deck and glanced around. The quarters were empty. *"Yes,"* she thought, *"We're here!"* She dressed quickly, pulling on the merchant's clothing that had replaced her armor, now long-gone to the scrap heap. The thought brought memories back to the forefront. The black daemons surrounding her, their iron blades and oaken staves bringing her down. T'Pani, the Land-Nymph child, flying free of her arms. Then, darkness and pain. They had her, they had the baby. The daemons had taken her back to the forest where the Tree Daemons no doubt took their prize, leaving D'Mique for dead.

If she'd been with Genow, the elfin healer—and truth be told, one of her best friends—she would have been patched up quickly, no scars, no tales, barely any time to worry or rest. But Genow was far, far away. She had a bright, beautiful, pink set of scars now. Stories to shut down the goblin soldiers in Myrth's halls and tales to tell to children. The chiurgeon had removed the stitches only a few days before, and D'Mique worried that the wounds along her chest, down her back and across her side still struggled to stay closed.

Covered now in a red brocade robe and off-white sailor's trousers, she slipped into a pair of sturdy leather shoes and grabbed the black pack hanging near her bunk. There wasn't much in it, but each member of the merchant's crew had donated something to her. A tinderbox, a flask of mead, some healing herbs, and a handful of coins needed to be enough to get her to Fortress Nightmare, home of the Fire Master. *"Maybe I can get a horse,"* she thought. Was Ebony Bay the Fire Master's territory? She didn't know, but she worried it was not and that the merchants and farmers would do little to help her. She shouldered the pack, moving her long black braid out of the way. The feather-and-bell goblin good-luck charm at the end of her braid tinkled merrily as it fell down her back and rolled side to side as she made her way to the stairs that led up out of the ship's belly.

D'Mique paused at the top of the ladder to close her eyes and take in the warm light of the recently risen Fiery Sisters. The twin suns marked each day the same, only their blue companion varied as he pursued them. She glanced around for the Ghost Moon, the blue sun Rysk, out of habit, though she knew he wouldn't rise until closer to midday. She'd spent nearly half a season at sea, watching Rysk process across the sky. The Ghost Moon rose after sunset, then rose after midnight, rising later and later each day until he was rising with the Sisters less than a cycle ago, and now trailed behind them.

"We've brought you to land, Daemon Slayer," Dris said, approaching, breaking into her meditation. "I know it was a longer trip than you anticipated."

"Lives are at stake, Captain," D'Mique said, green eyes glaring at him.

The sturdy human male frowned, his wrinkles burrowing deeper into his thick face. "As was yours," he replied. She sighed, knowing that they'd had this argument before. "You are but one soldier in a vast army. Let others do the work too."

"I am grateful for your charity in my time of need, Captain. You and your crew," D'Mique added with a glance around at the sailors and guards about her. Her eyes landed on Karok and Sabi, the second mate, a gruff old Canine Semian roughly a foot shorter than D'Mique. Sabi nodded in greeting. The canine smile that ruled Sabi's face pulled an answering smile from D'Mique. Startling blue eyes surrounded by white fur turned to glare sharply up at the sails and the crew clambering about in the rigging. Although her head and face were canine, the rest of Sabi's form was human and, according to Semian tradition, remained covered in light, billowing clothes. D'Mique had only seen her fine-boned hands uncovered once during the journey, and that had been one night when Sabi had helped the chiurgeon bathe D'Mique's wounds. Karok approached with a sheepish grin. D'Mique sighed again, certain of what he was about to say.

"You will be first ashore, Daemon Slayer," he said.

"I would think so."

"I would also be bitter, if I were a young soldier with few battles and fewer wars written on my skin," he acknowledged. "But now, as an old hand, I know the gift we have given you."

"I have thanked you and Captain Dris. Truly, I am grateful," D'Mique replied. "But it was a costly gift and we may never know the true cost."

Karok shifted uncomfortably and looked askance a moment. "Dear, yes, but not priceless and a cost that was not paid selfishly." He grimaced, turning thoughts in his head. "The Masters have vast power, Lady Warrior. Do not be fooled into thinking they are powerless without you. You were given a mission and, from what I gather, failed in it. It is noble to return and report that failure, but a power such as the Earth Master will have planned for that contingency. When you did not report in on time, he would have assumed your failure and moved on to the next option." Karok met her eyes as he spoke. Although his words were guarded, he spoke with conviction. As a goblin speaking about the Earth Master, Karok had to choose his words carefully. He, like all goblins, belonged to the Earth Master. From rocks, sands, and soil they sprung, and to dust they would return. While they lived, they served first their clan and kin, then any lord, sailor, or merchant with coin enough, but always, above all else, even self, they set the Master of Earth and lived and died at his whim.

D'Mique watched Karok fidget again from one foot to the other, then nodded. "There is wisdom in your words, friend," she said.

"Hard won," he agreed, sneering, his fangs gleaming between black lips. "Now, from Ebony Bay, you will need a horse."

"I do not think I have enough coin for one," she admitted. "What advice do you have?" Karok smiled at Dris.

The captain returned the smile and took D'Mique's hand. "I have a string of ponies. We can send you to Nightmare with one, provided it is returned."

Relief painting her face, D'Mique nodded. "Of course," she said. *"Well,"* she thought, *"I'll make good time."*

"Coming 'round!" Sabi shouted. "Pilot!"

"Ah," Dris said. He took his leave as Karok and D'Mique hurried to the bow to watch them close on Ebony Bay.

They'd kept relatively close to the shore as they'd sailed south from Freeport. Though rarely close enough to see beaches, D'Mique had been able to see distant mountains along the horizon from time to time. This morning, the ship had changed heading, veering westward to bring them in close to shore. The headland of the bay was visible to the north, to D'Mique's right. High Spring was bleeding into High Summer, filling the land with green, a starkly different land than the blasted plains and basalt deserts she'd left behind. From the headland, the port city of Ebony Bay slowly crept out of the green forest and frolicked along the heights above the shore. It was larger than most other places D'Mique had been. The only city rivaling it in size was Olimidia, the last of the Shining Cities, home of the Land-Nymphs. However, many more people lived here. D'Mique had been here once before, briefly, on her way to Nightmare the first time. The cold breeze that danced along the waves and played across the ship's deck joined the chill that crept from D'Mique's heart. *"What are you supposed to be?"* the Greater Daemon had hissed, dark, mantis-like head cocked to one side, eyes glowing eerily in the shadows of the throne room. She had no answer for it then. Now? *I am the Daemon Slayer,* she thought in response to the remembered hiss.

Ebony Bay's port held all manner of ships, from fishing boats to large sea-faring galleys. Most of the ships were smaller merchant vessels that plied the waters just offshore, moving goods and people from port to port around the Great Southern Peninsula. Aboard the *Feather and Bell,* D'Mique realized for the first time that the ship was a fair bit larger than many of the other merchant ships. This ship could brave the open oceans and probably made its way out to the island homes of the piscine Semians from time to time. Smaller boats hurried to move away from them as they turned and made their way toward the piers jutting out into the Bay. The *Feather and Bell's* goblin pilot appeared at her elbow, surveying the land and ships around them, his eyes lingering on the small fishing boats that rushed out of their way. Like Karok, his goblin-dark hair had started turning a steely gray and his moss-green skin was rough and weathered by sun, wind, and sea. He looked at D'Mique, smiling when he caught her studying him, his green eyes—almost the twin of hers in color—flashing with merriment. "We'll be in soon enough, Lady," he said before nodding and turning away. She returned the smile and watched him cross the length of the ship to the steering wheel, where he took control. Sabi stood next to him and barked orders to the crew in the rigging as he commanded the ship to slow.

With all the sails furled, the ship slowed and was soon drifting toward the shore. "I think we scared them, Dris!" the pilot shouted. Captain Dris chuckled. He stood midship, surveying both the crew and the port ahead of them. D'Mique smiled at the path that had been cleared for their ship, a watery blue track straight to port. Every ship had scurried aside for the fast-approaching brigantine. The ship continued slowing as they approached a pair of anchored galleys.

Dris, nodding at the sailors' work, moved to stand beside D'Mique. He watched the galleys pass by on their right. "We're still fast, Rol," he shouted at the pilot.

"Bah!" the goblin pilot returned. "We'll slow, we always do."

Dris gave a derisive snort and muttered to D'Mique, "He won't tell you how many times we've had to repair that dock." He motioned vaguely ahead of them. She giggled nervously, her smile fading as a tickle of fear raced through her. She started nervously glancing around at the other ships and small fishing boats, trying to judge how quickly they were losing speed. "It's going to be close, Lady. Prepare for a bit of a bump." Dris continued grumbling and started back toward the pilot and wheel.

"Prepare to dock," Sabi barked.

"Keep 'er steady!" Rol shouted, leaving the wheel and rushing forward to stand beside D'Mique. He leaned out to look down into the water before them. D'Mique followed his gaze. Billowy shapes passed beneath them. "That Dris," Rol muttered before spinning around and rushing back to the wheel. "Bringing her broad," he shouted. Karok followed his words with three short blasts on his whistle, and the crew started running around behind D'Mique, grabbing ropes. Three of them ran forward with the anchor. "Away on my word!" Rol shouted.

"By the pilot's order," Sabi commanded twice, grabbing hold of the mast nearest her, a sudden worried look flashing over her canine brow. "Look alive, Lady!" she called pointing to D'Mique. "Hold on!"

Rol turned the wheel then, slowly, and the *Feather and Bell* started veering south, then he turned it back the other way and they veered back north, as if the great ship had suddenly found itself on a slalom course. More ships had moved out of their way and they were starting to close on the nearest jetties and piers. Rol returned them to their original course, straight toward the docks of Ebony Bay. "Midship!" he shouted, "Away!" The trio holding the anchor threw it overboard midship to D'Mique's left, and Rol turned the ship in that direction once again. They didn't seem to be going very fast, to her eye, as they closed on the dock.

She watched as people started running from the end of the pier nearest them, scurrying out of the way of the oncoming ship. One dour elf remained behind, hands on his hips, scowling as the brigantine weaved its way into port. The dock grew closer and the ship continued, now bearing straight toward it once again. "Oh no," D'Mique breathed, bracing and grabbing onto the railing at her waist. They were coming up to the dock and the ship was not stopping. She expected the crash to come from the front, but instead, the ship suddenly floundered from behind. D'Mique continued forward, her momentum nearly toppling her overboard. She flailed at the wood and managed to stay aboard. The anchor behind them had caught the ship at last and nearly arrested her movement. The *Feather and Bell* bumped hard into the dock, first at the bow then along the left side.

"Tie off port!" Sabi shouted as sailors hustled to secure the ship. Four goblins jumped over the side, falling about four feet to the rolling boards beside the *Feather and Bell*, their Semian and human shipmates casting lines to them.

"Dris!" the glowering elf shouted from near the bow. "There's a reason sane captains don't let goblins pilot! Rol! You mange-spawn!

This is the last time you come barreling into port here! I'll ban the *Feather and Bell* and all your crew from my wharves!"

"Relax, Master Karvyx," Dris returned, "No damage done!"

"You'd ban Rol from the wheel if you want it to stay that way!" the elf returned.

Dris shrugged, "My hands are tied, Master Karvyx. He owns the ship!"

"Ha!" the elf threw his hands up in contempt and turned away, stomping down the pier toward his quarters just offshore.

With the ship moored, the denizens of the jetties slowly returned to the work they'd been doing. Rol and Karok lowered the gangplank to the dock and Sabi anchored it. They studied D'Mique a moment when she approached them, both of them smiling. "We are happy to have served you and the Earth Master," Karok said. "We will not ask for forgiveness regarding the deception, but we hope you will think better of us in time."

"When we meet again, I will welcome you as friends," D'Mique decided after studying them. "Goodbye."

"Swift journey, Lady Warrior," Rol bade, holding out a hand to help her down the gangplank. D'Mique took it to steady herself and held onto him until she could reach Sabi's outstretched hand. Three more strides took her to the dock.

"I am glad we could help you, Lady," Sabi said. "Captain Dris will be with you in a moment and he'll take you to get a pony." D'Mique nodded her understanding. "He has to chat a bit with Karvyx before we can leave." Dris appeared with a stack of papers and a sealed scroll tube, marching down the gangplank to join D'Mique as Sabi bowed a final goodbye.

"Come, Lady. Let me pay Karvyx and we'll be on our way." D'Mique followed him down the pier toward where the elf had disappeared. She studied the dock and the ship as she passed where it'd banged into the dock. The wood looked the worse for wear on the ship. Dris caught her looking and scoffed. "It's his ship," he said. "I just captain for him."

"It surprises me that he's the owner and not you," she said.

"Aye. Pilots sometimes own their ships but usually as part of a company rather than in partnership. Rol and Karok are good owners, if a bit high risk. Why do you think they named her *Feather and Bell*?" he said with a chuckle. They reached the dock master's quarters. Karvyx glared at Dris, glancing at D'Mique for a split second before dismissing her. Like all elves, he had alabaster-white skin and black orblike eyes with no visible pupils or irises. His white hair was short, shaved from the sides of his head, forming a three inch crest down the center of his head. "Master Karvyx. I bear spice and ingots," Dris said as he handed over the papers and scroll, "and one passenger," he indicated D'Mique.

"And you are?" Karvyx asked, studying her.

"I am D'Mique, a member of the Earth Master's Honor Guard."

Karvyx' black orb-eyes narrowed, his pale brow furrowing. "Then you will know his lieutenant, Berle," he said.

"Master Myrth's elfin lieutenant is Commander Sylus." D'Mique corrected, recognizing the question as a test of her story.

"You know Sylus," Karvyx said, impressed.

"I was sent on a mission by Master Myrth and the Land-Nymphs of Olimidia. I am on my way to report back to him."

Karvyx nodded. "You are granted passage, Lady. Dris, against my better judgment, you have a week to move your cargo and reload." Dris bowed in acknowledgement.

"Come, Lady," Dris said. "We will find you a pony and you'll be on your way." They hurried from the dock.

Ebony Bay flowed from the port and climbed the rolling shores ahead of D'Mique. The single story merchant shops mingled with two and three story inns, cafés, and tea houses. The people here, as with many other large cities, were a mix of goblins in armor, human servants and merchants, and a menagerie of Semians—canine and feline being the most common. D'Mique followed Dris through the crowd. They passed wagons and market stalls, turning left and right as they wound their way through the city toward the southern outskirts. As they walked, the close-sitting buildings of the city were left behind and garden patches, small fields, and farmyards appeared.

One field held about ten horses and mules, many of them cinder-gray like the horse D'Mique had ridden in the Blasted Lands. Tears stung her eyes as the remembered screams of her little ashen horse echoed in her mind. "*I tried,*" D'Mique thought. She bit her tongue to remain composed and hurried to catch up to Dris. "Are these them?" she asked.

"Aye," he said, "You can have your pick of the lot, so long as someone from Nightmare is willing to bring her back."

"If I don't bring her back myself, I'll see to it that someone else does," she promised. Dris nodded and waited expectantly. D'Mique looked over the ponies in the field. She wasn't much of a horse-person and had been riding them with any regularity only for about a year. There was a dusky beige one with a flaxen mane, standing calmly in the corner of the yard. "How about that one?" she asked, pointing toward the horse.

"Aye, she'll make it to Nightmare," Dris said. "I'll get you a saddle." He went around to the house that was attached to the stable and disappeared inside. A moment later he reappeared with tack for the pony and was soon leading the mare toward the gate. "Here you are, Lady," he said, handing the reins to her. With his hands free he undid the latch and swung open a portion of the fence to let the pony out. He patted the horse on the neck. "She's sure of foot, won't spook easily. Good little trail pony."

"Hi, girl," D'Mique greeted, letting the horse see her and smell her. "I need your help." She smiled at Dris, "Does she have a name?" she asked.

"Nah, you only name pets, Lady, not working horses."

D'Mique renewed her smile and led the pony through the gate, mounting easily and turning her toward town. "Thanks once again, Dris, for all your aid in my time of need."

"Your forgiveness for delaying you is all I ask in return."

D'Mique nodded and urged the pony onward.

They made quick time through town and were soon at the trade route that ran north and south. Just to her left, D'Mique could see the outer verge of the Bantu stronghold, home to black daemon hordes. The creatures preyed on weak or solo travelers, sometimes mustering enough courage to attack wagons and even nearby settlements. Because the cliffs that tumbled down to the steel-colored waters of Ebony Bay limited the daemons' access to the city, residents and merchants found safe haven even close to the stronghold. Those who traveled through the forest itself, however, faced greater danger and needed to stay away during the night when the black daemons hunted and prowled about.

The road north, also heavily traveled, would be safe enough from the creatures. *"I can do this,"* D'Mique thought to herself. She closed her eyes for a moment and listened to the wind, waves, and birdsong. The Great Southern Wilds had also been a stronghold and the horde that had been born from it had grown up around her, eyes gold, flooded by the tree daemon's spell. She hadn't been able to outrun them in the end, losing T'Pani and nearly her life instead. Being so close to a stronghold once more brought back the fear and pain of that day. "I can do this," she muttered aloud, chasing away the memories.

"Come, Pony," she said, turning north along the road, staying on the coastal side, as far from Bantu as possible without leaving the track. The forest's whispering darkness also reminded her of home and she tried to focus on those memories instead. Her village, Dornak, lay at the heart of another black daemon stronghold called The Nesting by the elves and Semians, and the Dark Forest, by the humans who lived within it. It would take her three days to reach Nightmare. *Three days along the outskirts of this stronghold*, she thought. "I'd best make peace with it," she decided.

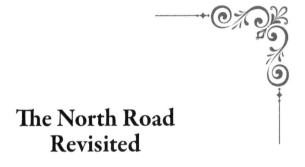

The North Road
Revisited

S he set a steady pace and the pony seemed happy with the quick
walk along the coastal road. It was a pace that would see the
work done, D'Mique decided. *"Get the work done and get back to the
paddock,"* she thought. "We'll be a few days," she said aloud, patting
the horse's neck. The longer she rode, the more certain she was that
this trail pony was the same type of horse as she'd ridden in the
Blasted Lands when she'd still been chasing tree daemons.

There were no other travelers along the road, in either direction.
For the first half of the day, she didn't think much of it. The last
time she'd traveled this way, there hadn't been any fellow travelers,
either. Despite Ebony Bay's status as a bustling port and this being
the main route to Fortress Nightmare and the Black Lands, it lay
empty. Wagons had worn the road, hardened it with their passage
over the months and years. In the winter, it was a difficult, muddy
trail for a laden wagon but now, as High Spring was turning to Mid
Summer, the road was perfect for trade. Yet, it lay empty.

D'Mique stopped midday and dismounted beside the road. The
last time she'd been this way, she and Trillip had stopped just often
enough to rest their horses. They'd pressed on through the days and
camped at night, not wanting to chance drawing black daemons
from the stronghold by walking in the dark. Now, she sat beside
the road, perched on a stump that she was certain others had used
in the same way. She ate berries and a hard biscuit from her pack,

chewing thoughtfully. She remembered Trillip sitting beside her in the light of the setting suns, his bright green eyes intent on the stronghold. While he sat, she'd strained to find any trail, track, or sign that the Greater Daemon had traveled the road in front of them. The Land-Nymph, his taut alabaster-white skin shimmering with pinks and oranges reflected from the setting suns, the light setting his bright pink hair on fire, looked at her and smiled knowingly. *"Oh Trillip,"* she thought, dismissing the memory and closing her eyes, sighing. *"Where are you?"*

He'd traded his life for that of his daughter, T'Pani. The Land-Nymph child wasn't his actual daughter, she was the daughter of the woman Trillip loved, Mara, who had died in childbirth. With Mara gone, Trillip's love and devotion had transferred to T'Pani. When the tree daemons kidnapped the child, Trillip had chased her across the Southern Peninsula to the edge of the Great Southern Wilds, a vast forest that lay north of the peninsula, cutting it off from the rest of the world. At the edge of the Wilds, Trillip had exchanged himself for T'Pani, agreeing to go with the tree daemons instead. Trusting D'Mique to keep T'Pani safe for him. A promise she hadn't been able to fulfill. Now, they were both gone, both of them lost. Every so often she allowed herself to hope that somehow they were both with the tree daemons, trudging north together. Heavy-hearted, D'Mique stood and mounted the pony. *"Report in,"* she told herself. *"Let Myrth know what happened."* She remembered what Karok had said, that Myrth would have had a back-up plan. That they would have moved on when she didn't return right away. She'd disappeared nearly a season ago. What had happened in that interim? Frowning, she urged the pony into a short canter.

As Nix and Col set, D'Mique pulled aside and made camp. The clearing she'd stopped at had been used for the same purpose before, the firepit well-defined and a horse line still strung between two pines. Finding a tinderbox in the saddlebag, she collected a few dead logs and some kindling to start a fire. Soon, its cheery light pushed away the wane shadows cast by Rysk, who was nearing its zenith. Unlike some, D'Mique counted day and night by the Fiery Sisters and when they rose and set. For many elves, "day" was when any of the three stars were in the sky, which led to some very long walks when Sylus was in charge. She sat staring at the stronghold across the road. Bantu's trees had pulled away from the road here, its stillness and the sense of unease it caused fading the further she was from it. She'd grown up in a daemon stronghold and had only noticed the sense of unease daemon strongholds caused when she'd been away from one for a long time. She studied the space between her and Bantu. "What do you think, Pony?" she asked aloud. "Do we sleep?" The horse continued clipping grass, silent. "Yeah," D'Mique thought. "I'll keep you safe. You sleep. Just stay on the road tomorrow while I doze," she added with a sigh.

D'Mique dozed while Rysk passed the hours. As the blue sun set, she forced herself to stand, hoping that the hours of fitful dozing would be enough to keep her awake while she waited out the true night hours. Nothing stirred in the darkness and no black daemons crawled from the forest across the road, beyond the clearing. Just as the coastal chill was burrowing into her bones, the stars started to fade. Dawn was coming. She moved away from the pine where she'd been standing near the pony, and stirred the fire to life. Then she found a few more dead branches to pile on it, enough to chase the cold from the campsite. To the west, Nix and Col would soon rise. Given how late he'd been up at night, Rysk would still be some hours behind them. D'Mique's activity woke the pony, who seemed happy enough to clip grass as D'Mique ate biscuits and berries for the second day.

She'd cleared camp and was on the road north again before the Fiery Sisters touched the sky, throwing their red-gold light across the plains. A short time later, she left the coast behind and the road turned inland as Bantu dropped away behind her, the wide grass plains replaced by black outcrops of basalt and stands of scrub oak. The road rose steadily as she traveled that day. She stopped near a creek that was making its way out of the foothills so that the pony could drink. Dismounting, she pulled nuts and a wrapped wedge of cheese from the pack for a quick lunch. She surveyed the food remaining. It was just enough to see her to Nightmare. Stooping, she took a drink from the creek, then mounted again and urged the pony onward.

As Nix and Col closed the day, D'Mique pulled off the road again. She'd reached the higher plains where the volcanic deserts of the Black Lands tumbled down to the Fanterra Plain. Ahead of her, the land peaked in a smooth ridge that ran east to west as far as she could see. She knew from her last journey that the ridge marked the beginning of the Black Lands. Beyond, the land fell gently into a shallow bowl-shaped valley marked with large swaths of lava rock. "We'll stay here tonight," she whispered to the pony. The day had passed once again with no other person seen on the road. In the fading light, D'Mique studied the road, reading the signs of passage. She found wagons, horses, and people all heading north into the Black Lands. There had been so many she couldn't count them all. At least five laden wagons, an assortment of horses and their riders. Dozens of people on foot. All had passed along the road recently, although none were here now. "There's something going on," she said to herself. There were no signs that pointed to trouble or strife, no battles and no blood. Worried, D'Mique dozed fitfully through the night.

The next day, she grimly carried on. The road entered the foothills, winding between black outcrops as it climbed the ridge. At the top, the land fell away into the Black Lands' valley bowl. At the center, visible in the mid-morning light, sat the obsidian fortress, Nightmare, the Fire Master's seat of power. When she'd first entered the valley the year before, the fortress and its surroundings had been lost in a fog. Now, she could see its towers gleaming far below her. Farmland and towns ringed the fortress in contrast to the other Masters' palaces. Dragon Ridge stood on a lonely mountain; Sea Spray sat on an island in the middle of a lake; and the Wind Mistress' Floating Castle was usually moored near a volcanic peak. Where other Masters seemed feared, Marladon seemed embraced.

The trail pony delivered her quickly down into the valley. Farms dotted the road, some of them with roadside stalls. Here, at long last, she found others. Furtive men and women barely glanced toward her, weighing her and the horse quickly before looking away and carrying on with their work. Occasional market stalls, laden with fruit and vegetables, were manned by the farmers' children—humans, Semians, and even elves comprised the Black Lands population. D'Mique kept her own eyes from straying and focused on the road and her pony instead. She hurried onward until the farms fell away and she entered a large, defensible perimeter. At the center sat the obsidian Fortress Nightmare. Large black walls sprang from the edge of a deep moat. Instead of water, the moat was full of a thick, deep gray fog. Mythical beasts filled it, according to the stories. The year before, as she and Trillip closed on Fortress Nightmare, they'd walked through the Moat Fog and even dropped into the moat without actually seeing any beasts. *"Maybe,"* she thought suddenly, *"they are a myth. One of the few myths that remained a myth,"* she continued, chagrined at how often things she thought were myth proved real once she'd left her walled village.

There were a few older guards at the drawbridge as she approached and they waved in greeting. She dismounted at the bridge and waited for the greeter to approach her. "Your business?" he asked.

"I am here to speak to Master Marladon. I'm with Myrth's Honor Guard," she said.

The human guard nodded at her words. "The Master is gone, but his steward is here. Come," he motioned her forward as he turned around. She followed him, leading the pony across the thick wooden bridge to the barbican, where the other guards were raising the portcullis. Passing through, she stepped into the cobblestone courtyard. For a moment, she remembered the four human guards who had greeted her and Trillip seasons before. How they'd disarmed the pair and then led them in to see the "Fire Master," the Greater Daemon, who'd taken the fortress and enslaved Marladon's dragon army, throwing the real Fire Master in the dungeon to die. Now, there were no guards at the door. The older human signaled for her to wait, and he stood at his ease beside her.

A moment later, Kryoso exited the fortress and hurried down to her, calling out her name. As all elves were basically the same—pale white skin, black orb-eyes, and white hair—Mortaks were also similar. Kryoso's black hair had grown longer since she'd last seen him, his lightly bronzed skin stretched taut over sculpted muscles that D'Mique had rarely seen on any other fighter. His bulk had always seemed misplaced to her, since he was a mage. She smiled and waved at him. His lilting voice also jarred against the male perfection of his physical stature. "What are you doing here?" he asked. D'Mique hesitated, mouth open but no words would come. Tears welled in her eyes and she caught a sob in her throat. He was in front of her, his silver orb-eyes, pupilless, irisless, but full of shine that reflected her face back at her, filling with concern, his brows knitting and his mouth frowning. "Oh," he took her into his arms and held her close. "What happened?" he whispered against her ear. He pulled away and studied her, trying to find an answer in her clothing and the small pony she'd ridden.

"Come, sit," he led her toward a nearby crate. She dropped the pony's reins and allowed Kryoso to lead her to the crate where she sat. He wore black leggings and a red billowing shirt and black vest combination. It looked satiny and made for throne rooms and parties. Kryoso was Marladon's steward. The two Mortaks were nearly inseparable, even though she'd first met Kryoso when she'd joined Myrth's Honor Guard. The Mortak stood in front of her, schooling his face to a calm, respectful stillness.

"I need to talk to Myrth," D'Mique managed. "Is Marladon's jar here? Could you use it?"

"I can use it, but it's not here," Kryoso replied with a head shake. The Masters each had a set of three glass jars they could use to communicate with one another. No one had ever explained how the magic worked although it had something to do with forcelines. According to Marco, Myrth's human apprentice, each jar was a construct. He wasn't sure how the Air Mistress and Earth Master had made them and when he tried to explore their makeup, he grew lost and confused by them.

"It's an emergency, Kryoso," D'Mique whispered.

"Everything is," Kryoso said. "Marladon marches north with the dragon army. If you hurry, you can catch them," Kryoso suggested, "they left yesterday morning but are slow and heavy. I can get you a fresh horse."

D'Mique sat in thought a moment, his words sinking in. "I promised to return this pony to Captain Dris, to a paddock on the southern outskirts of Ebony Bay," she said at last. "Can someone take her back?"

Kryoso bowed his head. "I will see to her personally," he promised. "Let's stable her for now and I'll get you some provisions. Maybe some armor and weapons?" he suggested, his silver orb-eyes traveling the length of her, brows knitting in concern. She nodded, standing. "And a sturdy mount for the coming war," he added with a sigh.

"What happened here, Kryoso?" she asked, following him at last into the unnaturally silent fortress.

"It's a long story, Lady," he said with a wry smile. "Come inside and I'll tell you all I know."

The Guard in Gaity

Sunlight bathed the Earth Master's workroom but it did not drive the chill from the air. The large, plate glass, transom-like windows were open, letting errant breezes in to dance through the drying herbs that hung from the rafters, and play in the chains and metal baubles that cascaded from a series of hooks near the Master's jewelry-making equipment. The Earth Master's hobbies, jewelry-making and herbology, belied the power held by the hawk Semian, Myrth. He sat now on the tall stool, his half-made bracelets forgotten while his pearl-gray eyes lingered on the water-filled jar near his elbow. His apprentice, Marco, remained motionless, the odd conversation Myrth had just had with the Water Master Nepo playing over in his head. *"He seems happy enough to play the part of prisoner at the moment,"* Nepo had said. Marco had the impression that the arrangement was tenuous. Tekalo had captured a Nura—whatever that was—the one responsible for killing the Matriarch in Olimidia. It was at Sea Spray but Nepo wanted the Masters to escort it to Olimidia or Gaity to stand trial for murder.

Marco reached out tentatively along the forcelines, feeling Myrth's weight beside him, judging the hawk-man's mood. The Master schooled his emotions to a calm stillness out of habit. When he became agitated, the earth shook around him and mountains could tumble down or the surface of the planet open up beneath his feet. The Earth forcelines that crisscrossed the Fanterra Plain intertwined with his soul, giving him control over everything from the fertility of the farmer's fields to the free-flowing patterns of the dunes in the Southern Desert. Myrth, like the other elemental Masters, used this vast power to steady the Plain and maintain the calm, predictable patterns of everyday life for those who lived on the Southern Peninsula and beyond. As his apprentice, Marco still had a lot to learn regarding the stillness of the earth. Through the winter, he'd learned to keep the Soil line steady. Over the last several days, Myrth had started allowing him to enter the Mage Realm once more, teaching him to end each session by smoothing the forcelines and calming the Earth Cloud. Normally, Myrth paced to expend his nervous energy as it bled off in small earthquakes but now, he just sat quietly still, staring at his communication jar.

"Master?" Marco asked.

Myrth stirred. "Prepare my honor guard, Marco. Choose two elves and two goblins; Genow should come with us. We need to travel quick and light," he ordered.

"Yes, Master," Marco ducked his head in a slight bow and left quickly. He exited the workroom through a thick oaken door and crossed a small antechamber to Myrth's throneroom. Goblin guards tossed him glances as he entered the sepulcherian chamber. Myrth's throne, carved from solid rock, hid a stairway down to his living quarters. Torches threw their weak light across the room, striving to drive the shadows into the corners. However, to Marco's eyes, the world was bathed in the golden light of the Earth Cloud superimposed over the darkness and the torches mattered little. Marco hurried behind the throne and disappeared down the stairway into the Earth.

Warm wood and deep, lavish, red and gold carpeting and wall hangings decorated the living quarters. From the bottom of the stairs, halls ran to the left and right, forming a square around Myrth's private suite. Marco's room was to the right, but he started left instead, stopping at the first room and knocking. The Sun Goblin,

Auros, opened the door, smiling when he saw Marco. "Chosen One, we felt your approach. I thought you were supposed to be sneaking?" he said. Marco returned the smile. He liked the jovial goblin who had taken Tierren's position after the defeat of the Greater Daemon the previous year. Auros and his blood brother and roommate, Gado, had relished testing Marco's growing power through the winter. They could feel him in the forcelines as a strong echo to Myrth but if he concentrated, he could hide from them.

"No time for games, Auros," Marco said. "Pack for travel, light and quick, you and Gado."

"Yes, Chosen," he said, his smile fading and his demeanor switching instantly from convivial to a disinterested aloofness.

Marco nodded and turned away, impressed by how quickly the goblin could change between his friendly off-duty personality to his no nonsense, on-duty, Honor Guard one. He continued around the square, stopping at the door near the next turning. A soft knock brought Vellin to the door. The elf opened it cautiously, glancing up at Marco, studiously assessing his expression with black orb eyes that reflected the diffuse light of the corridor back at the human. "Vellin, Myrth needs you and Squirm. Pack light and quick. We need to leave."

"Where?" the elf asked. His thin white hair made a wispy halo in the dancing lantern light behind him.

Marco thought through the conversation he'd heard. Nepo wanted to move the Nura to Olimidia or Gaity. "Sea Spray," Marco said, turning away. He did not wait for the elf's response.

Beyond Vellin's room, a rough-hewn corridor branched away from the private quarters. At its far end, a massive stone door sat closed, defended by Mud Goblins. Through the door lay the keep of the Earth Master, Dragon Ridge with its contingency of goblins and enough human, elfin, and Semian soldiers to support the keep. Past the rough-hewn corridor sat D'Mique's unused room and, leading to the center of the square, the door to Myrth's quarters. Marco sighed, stopping at D'Mique's door. Nepo hadn't mentioned anyone except Tekalo but he knew from Clippen that D'Mique, Burl, and a handful of mages from the Academy had set off with Trillip and Tekalo in pursuit of the Matriarch's killers two cycles ago. He smiled, memories of the spunky Lady Warrior playing through his mind as he pressed on. The room beyond hers was Genow's, his last stop. He knocked on Genow's door.

"Oh, Marco," Genow greeted. "How are you?" Genow had been the first to befriend him last summer when he and D'Mique had joined Myrth's Honor Guard in Dragon Ridge. When the rest of the honor guards had teased them and dismissed them because they were human, Genow had chosen to stand beside them. He was short for an elf, only slightly taller than the diminutive commander, Sylus. As other elves, he kept his white hair cut long, pulled back away from his face. His black orb-eyes beamed at Marco.

"We need to pack quickly and travel light, Genow. Myrth had a message from Nepo and we need to hurry to Sea Spray." Marco said, cutting off the elf's friendly greeting.

"Now?" he asked.

"Yes, now. I'll meet you and the others at the throne."

"Who?" Genow asked, a pout threatening to darken his light-heartedness.

Marco passed the elf a smile. He knew who Genow was partial to and had let that dictate whom he chose. "Auros-Gado, Vellin, and Squirm."

Genow clicked his tongue and rolled his eyes at the use of the nickname "Squirm." "He hates it when you call him that."

"Squirm is a good nickname," Marco said, burying his smile. "It's apropos."

"It—"

Marco cut him off with a wave. "Hurry, Myrth will be ready soon." He chuckled to himself at the elf's exasperation as he turned the corner and made for his room, leaving Genow to harumph at his back. Marco's room sat in the corner of the square opposite Auros-Gado. Like Tierren and Rogan, Auros and Gado were sworn by blood to protect one another, even unto death. For Tierren and Rogan, it was a one-sided affair with Rogan swearing to repay Tierren for saving his life. With Auros and Gado, the bond was two-way, making them painfully, exquisitely, inseparable. So much so, that they were nearly a single entity. They were both master swordsmen and Earth Mages, although neither of them wielded much power. It took Gado nearly twenty minutes to enter the Mage Realm without any interruptions. While they'd both studied enough magic to be safe, neither of them would bother working spells defensively or offensively, focusing instead on the odd parlor trick. Marco secretly believed that Myrth had brought them to Dragon Ridge in order to give Marco practice at soothing the Earth forcelines.

At his door, Marco reached out to the Earth Cloud and changed its pattern, unlocking his door. He paused momentarily to check the forcelines. Closing his eyes, he mentally glanced down at his body. Earth shimmered along his skin, changing it from soft brown to golden. From Marco's core, Earth formed strands of golden power that trailed off into the Mage Realm before joining with others. The strands formed currents, like rivulets, coming together to create a river. The flow of Earth eventually ran from Dragon Ridge to the World Dome at Gaity where it spilled into the Void. The lines passing through Marco danced and bounced, tracing undulating waves through the air. With a deep, slow breath, Marco willed them to stay still and they responded, the waves decreasing until each line moved languidly through space. There were six total now, he'd started with a single one, Soil, last autumn. While Myrth continued to maintain the largest cords, the Bedrock and Plates, he called them, he'd passed Marco a few regional areas to go along with his Soil. Now, the apprentice held the sand of the Southern Desert and the lava rocks of the Blasted Lands, Black Lands, and Broodlands. Most recently, Myrth had given him control of the forest mud of the Nesting. When they were smooth and languid, which took only a moment of concentration, Marco opened his eyes and opened his door.

At first, the room had been set up for him and a roommate, but after the death of the Greater Daemon, it had been upgraded to a private room. Like the other rooms in the underground keep, magic windows brought light and life to those who lived below. Here, Marco's windows looked out on the Nesting and his village, Trinik. In the village window, a large plate glass that nearly covered the entire wall to his left, he occasionally saw his mother and father. He knew there was no way to communicate with them, but watching his mother chase the village boys around the green or catching a glimpse of his father with the town leaders brought a smile to his face. Opposite the village window, Marco had arranged three large bookshelves and his table and chairs. Between the door and the bookshelves, he'd hung a map of the forcelines, one he'd seen before in Tekalo's room.

He pulled a travel pack from his wardrobe and opened it to stare in at the contents. He'd packed it months before and set it aside at Auros' urging. It held a change of clothes, a small knife, tinderbox, and suturing materials. He glanced around the room, his eyes lighting on other clothes, his cloak, a comb for his hair, and a handful of scrolls he'd been reading. He added the comb, and a second shirt to the pack, then grabbed a black, feathered cap that hung from a hook near the village window. Proudly, he smoothed the three red feathers by running them between his fingers before he donned the Potent cap. Last year, his cap had held only two red

feathers but once he'd been apprenticed to Myrth, Palo, the Grand
Syra, leader of the Fanterra Plain, had insisted Marco add a third to
show his true level of skill.

Commander Sylus despised the Potent cap but Myrth didn't
seem to mind. Marco had earned it while training in Gaity with
the Grand Syra's mage army, the Potentate. Like others before him,
although he was a member of the Potentate and answerable to the
Grand Syra Palo, he was first the Chosen of Earth and served Myrth
before all others. Marco was certain that Sylus only disapproved of
him wearing the cap because he was a commander in the rival army
at Olimidia and the Academy had lost bragging rights to a powerful
Earth Mage when Marco joined the Potentate. Marco smiled at his
reflection in the mirror that hung on the wardrobe's door before
turning and leaving with his pack. *"Sylus is staying here to look after
the keep,"* he said to himself while giving his cap a jaunty tilt. He
turned back the way he'd come, away from the throne room exit and
caught Genow as the Healer exited his own room, a similar pack
slung over his narrow shoulder.

Genow's orb-eyes landed briefly on Marco's cap and the three
feathers, pulling a smile from the elf's thin lips. "Sylus is staying
behind, then?" Genow noted.

"Someone has to be in charge," Marco replied. They reached the
corridor that led to the keep just as Vellin and Squirm exited their
room. The pair of elves could have been Genow's relatives, although
they were not. Vellin, who was older than Genow, had grown ageless
in appearance. His pale skin had lost any wrinkles or blemishes,
while his black orb-eyes felt immensely heavy as he gazed upon the
world. This agelessness coupled with the elfin natural affinity for Life
magic and seemingly supernatural healing abilities had given rise to
the myth that immortal elfin warriors existed. While they did not,
Vellin came close. The accomplished swordsman was accompanied
by Sennet, his young charge. When Sennet and Vellin had first

joined them at Dragon Ridge, the young elf had squirmed at each introduction, practically fainting from nervousness when Marco and the Land-Nymph Trillip had greeted him. He'd nearly keeled over at the sight of D'Mique. Although he had calmed over the winter and could even hold a conversation with one of the warriors without turning bright pink from embarrassment, not before earning his nickname, "Squirm."

Marco and Genow turned down the rough-hewn corridor toward the Keep, walking quickly. As they neared the stone door, Marco grabbed hold of the Earth Cloud and used his will to move the boulder aside, startling the Mud Goblin that stood on the other side in the center of the doorway. The large brute stepped aside, bowing, "Chosen," he rumbled. Marco paused, closing his eyes as he returned the bow. A quick glance at the forcelines and he was able to smooth them, falling only a step behind Genow. Opening his eyes again, he hurried on, catching up to the shorter elf in a matter of steps.

At the next juncture, Genow and Marco turned toward the kitchen and the stores. Ahead of them, Auros-Gado were already outside the storeroom, collecting rations for a swift journey. Auros scratched his thin white nose. "Not too slow," he said, approvingly. Gado smiled at them, acknowledging Marco from where he crouched, working with the straps on his travel pack. Like Auros, he was a Sun Goblin. Whereas most of the goblins Marco knew were Mountain Goblins—their skin coming in various greens, browns, and oranges and their hair black—these two were Sun Goblins, with pale skin and hair. Gado's pale orange hair was plaited tight against his skin, his long braid decorated with a bell and feather. D'Mique had worn the same, Marco knew, although he hadn't understood the significance of the objects until the winter nights grew long and Auros-Gado had started spending time with him. They'd shared stories of their homes and past adventures with one another through those dreary, wet evenings.

Gado's good luck charm tinkled as he stood and smiled at Marco. "We ordered yours for you," he said with a sly grin. He had a clipped accent—as if each word was being bitten off right as it ended—that Marco had never heard before. Gado patted Marco's chest in a friendly manner twice as he passed. Marco's quick glance down showed the Earth Cloud embracing Gado where he touched Marco, an oddity that Marco had only noticed with goblins. When others touched him, they sent the Earth Cloud shimmering away in waves and billows.

Genow, closest to the counter, turned to the quartermaster and asked, "Did they order us birdseed or anything like that?" Auros laughed at the question then nodded to Vellin and Squirm who were just arriving, before bidding Marco adieu with a touch of his finger to his forehead and following Gado back the way they'd come.

Vellin sighed, stopping next to Marco as the quartermaster assured Genow the goblins had ordered them all the same rations: meat, bread, berries, and fish for five days. "Is that the party, then?" he asked. "Auros-Gado, and us?" Marco nodded, opening his pack and passing it to Genow who returned to the quartermaster to fill it. Next to Genow, Squirm collected the rations for himself and Vellin. "It will be a good trip then," Vellin concluded under his breath.

"My goal was to keep Genow happy," Marco whispered, low enough that the Healer wouldn't hear. Vellin bit back a chuckle as Squirm rejoined them. The thin, young elf had barely enough muscle on his bones to hold himself up, never mind any sort of weapon. From what Marco could tell, he wasn't magically inclined either. Familial obligations had sent him to Vellin as a charge and Marco suspected the ageless elf kept Squirm out of loyalty, not love. Yet, except for calling him by the nickname he hated, everyone treated the young elf well, especially Vellin.

"Do you know why we are going to Sea Spray, Chosen One?" Squirm asked. His black orb-eyes wide with excitement.

Marco hesitated. "I do," he started cautiously, "sort of. Myrth will explain before we leave." He added, "This is just an escort," to set the elves at ease. Vellin nodded and motioned for Squirm to follow him. They left as Genow rejoined Marco, travel packs full, one slung over his shoulder.

"My thanks, Marco, for choosing the party you did," Genow said with a look that said he'd heard Marco's and Vellin's exchange. While the Healer had no qualms against any of the goblins, for some unknown personal reason, he disliked the other two elves whom Myrth had chosen to serve in his Honor Guard after the Greater Daemon had died. Marco nodded at the Healer's words.

They hurried back the way they'd come, the Mud Goblin sliding the heavy stone door closed behind them, sealing Myrth's private residence away from the remainder of the Keep once again. Once they'd reached the throne room, they joined the remaining Honor Guard before Myrth's throne. He sat there, his dragon fairy, Jerrold, draped across his lap. Myrth ran his three fingered, taloned hands through the dragon's mane, eyes closed. Marco could feel him in the Earth Cloud all around them and knew his Master was working to smooth forcelines and maintain the deeper currents. Sylus stood with the three unchosen guards, Burl's roommate Chay, and the elves, Nayoren and Leeto. His brow furrowed when he noticed the Potent Cap but he remained silent. Myrth withdrew from the forcelines and surveyed the group who stood with Marco, weighing them.

He nodded. "That will do," he said, his deep voice rumbling through the gloom. As he spoke, his thickened lips and hawk beak moved very little, his words forming in his throat instead. His pearl gray eyes flicked to Sylus. "You are in charge, Sylus. Stay ready to join us."

"Master," the elfin commander acknowledged with a bow. Myrth rose, moving Jerrold from his lap to his shoulder. The long dragon wrapped around from one shoulder to the other, draping his front legs over one shoulder and his back over the other, his tail coiling under Myrth's chin. The Master wore a long-sleeve white shirt that billowed around his human body and was tucked into sturdy black pants. His black palace boots made no sound as he led the way out of his throne room through the main door and into Dragon Ridge's courtyard. Gray cobblestones formed a veranda that fanned outward toward the base of a large white, marble tower, the Tower of the Elements, and a burbling fountain full of cavorting statuary. Horses for the Honor Guards, Genow, and Marco stood ready near the rose garden that surrounded the tower and fountain. Myrth whispered to his dragon and bent to let the fairy slink off his shoulders and onto the cobblestones. With a shimmer, Jerrold began to grow, transforming from the snakelike lap dragon to a horse-sized riding dragon. His sharp ivory horns and white mane remained distinctive. When the shimmering stopped, Myrth mounted the dragon. Sylus handed him a black silk cushion and his travel pack. "Safe journey to you all," he said.

"Gaity, then," Myrth instructed, urging Jerrold toward the gate. At the command, eyes all around flicked to Marco. Marco gave them all an exaggerated frown and shrug. Vellin and Auros chuckled as they fell in line behind Myrth.

They moved quickly. Leaving the Keep, they took the disused track down through the rolling mountains and at the first fork, turned west. The spring morning was still heading toward noon as they hurried through the forest. Marco and Genow flanked Myrth, while Auros-Gado took the rear. Vellin led the way, followed by his charge. A few hours travel and they left the Dragon Hills and Forest behind.

The Fanterra Plain stretched before them to the north, south and west. The track they followed led from the Dragon Hills Forest to Gaity, the capital city of the Southern Peninsula. Roughly halfway to Gaity, another road turned north. Following that track, which is the path the guards normally took, would take them northeast to Olimidia, the city of the Land-Nymphs.

They rode on through the day until Nix and Col began to set. The twin red suns sat near the horizon while Rysk, which had risen near noon, had just passed the zenith. Myrth stopped at a well-worn campsite. "We'll rest a moment but we need to hasten to Gaity so that I can consult Palo." As he spoke, the company clambered out of their saddles to stretch and rummage in packs for food.

"A long ride and then sleep, Master?" Vellin asked with a quick glance toward Squirm. Myrth nodded and Vellin returned it, contemplatively.

Genow frowned at Marco, "Do you know why?" he whispered. Marco shook his head no. "Hmm," Genow studied him, "That is the 'I can't talk about it' denial," he said. Marco frowned at him in turn but could think of nothing else to say.

Squirm hovered near Genow, eating berries from his pack. "It's a mystery then," he said. "We are pulled from our cozy beds, and rushed off across the plains to the capital for a secret meeting."

"Welcome to the life of a soldier," Marco said to the young elf with a smile.

Genow chuckled, "You'll get used to it, Sennet. Not everything is worth knowing. The burdens that move Myrth and Marco to action are not ones you need to carry."

"Do we need to know them?" Vellin asked, looking at Myrth instead of Marco and Genow.

"No," Myrth said without thought. "Your charge is safe, Captain." Vellin ducked his head in acknowledgment. Myrth's use of the elf's title caught Marco's attention. Over the winter, the hawk Semian had rarely used it, referring to him instead simply by name. Given the elfin custom of not using names except between close friends and family, its use suggested that Myrth and Vellin had been friends for years.

"We'll reach Gaity in the early morning," Auros said after a moment, "Before the suns rise. I've never been ferried across in the dark."

"We'll be fine," Marco said. For a moment, he remembered the last night crossing he'd made and the shielding he'd created to keep the light, flat ferry safe from the probing korsks—whale-sized daemon-spawn creatures who hunted in the channel at night.

"No doubt, no doubt," Auros replied, holding a hand up defensively. "We should carry on then, Master." He mounted, joining Gado on the track. Not waiting for Myrth and the others, the two goblins started westward. Myrth nodded and remounted the dragon, following them, flanked by Vellin and Squirm. Genow and Marco climbed into their saddles and took the rear guard.

"Is Sennet really safe?" Genow asked when he was certain they were far enough away from Myrth that the Master wouldn't hear.

"I think so, Genow," Marco said, watching the pale elves ahead of him, their Palace Blacks on either side of the blue and green scaled dragon. "I'm not sure we are, but I know Vellin and Myrth won't put Squirm in harm's way if they can help it." Genow chuckled. To Marco, it held a bitter edge. He looked at the Healer then. The elf's black orb eyes gave away little. Genow's inviting, jovial face held clouds of concern, his brows furrowed. "Sennet will be safe," Marco reiterated, "but Myrth did request you come with us. This isn't a simple message delivery or minor dispute. Something big is happening." Genow sighed and nodded.

They rode through the night, dozing in their saddles in turn. Crossing the plains with such a large party was generally safe. Any ne-er-do-wells that hunted this road with regularity would know Myrth at first sight and none would be willing to take on the Master of Earth. Additionally, less sentient beings would think twice about attacking such a strong party. That only left animals and daemon-spawn to harass them, but none did. They rested in the early morning hours with Rysk long set, just a few miles shy of Gaity Banks and the ferries to Gaity. Doing so, they decided, would be a wiser choice than rushing to Gaity, only to be turned away by a half-asleep Grand Syra.

Marco lay on the grass, wrapped in a wool blanket and the Earth Cloud, his head on his saddle. Myrth sat near him, dozing and meditating, tending the forcelines when awake. Marco could feel his work in the surrounding Earth Cloud. Over the weeks, it had become comforting to Marco to feel Myrth in the forcelines. Myrth stirred next to him and their eyes met. The hawk-man's face was unreadable. Marco smiled, encouragingly. "They're tended well," his Master admitted. Marco's smile grew smug. "Another week, and I'll give you a couple more."

"Does Tekalo tend forcelines?" Marco asked, a sudden thought occurring to him. He'd befriended the Chosen of Water while hunting down the Greater Daemon last year, and had never known the Land-Nymph to meditate.

"No," Myrth said. "Water doesn't form forcelines that need to be tended." Myrth sighed. "Also, Nepo has kept all his power until Tekalo matures. Once he can trust his apprentice, he will begin teaching him."

Marco chewed on Myrth's words for a moment. "Thank you for your trust, Master," he said at last.

"Hmph," Myrth chuckled darkly, the earth rumbling under him and eddying toward the others. Marco watched the Earth Cloud bounce up and down and ripple outward from the Semian. "If I recall, you stole my power. I am making the best of a bad situation." Marco's mood fell and he had to catch his own forcelines to stop them from furrowing as well. "Yet," Myrth continued, "I do appreciate your serious study and dedication to your work."

"Thank you," Marco whispered, half-aware of the world around him as he smoothed his forcelines. "I am grateful for your lessons." He finished his work and turned his full attention to Myrth. Myrth was still looking at him.

Myrth whispered through his mind, *"Be very careful, Marco. Step into the Mage Realm. Do that first, deliberately, before you do the work. Mages that don't have to step into the Mage Realm do not live long. Powerful people need to think we are controllable and counter-able."* The deep, gravelly voice shushing through his head sent shivers down Marco's spine. He nodded his understanding. Mages needed to step into the Mage Realm to work. Spells lasted only as long as the mage concentrated on it and remained focused on the Mage Realm. Everyone learned at a young age that the way to stay safe from a mage was to distract them and break their concentration. Yet some mages, those with the greatest power, could permanently change the Physical Realm, their spells continuing after they'd left the Mage Realm. These were the Masters. Few and far between, they were often feared beyond their small circle of friends and acquaintances. Finally, although there was no proof, rumors persisted about mages who could work magic from the Physical Realm. They didn't have to step into the Mage Realm to call the power to their will. Unstoppable boogeymen, these overpowered mages would be put to death if ever discovered. Marco knew that only another powerful mage would realize he was working with the forcelines from the Physical Realm but Myrth was right to admonish him. It wouldn't take much to turn allies against him. The fear of the Masters beyond their small circle of friends and acquaintances would pale beside the need for self-preservation that would bring Marco a swift death if someone ever realized how powerful the Mage of Man truly was.

As the Fiery Sisters rose, the party returned to the road, assuring they'd reach the ferry after sunrise. As they neared the shore, Myrth stopped, dismounted, and spoke to Jerrold. With a trill, like a songbird, the dragon fairy shrank, returning to his original size. Myrth took the saddle pack from the ground and replaced it with the black cushion, standing back as the dragon curled up on the pillow.

With a shimmer of magic, the dragon fairy changed. Starting at its tail, the scales turned to embroidery, stitching the dragon fairy onto the cushion. Marco and the other guards had seen the transformation often enough that it did not elicit the gasps and fear Marco remembered from the first time he'd ever seen the fairy change. The red and gold scales of Jerrold's toes turned into tiny cross-hatched stitching, as his blue and green scales turned into satiny patches of floss. The magic traveled up his body, trapping his head to the pillow last. The dragon smiled and winked, the mischievous expression caught forever on the silk pillow. Myrth bent and picked up the fairy embroidered pillow, tucking it under one arm. He stood next to the Palace Black Squirm rode and waited while the young elf dropped out of the saddle. Myrth then mounted and started down the road, Auros-Gado flanking him. Vellin reached down and helped Squirm up onto the second Palace Black before following the others, Marco and Genow bringing up the rear.

The road crested a hill and spilled down to the shore; the Endless Ocean greeting them. Here, the plains rolled from grass to a rocky bay. A long, sturdy pier ventured out into the shallow channel, pointing toward a large wooded island beyond. Enormous white banners bearing black circles, signaling that the ferry port was open, covered the island's granite cliffs. A half-dozen ferries plied the waters between the mainland and the cliffs of Master Island. There, the capital city Gaity nestled under the boughs of an ancient pine forest. North of the ferries, a small group of inns and market stalls called Gaity Banks huddled near the shore as well.

In the time of the Hero Masters, when the first Greater Daemon had broken the forcelines and the elements ran rampant, the first Masters had retreated to this island. Hoping to distance themselves from the rift made by the daemon as they wrestled with their newfound powers, giving the island its lofty-sounding name. The city, along with the representative government that ruled the Southern Peninsula, had been the creation of the First Water Mistress, Syra. The elf had given her name to the position she'd created, overseeing the government as the Grand Syra.

Nearing the ferry docks, the party dismounted and led their horses down to the goblin who was directing traffic. He wore a black on black uniform with the same black cap that Marco wore. Where Marco's hat had three red feathers, his had two white ones. "Dock Master," Myrth greeted. The goblin gaped for a split second at seeing Myrth. "How soon can we cross?"

"I will send you with the next merchants," he said with a deep bow.

"Very good," Myrth said with a nod.

"Potent," the goblin added a second bow in acknowledgment of Marco's rank. Marco returned the acknowledgment, then followed Myrth down the pier. A ferry soon reached the dock and disgorged its merchant passengers. When they'd left the ship, a handful of merchants going to Gaity took their place. Myrth followed them aboard, leading his horse and the Honor Guard.

Marco went to the bow to greet the crew's mage, a goblin with a single red feather in her cap. "Potent," he greeted, catching her eye. Her pale orange eyes widened for a moment and she nodded in greetings, taking in Marco's own feathers. "Are the korsks an issue in the day?"

"No, but they get frisky occasionally," she answered with a smile. Marco returned the smile and stood aside as she stepped into the Mage Realm and endowed the ferry with Earth, strengthening the wood. She then reached out to the Water and formed a shield around the bottom of the boat.

"Potent," another goblin greeted, standing near the mage. Marco nodded in greeting, studying this new goblin. He was armed with a halberd and took up a defensive position next to the mage. He was there to protect her, allowing her to remain in the Mage Realm and continue working her spells while they made the crossing. With him in place and everyone aboard, the ferrymen pulled away from the pier, working oars on either side of the boat. They crossed quickly to the cliffs of Gaity, the crew disembarking with them, ready for a rest after working several crossings in a row. Myrth led the party through a cut in the cliff and up a steep path, entering the dense forest that sheltered the capital city.

White stone walls and a sturdy wooden gate greeted them when they reached the outer city wall. Elfin guards stood watch, questioning everyone who entered. "Palo has shut the city?" Myrth asked when it was their turn at the gate.

"Aye, Master," the elf greeted. "He says Oracle is spooked."

"I have business with both. You know my apprentice, my retainer," Myrth said, indicating Marco and Genow, "And my guard."

"Captain Vellin," the elf said with a deep bow. "Proceed, please," he added to Myrth. "You will find another closed gate at the inner keep." Myrth acknowledged his words and they hurried through.

Here in Gaity, the houses were one or two stories tall, similar to those built by the Land-Nymphs in Olimidia. The cobblestone streets bustled with people from across the Fanterra Plain, Semians of all varieties, Mortaks, goblins and elves made their way between market stalls, businesses, and homes. Marco saw no other humans as they passed through the central plaza and on to the inner keep. As the elf had said, the gate was closed. A large black tiger-man with white stripes, whom Marco knew well, stood guard, his massive arms crossed menacingly over his bulging chest, hands hidden by thick leather gloves, currently balled into fists. Like Marco, his black Potent cap held three red feathers.

"Pyko," Marco and Myrth greeted simultaneously.

The tiger-man smiled, his bestial face taking on a laughing countenance, "Master Myrth, Chosen of Earth. It is good of you to visit." His bright human eyes darted around the party and he quickly hid his disappointment. Pyko was a longtime friend of the Land-Nymph Clippen, who often accompanied Myrth and Marco to Gaity, despite Clippen being a member of Nepo's Honor Guard, not Myrth's. No Clippen meant no drinking buddy for the evening.

"I have urgent business with Oracle and Palo," Myrth said.

"The Grand Syra is not taking visitors today, Master of Earth, but Oracle is likely to know that you are coming and I'm sure he has set aside time to speak with you." The tiger opened one side of the double gate, allowing them to escort their horses into the inner keep. He winked at Marco as he passed and the apprentice nodded once. Pyko would settle for Marco's company this evening if possible. Inside the inner keep, the grounds were clean and orderly. Before them, a large white dome rose skyward. In attendance, at the four corners of the keep, sat a squat tower, each adorned with a black pennant.

Glowering, Myrth led the party across the cobblestones to the front entrance of the domed building. A large, white-feathered Stag Semian greeted them. "Palo is not taking visitors?" Myrth asked.

"My apologies, Master, he is not." The stag Semian's Potent uniform covered his entire body and his face was nearly human as well, although his square-pupil, blue eyes were larger than a normal human's eyes. Above them, spiraling horns rose several inches above his long deer-like ears. "Oracle did ask that I show you to his tower and make your entourage comfortable," he added, ignoring the slight quaking around them, which started the moment the stag's answer had registered with Myrth. Even the guard's gloved hand did not fidget along the staff he held slightly ahead of him and to the side.

"Very well, I will speak with Oracle. No need to take me there, I know the way." Myrth turned from the horned Semian and started around the dome, heading for the northwest tower where Oracle resided. Halfway there, a pair of stablehands appeared to take their horses, arranging to bring their packs to their rooms. Behind the dome, the cobblestones gave way to a large training ground. Three low buildings sat opposite the dome. These were the barracks of the Potentate, broken into three camps: elves, goblins, and Semians. Behind the barracks, at the base of the northwest tower, Myrth stopped and studied his companions. "Don't get comfortable," he said. "We'll be here until I can speak to Palo." Vellin and Auros bowed and took their leave along with Gado and Squirm, each of them returning the way they'd come to join friends and family in the Potentate barracks. Genow waited a beat. "We are safe here, Genow," Myrth continued with a nod.

"Yes, Master." He also bowed and left.

Marco waited as well. Myrth contemplated him. "You should sit with us but I suspect there's a certain Fire Mage you'd rather spend your time with." Marco felt himself blush and look away. Myrth smiled, "Go find your princess but remember to mind your forcelines as well."

"Thank you, Myrth," Marco said, allowing a thrill of excitement to run through him. He took a deep breath and turned away from his master before allowing his heart to flutter and his face to split in a grin. Schooling his steps to a quick steady beat, instead of the all-out run he wanted to break into, he hurried back toward the central grounds of the inner keep. Almost immediately, he felt Myrth smoothing the forcelines around him and heard the chiding at the edge of his mind, followed by the hawk-man's knowing chuckle. Marco broke into a run then, rushing toward the central barrack.

When Marco had trained here last year, the Semian barrack had been his home. He slowed to a walk as he neared the door into the round house. Like the dome behind him and the other two barracks to either side, it was made of white marble, though the roof was flat, rather than domed. No guards manned these doors. Anyone foolish enough to attack the Potentate deserved everything that was about to befall them. Guards would pay to see such a sight, so why discourage it? The Grand Syra's Potentate consisted of only the strongest, best trained mages. Those who wielded magic and tried to become a Potent at the end of every summer season, but failed, were given a consolation prize and shown the door. Pattern Mages who knew their business well, earned a single red feather, those with greater gifts could earn two feathers. With training, many of the two-feathered Potents would earn a third, rising to High Mage status. Others, like Marco, were already High Mages, wearing three feathers to denote their rank. This time of year, just as High Spring began, there would be no cadets or trainees in the barracks. Only a few dozen of the strongest mages on the peninsula would greet any intruder.

Marco let himself in and took a few steps away from the door, stopping to give his eyes time to adjust to the dimness within and to be recognized by the Potents inside. Colin was the first to acknowledge him and he raised a hand in greeting toward the stag Semian who sat playing cards at one of three central tables. Two more stags had joined her, all three of them wearing two-feathered caps. Marco had joined the Potentate at the same time as Colin, both of them Earth Mages. Turning to his left, he had just enough time to brace himself before another Semian leapt onto him. He caught her, hugging her close.

She wrapped her arms and legs around him, kissing him, forcing him to kiss her back. For a moment, the world shimmied around him, as the forcelines reacted to his excitement. He pulled back from her then, taking a deep breath to steady his heart and mind. Almira smiled at him. "I've missed you," she breathed in a deep velvet voice. Her dark skin, a few shades tanner than his, was golden in the lamplight. Dark human eyes, a wide human nose, and luscious human lips greeted him, smiling brilliantly.

"I've missed you too, my Princess," he breathed, kissing her again. He let her slide down to stand on her own feet before running a hand through her black curls. Every inch of her seemed human and, according to Semian custom, she covered all her humanity when she was in public, even wearing a veil beyond these walls. Marco's fingers found the thin stripe of downy feathers at the nape of her neck and stroked them, causing her to giggle and pull away from him. Avian Semian, Almira's only animalia, her only animal feature, was a small stripe of downy, iridescent feathers running along her spine from her neck to her lower back. The first time they'd met, she'd been willing to burn him alive, refusing to believe that a human could be a mage and certain that his animalia were simply hidden and small like her own.

"How long are you here for this time?" she asked, her hands firm on his chest.

"Not long, tomorrow."

"So long as that, Chosen?" she asked. "We shouldn't waste time, then." Her black eyes burned with desire, mirroring his own deep brown ones.

He kissed her again, leading her back toward her bunk. When they reached the small table beside her bed, Marco pulled away and, stepping quickly into the Mage Realm pulled the Earth Cloud into a high wall, adding a stone roof above with a smoke hole. There were no doors or windows. He smoothed the forcelines at his chest and opened his eyes. Almira lit the lamp on the table with a wave of her hand. Like Marco, she stepped quickly between the two Realms, working Fire from her hand to the oil in the wick of the lamp and then dropping back to the Physical Realm within a single breath. She smiled, hugging Marco close again, exploring the straps and buttons of his uniform. He felt for the same straps and ties on hers, maneuvering toward her bunk.

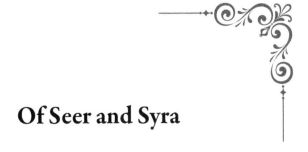

Of Seer and Syra

Myrth ascended the tower stairs. The occasional floor opened up around him, giving space for defensive armaments and guards. Bedchambers for guests and dignitaries could also be found on some floors, along with servant's quarters. The white stone walls remained bare in the stairwells but were covered with bright tapestries and subdued paintings and portraits on each floor. At the top, Myrth knocked on the single door in the center of the floor.

"Friend Myrth," Oracle called from inside. His voice held a growl that rivaled Myrth's own bass tones. The hawk Semian opened the door, knowing it would be unlocked. His friend sat at the table, lunch laid out for the pair of them. "You rode hard to get here," the wolf Semian said. Myrth bowed his head in acknowledgment, closing the door behind him. Oracle was a rare Semian, having almost no visible humanity. Because of this, he often went with very little clothing. His black fur bristled and he grinned at Myrth, fangs bared. "Sit, please," he said. As a seer, Oracle had no equal on the Fanterra Plain. His prophetic dreams and the hunches he followed often had him roaming across the Plain to meet people. However, sometimes, he was able to sit and wait for them to come to him.

"What brings me here?" Myrth asked, removing his cloak and laying it across the back of the empty chair. He studied the eggs and toast in front of him. He hadn't eaten much over the last cycle, not since a runner from Olimidia had brought news of Mara's death and D'Mique and Burl's hasty pursuit of the creatures that had kidnapped a Land-Nymph child. He sighed, frowning at the food.

"Time is unsettled," Oracle said with an echoing weary sigh. "My dreams are scattered, like looking in a broken mirror that shows a different person in each shard."

"And down deep? In the *Hisseth*?" Myrth had never been there, of course, but Oracle had described it and tried to help Myrth understand.

Oracle hesitated. "Time is unsettled," he said again. "There are forces at work that I cannot track and cannot see."

"As in "Greater Daemon" cannot see?" Myrth asked in a whisper. The year before, Oracle had said nearly the same thing, that he could not see, before realizing that a Greater Daemon was upon them. They'd had a mere handful of cycles to find and train those whom Oracle had predicted would be victorious over the Daemon before it invaded the Physical Realm.

Oracle's initial reaction to Myrth's whispered question was denial, but he stopped mid-head shake and thought about it. "No," he said after a moment. "No, not a Greater Daemon."

"Where do you see me?" Myrth asked after pushing his eggs around on his plate in silence for two full minutes. He looked up at his friend.

Oracle's amber wolf eyes closed and he grew still. Myrth felt him move through the forcelines as Oracle dropped away from first the Physical Realm and then the Mage Realm. Afte a moment, Oracle returned and opened his eyes. "Where do you want to be?" he asked.

"Dragon Ridge," Myrth said with a forlorn chuckle.

"I can't see you, Myrth. Your time is mixed up in the unsettled strands." He chewed a piece of toast for a moment, watching Myrth turn his eggs over on his plate. "Why are you here?" he asked.

"I need to speak to Palo." He stopped playing with the eggs and set his fork down. "Do you know of the Nura?" he asked.

"I know of them. They're daemon-kin from the north. They don't cross through the Vast Wildlands."

"There is one at Sea Spray, according to Nepo."

Oracle closed his eyes, dropping into the *Hisseth* again. When he returned, he spoke quietly, "Knowing this helps but I am only able to see me and I do not see me at Sea Spray." He paused for a moment, thinking. "Is that what you have come to talk about?" he asked, amber eyes flashing open and drilling into Myrth. The master nodded. Oracle sighed and closed his eyes again. "I cannot see the Nura."

"Could they be shattering your vision?"

"No." Oracle dismissed the idea with a huff and a shake of his head. The pair sat in thought, staring at each other and the food before them. "You came to speak to Palo about the Nura," Oracle restated at last, hoping Myrth would add more.

"Yes," Myrth said. "I was hoping you would offer guidance, as well." Oracle nodded once, an acknowledgment of the service he normally provided. Myrth continued, "and Palo, he is...?" Myrth waited for Oracle to finish the sentence.

The wolf snuffled and coughed. "Not worth viewing! Scoundrel," the seer growled. Concern and humor chased each other across Myrth's face. He waited for Oracle to elaborate. "Two...nubile elves thought they would try to wile their way into the Potentate. Palo took them up on their offer. Not enough magic between them to fill a tea cup."

"Palo doesn't decide who becomes a Potent," Myrth said, shaking his head, "the High Mages do."

"Hmph," Oracle rolled his eyes. "Palo did not mention that bit of trivia to the elves."

"Ho," Myrth studied Oracle for a moment. "You're joking, surely."

The wolf shook his head, no. "You'll have to wait with the rest of the city for his Grand Lordship to satisfy his appetite." The tower swayed in a small quake as Myrth digested the news. Then it settled. Myrth sighed, closing his eyes and stepping into the Mage Realm. Here, the maelstrom of the Earth forcelines overwhelmed all other senses and he could see only the golden clouds and eddies as they funneled into the World Gate at the top of Gaity Dome, bleeding out into the Void. He smoothed both his forcelines and Marco's before opening his eyes again, returning to the Physical Realm.

"I suppose we might as well have breakfast then," he said, picking up his fork.

The Fiery Sisters had just risen when Myrth returned to the dome. The no-nonsense guards had been replaced by low-ranking non-mage avian Semians. Recognizing Myrth, they bowed and allowed him to pass, opening the door for him. The door opened directly into the dome's central room, known as The Pit, where the syraes from across the southern peninsula met to discuss politics and economics. The syraes themselves lived here, on the island, occasionally returning to their homes to meet with various magistrates and warlords. The master of all, the Grand Syra, Palo, lived here in the dome itself. The door to his private residence lay across the Pit from the door Myrth had entered. Myrth crossed the sand floor quickly and rapped on the glass door that led to Palo's meeting room. He waited, hoping the door would be answered, that Palo was awake and not still lying abed with the two elves.

With a sigh, Myrth reached for the knob and the door opened beneath his hand. Palo peeked cautiously out. The dangerous, steady gleam in his gold-green cat eyes turned joyful when he saw Myrth. "Why Myrth," he purred low, "Good morning." He opened the door and turned away, strolling languidly back toward his throne. Here, in private, he remained in a state of partial undress, his feline Semian animalia and humanity all in plain view. Palo's snow leopard tail twitched as he walked, accentuating each fluid move he made. Myrth followed him, closing the door behind him. Palo's bare torso, human in form but covered in a downy gray and black mottled fur, held an intricate lacework of white scars, marring the pattern of his fur, crossing his back, sides, and front. Palo lived well now, safe in his island castle, the entire southern peninsula at his call, but once, he'd been a warlord. Standing naked, Palo's profile shadowed and lined in sharp relief by the lamplight thrown round the room, Myrth remembered how dangerous he could be.

Like most feline Semians, Palo had a natural affinity for Water. Decades before, he'd been one of three High Mages apprenticed to the Water Master. When his fellow apprentice, Nepo, had been named Chosen instead, Palo had disappeared into the fog of his native Misty Lands. Years later, he'd returned to the Fanterra Plain with a legion of High Mages, gathering power as he traveled, pulling all the magistrates under his black-on-black banner as he went. Palo'd left the Masters alone, seeing them as separate from all else. Myrth had been grateful for that, mostly because he had always liked Palo, and didn't want to stand against him over something so petty as who was in charge. The Wind Mistress Jay, too, had no qualms about Palo naming himself Grand Syra and setting up a loosely governed kingdom. Now, Palo had been in charge so long that it seemed natural to consult him when issues arose. His languid joviality rarely gave way to the bloodthirsty pragmatism that had driven him to take control so long ago. Yet, it lingered there in the half-light, tales told in scars.

"Are your visitors still here?" Myrth asked, pitching his voice low and indicating the door into Palo's private chambers.

Palo sat down on his throne, lazily scratching a forearm with his furred human-like hand, his thick claws just visible. His leopard face parted into a sultry grin. "Would you like some?" he purred. Myrth glared at him, pearly eyes turning hard. "Yes, they are still here," Palo continued, cutting off Myrth's retort, "Sleeping. I was hoping to turn them out later, after having another go. Do they need to leave now?" Palo's glowing eyes clouded, and he frowned, whiskers drooping.

"You're incorrigible," Myrth rumbled, shaking his head.

"You haven't seen them, old man."

Myrth snorted at that. "I've no doubt they're young enough to be my grandchildren."

Palo chuckled, rubbing the black paw pads on his palms together. "Do we need privacy?" Palo asked, setting aside the jesting in the blink of an eye.

"I would prefer we had privacy. I do not know the extent of the news I bear and Oracle cannot see it either."

With a nod Palo stood again and returned to his private quarters. He was gone longer than a few minutes. When he emerged, he followed a young pair of elves out of his room and around Myrth to the door. The women were young, perhaps only slightly older than Sennet. While they were old enough to be making their own way in the world, they should have been with a chaperone. "Where is your chaperone?" Myrth asked, doing his best to look disapproving. Palo's eyes grew wide.

The women looked chagrined for a moment then Palo draped an arm over each of them, "Ignore him," he purred, "He's just jealous." The young women's giggles returned and they each made a show of kissing Palo's furry cheeks. He nuzzled each of them in turn, spinning away from Myrth and hurrying them out the door. He returned a moment later, leaning against the closed door, now half dressed, wearing a light silk robe that he belted around his waist.

"I should send them to Vellin," Myrth said.

"They're adults, Myrth, and free to make their own choices."

"Oracle says there's not enough magic between them to fill a tea cup, that they wanted an easy way into the Potentate. You took advantage of them."

"Hard lessons are learned in life," Palo growled, "best to learn them early." The snow leopard's gold-green eyes glinted dangerously. In the half-light of the throne room, with his scar-covered torso, Palo was once again the warlord who'd brought the Southern Peninsula to heel. Myrth weighed the Grand Syra in his mind. He was a Water Master, though not THE Water Master. He worked magic very little, out of respect for Nepo, who had to wrestle power away from the Grand Syra afterward. However, when Palo did step into the Mage Realm, he had no qualms about destroying his opponents, the surrounding cities, and any innocents who should have known better than to be in the way.

Myrth blinked slowly, waving away the Grand Syra's threat. "There are more important things. I didn't come here to pass moral judgment on you, Palo." The two studied each other for a quiet moment. Myrth felt the feline Semian doing his own weighing of the situation.

"Why are you here, friend?" Palo asked, his voice turning languid and his rigid stance softening. The two looked at each other for a moment. "Oracle cannot see, you said. He has been a terrible bore. I had to ban him from my sight for a few days."

"Do you know of the Nura?" Myrth asked, voice barely a rumble above a whisper.

"Nura?" Palo sat down on the throne and closed his eyes. "No," he said after a moment.

"Once, when I was young, I journeyed north beyond the Vast Wildlands to the main continent," Myrth whispered.

"I've heard this rumor," Palo said with a nod. "That's where your dragon is from."

Myrth nodded. "Dragon fairies are rare there too, but I made an impression on the lord who had acted as my host and guide." He paused a moment, picking his words. "As the goblins form our armies here on the Fanterra Plain, the Nura form the armies there. They are daemon-kin, warriors of the highest quality who wield magics that we cannot sense, understand, or even see." Myrth paused, letting Palo chew on the information.

"And?" Palo asked.

"Tekalo captured one. It's at Sea Spray."

"Ha! Our Tekalo! Excellent!" Palo crowed, chuckling. He continued smiling, waiting for Myrth's glare to turn into further information.

"The Nura killed the Matriarch and a number of other Land-Nymphs in Olimidia less than two cycles ago," the Earth Master paused, "Surely you knew your magistrate had died?"

Palo nodded, face somber. "Yes, of course." He didn't rise to Myrth's goading.

The Earth Master continued, "Clippen sent news shortly afterward to let me know that my retainers had left the city in an attempt to rescue a kidnapped Land-Nymph baby and her nurse." Palo blinked at the information, caught unaware.

"So the Nura is a kidnapper and a murderer. Good that it was captured. I want none of the justice. Clippen can handle that. Did you know he is interim Magistrate until they decide which Mother will become the new Matriarch?"

"I did not, Grand Syra," Myrth admitted. He smiled and Palo returned it. "That is not the problem. The problem lies in the fact that it is a Nura."

"Explain," Palo commanded. "Short version," he added with a widening smile.

Myrth snapped his beak at the Grand Syra then closed his eyes to collect his thoughts. He began, "The Nura never travel alone, they are warriors and live in tight-knit squads of about a dozen. Tekalo captured one, that means at least eleven more are still roaming the Southern Peninsula. Also, they never cross the Vast Wildlands, they shouldn't even be here. Finally, there is no real reason for the Nura that was captured to stay here, imprisoned. It is only still a prisoner because it is honoring the fact that it was captured in a fair fight and returned to its opponent's base."

Palo contemplated the Earth Master. "Thank you, for the short version. I think it needs some elaboration," he admitted, a smile creeping over his face as Myrth scowled.

"Why am I friends with you?" the hawk-man asked.

Palo chuckled. "I think you have a soft spot for me."

"Nepo has been to the North as well, although many do not know about his trip," Myrth said. Palo nodded. "We agree that the Nura should be taken to Olimidia to face justice for its crimes. We *might* be able to take it there without any problems but when it understands why we are taking it there, it might just decide to leave. We won't be able to stop it.

"Do you need the Potentate?" Palo asked. "It *was* captured by Tekalo."

"No. Marladon, Jay, Nepo and I along with Marco will suffice. But the Nura have magic we do not understand and cannot counter. We can't even see it."

"They're daemonic. It's not Shadow?"

"No," Myrth shook his head. "Yes, they do use Shadow and we can see that, but they use others that we cannot see. Whether we keep it prisoner in Sea Spray, move it to Olimidia, kill it in revenge or it simply leaves, the problem is bigger than that and I suspect it is why Oracle has been so on edge. The Nura are the backbone of the Northern armies, meaning that this one has hundreds of friends and a Master of its own."

Palo glared, sitting up. "Are you saying...?" he asked.

Myrth interrupted him, "Tekalo may have inadvertently started a war." Myrth waited for Palo to speak.

The Grand Syra sat with his eyes closed thinking for a long time, the tip of his tail twitching. Then he spoke, "Take it to Olimidia, I will send a message to Clippen not to harm it. I will meet you all there in about a cycle with a retinue of my own. I want to speak to it. If it really is here just because Tekalo captured it, ask it to stay long enough to talk to me."

Myrth frowned, but nodded. "I will do as you ask, friend," he said. Palo returned the nod and sat scratching his arm once again, his tail twitching languidly. Myrth had the feeling that Palo was weighing him again. Myrth rose, bowing his head.

"Safe travels, Myrth," Palo purred.

Myrth turned and left quickly without another word. His feathers ruffled as he crossed the Pit's sandy floor. *"How close was I to feeling those claws,"* he wondered, followed by, *"Would he dare attack the Earth Master?"* He knew undoubtedly that Palo would, even as he thought it. He paused before leaving the Dome, closing his eyes and falling into the Mage Realm. The Earth Cloud rippled around him and it took a moment of deep calming breaths before he was able to soothe the Power. He then reached out along the line that tied him to Marco. *"Time to go, Apprentice,"* he said in Marco's head, catching a quick glimpse of Almira in his arms, the pair awake and waiting for Myrth to take Marco away. Myrth smiled. *"Say your goodbyes quickly, we cannot dawdle,"* he added. Turning away from Marco, Myrth reached out to Auros-Gado. *"Auros, Gado, come to me. We travel light and swift toward danger."*

"Your command, Master," Auros said aloud. Myrth opened his eyes, dropping from the Mage Realm. Auros was just outside the door. Myrth opened it, schooling himself to the deep stillness of the bedrock. "Gado is fetching horses and supplies. We felt your agitation and figured we would be leaving soon," the goblin explained with a smile.

Myrth nodded, impressed with the goblin. The bonded goblins had offered to take Tierren and Rogan's place when his former

Guards had returned to Hawkethorne Valley and he had enjoyed their companionship ever since. "And Vellin? Genow?" Myrth asked.

"Gado sent a white-feather to let them know we were preparing to leave. I'm sure the captain and Squirm will be along shortly, along with Genow."

"Good," Myrth said. "I will pack and meet you at the inner keep's gate."

"Yes, Master," Auros said with a deep bow.

The party reassembled at the gate, Marco joined by the veiled Fire Mage Almira. She stood nearly a head shorter than him, but anyone foolish enough to dismiss her as nonthreatening regretted the decision. "Has Palo given you leave to join us, Princess?" Myrth asked. He glanced around, searching for Temeres, the Princess' bodyguard.

"Not today, Master. I'm merely seeing my man off."

"I look forward to your company in the future, Potent."

"And I yours," Almira returned, her expression hidden by the veil but a smile on her voice. With a last hug, she saw Marco into his saddle and then turned and walked away, refusing to watch him leave. Marco watched her a moment.

"Bad luck, human," Gado whispered. "Lovers should never watch one another leave if they wish to return to each other's arms." Marco turned to look at him then followed him out the gate. "You mean a great deal to her or she wouldn't have walked away. To have one so fierce as the Mage Princess as a defender is a statement of your own strength," Gado continued.

"Are these all goblin tales?" Marco asked, following Myrth, who was walking and carrying Jerrold on his shoulders.

"Goblin? No, Hawkethorne and Vale, yes." Gado said, keeping pace with Marco as they made their way through Gaity to the cliffs of Master Island.

As they waited for the ferry, Myrth turned to Vellin. "You and Sennet return to Dragon Ridge, Captain," Myrth ordered. Vellin studied the Semian then looked at Sennet. "I cannot take your ward into this," Myrth added. "Take him out on the next goblin patrol."

"Very well, Master," the elf said.

"We part ways at Gaity Banks," Myrth added. They were silent for a moment. "Can you be severed from your ward, Captain?" Myrth asked under his breath, thoughts turning in his head.

"Only by death, Master." Myrth sighed and nodded his understanding. Vellin would die for Sennet, yet could not leave him behind if a dangerous situation arose. They would both have to flee. "I will stay close to Sylus," Vellin continued. "Call for me and we will come."

Marco caught Gado's eye and frowned. Gado returned it. A silent confirmation that things did not look well and the path seemed inevitable. *"Are we in danger, Myrth?"* Marco asked silently, his thoughts carried on the forceline that tied them together.

"Not today," Myrth replied.

Imprisoned by Honor

Ryn added some shading to the hands he'd been drawing, deftly blending the charcoal shading with a pale finger. He looked up at the prisoner, focusing on the tree daemon's hands, trying to decide if the sketch was now accurate. The elf shifted slightly, stretching his shoulders. His movement brought the prisoner's attention to him. The elf's black orb eyes reflected the tree daemon's fiery pupils as they studied each other silently. The Air Mage Ryn had been there when the prisoner was captured. He still could not fathom leaving the daemon free to wander at will, to work its odd Void-tainted magic whenever it wanted. He didn't trust it, not so far as the goblin Kita could throw it. When nothing further happened, the daemon turned away from Ryn and closed his eyes again. Ryn looked back down at his sketch and the notes he'd penned this morning. His thick white hair curtained around him as he bent close to the sketchpad. He'd stopped wearing his hair in a top-knot two days before. He didn't trust the daemon, but for some reason, Nepo believed it would not cause any further problems. And Ryn trusted Nepo. The sketch held the prisoner's likeness. The tree daemon's bald head had started growing black stubble. Fiery daemon-spawn eyes were deep-set above a wide, flat nose. His ears, similar to an elf's, were short and pointed. He no longer wore the gray, flowing clothes he'd been captured in. Nepo had provided his "guest" with a wardrobe of skirts, pants, flowing robes, and tunics. The tree daemon had chosen a robe and linen skirt to wear today. It left his muscular torso bare, his skin scintillated as he breathed, the sunlight gleaming on the smooth scales that covered him.

"*Shuwarr DJar,*" Ryn called softly. The tree daemon looked at him, face blank. Ryn chose his words carefully, "*Comsha bala?*"

DJar's brows furrowed and he frowned, shaking his head. "*Ur,*" he began, "*Comqui bala do?*"

"'*Comqui bala do,*'"Ryn repeated. "*Comqui bala do?*"

"*Ah,*" DJar nodded.

"What did I say before?" Ryn asked, standing.

"What do I eat," DJar said, also gaining his feet. The tree daemon stood slightly shorter than the elf. "You are a quick study, Fae," the daemon-kin added. Ryn shrugged in response. He stood back, allowing DJar to exit the room first. The Nura moved sedately, seemingly unperturbed. Ryn followed, guarded. For several days now, DJar had passed the time teaching Ryn his language. As they'd conversed, it became obvious to the elf that the tree daemon, or rather, the Nura, understood Fae well enough to survive so long as the conversations were not complex. Ryn, on the other hand, would barely be able to find food in the Northern lands.

They made their way down the spiraling tower stairs toward an arched doorway that opened out into the Water Master's throne room. Burnished wooden walls that glowed red and gold greeted them. Above them, the glass dome of Sea Spray was a mix of plain glass and stained-glass windows. Where the sunlight streamed through the stained-glass, it painted mottled colors across the floors and walls. The Water Master's throne sat at the top of a tall dais, empty. Near the base of the dais, a small round table had been laid out for guests and denizens of Sea Spray with meats, cheeses, and a variety of fruits and vegetables. Ryn watched as DJar took meat and cheese, bypassing grains, fruits, and vegetables. The tree daemon carefully avoided any utensils. When he'd filled his plate, he stepped back from the table, standing still while Ryn filled his own plate.

When the elf had his food, they both turned and left the throne room through the main door. The Great Hall's ceiling above them, like the throne room they'd just left, was made of stained-glass panels. The polished wood floor reflected golds and reds along its grain. At the end of the hall, Ryn and DJar exited the main keep and stepped out into a lush, water garden full of ferns, mossy stones, and fruit trees. They started through the garden to the left. DJar was looking for Nepo.

Halfway around to the training grounds at the back of the castle, they found him. The lion-man was conversing with the Wind Mistress under a pergola laden with flowering vines. Although they were both Semian, the pair were a study in opposites. Nepo, a feline Semian0, was human in form, every visible inch of his upper body and arms covered in a tawny, velvet fur. His hair formed a luxurious mane, hiding human ears from any onlookers. His face, however, was leonine, with a wide black cat-nose and mahogany eyes. At nearly seven feet tall, he barely fit beneath the pergola. Beside him, the Wind Mistress Jay barely reached his chest. Being a piscine Semian, like the sharks she resembled, she had no fur. Human in form, she was covered by sandpapery gray and white skin. Her mouth, lined with sharp triangular teeth, was thin-lipped. What hair she did have was a bright fuchsia and formed a tall ridge at the top of her head, trailing down her back like a horse's tail. Flat, alien gray eyes greeted them when DJar stopped.

"*Shuwarr DJar,*" Nepo greeted with a slight nod.

"*Hethdi djo ee,*" DJar greeted, "*Dreetaal ee do?*"

Nepo shook his head, "No, I will not," he said, "*Ur, dreeteth do.*"

Djar bowed his head and sighed, shaking it. He looked up at Nepo, "*Tepok Nepo, tekdi nal ee garpokcho.*"

"I have no doubt, *Shuwarr.* You are valuable," Nepo responded.

Ryn sighed. He'd heard this exchange every morning for nearly a full cycle. After the second day, he'd asked Nepo about it and the

Master had explained that it was a customary request—DJar asking to be set free and reminding Nepo that his master would come for him. One day Nepo would honor the request, but for now, he was waiting for Myrth to meet the Nura.

Nepo continued, speaking to Ryn, "Has he been good?"

"Yes, Master Nepo," the elf supplied, "*Shuwarr* DJar is a model prisoner." He held up his sketchpad to emphasize the pun. The sketch showed DJar in meditation, sedate, surrounded by pillows and billowing curtains, the intricate mudra of his hands the obvious focus of the elf's work. The Wind Mistress giggled appreciatively, her lilting voice like birdsong.

"A fair sea, Little Sister," DJar greeted Jay as he had done upon her arrival the day before.

"Major," she returned with a formal nod. DJar bowed low to the pair of them then continued down the path. Ryn copied his bow and hurried to catch up to the prisoner. As he had done since the Fire Master's arrival, DJar was looking for him to eat with and knew he'd be out back. Marladon sat alone under a tree on the grass at the edge of the dirt training field. When he saw them approaching, he stood.

"Brother," DJar greeted, saluting with his fist to his chest. Marladon copied the gesture.

"*Shuwarr*," Marladon returned. "Join me?"

"I welcome. Mortaks are good friends," the Nura said, sitting down near Marladon. The Fire Master returned to his seat. His silver orb eyes met Ryn's dark ones as the elf sat as well, near enough that he could intervene if DJar decided to do more than eat and converse. "Your people," DJar began as he started on the mound of meat and cheese on his plate, "are from the Embers?"

Marladon nodded, the shiny scar that sliced across his left cheek from his jaw to the outer corner of his eye danced as he chewed and swallowed his mouthful of food. "We are. When I was a boy, an emissary came to check on us. He was a Molbdyn."

"Of the Ruby Hills?" DJar asked.

Marladon shrugged. "I do not know." They fell into silence, eating and watching each other in turn.

"Do you speak Nura?" Ryn asked Marladon.

The Fire Master shook his head, "No. My understanding is that only the Nura offer such instruction and only to certain outsiders." He eyed DJar and Ryn. "True?"

DJar studied them, brows furrowed. "My Fae is little," he said after a moment.

Marladon thought for a moment. He looked at Ryn. "Well, he's teaching you,"

"I know very little," Ryn said, then added with a smile, "My Nura is little."

"Ah, oh!" DJar said with a smile. His thick fangs glistened between his black lips and the flames in his eyes flared, a reminder that they were speaking to a daemon-kin.

"Try," Marladon said, waving Ryn onward.

"*Vorbash-Nura...*" Ryn paused. "Sorry, I don't know the verbs," he said to Marladon. DJar studied him and looked between Ryn and Marladon.

The Fire Master shrugged and smiled. "Oh well." He sat for a moment then sighed deeply, "Our perfect afternoon is about to be ruined."

Before Ryn could ask why, a messenger came running. "The Earth Master is crossing the Sea of Scorn, Master. Nepo has requested your and the prisoner's presence in the throne room."

"We will be there shortly," Marladon said, waving the messenger away. He turned to DJar, "We have time to finish our meal if we hurry."

The three ate quickly and then Marladon stood and the other two followed him back the way they'd come. Marladon's red and white outfit matched the burnished red wood of the Great Hall.

While DJar's white robe and skirt matched Marladon's trousers and Ryn's hair, Ryn's own functional brown and green linen outfit seemed out of place following the two richly clothed people before him through the opulent hall.

Marladon stopped just short of the doors into the throne room and turned to DJar. "Wait a few beats before entering," he said, holding out a hand, nearly touching the tree daemon. "Ryn, keep him here," he added to the elf.

"Master," Ryn said, with a bow. He took Marladon's place and stood between DJar and the door. Marladon disappeared into the throne room. Ryn waited for a long three minutes, then turned and motioned for DJar to enter, following him through the door. Before them, Nepo had arranged the room in order to maximize his importance and the power the Masters had over the prisoner.

Nepo sat on his throne at the top of the dais. Beside him, three more thrones had been brought in, one for each of the other Masters. Jay sat to Nepo's left and Myrth to his right. Marladon flanked Myrth on the other side. Several others stood near the dais. Ryn recognized them as some of Myrth's honor guard, his retainer Genow, and his apprentice, the human Marco. They all looked nervous.

"*Tlii!*" DJar suddenly cooed. Ryn felt the power gather around him, and took a calming breath, ready to attack or drop into the Mage Realm in an instance. Myrth's dragon fairy, which was curled around the Earth Master's shoulders, raised his head and hissed at DJar, his fangs large and bright in the stained glass light. DJar came to a stop, eyes glued on the dragon. He was so mesmerized by the dragon he hardly noticed the introductions that Nepo made.

"*Shuwarr DJar,*" Nepo said, presenting him to the others.

DJar pulled his eyes away from Jerrold. He bowed low from the waist, "*Tepok* Nepo, warm sands greet you. *Tepok* Jay, fair seas greet you, Brother Mortak," DJar saluted Marladon once again. He turned to Myrth, beginning to speak "Swift winds, little broth—." He stopped and his eyes flared, flames leaping wildly.

"*Tepok* M—," Nepo introduced.

"Myrth," DJar finished.

The room swayed slightly around them as the Earth Master and his apprentice reacted, surprised. DJar held up his hands, empty. He stepped forward twice and addressed Master Myrth in Nura.

Comqui so ee do? Myrth asked, "*Tla comqui so do ee?*"

DJar answered in Nura, "I know you, *Tepok*. A bird-of-prey Semian with a *tlii* in stitchery. When I was a boy, just born to the dream, my master's father told tales of the Maelstrom-born bird of prey Little Brother with pearl eyes. He was so impressed with you that he gave to you a prized *tlii* trained in stitchery."

Myrth stood and walked down the steps, Jerrold hissing at the Nura as they closed the distance. "And how is your master?" Myrth asked, the others watching him curiously as he spoke to the Nura. "Sybon was a dear friend."

"He awoke many years ago, *Tepok*. His son rules now and holds my bond. He is as worthy of your thoughts as his father."

"When I knew Sybon he had no children. It is good he has a son to be proud of." Myrth glanced at Jerrold who had remained perturbed by the Nura. "My *tlii* doesn't like you."

"He wishes merely to protect you," DJar surmised, eyes flaring as he smiled.

"Does he need to?" Myrth's voice turned hard, his eyes granite.

DJar shifted slightly, as a fighter readying for a fight would do, before replying, "I am honorable. I was captured in battle and taken prisoner. When my squad returns to the Crystal Hills without me, others will come. I am assured by *Tepok* Nepo that I will not be held so long as that. I trust his honor as well, thus, I remain and I play my role as prisoner."

"What did he say about me?" Nepo interrupted, hearing the Nura refer to him.

"He says you said you'd let him go," Myrth relayed switching to Fae, turning to face Nepo with an incredulous look on his face. "Is that true?"

Nepo held out his hands in surrender. "Yes," he admitted, "I know how the game is played, Myrth," he continued defensively.

"Ruby Hills game, not Crystal Hills game, Nepo," Myrth hissed.

"Masters!" Ryn shouted. Myrth turned back to DJar, who had closed his eyes and was gathering magic power to his will.

"Shuwarr DJar," Myrth said, pitching his voice calm and closing the distance between them, "I am honorable."

DJar opened his eyes, daemon-fire blazing where his pupils should have been. "You do not hold my bond, *Tepok*," he said.

Myrth hissed under his breath in Nura, indicating Nepo. "*Tepok* Nepo spent a year in the Ruby Hills as an emissary, but I lived in the Crystal Hills Kingdoms for nearly a decade, apprenticed to Sybon. I *am* honorable."

"Would you win my bond?" DJar asked. Myrth pulled away, stepping back from the Nura. A sudden spike of fear whipped through Marco and the goblins as it poured from Myrth, bringing them rushing to stand beside the Earth Master. DJar smiled. Marco took a deep breath, steadying himself as the room began to rumble. Auros-Gado reached for their blades but DJar held out his hands, repeating Nepo's gesture from earlier, signaling his unwillingness to fight.

"Be at ease, Marco," Myrth soothed in Fae. "Auros-Gado, stay your hands." The rumbling slowly subsided.

"There was one of his kind with the Fae who captured me," DJar said, conversing in Fae, pointing at Marco.

"My retainer, D'Mique?" Myrth asked after a moment. "Female, long black hair like a goblin-maid."

"*Ah,*" DJar confirmed. "They are Fae as well?" he asked in Nura.

"No, they are not Fae, nor daemon-kin."

"They look like the Pale Ones. Maelstrom-born beast-kin," DJar said, contemplative.

"My retainer captured you as well?" Myrth asked. "If so, I have equal claim to your bond and do not have to win it."

DJar turned away from his study of Marco and looked directly at Myrth. "There were several in the party." He pointed to Ryn, "This one, your beast-kin maid, his apprentice," he continued, pointing at Nepo. "Others," he said, shaking his head.

Myrth turned to Ryn. "Do you remember who fought against DJar when he was captured?" he asked, switching languages.

"We were all there," Ryn said, "Trillip, Tekalo, the Lady D'Mique, Derik, Gera, and I."

"Nepo," Myrth said, "You are not the only one who can lay claim to DJar's bond. Trillip and D'Mique are mine, Derik, Gera and Ryn, all serve the Academy and Olimidia."

"Tekalo landed the blow that brought him down," Ryn added. "He saved him from Trillip's revenge."

"*Shuwarr* DJar," Myrth said, "I ask you to return to your quarters. I would have a word with my fellows."

DJar rubbed his fingers with his thumbs, before bowing his head and speaking in Fae. "You are honorable, *Tepok* Myrth, and I will retire as you ask." He turned and left without further incident and Ryn followed him with a nod.

Myrth waited for them to leave before turning to study Nepo and the other Masters. "Is Ryn the only one here," he asked, "of the group?"

Nepo nodded once, "The others returned to Olimidia. Ryn stayed to study the Nura. He said his commander gave him leave."

"Who brought DJar here?"

"Derik, Kita, Sai, Shuri, and Ryn."

"All Air Mages from the Academy," Myrth pondered.

"Will you be explaining what is going on?" Marladon interrupted. "Or should I just return home." His outburst brought a *tsk* from Jay. Nepo looked between Marladon and Myrth.

"I did what I could, Myrth," Nepo claimed, "A handful of soldier mages walk into my throne room with a NURA prisoner and I did what I could! I told it at the very beginning, 'I've seen the Crystal Hills turn red.' That's a Ruby Hills greeting and it's its own shortsightedness if it didn't realize that."

"This isn't helping me," Marladon warned. "I know some about the Hills Kingdoms. That rot-bog daemon-kin Krindin was from the Ruby Hills."

"The Ruby Hills and the Crystal Hills have similar customs regarding prisoners taken in battle, but not exactly the same," Myrth explained. "You couldn't have known he was not from the Ruby Hills, Nepo; nearly all our contact comes from there." Nepo nodded.

"Well, the Embers is technically a Ruby Hills colony," Marladon added with a dismissive frown. "Please continue, Myrth," he added.

"The Crystal Hills tradition states that a prisoner taken in one-on-one combat and returned to a throne, is bonded to the new throne. If a prisoner is taken by a group, each combatant can lay a claim to the prisoner, regardless of which throne it is taken to. In the Ruby Hills tradition, only the throne that holds the prisoner has a claim to its bond."

Jay cleared her throat, speaking in a lilting voice, "So you, Nepo, and the Academy all have a claim to DJar?" Myrth nodded.

"Then why the sudden threat of combat?" Marco asked.

"He didn't know I already had claim through Trillip and D'Mique," Myrth answered. "He was offering himself to me as prisoner if I could best him."

"A battle sure to drown half of us," Nepo added under his breath.

"Likely," Myrth agreed. "Things are going to get complicated when Palo meets us in Olimidia. DJar belongs to a Crystal Hills *Garpok*. People will come for him. We don't want a war with the Hills Kingdoms."

"Yet, Olimidia has a claim to him," Jay said. "They aren't going to let him go, he killed the Matriarch." They all agreed, nodding and falling silent. As the silence settled over the throne room, Myrth returned to his seat, followed up the dais by Marco. The extended silence seemed to mark an end to the discussion of the Nura prisoner.

"What news?" Myrth asked. "As we are all here." Silence stretched around his question for a moment.

"Farmers are moving back to the vale. I'm happy about that," Marladon said after a moment's thought.

"There is an Air Master born on the plain," Jay said.

"So strong you felt them?" Marladon asked.

"Indeed."

"An infant Air Master will cause a stir," Nepo said. "They will be brought forward soon enough." Jay nodded, smiling at his words.

"And you, Myrth?" Nepo asked.

"Marco is doing well in his studies," Myrth said, with a nod to Marco.

"Speaking of apprentices, mine keeps disappearing," Nepo admitted in response.

"Disappearing? How?" Myrth asked.

"From the forcelines?" Jay asked simultaneously.

"Yes, his weight has been disappearing from the forcelines for brief periods of time," Nepo replied, choosing to answer Jay instead of Myrth. "He is there right now but he was gone this morning for quite some time. I can still feel an echo of him, so I know he isn't dead but it's unnerving."

"Your bond with him is tenuous at best," Myrth said. "DJar was taken prisoner at the Crest. If he is further away from you, the forcelines may be stretched thin."

"Tekalo is strong and talented," Marco said, "Try not to worry about him, Nepo."

Marladon smiled at the glare Myrth passed to Marco. "Your apprentice speaks true, Myrth," Marladon added. "Tekalo captured a Nura. I'm sure he is well." Nepo nodded and sighed, acknowledging their attempts to assuage his concern.

"We should start for Olimidia in the morning," Myrth suggested. "I'll have a talk with DJar. Can you see my guard to some rooms?" he asked Nepo.

"Of course," Nepo said, standing. "Genow, Marco, your rooms are still set up. I'll find one for the goblins." A chorus of thank-yous followed the lion-man down the dais and over to the secret door that led from the throne room to the private quarters.

Myrth and Jay stood as well. "Marco, take Jerrold, please," Myrth said, and Marco coaxed the dragon fairy from Myrth's shoulders before hurrying after Nepo.

"What are you going to say to the Nura?" Marladon asked from where he remained sitting.

"That there is more than one claim on him and that only Nepo agreed to forfeit it." Myrth supplied.

"Will that be enough to keep him here?"

"I don't know." Myrth sighed and continued down the steps. He went around to the wall opposite of where Nepo and his guard had disappeared. As with the other walls in the throne room, this was decorated by patches of colored light streaming in from the ceiling. A pentagonal patch of blue light marked the secret panel that led to the fan towers on the back side of Sea Spray Castle. He pressed on the button and waited for the panel to swing open on silent hinges, lost in thought.

Seeing the Nura had brought back memories of long-gone years. His time in the Crystal Hills Kingdom had been fraught with sorrow, pain, and confusion. Yet, the days spent with the Nura, learning their customs and their language, had been a bright spot. That DJar had come from Sybon's estate felt too much of a coincidence. "*I wish Oracle could see,*" Myrth muttered to himself as he shut the door behind him.

There were no guards here in the domed room that lay beyond the panel. Five spiraling staircases led away from the dome up to five separate towers. Contemplating for a moment, Myrth chose the center staircase and the tallest tower, hoping that they would have taken a high-ranking prisoner to the tallest tower. He climbed quickly, his guess rewarded by seeing Ryn perched on the stairs a few feet from the door.

"Master," the elf greeted, standing.

"Good Elf," Myrth nodded in return. "Is he still in there?"

"Ryn, please, and last I checked," the elf said, his brows furrowing and his eyes narrowing. "Shouldn't he be? He has shown no sign of wanting to escape." Worry and guilt ran through the elf as he frowned.

"By rights he should be," Myrth agreed and stepped around the Air Mage guard to enter the room. Djar sat in meditation in the middle of a pile of pillows and blankets that had been strewn upon the floor. "Yes, he's here." Myrth said. Ryn visibly relaxed. "I'll only be a moment. I am safe with him alone." Myrth assured the elf, closing the door between them. Worry returned to the elf's face as the door clicked shut.

Myrth stepped into the Mage Realm and surveyed the room. DJar sat before him, a hollow, glasslike body that wasn't really in the Mage Realm. Myrth opened his eyes and made his way to the physical daemon-kin. He sat across from DJar, folding his legs in a meditative stance, just shy of arm's length distance between them.

Myrth took note of the mudra the Nura was using. "*Calming but not meditative,*" he thought. He sighed loudly, as he'd been taught so many decades before. DJar's eyes slid open, his daemon-fire banked low smoldering in his pupils.

"*Shuwarr DJar,*" Myrth began, speaking in Nura. "We have discussed your bond. While Nepo follows the Ruby Hills Traditions, I follow those of the Crystal Hills. I and others agree that as you are also of the Crystal Hills, we should follow those traditions as well. We believe that there are other claims on your bond than just Nepo's."

"Who has claim to me?" DJar asked in a whisper, sibilant foreign sounds raising Myrth's feathers along his neck.

"I do, and so does Palo, the Grand Syra, *Tepok-Myir* of the Southern Peninsula.

"*Tepok-Myir?*" DJar's eyes flared.

Myrth nodded. "He will meet you in Olimidia."

"The Fae city," DJar said, voice low.

"You are honorable, *Shuwarr DJar.* I am honorable," Myrth said, willing his words to have enough weight to keep DJar here. "You are believed to be a murderer. Kin-killer."

"Ha!" DJar barked, causing a spike of adrenaline to rush through Myrth, and his heart to leap into his throat. "The Fae are not kin."

"They are not beast," Myrth whispered, eyes hardening.

"Says you, who lives here in the Maelstrom."

"I know that I cannot stop you from leaving, *Shuwarr,*" Myrth admitted. "I do not understand your ways but I know that the Nura cannot be held to the physical realm. I ask you, on your honor and for Sybon's, to stay this course."

DJar studied him, daemon-fire eyes glowing brightly even in the sunlit room. "I will stay but I will not awaken at the hands of a Fae-beast," DJar said.

"I can ask no more from an honorable prisoner who is not my retainer," Myrth agreed. They studied each other a moment longer before DJar nodded and closed his eyes. Myrth watched him, waiting for more but his mudra changed and the Nura was gone in meditation. Myrth sighed quietly and stood, backing away from the Nura before turning his back on the daemon-kin. At the door, he laid a hand on Ryn's shoulder.

"Watch carefully, Ryn, but do not attempt to capture him if he leaves."

"Yes, Master." As Myrth descended the stairs, Ryn pulled his hair into a top knot, wrapping it in leather so it would stand up out of his way.

Nothing Owed

As the suns were rising, Myrth woke Ryn, who was dozing outside DJar's room. "Master," the elf greeted.

"We are off to Olimidia this morning. You are welcome to join us. Ready quickly while I entertain DJar."

"I will, and I will meet you in the Great Hall," Ryn said, standing stiffly. "It was a quiet night."

Myrth nodded and let himself into the tower room. DJar was as he'd been before, but dressed in the gray uniform Myrth remembered from his time in the north. "Are you armed, *Shuwarr?*" he asked without introduction.

"I have my faculties, Little Brother." He opened his eyes, ablaze in the dim pre-dawn light of the room, "And my skill."

"Only the strong survive the Maelstrom, *Shuwarr,*" Myrth said. "Our skills and blades are honed. Do not try us. Even the Fae among us are strong as you have seen."

"I am bound by honor, *Tepok* Myrth. You lead, I follow." He stood then, a study in fluid grace.

"Was it a worthy battle?" Myrth asked. "When you were taken?"

DJar smiled. "It was a worthy chase. Your retainer was tenacious. The Fae with the flower hair awakened my brother-in-arms, Shirk." DJar's glowing eyes watched Myrth, waiting. Myrth nodded and turned away from the Nura. Together, they started down the spiral stairs. Myrth spent the few moments it took to descend composing himself, breathing steadily to keep the forcelines smooth. The Nura's nonchalance around battle and death still unnerved him, even after all this time.

"I am certain Shirk was prized," Myrth added when they reached the hub and stepped out into the throne room.

"He was," DJar agreed. They continued across the empty throne room and out into the Great Hall where the others had gathered. Marco held Jerrold's cushion, the dragon fairy returned to stitches roiling across the black silk. Auros-Gado, and Genow stood beside him. They'd been joined by Nepo's remaining Honor Guards and retainers. His elfin captain, Leona, stood near the Sun Goblin Jenna and the fairy Pallan. Leona's shock of short white hair mirrored Jenna's green hair. Pallan, a lithe, lavender-skinned fairy, flitted near Marco on three-foot wings. Marladon leaned against the wall, his elegant silhouette setting him apart from the soldiers around him as much as his physical distance from them. Nepo folded his arms across his bare chest as they approached. Everyone carried a pack filled with supplies for the journey. Sage and Ryn stood at the doors. DJar hissed at the sight of Sage.

"You mistake him," Myrth warned in Nura, holding up a three-fingered hand. "He is Fae not kin." DJar scowled and studied the creature at the door. Sage had the appearance of a Gray Daemon, a human body, though bent with age, with satyr-like hind legs ending in large paws. His hands were clawed, leaning on a staff that was as tall as his bent frame. The goat-like face and long velvety ears were surrounded by wiry white hair that joined with a beard so long it dragged along the floor. Jay joined them, lightly stepping around DJar and Myrth, to stand with Ryn and Sage near the door.

"The idea is to use our flying disc spells," Jay said to DJar. We won't be able to keep pace with the dragon so Master Marladon will fly on ahead to inform Olimidia of our arrival."

"Seek out Clippen," Myrth added. "He is acting Magistrate." Marladon nodded in understanding.

"Fair flight, Brother," DJar said to Marladon as the Fire Master picked up his backpack and turned to the door. Marladon looked back and saluted DJar as they had been doing at mealtime. DJar returned the salute, remaining motionless until the Fire Master disappeared out the door.

Jay borrowed Sage's staff and used it to trace a large circle in the air around her, just above the ground. Where she traced, the air began to glow and as she finished the circle, she stepped up onto a disc of Air that hovered about three inches from the ground. She passed Sage his staff then sat in the center of the disc, concentrating, standing with one metaphorical foot in the Mage Realm and one in the Physical Realm. Ryn traced the same circle around himself, using his sword as a focus. As the disc formed, he stepped up onto it. He stood in the center, balanced on the balls of his feet. Sage tossed a pillow into the center of the hall and drew a circle around it, shuffling near DJar and Myrth as he drew the circle of the flying disc. When he'd finished, the pillow floated about an inch off the ground. Sage climbed aboard and settled onto the pillow. Pallan, Leona, and Jenna joined him. Marco stepped up onto Ryn's disc, followed by Genow who took a seat near the center where Ryn stood. "We'll board Jay's," Myrth directed and he waited for DJar to lead the way to the glowing disc. Nepo and Myrth flanked the Nura as he climbed aboard. He sat near the Wind Mistress, closed his eyes and retreated into meditation. Auros-Gado stepped up onto the Wind Mistress' disc, sitting between DJar and Myrth, blades at the ready. Jay's disc moved first, followed by Ryn and then Sage.

They flew through the water garden to the main gate then out over the interior lake. Looking down through the crystal clear waters, Marco could see all the way to the sandy bottom. Behind them, domed rooms and hallways spiraled out from the central island.

Much of Sea Spray was actually underwater. Beyond this crater lake, a ring island called Hope Island sheltered the castle from the Sea of Scorn beyond. The discs passed through the trees to the inland sea. Here, the water was deeper, murky, home to a half-dozen korsks that guarded the Water Master's realm, acting as ferries for the guests Nepo welcomed and a fierce deterrent for those that the Semian didn't want to talk to.

At the shore, the discs slowed, entering the Wild Wood forest. Tracks and wagon trails penetrated the forest, giving passage through it, and Jay started south along a wide road. They'd passed into a black daemon stronghold when they entered the forest and, despite the sunshine and freshness of the morning, the party members fell into a sullen silence. Dread and the feeling of being watched joined them on their discs.

"Watch him, Masters," Ryn warned. Auros turned to look at Ryn and DJar's eyes slid open. "The last time he was here, he called the black daemons to his aid." Myrth looked from Ryn to DJar. The Nura smiled and closed his eyes again.

Marco stepped into the Mage Realm. Where DJar should have been, there was a smoky hint of a body. Marco had seen it before, when Kryoso first started working in the Mage Realm. *"It's like he's not all the way here."* Marco contemplated the creature, *"Are all the Nura see-through?"* he thought to Myrth.

"Yes," Myrth replied. *"They do not work magic from the Mage Realm."*

"Not—," Marco gasped.

Myrth interrupted him, *"No, not from the Physical Realm either. A decade of study and I can't explain it any more than by saying they step away."*

"You never just asked them?" he chided.

"Mind your tone," Myrth snapped aloud, glaring back at Marco.

Marco bowed his head quickly, face flaring red as Gado suppressed a chuckle and DJar's eyes found him. "I apologize, Master," he said. He felt a sudden weight on the forcelines around him, as if a large boulder had been gently rolled into a basket he was carrying in his arms. Then it was gone, as quickly as it'd come. The goblins had drawn their weapons, eyes fixed on DJar now. The Nura held up his hands, empty. *"That weight just now was the Nura?"* Marco thought at Myrth.

"Yes," Myrth responded. *"He was testing the lines between us—you, me, and the goblins."* Aloud, Myrth continued, "Be at ease, Auros-Gado. DJar was just curious." In his own language, Myrth addressed DJar, "Anything else you'd like to test, I suggest you warn us first, or you may end up joining Shirk in the Sands."

"They are all bound to you, except the green one." DJar replied. He thought a moment before adding, "I find the weight of your power satisfying, Little Brother Myrth."

Myrth glared at him but said no more.

Ryn leaned into Marco, "Watch that one," he said. "He's slippery, regardless of what the Earth Master says."

The discs flew for a few hours before Ryn called a halt and they took a break. "I'm a strong Air Mage," he admitted with a chuckle, "but I'm not a Master."

"Do not strain yourself, Elf Ryn," Jay said, approaching him. "You carry Genow and he can sustain you if needed but we are making good time and we can allow you rest. Save your strength for when it's needed."

"Thank you, Mistress," he said, bowing his head. Marco followed him to where DJar and Myrth sat near a small spring, sipping water they'd scooped from the basin. "Did you use flying discs?" Ryn asked DJar, pointing to where they'd landed and Sage still sat with Pallan.

"I can make one, if allowed," DJar said. "Bonded, I only dream."

Myrth added, "He means meditate. DJar is not allowed to work magic unless I say he can."

"Didn't he work magic earlier?" Marco asked, remembering the weight of the Nura in the forcelines.

"No, he was simply exploring, he didn't work." Myrth then added clarification of Ryn's question, translating for DJar, and explaining that the elf was asking if DJar had used flying discs in the past.

"Ho," DJar said, falling silent briefly. "I can make one," he repeated, smiling. "I do understand some Fae, Little Brother," the Nura added with an acknowledging bow of his head. "But," he added, switching to Nura, "your translations are appreciated."

Myrth studied him then returned the bow. "Then I will continue them," he offered.

"He's not going to tell you, Ryn," Marco supplied as the conversation between Myrth and DJar ended. Marco bent down near Myrth to scoop water, avoiding being too close to the prisoner. Ryn scoffed and followed Marco's example. Marco thought to Myrth, *"If he can work magic we cannot see or understand, how do you know he did not work any?"* Myrth frowned at Marco's question but did not supply an answer.

"Do you work Air, Marco?" Ryn asked as they sat near Myrth, sipping water from their cups.

"It is hard for me," Marco admitted. "I am attuned to Earth and have been all my life. I can work Fire and use basic patterns with Water, nothing fancy. You, I think, are an Air Mage. Flying discs are a specialty of yours."

"Of Air Mages, yes," Ryn added. "My personal specialty is barrier spells. Do you have a favored spell?"

Marco thought for several minutes before answering, "I don't know if it has a name. I call it liquid sand." He reached out then to the Earth Cloud, closing his eyes just before he touched it and retreating into the Mage Realm. He pulled the cloud to heel and thought of ribbons of earth, the cloud obeyed his will, forming into ribbons. Ryn gasped and Marco felt the clearing tense around him. He wove the ribbons together—over, under, over, under—then opened his eyes. The soil had flowed into ribbons of rock that bent and swayed as he wove them together. When he was done and the rock ribbons no longer moved, he'd created a woven stone mat. He blinked and released the Earth Cloud. The stone turned back to dirt that slumped to the ground and retreated to the forest floor where it belonged. With a sigh, he closed his eyes and looked to the forcelines at his core, smoothing them. He studied the eddies he'd made around Myrth and smoothed them as well.

"Impressive?" Auros asked, smiling at Ryn as he and Gado joined them for a drink. The elf nodded. Marco caught DJar looking at him, weighing him.

Marco smiled at the Nura. Auros glanced over his shoulder at DJar, locking eyes with the prisoner until DJar looked away.

Myrth supplied an answer to Marco's previous question into the silence that spread around them. *"I do not know that he did not work any magic. However, Nura do work Shadow and Air, which we can see."*

"How does he press on the forcelines?"

"His will bends magic toward him. You feel the same to others when you gather the Earth Cloud and prepare to work." Marco swallowed and blinked at the Earth Master.

"Marladon is going to get too far ahead at this rate," Myrth rumbled aloud, standing. "Let's move."

Jay and Sage took turns with his staff forming their Air discs, and their passengers climbed aboard. DJar, sitting comfortably near Jay and Nepo, closed his eyes and returned to his meditation. Ryn drew his sword and formed his disc where he stood. Marco and Genow climbed aboard and they started along the track once more.

"We should reach the edge of the Wild Wood before Rysk sets," Ryn muttered. Even if we stop once more."

True to his estimate, they reached the edge of the Woods and stopped for the night as Rysk neared the horizon, following behind the Fiery Sisters. They set camp quickly and decided on two watches, one to watch DJar and one to watch the Woods. Ryn explained to the mages who would be taking turns watching DJar what he had experienced bringing the Nura to Sea Spray, wrapped in complex matrices of magic that had to be maintained the entire way, and what he'd seen since, a sedate DJar happy to meditate and not reach out for any magic. While Myrth felt that there was no chance DJar would work magic, it was still worthwhile watching him through the night.

After dinner, Myrth took his jars from his pack and set Marladon's down between himself and Jay. Nepo drifted near enough to hear the conversation. "Marladon," Myrth called, concentrating on the Fire jar. "A quick check-in?"

"Myrth," Marladon responded almost instantly. "How is my brother?"

Myrth grimaced at the jar, "DJar is behaving himself."

"Where are you?" Jay asked.

"The Crossroad's Inn," he said. "They were accommodating of my dragon," he added with a smile in his voice. "You'll be here tomorrow, I imagine."

"Yes," Nepo and Jay said. Myrth nodded.

"Sleep well," Marladon finished, cutting off further discussion. Myrth picked up the jar and set it gingerly back in his pack.

Marco had pulled the late night watch, splitting his time between watching the edge of the Wild Woods for black daemons and stepping into the Mage Realm to study DJar. Although awake, the Nura did not try to converse with Marco. The Ghost Moon had set long hours before, and the Fiery Sisters were not yet ready to rise. From the Mage Realm, Marco could see the puddles of Shadow magic that marked black daemons foraging in the Wild Woods. Some drifted close to the edge of their stronghold but none crossed through the barrier of discomfort that marked the edge of their territory. Marco had been watching a group of ten meandering toward them for half his shift. They moved resolutely toward the edge of the woods and sporadically one or two would put on a burst of speed. *"Hunting rabbits,"* Marco decided. *"Or birds."* As they neared the edge of the woods, Marco heard a slow, deliberate clicking, followed by a low whistle. He stepped out of the Mage Realm, eyes falling on DJar. The Nura's eyes were open, burning with orange daemon fire. He did it again, three clicks of his tongue followed by a long, low whistle.

"What are you doing?" Marco asked. He was expecting a smile, maybe a chagrined look away.

The Nura deliberately ignored him, giving three clicks of the tongue and a low whistle followed by a single word barely whispered, *"Haath."*

Marco stepped away from his post and nudged the nearest body. Auros awakened almost instantly, catching the Nura's next iteration. "What?" Marco felt the goblin reach out on the forcelines to wake Myrth. Myrth stirred, sitting up to stare at DJar. The Nura fell silent as Auros-Gado stood, drawing two daggers apiece, each as long as their forearms.

The Nura closed his eyes but he didn't relax into meditation. Marco stepped into the Mage Realm. DJar appeared the same, smoky glass and burning eyes that sat watching him.

"He's called daemons!" Ryn suddenly shouted. "He did it before!"

Marco looked up at the Wild Woods. The ten daemons who'd been hunting near the edge of the forest stronghold had now left the woods and were barreling toward their camp. The party had only a moment before the daemons reached their encampment.

"Release them!" Myrth hissed, snapping his beak an inch from DJar's nose.

DJar held out his hands, empty palms outward. "I do not hold them," he said matter-of-factly.

Myrth hmphed in disbelief. "Auros, Gado, to me!" he shouted. The goblins leapt for him, blades in both hands, and Myrth pulled the Earth up around himself, the goblins, and DJar, shielding them all, safe from the daemons.

Marco checked the forcelines, smoothing them after Myrth's work. Around him, guards leapt from their beds, grabbing blades and rushing forward to meet the charging daemons. Jay and Nepo closed in on him. "Remember," Nepo chided, "Let the guards do their job. Your power is too great for trifles."

"Genow," Marco snapped, "Help Ryn, he's a Barrier Mage!"

"Aye!" the healer rushed to where Ryn stood near the fire. Marco felt the Air press outward around them. Stepping into the Mage Realm, he could see the blue wall of Air solidify around the camp, a yard in front of the nearest black daemon, just shy of the green whirling Life energy that marked the advancing elf Captain Leona.

Marco returned to the Physical Realm, trying to suppress the adrenaline that rushed through him and caused eddies and waves in the nearby Earth Cloud. Nepo laid a warm hand on his shoulder. "Breathe, Marco," he urged. "Calm yourself." It was then he noticed the queasy swaying of the earth beneath his feet. He felt Myrth on the forcelines, steadying his emotions and working to smooth the Earth.

"Open here, Ryn!" Leona shouted. The Air Mage complied, and Leona and her partner Jenna rushed through the barrier, bristling with daggers and the same long knives Auros-Gado used. Their steel crashed into the blades of the nearest daemons. By firelight, the black daemons' iron blades sparkled. Their burnished human torsos gave way to black coarse hair on their arms and shoulders, where their human features turned goat-like. Instead of human or bestial legs, however, the daemons ran forward on four blade-like limbs, each one ending in a dagger-like point. They cried out as Leona and Jenna joined the battle, goat-like faces snarling, and bleating. Others crashed into Ryn's barrier but it held solid despite their attacks against it.

Marco watched as the elf Leona and goblin Jenna dispatched two black daemons in quick succession. They turned and spread out from where they'd exited the barrier, protecting each other's back but driving deeper into the daemon force. With another three dead at the hands of the vicious pair of guards, the remaining daemons retreated, bleating and shaking burly arms high overhead in a show of force and bravado. Jenna and Leona did not follow them. When he was certain there were no more attackers, Ryn dropped his barrier. Genow sheathed his sword and laid a healing hand on the mage's shoulder, renewing his energy. Myrth's barrier dropped as quickly as it'd formed. Inside, he'd remained standing, back to Marco and Nepo, eyes fixed on DJar. Auros-Gado sheathed their blades after a brief look around. In all, the attack and driving off the daemons had lasted only a few short minutes.

Myrth's glare would have withered Marco or anyone who knew him well. DJar appeared unfazed by it. "I thought he couldn't work," Marco spat, closing the distance between them so that he stood one step closer to the Nura than the others, but still behind Auros-Gado.

"He didn't," Myrth grumbled.

"That wasn't magic?" Marco asked, incredulous.

Myrth shook his head, "No, not that I can discern."

"Do not be too hasty to dismiss him, Master," Ryn warned. "They work magic we cannot see from the Mage Realm or Physical one."

"I am bound, it is dishonorable to work magic," DJar offered.

"Are you honorable, *Shuwarr DJar*?" Nepo asked in Nura, moving to stand beside Marco.

DJar glared, his eyes flaring. "Do not question my honor, Little Brother," he returned vehemently.

Nepo roared and leapt for the Nura, stopping with their noses touching. DJar had his hands up again, palms out, empty and nonthreatening. *"Tepok* Nepo!" Nepo demanded, pounding his chest. The daemon-fire of DJar's eyes lit the Semian's furry face, casting the Water Master's honey-colored eyes red. Nepo bared fangs in the Nura's face.

"*Tepok* Nepo," DJar acknowledged, blinking slowly. Nepo straightened, backing away as he reached his full seven foot height.

"When he called them before," Ryn offered, "he was bound. We used an endowment of Water, Air and Earth to hold him. He still managed to call the black daemons to his aid. Once he'd distracted us with the daemons, he slipped his bonds and attacked."

"How did you stop him?" Marco asked.

"Kita clobbered him, bounced his brain making it impossible for him to work magic," Ryn supplied, unsuccessfully hiding the smile on his face and unable or unwilling to keep it out of his voice.

DJar studied the elf mage.

"Gag him," Myrth said, indicating DJar before turning away.

Auros-Gado watched their Master until Myrth reached the fire, then they turned to DJar and smiled. Ryn threw an endowment of Air and Water around the Nura, holding the Nura's hands at his sides, binding his arms tight to his torso. Marco stepped up to DJar, a handful of Earth already formed into a rock ball to act as the gag. "Don't make this difficult," he said.

"Or do, and see what happens," Gado added, his smile growing feral. A blade glinted in his hand and he danced forward to place the gleaming metal on DJar's cheek, the tip near his smoldering, daemon-fire eye.

"Shhh," DJar hissed quietly through clenched teeth.

"Are you going to open up or does Gado carve?" Marco asked.

DJar smiled and then opened his mouth for the gag.

Myrth, Nepo, Jay and Sage stood to one side, watching Marco, Ryn and the goblins bind and gag the Nura. "I thought he was honorable," Nepo muttered. "All this talk of Ruby Hills and Crystal Hills and honor."

"He said he wouldn't use magic and from what I can tell, he didn't," Myrth supplied. "He agreed to come with us to Olimidia, and he is still coming with us."

Sage leaned close, his rough voice just above a whisper, "That was an incantation, Myrth. The Grays use them." Myrth, Nepo, and Jay studied the gray daemon. Sage hadn't always been a gray daemon. Once, he'd been the Land-Nymph Donatan, a daemon hunter who lost his way both figuratively and literally in the Vast Wildlands. Returning to his home, he had spent several seasons trying to convince anyone who'd listen that he was really Donatan, trying to convince them not to kill him. "The last word, *Haath*, what does that mean?"

"Meat," Myrth and Nepo translated in unison.

"He called them over here and told them there was meat here? They were hunting in the night," Jay surmised. She turned to where Pallan and Leona were disposing of the five bodies, drawing the corpses far away, upwind, and piling them into a large pile before setting them alight so that they wouldn't spoil the encampment.

Marco and Ryn joined the Masters and Sage. They'd left the Nura with the Sun Goblins, Jenna having joined Gado and Auros in taunting their prisoner. Jeers and verbal jabs took the place of blades as the soldiers worked through the adrenaline rush that the attack had brought on. "Ryn," Myrth said, "He did this before when you were taking him to Sea Spray?"

"Yes, Master. Clicking and whistling to call the daemons," Ryn nodded. "I did say that before."

"You did." Myrth pondered the Nura. "I was lulled by his talk of honor," he admitted. "He stays that way until we reach Olimidia," he finished. "If I thought it'd do any good, I'd blindfold him." Then he snapped at Auros-Gado to stop pestering the prisoner and get some rest. They did as he said, Jenna reluctantly returning to Leona's side, helping with the last of the corpses.

With their rest disturbed, Sage and Pallan agreed to take over the watch, letting Marco return to his bed. He lay down near Nepo, turning away from the lion Semian and the fire to stare at DJar. "Trust Sage and Pallan, Marco," Nepo breathed. "Sage isn't as dottering and old as he plays." Marco turned over and met the Master's honey-colored eyes. "Breathe easy and rest now; it's a luxury you won't always have."

"It won't be easy," Marco admitted.

Nepo smiled, "It never is," he said, a soft purr in his voice.

Marco woke early, the camp breaking around him. He rose and hurriedly prepared for the day's journey. DJar remained bound and gagged. When it was time to move from the fireside to the Air disc, he refused to budge. Nepo leaned in close to the Nura and whispered something to him. For a moment, they stared at each other, then DJar stood and moved to Jay's disc where he sat once again. They were soon on their way, skimming across the grass of the plains, making good time with no trees to dodge. Before noon, they reached the Crossroads Inn where Marladon had spent the night. They stopped briefly, Pallan, Jenna, and Leona foraging for fresh fruit while Ryn rested. When the Air Mage was ready, they boarded their discs again and started across the plains, continuing through the rest of the day, and stopping as the Fiery Sisters touched the horizon. As dinner cooked, Myrth removed DJar's gag. "Will we have any more problems from you?" Myrth asked in the Nura language.

"Only the ones you allow me to get away with," DJar said, spitting dirt from his mouth, aiming away from the Earth Master, glaring at Gado when the red-headed goblin caught his eye. Daemon-fire flared bright, lighting the Nura's face.

"Is that honorable?" Myrth asked.

"I am a prisoner of war. My respect and love of Sybon stays my hand, *Tepok* Myrth."

"I hold your bond," Myrth said.

"As does *Tepok* Nepo and the *Tepok-Myir.*" DJar added. "I remember this well enough. I owe them nothing."

Myrth stood, "I will bring you some dinner," he said. DJar lowered his head in thanks.

They ate quickly and set the same watch rotation, each mage set to watch DJar now with the understanding that short of magic and actual escape, the Nura would try anything to injure, slow or delay the party. Once again, Marco found himself watching DJar and the dark night around them in the early morning hours.

DJar was awake, watching him. "You," he said at last, "Pale One, I would like some water." He spoke hesitantly, thinking through the Fae words before speaking them.

Marco scoffed at the Nura. "I'm not a Pale One," he said, "And no water."

"To deny a prisoner..." DJar trailed off, shaking his head.

"You've never asked for water before."

"It is dry here," he said.

"You'll have to ask Myrth in the morning."

The daemon-kin fell silent for a moment. "When do we arrive at the Fae city?"

Marco thought for a moment before answering, "About a day." DJar nodded, stretched his hands, fanning out his fingers, the only part of his upper body he could move. He shifted his weight around and then closed his eyes, retreating to meditation again. Marco watched him for a moment then slipped into the Mage Realm and studied him and their surroundings. Satisfied that the Nura wasn't up to anything, Marco returned to the Physical Realm. An hour passed before he woke Sage and Pallan to take his place, relaying to them the water conversation he'd had with DJar. Sage nodded and shooed Marco to bed.

Pallan took flight, scouting the surrounding area while Sage hunkered down near DJar, watching him. "You meditate more than the Masters," he said in a wheezy half-whisper.

DJar opened his eyes and studied Sage, lips curling in a snarl. "You are Fae?" he asked.

"I am Sage," Sage said.

"*Tepok* Myrth says you are Fae, not Gray."

"I was once Fae. Now I am Sage." DJar frowned and then closed his eyes. Sage felt him step away. He knew that he looked like a gray daemon in the Mage Realm and that his specialty as a Time Mage would not be readable there. Sage waited for DJar to return.

DJar opened his eyes again, contemplating the creature in front of him. "And when you *were* Fae, how did you become Gray?"

"Gray daemons are not to be trifled with," Sage said with a bitter smile.

DJar returned the smile and nodded, "Ah, yes," he said. "I am sleeping now, Gray." DJar closed his eyes again and fell into silence. Sage sat quietly as well, watching and waiting.

A Prisoner's Welcome

M yrth!" Nepo shouted suddenly. He'd fallen to his knees near Sage and Pallan as they stopped for their first break the next morning. Nepo's Honor Guard ran to him, Myrth and Marco joining them, leaving Auros and Gado to watch the prisoner.

"Nepo," Myrth soothed, "What is it?"

"Tekalo," he whispered, "He's gone. GONE!"

"Gone how?" Myrth asked. "Dead?"

"I...I don't know," His voice hitched in his throat.

"You said before he was disappearing," Marco said. "Is this different?"

"Yes," Nepo whispered, "it hurt, here," he touched his stomach and his head, "and here."

"Call to him," Myth whispered. "Try," Nepo dropped into the Mage Realm, his body unmoving, but Marco could feel the Master drifting through the Earth Cloud. Water responded to its Master and the water vapor in the air began to condense, forming droplets and raining without a cloud.

"I can try an Eye," Jay offered.

"How?" Myrth asked, "We do not know where he is or where he was last."

"He may know," she said, nodding to DJar. Wet from Nepo's condensation rain, DJar frowned at them. "If he tells us where he was going, I can set an Eye in that direction."

"You were returning to the Crystal Hills," Myrth said to the Nura.

"Was I?" DJar asked. Myrth glared at the Nura.

"I can start with the Blasted Lands," Jay said with a frown.

"Let's get him to Olimidia. We can try an Eye from there," Myrth said after a moment's thought. They all nodded and returned to their respective discs.

They stayed the course throughout the day, stopping late in the afternoon for a quick meal. Myrth pulled Marladon's jar from his pack. "Marladon," he called and then waited for the Fire Master to respond. "We're a few hours out and making good time."

"Good to hear," Marladon said. "Clippen has asked you not to make a scene bringing the prisoner in. He wants DJar brought to the Matriarch's Palace, to her dungeon.

"Not make a scene? We're the Masters. They're going to notice us," Nepo said.

"I'll meet you at the crater's edge. Come in from the north and few will notice you," Marladon replied.

Myrth checked the sky. "We'll be there near sunset," he confirmed.

"Let's go!" Myrth shouted to the others after the jar had gone dark. He dropped to Jay's disc near DJar and his guard climbed aboard. "Nepo," he said as the Water Master knelt beside him, facing away from the Nura. "Let us know if Tekalo returns."

Nepo nodded, a short, quick gesture to let Myrth know he'd heard.

Marco felt a knot form in his throat. "*Please be well,*" he thought, a sudden fear for his best friend's life blossoming in his chest. They raced southward, following a well-used trade route as the Fiery Sisters continued their descent toward the horizon. Rysk trailed them by several hours and wouldn't yet be at his zenith when they disappeared for the night. The hours passed and as they neared

Olimidia, they could see in their red-gold light, Marladon and his dragon glinting, marking the northern rim of the crater that held the last of the Shining Cities, Olimidia. The Land-Nymph city had once glittered in the night. At the bottom of the large crater, its lights had mirrored the starry skies above. Now, nearly empty of life, only the occasional firelight would shine out in the coming darkness.

From both the north and south, the road down into the crater was steep, although the northern route climbed higher, faster, and held many switchbacks. Wagons generally entered and exited from the south, where the road fell gradually to the crater's floor. Because of this, the city fanned out to the west, east, and south, with almost no buildings along the northern slopes of the crater. Bringing DJar in via the north road did have the advantage that none of the few hundred Land-Nymphs living in the city were likely to see him.

Marladon's dragon landed as the flying discs reached the edge of the crater. Its white scales held a pearlescence, causing it to glitter and gleam in the light of the setting suns. Unlike the burly dragons of Marladon's army, the riding dragons were slim and delicate-boned. It was twice as tall as a horse at the shoulders and three times as long from tip to tail. Its narrow jaws were made for eating insects and fruit. The bridle and halter looped loosely around its jaws and over thin branching, stag-like horns above its bright blue eyes. Marladon's saddle sat at the base of the dragon's neck, keeping any riders and packs well away from the four leathery wings that beat in figure eights, paddling their way through the sky. The dragon bowed low, allowing Marladon to slide to the ground. Its thin body folded into thirds as it perched, waiting for its rider to return, its thin legs under it like a cat's, while its rudder tail whipped around its feet and it buried its nose in the grass, snuffling for grubs and insects in the spring greenery near its chest.

Marladon cooed, patting the dragon's neck quickly as he stepped away to meet Jay and Myrth. "Safely arrived?" he asked.

"Mostly," Nepo replied. "The sooner we are done with this," he indicated DJar, "the sooner we can get on with other things."

Marladon nodded and approached DJar, saluting, "Brother," he greeted.

"Forgive my rudeness, Brother Mortak. I am bound." DJar said with a nod.

Marladon returned the nod in understanding. "You are ordered to the dungeon here," he said. "I asked for a more suitable prison but the Magistrate would not entertain such an idea." DJar nodded then turned to Myrth for further explanation in his own language.

"The Magistrate is securing you in the palace dungeon. Your bond is held by the Magistrate through the *Tepok-Myir*," Myrth supplied.

DJar nodded once, bowing his head. "I understand," he said to Marladon.

"I have no claim over you, Brother," Marladon added. "I ask you not to cause me trouble on the way to the dungeon." He indicated the dragon. "Reirdra is precious to me."

"I understand," DJar said again, "*Wuatli* are precious to all."

Marladon nodded. "Jay, stay with us?" he asked. "Clippen will meet us at the inner Grand Courtyard." He turned to Nepo and Myrth. "We will need a translator."

"I will translate for you," Myrth said. "Marco, Auros, Gado, Genow, settle yourselves at the Academy. Ryn, you are released to return to your duties here." They all bowed. "Nepo?" he asked.

"Still nothing, Myrth. I should speak to Basskin."

"Basskin has taken quarters in the Palace," Marladon supplied, "I will fetch him if you'd like." Nepo nodded.

As the party broke up, Myrth released DJar's bonds. The Nura stretched his arms, balled his hands into fists a few times, and rolled his shoulders and neck. The Nura and Mortak climbed up onto the dragon's delicate neck. With a nudge from Marladon, the dragon sprang into the air, beating its wings and stirring up a windstorm. Jay formed a disc large enough for the other three Masters and they followed the dragon, close enough to intervene if there was a problem but far enough that the wash of its wings didn't upset their disc.

Marco watched them leave, the other guard members standing close beside him. "I am glad we were able to serve together, Marco," Ryn said. "You are an interesting counter to the feisty Lady Warrior Myrth also keeps on retainer. I look forward to serving with you both again." He bowed, saluted, and then started down the switchback northern road to the bottom of the crater. Marco watched him for a while then looked up, noticing that everyone was looking at him expectantly, even Sage and Pallan.

Marco sighed and shrugged before following Ryn down the road. The others fanned out behind him, Sage forming another disc and plying the Air beside them instead of walking.

Marladon and Jay flew directly down into the crater and toward the central peak. The flattened top of the peak held two large buildings and their walled grounds. To the east sat the Academy, to the west, the Matriarch's Palace. When Palo had first swooped into the Shining City with his Potentate army, the Matriarch had put up no resistance. In the negotiations that followed, she'd agreed to house a training grounds for Palo's future cadets in exchange for the Land-Nymphs' continued autonomy. The small armies that manned either building had been rivals ever since.

From above, it was possible to see the odd concentric building style of the Matriarch's Palace. Walls, gardens, and open-air courtyards flowed along the inner perimeter of the building, seemingly cut off from the rest of it. These were the Ways, the women's quarters within the palace. Large rooms and still more courtyards filled the inner areas of the Palace as well, equally inaccessible to the Ways. This inner world was home to the Matriarch and her sons alone. Currently, there was no Matriarch as debate still raged between the Land-Nymph clans over which Clan Mother was elder, Moon Clan Mother or Star Clan Mother. All records indicated they were born on the same day in the same year and now vague memories were being questioned, village elders and visitors to the city from long ago sought, who might supply evidence of one baby born in the morning and one born in the afternoon.

Three bright fires lit the courtyard where Clippen waited and Marladon and Jay angled toward them. The dragon moved to one side of the fires while Jay dropped down in the center. Clippen approached them from an alcove to the east. He was Moon Clan, tall and thin but well-muscled. Human in form, his pointy, reed-thin ears rose a few inches above his head and he'd decorated their length with thin gold hoops that blazed in the firelight and tinkled like tiny bells when he moved. Like all Moon Clan, his sharply angled cheeks and chin looked carved from alabaster. While the Star clan's complexion was similar, the Sun Clan ran toward tawny yellows and tallowy off-whites. Clippen had bright pink eyes and a thick mane of white hair the same color as his skin, but Land-Nymph hair and eyes appeared in any color imaginable. Clippen was dressed in a blue and green tunic with black trousers and knee-high palace boots. He'd once fought alongside Myrth, though he technically belonged to Nepo's Honor Guard and often trained with the Potentate; a skilled Air Mage well on his way to earning a second red feather in a cap he refused to wear. Land-Nymphs, by tradition, did not join the Potentate, although they were free to train with them.

Marladon and DJar slid from the dragon and turned to face Clippen who was covering the ground between them with long, determined strides. "Clippen," Marladon greeted as the taller person approached.

Further words were cut off by a dagger-like glare. "Is this it?" Clippen hissed, voice barely above a whisper, tiny fangs bared in a snarl. Marladon nodded. Clippen closed on DJar in two strides and with a rage-filled scream, punched him square in the jaw, throwing his entire weight into the blow. DJar spun away with the force of the punch and dropped to one knee. Myrth appeared between the Land-Nymph and the Nura, one clawed hand to each of them. DJar raised his hands, palms out in his now-familiar unarmed, defenseless position and he slowly stood again. He faced Clippen, unflinching.

DJar's eyes smoldered, the daemon-fire banked low, and his thick tongue snaked out between his fangs to lick the blood from his lips. Clippen screamed again but made no attempt to move around Myrth for another attack. The Land-Nymph visibly rallied his self-control before addressing Myrth, "Get it out of my sight," he hissed. "Palo will be here within a day or two to deal with it." He turned on his toes and disappeared back the way he'd come.

Myrth looked to DJar then, remembering what the Nura had said about the Fae. The daemon-kin was still licking blood from his lips but remained silent.

"And that's the calm one," Nepo added, smiling down at the Nura.

DJar held his hands up again for a moment before balling them into fists and speaking, "I am bound by Sybon's honor to see this through, *Tepok* Myrth, *Tepok* Nepo. Lead and I will follow. I will await the *Tepok-Myir*. I will *not* suffer abuse at the hands of a Fae."

"They do not intend to abuse you, I am certain," Myrth replied. He turned to Marladon. "Jay and I will see to DJar if you'd like to take Nepo to Basskin."

Marladon nodded and gestured for Nepo to follow him. They left the courtyard through the same doors that Clippen had used.

Myrth motioned for DJar to follow them. Within, the Palace was elegant but functional. There were no bare stone walls but there were also no garish art pieces festooning the corridors. Lush carpeting and polished wooden walls held the occasional piece of decor. Some sat on display in alcoves, while others occupied places of prominence on the walls of a t-junction or at the end of a corridor. Some, Myrth knew, were secret panels, doors, and locks that led into the Ways or out to the public areas of the palace.

While Nepo and Marladon journeyed deeper into the private quarters, the others turned toward the front of the palace. Their path took them to a spiral staircase that burrowed down underground. Jay excused herself, remaining behind in the hall as Myrth and DJar descended the stairs. The way was close and cramped, meant to be guarded by a single soldier at most, although there were no guards now. At the bottom, a lamp-lit room greeted them. Two Moon Clan Land-Nymphs stood as they entered. Their chiseled features mirrored Clippen's, their brightly colored hair and eyes relieving the white alabaster of their skin. Rage filled their faces when they saw DJar and the Nura hesitated to approach. They knew who their prisoner was. The Nura held out his hands, placating them as Myrth stepped around him and up to the nearest guard. Surprised at the appearance of the Earth Master, the pair of Land-Nymph's faltered, their anger replaced by surprise and then fear.

"The Nura is a prisoner of the Grand Syra," Myrth said. "Palo will not appreciate it if you are abusive toward him and neither will I."

"Master," the blue-haired Land-Nymph said with a bow of his head. His companion followed suit, his red hair washed out in the yellow lamp light. Myrth knew these two, although he didn't know their names. They were good soldiers. The red-haired one turned and opened a cage door, stepping aside and motioning for DJar to enter.

The Nura ducked through the low door. Beyond, the metal cube was just tall enough for him to stand. If he'd been a Land-Nymph, he would have had to stoop to fit. The straw bedding looked fresh but the water bucket was empty. "There is no water," DJar informed Myrth.

"I will ask for some to be brought," Myrth replied.

The guards' eyes widened at the exchange. "You speak its language?" the blue-haired one squeaked.

Myrth nodded. "Yes, and I know their customs. Have fresh water brought."

"Clippen ordered no food or water," the blue-haired one replied.

"Are you defying the Earth Master?" Myrth asked, his voice dropping an octave, the stone floor beneath them shivering.

"No, Master!" the red-haired one hurriedly answered. "I will get the water now." He rushed to leave, grabbing a fresh bucket from a stack near the door.

Myrth turned to DJar, "They will bring water. Clippen ordered no food."

"I will continue to feast," DJar said. Myrth nodded, then frowned. He knew tales of Nura not eating for months when they were on sacred journeys. They always responded to the lack of food by saying they were feasting on the Dream or eating of Sand. Myrth studied the daemon-kin. He knew it was rude to ask one of these fasting warriors when they'd last eaten. DJar met his eyes and the daemon-fire flames brightened. The red-haired Land-Nymph returned then, a full bucket sloshing water as he passed it to Myrth. Myrth held the bucket to his mouth and drank from it. He then handed it to DJar. DJar took the water and waited, watching Myrth. When no sign of a fast-acting poison appeared, he sipped the water also, then turned away from the door. The blue-haired one closed the cell and locked it.

Myrth turned to the Land-Nymphs, studying them in turn. "I know you to be level-headed, good soldiers," he began. "His name," he indicated DJar, "is DJar. He is a major in his home army. He may be our only prisoner, but he was not the only one of his kind here. *He* might not be the one who killed our fair Matriarch. Do not abuse him." Myrth paused, then added, "If he chooses to leave, you won't be able to stop him. Remember, you are each precious." The Land-Nymphs studied their prisoner, who'd settled into the straw and appeared to be meditating. "We are holding him for the Grand Syra, who will be here in a day or two. Pass on my message to the other guards when they come on duty."

"Yes, Master," they chorused. Myrth quashed the sudden fear that ran through him and closed his eyes to smooth the forcelines. He checked DJar in the Mage Realm but couldn't see him there. Myrth opened his eyes. The Nura's body was still there, but he'd stepped away.

Above ground again, Myrth noticed that Jay had not stayed. He traced his way along the forcelines. Marco and the goblins were at the Academy, along with the faint echoes of a dozen other goblins who served there. He could feel Jay on the forcelines as she walked with Nepo toward the Academy. Further away still, Sylus felt nervous, his agitation echoing along the bond Myrth shared with his servant. "*Are you well, Sylus?*" Myrth asked.

"*I am,*" came the elf's thought, "*Vellin and Sennet arrived with no answers.*"

"*Stay ready,*" Myrth supplied, unwilling to deal with the commander's worries. As they forced their way into Myrth's mind, he closed the connection and delved deeper into the forcelines tied to his soul for one more: Oracle. The bond between them was nearly as old as they were, formed when the wildling Oracle, driven mad by Time magic, had found his way to sanity with a hawk-boy's help. Oracle was agitated as well, traveling as fast as his horse could run. Myrth frowned, backing away from the seer without speaking.

"*Things are in motion,*" he thought to himself. With a sigh, Myrth pressed on down the corridor and along another flight of stairs to a door. He let himself out, passing from the private residence to a public drawing room at the front of the palace.

He hurried through the drawing room, down a hall and out the front door where four Land-Nymphs stood guard. They bowed low when they noticed the Master, allowing him to pass. He wasn't able to catch up to Jay and Nepo before they entered the Academy across the road. He followed Jay's presence until he found them in her quarters at the back of the Academy on the highest floor. He entered without knocking, knowing Jay and Nepo would sense him.

With a sigh, he joined them, slumping in a chair. The three sat there without talking or moving for some time. "Still no Tekalo," Nepo muttered after a few moments. "Basskin took it well enough. He doesn't believe his son is dead either."

"Do you?" Myrth asked.

"No, I don't think he is. He's gone, but he's not dead."

"*He's stepped away,*" Myrth thought before dismissing it. "*DJar has stepped away.*" he said to himself. "We're tired," he said aloud. "We should sleep." Jay nodded. Nepo stood slowly and Myrth followed him to his feet. "I don't anticipate problems before Palo reaches us," he added.

"Good," Jay lilted. "I can sleep in tomorrow."

"Thank you for your help, Mistress of the Wind," Myrth said with a bow. She returned the gesture and watched Nepo and Myrth leave without standing. Nepo's own quarters were back across the way at the Palace. Given that Tekalo was his Chosen One, apprentice to Water, the Land-Nymphs had unofficially adopted the lion-man. Together, Myrth and Nepo descended to the front door and then Myrth watched the Water Master through the gate and across the road to the Palace before he sought his own bed. Closing the door,

Myrth turned and stopped at the quartermaster's desk. An elf looked up at him, waiting.

"I am going to take Sylus' quarters," he informed the elf.

"Very good, Master," the elf said. "As I told your apprentice, it should be made up. The Lady Warrior and her goblin partner were there most recently. They left quickly and some of their equipment is still there."

Myrth nodded in response and climbed the northern stairs to the fourth floor of the North Wing. At the end of the corridor, he reached out to the Earth Cloud and unlocked the door to Sylus' suite. Myrth pulled Fire from his hands and lit the flames in the lamps around the room. The bed had been made up since D'Mique and Burl had left to chase after T'Pani. Their gear, two packs that looked stuffed with clothes, was sitting near the couch where Marco lay sleeping. Myrth frowned at the packs and sank onto the foot of the bed. For the first time, he found himself wondering where D'Mique and the others were. *"Have you also disappeared? Are you with Tekalo?"* He concentrated on Burl but knew he had no real bond to the goblin and there was no way of knowing if any faint goblin echo was him or any other goblin. He yawned suddenly and laid back onto the bed. *"Perhaps I'll sleep in tomorrow too."*

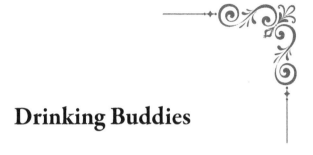

Drinking Buddies

Clippen stared at his breakfast. He'd been joined this morning by Ryn and the other Air Mages who'd captured the daemon-kin. They called it a tree daemon although Ryn had reminded them all this morning that the real name was Nura. The black-skinned goblin Kita had approved of Clippen's attack on the daemon when Clippen had admitted to it. His hand was bruised, perhaps even broken, and he sat with it wrapped in a cold, wet towel. The servants this morning had offered more than once to find him a healer but he'd refused. The two avian Semians, Shuri and Sai, sat across from him, and the elves, Derik and Ryn, beside him across from Kita.

Ryn broke the silence, "It called black daemons again while we were transporting it."

"Did you concuss it too?" Kita asked with a feral grin.

"I'm surprised it tried with the Masters," Sai said, his black and white barred feathers matched the decor of the table, marching across his cheekbones and forehead, replacing his hair with a snow-white dome. Bright yellow eyes matched the gold settings on the table as he looked to Ryn. The elf shrugged.

"Maybe it had to try," Shuri said, his Misty Realms accent still heavy after years in Olimidia, clipping his words off succinctly as they ended. The wood duck Semian picked up his tea and sipped at it, his beak making delicate drinking an art form.

Ryn shrugged his thin shoulders again, picking over a plate of berries. "It, Master Myrth, and Auros-Gado were shielded during the fight with the black daemons. Who knows what happened and how many punches were thrown. I was busy with my barrier."

"And Marco?" Clippen asked.

"Nepo held him back," Ryn said.

"Wise," Derik said, as the others nodded in agreement. "He's still only half-trained at best."

A quick knock at the door brought all eyes to the newcomer. Myrth entered, plainly startled to see the group at meal. "Oh," he started. "My apologies. Your doormen need more training," he said. "They didn't mention that you had company or that you were eating."

"Did you come to scold or discuss better accommodations for the prisoner?" Clippen asked, his voice turning dangerous.

Myrth shook his head, "No. Simply to talk." Clippen studied him judiciously for a long minute before nodding in welcome.

"We will make room, Master," Kita offered. After a moment's hesitation, Myrth returned the nod and crossed the room to where Kita was shifting his plates and Derik positioning another chair. Clippen rang a small silver bell. When the servant appeared, he requested one more setting for the Master. As Myrth settled in, the others watched him, waiting for him to speak. He did not until his own breakfast had been delivered.

"I stayed the night in Sylus' suite," he started. "D'Mique and Burl left some gear behind. Did you see them before they left?"

Clippen thought for a moment before answering, The days had passed in a blur since they'd left. "No. Everything they did was on Tekalo's orders. I knew they were investigating and I knew they were on to something, but..." he trailed off, replaying the stories the Air mages had relayed to him—tales of daemons and lost Land-Nymphs, and the visits he'd had with the distraught father, Timmil, demanding his daughter be found. "Should I have?" he asked, genuinely concerned.

"*We* didn't even know what was happening," Sai said. "They came barreling in asking for volunteer Air Mages and we went."

"I think it was a day or two in the saddle before we were able to put together why we were there and what we were hunting," Shuri continued. "And then we," he indicated Sai and Kita, "doubled back with Burl for supplies at the Crossroads Inn."

"When we reached them again, they already had the prisoner and had killed another," Sai said. Unlike Shuri, his Misty Realms accent had faded and only hints of it remained. Shuri ran a hand through the black feathers that flowed across his head.

Myrth nodded, "You have done well, Clippen. Few would want to take this job under any circumstance, but you have shouldered the burden of leadership in a time of chaos, and you shine in the role."

Clippen ducked his head at Myrth's words and his eyes fell on his wrapped hand. Clippen looked to the ceiling before closing his eyes. "Moon Clan's claim to the throne is stronger than Star Clan's claim," he said. "I will be able to step aside soon enough, and Moon Clan Mother will become the Matriarch. I am too young yet to advise her and too far removed to attend court here." He smiled and looked at Myrth. "Thank you, Myrth. I am glad I am only an interim Magistrate and can return to Sea Spray soon." Kita banged his mug on the table three times in support of Clippen's words. "Until then, we do have a problem to discuss."

"Palo will be here this evening, I believe. I would prefer to answer all the questions at once," Myrth said.

"I would prefer to have my answers first," Clippen pressed.

Myrth studied the Land-Nymph, weighing the authority that now sat upon him. "Ask, and I will do my best to answer then," Myrth said with a bemused smile. He sipped his tea, his own hawk beak better suited to drinking from tea cups than Shuri's duckbill.

"You speak its language," Clippen began.

"In my youth, I spent a decade in the north, beyond the Vast Wildlands and the Great Southern Wilds."

"I knew that Nepo went once to the Ruby Hills, but I did not know that you'd been as well," Clippen responded. Myrth nodded.

"I went in search of a rumored gray daemon whom I could train with. I found him, and he agreed to teach me for a year. Ten years later, he'd taught me all he could." Myrth smiled at the memories. "The Nura are to the northern Hills Kingdoms what the goblins are to the Fanterra Plain, the backbone of every army."

"The gray daemons rule the Hills Kingdoms?" Kita asked. Myrth nodded. "Was Donatan there when he was cursed?"

Clippen answered, "Donatan was lost both figuratively and literally when he was cursed. Not even he knows where he was."

"I don't think he was so far north," Myrth said. "If he had been slaughtering innocents in the Hills Kingdoms, he would have been executed, not cursed."

"And yet," Clippen whispered, "they come here and slaughter innocents, kidnap a child and her nurse, and then don't expect to face punishment?"

Myrth met pain-filled pink eyes that glittered with hatred and tears. *It's been over two cycles,* Myrth thought, *since Mara's death and the loss of her child.* "It's complicated," he said aloud. "I don't think DJar expects to go unpunished. But he won't stick around by choice to face death."

"What would he do?" Clippen and Ryn asked simultaneously. Ryn continued, "You've warned me and others that if he tries to escape we won't be able to stop him."

"Nura are daemon-kin, they don't work magic as we do. They don't use the Mage Realm. We can only hope to counter them by stopping them from leaving the Physical Realm. But you've hunted them. You've seen their disappearing trick," Myrth said to Ryn.

"Air magic," Sai and Shuri said in unison. "A spell we simply don't know," Sai finished.

"No, not Air. Nura magic that we don't know and that we can't use," Myrth warned, "But that can still kill us."

"You lived with them for a decade, and you don't know what they work?" Clippen asked.

"I lived with the gray daemons for a decade. The Nura are servants and soldiers. I learned what I could from them, their language and their customs. They don't normally teach the noble tongue to outsiders. Nepo speaks a little that he picked up as an emissary, and there are maybe a handful of Mortak near Mount Myrs who know some phrases."

"He was teaching me," Ryn noted.

"I suspect it passed the time," Myrth said with a nod. "Those who taught me were off-duty guards along the outer estate walls."

"He has *chosen* to stay," Clippen continued, changing the subject.

"No, he is honor-bound to stay," Myrth corrected. "He was captured in a fair fight and returned to a king's throne. He is in bond now to that throne and to the thrones of all the combatants who captured him."

"What does that mean?" Clippen asked as confused looks crossed the faces around the table.

"The party that D'Mique and Burl took with them, including Tekalo, have a claim on DJar. They represent me, Nepo, Palo, and arguably, Olimidia...which is you," he indicated Clippen.

"We have a claim on him?" Clippen repeated.

"Yes. Nura are servants and soldiers. They serve at the whim of a master. Right now, we all can claim to be DJar's master."

"But, that would mean we owe him life and sustenance," Clippen said, "As any other who serves is afforded."

Myrth shook his head, "No, not according to gray daemon and Nura tradition. He simply belongs to us. We can demand anything reasonable and honorable. We do not have enough sway over him to command him to kill himself or stand still while we kill him, but short of that, he is ours to control *if* we are able."

"Slavery?" Ryn asked, a frown deepening his whisper.

"Not really," Myrth said hesitantly. "It's moot though, as the point of holding his bond is to return it to his true master, not keep him as our servant. He is a prisoner of war and his master will want to reclaim him. We can demand anything for his return, and if DJar's master is honorable, he will agree to our terms."

"Retribution in some way for the deaths we have suffered?" Clippen asked. Myrth nodded.

"And if he is not honorable?" Derik asked.

"He could send an army to retrieve DJar instead, or allow his servant to die at our hands." The table fell silent at Myrth's words. "That isn't likely," Myrth said after a moment. He hesitated before adding his final explanation, "The gray daemon I studied with was named Sybon. DJar is a commander in the army that serves Sybon's son."

"You know each other?" Clippen asked, incredulous.

"No," Myrth held up a hand to the Land-Nymph. "I knew Sybon. DJar came into Sybon's service long after I had returned to the Southern Peninsula. DJar knows me from stories Sybon used to tell him."

"That's quite the coincidence," Sai said. Shuri nodded, studying Myrth closely.

Myrth stared them down. "Yes, it is," he said, his voice dangerously low. The water in the glasses on the table began to ripple and sway as a shiver ran through the room.

"I do not believe for a moment that Master Myrth had anything to do with the creatures that killed our Mother," Clippen hissed, also glaring at the two avian Semians.

"Stop being ridiculous," Kita said, reaching over and lightly smacking Sai on the back of the head.

"Forgive us, Master," Shuri said.

Myrth sighed and closed his eyes, the small quake subsiding as he smoothed the forcelines. "It is fair to wonder, as I have," he admitted. "But I choose to see it as an advantage. I have some sway over DJar because of these stories."

"Does that make your claim strongest?" Clippen asked.

"No, Tekalo is the one who brought him down. The throne he serves has the strongest claim. Tekalo sent him to Nepo but my understanding is he did so because Sea Spray was the closest and he knew a Master's strength would be needed to hold the daemon-kin prisoner. Therefore, we have to determine who Tekalo was serving at the time."

Clippen thought for a moment, "I barely knew he left, he couldn't have been serving me."

"He could have if you trusted him to do his job and gave him full rein," Derik said.

"He is also a Moon Clan Land-Nymph, son of the Marshal Basskin. He could have been serving the Marshal, who serves you," Sai added.

"But he is Chosen of Water," Ryn said. "He was serving Nepo in name."

"It is complicated further, Clippen," Myrth said. "Nepo already promised DJar that he would release the claim on him before parlaying with Sybon's son." Wide eyes met his words. "Nepo is trained in the Ruby Hills customs, so it could be argued that he was twisting the truth. We could argue that when Nepo said he would release his claim, he didn't mean to free DJar, only to pass that claim to another."

"Could he have meant Clippen when he said that?" Ryn asked. Myrth nodded, his thick black lips at the edges of his beak pulled down in a frown.

"Who did Nepo mean?" Clippen asked. "Between us."

Myrth shrugged his bony shoulders, "He hasn't said."

"So he could have meant to free him," Clippen concluded. "Or," he continued after a moment, "he knew that the tree daemon wouldn't stay in custody anyway, so why fight it."

"That latter does sound more like the Water Master," Kita said. "You know him best of all of us, Clippen." His beady goblin eyes glanced once at Myrth but the Earth Master had no qualms admitting that he did not know Nepo as well as the Land-Nymph did. They were part of a cadre who had grown up together in the cities of Gaity, Olimidia, and Sea Spray Castle. Nepo, Clippen, Palo, and Pyko all powerful mages who enjoyed a tight friendship. That friendship had survived Nepo ascending to Water Master over Pyko and Palo as well as predicating Clippen serving in Nepo's Honor Guard.

With a sigh, Clippen rang his bell, signaling another servant and nodding at the table. Through the conversation, most of the breakfast plates had been emptied. Myrth signaled for his half-eaten plate to be taken away as well.

"I will need to speak to it," Clippen said. "You can translate?" he asked.

Myrth nodded. "That is why I'm here. Nepo and Jay also have their own questions for him."

"Thank you for your company, mages," Clippen said, "I appreciated your time and information." The five mages stood and bowed their heads. "Do you know the way out?" he asked, as they stepped away from the table.

Kita nodded, "Yes, I've been to breakfast and tea several times through the years." He struggled to hold his face still and his voice steady before turning and leading the others out.

Myrth waited for them to leave before he turned to study Clippen. "You should see to your hand," he muttered. "Do not dwell on your anger; you can't afford to if you want to be an effective leader."

"It didn't kill your Mother," Clippen whispered.

"You don't know that he did, Clippen. He is one of at least a dozen Nura who were here."

"You said it was the leader. That means it gave the order to kill." Glaring, Clippen stood, turned away from Myrth, and left.

Myrth trailed him down to the dungeon entrance, where they met Nepo and Jay, who were waiting to accompany them into the cramped prison. Nepo hugged Clippen close for a moment when he reached them, then stood at arm's length. "Have you heard?" he asked.

Clippen nodded. "You still can't feel him?" he asked. Nepo shook his head no. They hugged again while Jay and Myrth waited respectfully until they stepped away and broke the embrace. With a sigh and a determined frown, Clippen led the way down the stairs.

At the bottom, the blue-haired and red-haired Moon Clan guards had been replaced by a pair of green-haired Star Clan guards. Like Moon Clan, their skin was pale, though not as alabaster white as the Moon Clan. Additionally, they were shorter in stature, though not as small as the Sun Clan Land-Nymphs, and generally stockier in build. Like the Moon Clan, they all looked like they were siblings, the genetic pool shrinking as the species slipped toward extinction. They bowed to Clippen and the Masters. "Leave, but don't go far," Clippen instructed.

"Magistrate," they chorused before quickly leaving, closing the door behind them.

"Are you well?" Nepo asked DJar in his language, stepping close to the cell's bars. DJar's eyes slipped open, the darkness of the cell emphasizing the daemon-fire glow.

"How does one answer that?" DJar asked with a glance toward the other visitors. His eyes lingered on Clippen and he used his tongue to play with the large cut on his lip that was just beginning to heal. Clippen smiled unpleasantly at the Nura.

Myrth cut in, "Magistrate Clippen, *Garpok* Clippen," he introduced. "*Shuwarr* DJar, Major DJar." Myrth added, "I will translate," with a quick, sour, look to Nepo. Nepo shrugged and stepped back, the four visitors formed an arch around the cell. Clippen grabbed one of the guard's wooden chairs and sat in front of the cell's door. He gleamed from his hair to his black boots, out of place in the lamp-lit dungeon.

"I am grateful for the accommodations," DJar began, pausing between sentences to allow Myrth translation time. "I come before you and ask, will you release me?"

Myrth paused in the translation and added for Clippen's benefit, "This is a ritual greeting from one who is bonded. Your response should be a simple yes or no."

"No," Clippen said.

DJar responded, "*Tekdi nal ee garpokcho.*"

"His Master will come for him...that is a ritual response as well," Myrth added.

"Do you know why you are here?" Clippen asked.

DJar frowned, "I was taken prisoner in battle and returned to the king's throne. I am honor-bound to be here." He motioned toward Nepo when he spoke.

"Your bond is held by more than one," Myrth reminded him. "There are four holders."

"Four?" DJar asked. "I am allowed to know them and to bring my request before each in turn."

Myrth listed them, "Nepo, myself, the *Tepok-Myir* Grand Syra Palo, and Clippen."

"How does he hold a bond more than through the *Tepok-Myir?*" DJar asked.

"You killed our Mother," Clippen hissed in reply. "The City of Olimidia demands justice! You stole our child, we demand her returned!"

DJar shook his head, "No, not the claim, the bond."

"Tekalo, the Fae who captured you," Myrth supplied. "You were taken by retainers serving me, *Garpok* Clippen, and the *Tepok-Myir*. Nepo holds your bond because you were returned to him." Myrth then explained to Clippen and the others, "The demand for justice is a claim, it is why you wish to hold him. The power to hold him is the bond which comes to Olimidia because Tekalo captured him."

DJar fell silent a moment then asked, "and will either of you release me this day?" he looked to Myrth and Nepo.

"No," they choroused.

"Tekdi nal ee garpokcho," he responded.

"Yes, you are valued," Nepo replied, the Ruby Hills missive that was added at the end of the ritual exchange.

"And the last of the four?" DJar asked.

"Clippen stands for him until his arrival tonight or tomorrow," Myrth supplied.

DJar nodded his understanding. "I continue to feast, but I would like to request food. My kind are carnivorous."

Myrth added, "When he says 'feast' he means that he is fasting and sustaining himself through his faith."

Clippen shook his head, "No." DJar studied him and played with the cut on his lip again, then he nodded his understanding.

"You should start, Jay and Nepo," Clippen said.

"We need to know where you were going?" Nepo said, and Myrth translated for Clippen and Jay.

DJar smiled. He closed his eyes. "I am Major DJar of the Crystal Hills where the suns go to rest."

Nepo scoffed.

"That sounds like the end of the conversation," Clippen said after hearing the translation.

"You are here because you are honorable," Jay tried. DJar opened his eyes and studied the Wind Mistress. "The soldier who took you, is precious to me."

"He fought well. I was impressed by his strength. But the one that killed my brother-in-arms is the one you should celebrate," DJar said.

Clippen frowned at DJar's words and looked at Myrth. "What does that mean?"

"Trillip killed one of them," Myrth supplied, "before DJar was captured."

Clippen studied the tree daemon for a moment. "You are a soldier," he said. "I am a soldier, I know you aren't going to provide us information that will endanger your squad." He motioned to Jay and Nepo, "They are trying to find the soldier who captured you."

DJar shook his head. "I do not know where he is, I was captured and returned to the throne."

Jay continued, "If we know where you were going, I can try to find him with my Air Magic."

DJar sighed deeply and shook his head. "Steel your heart, Little Sister," he said. They all stared at one another, silent. Djar closed his eyes, retreating into meditation.

Myrth studied DJar's mudra and sighed. "He will not speak to us again today," he said. "We can try when Palo arrives or tomorrow morning."

Clippen stood. He replaced the chair and left covered in a dark cloud of anger and impotence.

"I'm disappointed, *Shuwarr*," Nepo whispered. He followed Clippen out and Jay trailed after him, patting Myrth on the shoulder as she passed him.

Myrth waited a long minute, watching the Nura. Then he bent close to the cell bars and whispered to DJar. "I value your honor, *Shuwarr*, we will return with the *Tepok-Myir*. There is a reason he is the *Tepok-Myir*, and not just another soldier in the armies of the Maelstrom." He left as the green-haired guards returned.

The remainder of the day passed in tense silence. Myrth had returned to the Academy and spent the day in the library watching Jay pour through scrolls and paintings, looking for a detailed map of the Blasted Plains and the Southern Peninsula. She needed them to form her Eyes. The shark-woman clambered up and down shelves in the large room, using solid air to reach the higher items or carry heavier tomes. Myrth found himself smiling at her more than once, enjoying her studious single-minded pursuit. By sunset, she'd narrowed it down to two large maps, one significantly older than the other. She called Myrth over to view them and he complied. "I know there are more cities now," she said, pointing to the older map, but I think the natural features are more accurate.

Myrth studied the pair. "I think you should have both copied," he said. "Do you know who is going to scribe them for you?"

Jay looked at him, her alien shark eyes emotionless but her brow furrowed and her mouth dropping into a frown. "No," she said. "I hadn't thought that far ahead."

"Ask for the best in the city," he said. "Perhaps Basskin will know whom to ask." Jay nodded at his words.

"Masters," a guard interrupted, "the Grand Syra is approaching." The female goblin waited as they looked at one another. Jay set the maps aside. She and Myrth then turned and left the library, the guard stepping aside to let them lead the way out to the main entrance.

Outside, the upper echelon of soldiers in the Academy had rapidly assembled in the front yard. At the head of the formation the five captains in charge of the Academy stood ready to receive the Grand Syra. They represented the three most common peoples found in Palo's armies: two goblins, one elf, and two stag Semians. Myrth and Jay joined Nepo, Marladon and Marco near the front, deferring to the captains and standing behind them. Palo reached them a few minutes later, riding a large palace black, the horse a tall, elegant steed that was trained to stay calm in the midst of battle. The snow leopard Semian dismounted easily at the gate and stepped through, leading his horse behind him and handing the reins to a canine Semian stablehand who melted from mustered troops.

"Captains," he greeted with a nod. The five dropped to their knee, hands on their hearts in salute, in unison. "Masters," he said with a nod. They bowed to him as a group. "I rarely see you, Mistress of Air. Welcome," he added.

"I enjoy our talks when we do meet, Grand Syra," Jay said with a lilting smile.

"Marco, Nepo," he greeted.

"Palo," Nepo returned.

"It's been a long ride," Palo continued, "I'd like to eat and talk of your travels." He turned to the nearby elfin captain. "Can you send a messenger to Clippen? Ask him to join us for dinner."

"Yes, Grand Syra," she said before hurrying away.

One of the stag Semians stepped forward, ducking his head slightly, his moose-like antlers making the movement unbalanced and oddly unnatural. "I will show you to your suite, Grand Syra," he said.

"If you'd like," he said with a purring smile. He waited for the captains to lead the way and bowed to the cadets who all bowed low as he walked past. The Masters and Marco followed him. They made their way to the southern Wing, back near the library, and up a short flight of stairs to a grand suite at the rear of the Academy.

"We will see food brought for you and your guests, Grand Syra," the moose said.

Palo nodded his approval and started removing his clothes as the captain left. He laid his travel-worn jacket and shirt across a chair and motioned to a settee and couch. "Sit, please," he said. "Marco, how are your studies?" He paused to eye the Chosen of Earth.

"They are going well," Marco said, his eyes drifting along the Grand Syra's fur-covered torso, tracing scars along his ribs and across his spine. The suite's lamps all glowed brightly and few shadows lingered in the plush room. There were two sofas and a settee along with a low table, three overstuffed chairs, and a large four-poster bed festooned with thick curtains.

"Is that true, friend Myrth?" Palo asked, smiling at the pair.

"Yes, Marco is studious and responsible," Myrth confirmed, taking a seat on one of the sofas.

"Shame," Palo purred. "I had high hopes for you, Mage of Man." He smiled and winked a gold-green eye at Marco. Marco stifled his own laugh and smile at Myrth's glare. Marladon did not stifle his chuckle. He sat down in an overstuffed chair near the table still laughing at Myrth's glare as a sharp knock echoed through the room. "Come!" Palo called and Clippen hurried in, closing the door behind him. He was dressed in the same elegant blue and green tunic he'd worn this morning, his face more careworn than before. His long legs carried him into the room and straight up to Palo where he fell into a fierce hug. They embraced for a moment before stepping away from each other.

Palo studied the Land-Nymph. "Leadership suits you," he said. Clippen sighed then turned away from Palo and slumped into one of the other overstuffed chairs near Marladon. He closed his eyes. Palo turned his back to the room and rifled through a wardrobe stuffed with clothing. He chose a white silk robe, donning it before slipping out of his boots and pants. He pulled the robe closed around him, tying the belt in place before returning to his guests. Jay perched near Myrth on the sofa.

"The tree daemon—" Clippen started but Palo shook his head and made a cutting gesture.

"No. Tonight, it is just us. You, me, Nepo, Marco if he's up to it. I want none of tree daemons and wars. No talk of prisoners, death, loss." He paused. "We'll have to send Myrth to bed early." He smiled wide and his eyes twinkled at the exasperated noise that choked Myrth. Marladon laughed under his breath, pointedly not looking at the Earth Master. Clippen closed his eyes and then nodded slowly. Another knock signaled the arrival of their dinner, a simple selection of meats, vegetables, and sauces along with fresh baked bread.

They helped themselves to the food and did their best to keep their talk to simple conversations about the weather and doings in their respective households. When they'd eaten their fill, Palo looked pointedly at Myrth, Marladon, and Jay in turn. They were being dismissed, as politely as the Grand Syra was going to do so.

"I will take my leave," Myrth said, standing. "Tomorrow, when you are rested from your journey, we will talk again." Palo smiled and bowed his head.

"I have my own preparations to make," Jay said, also standing and Marladon followed quickly behind her without a word.

When they'd gone, the Grand Syra pulled on a bellrope and waited for a servant to appear. Ordering wine and spirits, he sent the elf away and then perched on the edge of a high-backed chair, his long tail twitching at the lower edge of his robe. "Who wants to play a game," he asked, his smile a little too wild and wide for comfort.

Myrth moved about the suite quietly, trying not to disturb Marco who'd climbed into bed with the Ghost Moon near setting. Despite his efforts, Marco groaned and turned to face him. Myrth studied him without expression. Marco closed his eyes and moaned, "You could have warned me." Myrth thought about that for a moment. *"Warn you about drinking with the Grand Syra?"* he asked through their connection.

"I could have, but would you have left? Even if you believed me when I said, 'Don't party with Palo if you want to be functioning the next day,' would you have left?" Marco thought about it a moment and shook his head. Myrth smiled. "You could do worse for friends, Marco. The Grand Syra, Clippen, the Water Master. Just remember your place and yourself. Besides, don't you drink with Pyko? I thought he was the true champion of the lot."

Marco scoffed lightly, "Pyko sips his whiskey. He enjoys storytelling," Marco whispered. Myrth shrugged in response but didn't think Marco saw.

Myrth left him to sleep and recover. He went down the stairs and around to Palo's suite where he knocked on the door. It took Palo a few minutes to answer, his robe tied loosely closed at his waist. He turned away from Myrth as the hawk-man entered and strode across the floor toward one of the overstuffed chairs. Palo sat and made a shushing noise, pointing to Clippen, who'd spent the night and was sound asleep in the bed.

"Marco could have left at any time, Myrth," Palo whispered, anticipating the Earth Master's admonishment as the hawk-man joined him in a nearby chair.

"He's my apprentice, but he's not my child. He chose freely to stay and I hope it was worth it for all of you," Myrth whispered in reply.

Palo smiled and looked to where Clippen slept. "He is worn thin," the Grand Syra said, indicating the Land-Nymph. "Leadership suits him but he is carrying a great weight for me. I owed him a night of play and a chance to forget his troubles."

Myrth nodded. "Never let it be said that the Grand Syra Palo did not care for his people and his servants." They exchanged smiles. "And Nepo?" Myrth asked.

"Better than Marco, slightly worse than me. Nowhere near as gone as Clippen." Palo paused, frowning. "They told me of Tekalo last night. All are certain he is not dead, despite his being ripped from his connection to Nepo?" Myrth nodded in response.

"Jay is setting some Eyes to watch for him in the Blasted Lands. I believe she will need to go there to set them up but currently she is exploring the area using maps."

"And the Nura?" Palo asked. With a frown, Myrth relayed their previous conversations and the journey to Olimidia from Sea Spray. As he spoke, Palo's brow furrowed and his frown deepened. When Myrth finished with their dead-end meeting from yesterday. Palo began scratching his forearm once again, his claws just visible, as he thought. "He doesn't yet know I am here. I will not speak to him today," he decided.

Myrth nodded at the decision. "I will wait for Clippen and Nepo to awaken and we will go together to speak to him once more before the Ghost Moon rises," he conceded. "Clippen can speak for you."

Palo whispered to himself, "Rysk just set," then nodded. "Yes, that will do. If that's all ..." he motioned toward the door.

Myrth sighed and shook his head then stood. "You're incorrigible," he said with a dry chuckle. Palo smiled at him, fangs gleaming. "I'll report tomorrow," Myrth added as he started for the door.

"If you'd like," Palo said.

It was past midday before Marco stirred. Myrth and Jay had been having a hushed conversation, pouring over the map she'd had made that morning. To the black inked lines showing the Vast Southern Wilds and the Blasted Lands, dominated by the volcano Mount Myrs, Myrth had been adding golden lines to show the Earth currents in the area. Jay had decided she would use the Earth Currents to carry vision from the Eyes back to Olimidia. As Marco woke, they were discussing objects that could be used to see what the Eyes saw. "Looking glasses," Jay said with finality. "I can gather them from the Ways, I'm sure."

"When you tell the women that it's for Tekalo, they'll find all they can," Myrth said with a nod. They were speaking low, but their voices pierced Marco's head and he closed his eyes, holding his hands to his temples. "Oh, you're awake," Myrth added when he saw Marco stir. "That means Clippen and Nepo won't be far behind."

"You need to come up with an excuse for the next time Palo invites you to stay late and drink with him," Jay said with a giggle. Her lilting songbird voice crashed in Marco's ears and echoed through his head, driving splinters into his brain.

"I'm going to be sick," Marco muttered.

"Lots of water, Man Child," Myrth said in a whisper, appearing before him with a cup and a waterskin.

Marco reached for them and had a moment of panic as his eye caught the muddled mess of his forcelines. He gasped, nearly dropping the full cup.

"*Peace, Marco,*" Myrth said in his head. "*I have seen to your lines and all is well.*"

"Thanks," Marco mumbled, meaning the forcelines as much as the water.

"I'll finish with your map first, Jay," Myrth continued, "Then I'll find the others and visit DJar. I'm sure he is anxious on some level."

"Do you need me with you?" Marco asked, sipping water and closing his eyes, waiting for the pain to subside.

"No," Myrth paused, "Recover. Tomorrow we will need to show our force when Palo meets DJar for the first time." Marco nodded, grateful.

"If you're up to it," Jay offered, "get dressed and help me find some looking glasses. I need at least two dozen."

"You were talking about Eyes and looking glasses," Marco remembered. Myrth returned to the table and his ink, continuing his work. He closed his eyes, stepped into the Mage Realm and rode the Earth Currents north. As he traced them, he opened his eyes, stepping halfway out of the Mage Realm, and drew golden paths on the map to show Jay where the Earth magic lay. As he worked, Jay moved and sat next to Marco on the bed.

"My specialty is constructs," she began, "I use Air and Earth for most of them. True, they are opposing forces, but that's what makes them so powerful when brought together." Marco drank and nodded, signaling that he was listening, despite his eyes being closed. "I'm going to make a series of Eyes through the Blasted Lands, so that we can look for Tekalo. It's similar to what I have done for the Broodlands. Air is everywhere and knows all things, sees all things. Harnessing that and sending the vision along the Earth Currents to a receptacle of some sort is a simple task once mastered."

Marco nodded again. Then he opened his eyes in realization, "You're the one who makes the magic windows." Jay nodded and smiled. "So we need looking glasses to see what's going on in the Blasted Lands." Again Jay nodded.

She turned to Myrth, "He catches on quick, Myrth" she giggled. Myrth fell out of the Mage Realm and glanced between them. Nodding at Jay's smile before returning to his work. "Dress quickly and we'll go over to the Palace to start our search," she ordered, standing and leaving the room.

Marco struggled out of bed, head pounding. "Looking for mirrors sounds like all I'm capable of today," he said. "Maybe I do need an excuse for next time."

Myrth fell out of the Mage Realm again and sighed, a slight quake shimmying through the room at his exasperation. "Don't sell yourself short," he began after smoothing the forcelines. "Palo chose you to be his friend, that's not done lightly. He chose you to be with Clippen when Clippen needed friends and to forget his troubles. Again, it wasn't a fickle whim." Marco nodded slowly. "Besides," Myrth continued with a grim smile, "Palo wouldn't believe any excuse you made up, and he won't allow you to leave next time. You have drinking buddies now, welcome to the Potentate." Marco snorted. He dressed slowly while Myrth worked and left to find Jay and the mirrors she needed for her new Eyes without another word to the Earth Master.

Not long after, Myrth finished his mapping and left the document to dry on the table. Then he left the Academy and crossed to the Palace. The Star Clan guard at the front door bowed as he approached. "Are Nepo and Clippen in?" he asked.

"Yes, Earth Master. They are at 'breakfast' in the main hall," the black haired, green-eyed Land-Nymph opened the door for him and bowed again as the Earth Master entered. Myrth crossed the foyer and passed into a large, central hall. The Matriarch had kept this space free but with her passing, it had become a convenient meeting space and Basskin and Clippen had brought in extra tables and chairs to accommodate visitors. When Myrth arrived, Clippen and Nepo were eating. They'd been joined by Marco who was picking at a dish of food as if worried that eating it might bring on an unwelcome reaction. The other two silently worked on their food. Clippen nodded in greeting when Myrth approached.

"Marco?" Myrth asked.

"Jay went with the women through a secret door. They said I had to wait here."

"We must present ourselves to DJar," Myrth said, sitting down at the table but waving away a nearby attendant's offer of food.

"And Palo?" Nepo asked. Myrth shook his head. Nepo, like Marco, looked like his head hurt. Clippen's pink eyes shone extra bright, bloodshot from his rough night. *"He does seem less careworn,"* Myrth admitted to himself.

"We will finish here and then go down," Clippen rasped.

They ate slowly and the suns were beginning to set when Clippen, Nepo, and Myrth finally descended into the Palace dungeon. The original guards were on duty once again. Clippen clasped the red-haired one's forearm in a brotherly gesture. "How are you, DJar?" Nepo asked as the guards left. The Nura opened his eyes and glanced at his visitors before closing them again.

"You are three," he said, "Not four."

"Tepok-Myir Palo will summon you tomorrow. He has journeyed long and just arrived," Nepo said.

"I speak for him here and now," Clippen added.

"My water dwindles and I continue to feast," DJar said, waiting for Myrth to translate for Clippen. "I ask, *Tepok* Myrth, *Tepok* Nepo, *Garpok* Clippen and Palo, will you release me?"

"No," they chorused.

"My master will come for me," DJar responded, eyes closing, the pinprick fires in them snuffed out in the near darkness.

"Yes," Nepo added, "You are valued."

DJar opened his eyes and studied Nepo a moment before saying, "You said you would release me. Are you honorable, *Tepok* Nepo?"

Nepo glared at him, "I am honorable," he said. "Tell me about Tekalo."

"He fought with ice, Air and Water. Your retainers," DJar said with a glance to Myrth, "and he are formidable, perhaps the most formidable Fae I could hope to hunt."

"You came to hunt," Myrth said. DJar blinked slowly. The Earth Master turned to Clippen, speaking low, "A hunting party is at least a dozen, sometimes as many as twenty."

"How many were in your party?" Clippen asked.

"I ask again," DJar said, daemon-fire flaring, "*Tepok* Nepo, are you honorable? Will you release me?"

Nepo shook his head no. "You have not told me enough about Tekalo."

"I am *Shuwarr* DJar of the Crystal Hills, where the suns go to rest, my master will come for me and you will return my bond to him. I have said all I will this day." DJar turned his head, facing away from them, eyes closed.

The three exchanged a glance and then stood and left. "Be careful with him, Moray," Clippen said to the blue-haired Land-Nymph. "He is starting to slip."

"Aye, Magistrate," the guard answered as he and his red-haired fellow took their place again.

At the top of the stairs, the three questioners paused. "Hunting Fae?" Clippen asked, he looked at Myrth and Nepo.

"The gray daemons of the Hills Kingdoms have hunted Fae for all of known time," Myrth whispered. "There are few Fae to be had in the north."

"So they came here to find some?" Nepo asked. Then he answered his own question with another, "But here? In the Maelstrom?"

"Could there be no Fae left in the north?" Myrth asked. The three of them exchanged long glances. "Sleep well tonight, we want to be a strong force to back up Palo tomorrow," Myrth said into the dread silence. Clippen and Nepo nodded their agreement. They remained standing by the dungeon door another long minute.

"What are you thinking, Myrth?" Nepo asked, watching the hawk man.

Chagrined, Myrth whispered, "I'm glad Palo is a Semian and not Fae." Clippen glared but Myrth pressed on. "Tomorrow, Nepo, if you intend to release DJar, we need to make certain that Clippen isn't the only one holding him as DJar will not honor a Fae bond."

"I'm not releasing him until I know what happened to Tekalo," Nepo growled. He pushed away from the wall where he'd been leaning, and left, heading back to his room, deeper into the palace. Clippen followed him without a word and Myrth was left to see himself out.

A Show of Force

A s the Fiery Sisters rose, Myrth returned to the dungeon. DJar stood, eyes burning low. "You come alone, Little Brother?" he whispered.

"I'm here to take you to Palo."

"As I am, then," he said. He stretched his hands and arms, balling his fists and rubbing his fingers with his thumbs. Then he stretched his back and legs. Myrth watched him, realizing the smell within the close quarters was beginning to sour, a reptilian smell that he associated with dragon stables, not daemon-kin. "I am honorable, Little Brother," he said, standing with his hands clasped in view at his waist.

Myrth nodded to Moray to unlock the cell and the blue-haired Land-Nymph did, stepping aside with his hand on his sword, ready for the prisoner to attack. DJar made a point of ignoring the two Land-Nymph guards and bowed his head to Myrth. They climbed the stairs, DJar following behind Myrth and the guards behind him, until they reached the main floor. Moray and the red-haired Land-Nymph then took a position on either side of the Nura, swords now drawn, and they followed Myrth down the main hall, up a flight of stairs and into a grand tea room. DJar squinted in the sunlight that streamed through the round, glass walls, the windows overlooking the Central courtyard where he'd landed a few days earlier. "*Tepok-Myir,* Grand Syra Palo, *Shuwarr,* Major DJar," Myrth introduced.

Palo had donned a Potentate uniform, black on black leather with brilliant steel rings and grommets that sent errant sparkles of sunlight across the room as he shifted in his high-backed chair. He had added leather vambraces to his forearms that were covered in small metal spikes. Atop his head, his Potentate cap held three large red feathers, denoting his master mage skill level. Beside him, three more ornate high-back wooden chairs had been arrayed, Nepo sat to his left, and Clippen to his right. Myrth's empty chair waited to Clippen's right. Behind the chairs and along the walls of the room, Palo had called up the mages and guards of the Academy, filling the room. The five Captains of the Academy sat at a table before the dais, facing DJar as he entered, while the five Air Mages who had brought him back to Sea Spray sat in chairs opposite the captains. Between these ten, a walkway large enough for three abreast had been left clear. Marladon, Jay, Marco, and Sage stood behind the chairs on the dais.

Myrth signaled DJar to stop then carried on up to his chair where he sat. "I will translate," he informed them all. "How are you, DJar?"

"I am honorable, Little Brother." DJar said, his voice just above a whisper. "I come before you to ask, will you release me from my bond?"

"No," Myrth said, "I will not release you this day."

"No," Clippen said.

"Tell me of Tekalo," Nepo said.

"There is nothing more I can tell, *Tepok* Nepo."

"Then my answer remains no."

DJar bowed his head at the lion-man's words and looked to the newcomer, Palo. "You are the fourth who holds my bond, *Tepok-Myir*, king of all. I ask you, Little Brother, will you release my bond?"

"No," Palo said.

"My master will come for me."

"Yes," Nepo intoned, "for you are precious."

"I ask you, *Tepok-Myir*, for food and water." He paused and glanced at Clippen. "The accommodations have been adequate," he added.

"No," Palo said. "Not yet."

"Then I will continue to feast," he bowed low. Myrth added a quick explanation for those gathered in the room.

"Do you know why you are here?" Palo asked.

"As I said before, I was captured in battle and sent to the throne of Nepo. I am honor-bound to serve out my bond."

"No," Palo said with a shake of his head, "You are here because I want to know what you know." Myrth and Nepo both looked between Palo and DJar as Myrth translated.

DJar pulled himself up straight, closed his eyes and took a deep breath. When he opened them, they blazed with daemon-fire. "I am *Shuwarr* DJar of the Crystal Hills, where the suns go to rest. I need not say more."

"Need not? I will give you that," Palo said, voice falling, claws unsheathing on the arms of the chair, "Will not?" he paused, "That remains to be seen."

DJar studied Palo, weighing the snow leopard man's intent. He turned to Myrth, "Is the *Tepok-Myir* honorable?"

Myrth thought for a moment before replying without translating for the room. "The Grand Syra protects his own. You destroyed what was his, his favored city and his favored people, the Land-Nymphs." Myrth paused, again, weighing his words. "I cannot guarantee that he will not abuse you, that he will not turn you naked and helpless over to the Land-Nymph clan most thirsty for your blood. But I can say, he is patient and an astute politician, even more so than he is a dangerous soldier and skilled mage. Answer his questions and he will treat you honorably."

DJar held up his hands, palms out, placating the surrounding crowd. "I understand my position here. I await your pleasure, *Tepok-Myir.*" Myrth translated his final missive.

Palo eyed him and then DJar, obviously wondering what the longer statement had been. "Take him back to the dungeon," Palo growled. I will see him when I am ready."

"Yes, Grand Syra," the two Land-Nymph guards said, and they waited for DJar to turn away, escorting him from the room and back down to the dungeon. For a long moment, the room remained as it had been then Palo signaled dismissal to the soldiers and the room slowly cleared. When the soldiers had gone, Myrth let out a breath he didn't know he'd been holding. "You do know," he said to Palo, "That he doesn't have to stay."

"You go on about their disappearing trick," Palo said. "Yet he is still here."

"He is starting to linger," Marladon said, holding his nose as an explanation for his comment. "It would be best to clean him up, to feed him."

"No," Clippen, Nepo, and Palo chorused.

"When he has had enough of us," Myrth added, "You will see. He will simply not be there anymore."

Jay cleared her throat, "Now that the posturing is over, I'm off to the Crest to set my Eyes on the Blasted Plains. If you're going to kill him, do it without me," she added, standing.

"I will see you off, Mistress," Marladon said standing as well.

Palo waited for them to disappear and turned to Clippen. "Let's let him wallow a couple more days, then we'll try again. No food, no water."

"We must present ourselves or bring him before us each morning in order to honor his bond," Myrth warned.

"I'll see him tomorrow at dawn then," Palo said, "and the next day as well." Then we'll see if he's more talkative.

For two days, the Land-Nymph guards marched DJar to the tea room to stand before his four bond-holders and a room full of soldiers as they denied DJar's request. On the morning of the third day, Moray woke DJar and brought him once again out of the dungeon and back to the tea room. There was no show of force today, only the four who held his bond. "Good morning, honorable DJar," Myrth greeted.

DJar stood, eyes banked low, clothes disheveled, the hair growing back across his pate now nearly a quarter inch long. His hands balled into fists as he stood. "I come before you to ask, will you release me this day?" DJar whispered.

"Will you speak of Tekalo?" Nepo asked.

"I have said all I am able to say, *Tepok* Nepo," DJar said with a shake of his head.

"I will not release your bond," Clippen said. "You have killed and we demand retribution."

"My suffering is just in your eyes," DJar whispered. Myrth blinked at him, surprised, as he translated. Clippen's glare deepened.

"I will not release your bond this day," Myrth said.

DJar nodded and looked to Palo who was dressed once again in his armored Potentate uniform.

"You came here to hunt my people," Palo said. "You slaughtered a dear friend. Why would I release you?"

"My master will reclaim my bond," DJar said.

"Yes, you are valuable," Nepo intoned.

"You may go, Myrth," Palo said. "Nepo can translate."

Myrth hesitated at the odd request but stood, taking a step away from his chair and turning so that he could see the entire room, back to the nearest wall. He looked around and his heart leapt to his throat. The room had been cleared of most furniture. The four bond-holders and a handful of Land-Nymph guards were the only occupants. "I do not think that is wise, Palo," Myrth said, studying the glowers on Clippen's and Palo's faces, catching Nepo's hardened honey eyes. *"This has been planned!"* he thought, heart leaping to his throat.

"I said, you may go." Palo stood then, Nepo and Clippen rising to flank him. The world swayed before Myrth could stifle his emotions. He took a step back, increasing the distance between himself and the other three. He looked at DJar. The Nura's eyes flared as the Grand Syra and his two friends stepped down from the dais. DJar glared at the three standing before him. A brief glance to either side showed that his Land-Nymph guard had backed away, swords still drawn.

Reading the room, DJar's composure changed. "Try your luck, Little Brother," DJar hissed, baring fangs in a challenge. He balled his fists, rubbing his thumbs along them then held his hands up, palms out. "I am unarmed, but not defenseless." As Nepo translated, DJar fell into a fighting stance that Myrth had seen used before, a low center of gravity, perfect for picking off strong, tall opponents. The earth rumbled again as Myrth's apprehension flooded the forcelines.

"Oh, I'm not worried about a fair fight," Palo growled, "I'm just going to beat you." He stepped forward, his menace rising. DJar relaxed into his stance, hissing again in challenge.

Myrth threw himself between the two. "I can't let you do this, Palo!" he shouted, hands up, hoping to hold both of them.

"Peace, Myrth, the Land-Nymphs won't be abusing him, they're just going to watch," Palo added, continuing forward, closing the distance between himself and Myrth until he was inches from Myrth's beak, Myrth's taloned hand pressed against his armor-covered chest.

"No, Palo," Myrth said, shaking his head. "No. You don't realize what you're doing."

"Stand aside, Myrth," Palo growled. A commotion started at the front door of the Palace and the room swayed. Myrth shook his head slowly, his pearl eyes hardening into granite shards. "I count you friend," Palo continued. "Move, or I will move you," the snow leopard man growled, voice low and slow. Myrth studied the Grand Syra's eyes and knew he would not stop. With a short hawk scream, Myrth snapped his beak in Palo's face, just shy of the leopard man's nose. Palo grabbed him suddenly and threw him across the room with a roar.

The commotion from the front door crescendoed and the room suddenly filled with goblins. Their appearance startled Palo and DJar, breaking the tension between them. As Myrth landed, Marco shouted, "Palo! What are you doing?" The Chosen One's power pulled on the forcelines, filling the room. DJar spun to face the newcomers. His eyes flared, daemon-fire dancing in his pupils as Marco's power filled the space. A large rock ball appeared in the human Mage's hands, burning, endowed by Fire. Goblins formed a wall between Myrth and Palo, weapons drawn, they faced the Grand Syra.

Palo turned to the Chosen One. "Check yourself, Marco," he shouted. "And you!" Palo pointed to Kita who had joined the wall of goblins protecting Myrth. "Who do you serve!"

Kita did not hesitate. "From soil I sprang and to soil I return. I serve the Earth Master."

Myrth had regained his feet and was fighting through the goblin wall, pushing them aside until he stood glaring at Palo, Auros-Gado and Kita, the only goblins between him and the Grand Syra.

"ENOUGH!" DJar shouted in Fae and he stood up straight, clapping his hands once. His voice and the crack of air from his hands brought everyone's eyes to him.

Then it was there. It took a moment for the eyes of the people in the room to realize they were seeing it, and they gasped and pulled back *en masse* as the figure that had suddenly appeared registered in their brains. It occupied the space between Palo and DJar. The large steel blade it carried was less than an inch from Palo's eye. Its metal tip glinted in the sunlight as did the serrated fins along its top edge. Six inches on, the blade was attached to a long staff being held steady at shoulder height by the dark figure. "Back off," the figure purred in perfect Fae, its voice higher pitched than DJar's.

"*Shi shi shi shi shi*," DJar shushed.

Myrth straightened, taking a deep breath. Palo took a step back so he could see the newcomer better. The goblins drew closer to the Master as Clippen and Nepo held up their hands, empty. No less tense, the room's attention spun to the figure that had suddenly appeared. The newcomer wore the same uniform as DJar, black linen on black skin. Scintillating scales covered its bare shoulders and upper arms. Where DJar's hair had been shaved, this one had long matted white dreadlocks, each one tied with a colorful ribbon at the end. Its eyes blazed bright with daemon-fire as it took stock of the room.

"I will NOT be abused," DJar claimed from behind the newcomer. "If I am abused, there is no bond." His daemon-fire eyes burned as he weighed Palo for a moment. Then DJar took a deep cleansing breath and released his stance. "*Tepok-Myir*, I invite you to challenge me," DJar waited for Nepo to translate before continuing, "but it will be a fair fight, when I am well rested, slaked, and fed."

Palo smiled at the daemon-kin and studied the one who had just appeared out of nowhere. "A bodyguard?" he asked DJar.

DJar glanced at Nepo and the Water Master translated. DJar shook his head no. "Shi'Shou is bound to me, sister-in-arms and Daughter of the Sands." They all looked to Myrth.

"She's a member of his squad, bound to him because he is the commander, and enlightened, according to their faith," Myrth explained.

"Marco, drop the rock," Palo said, "your Master is safe." Marco didn't move, eyes on the blade-wielding Nura who'd just appeared.

DJar called softly to Shi'Shou and when she glanced at him, he held his hands up, palms out. She lowered her spear and relaxed her stance, eyes still ablaze and wary. Marco released the Earth Cloud and the Fire endowed rock disappeared, the fire burning off in a quick burst. The rock became a pile of sand that slowly snaked away from Marco, returning to dusty corners and potted plants where the Earth had originally been.

Myrth screamed and suddenly dropped to his knees, holding his head. The goblins all around him instantly resumed their fighting stance. DJar fell into a crouch as Palo whirled toward the hawk-man, "Wait!" Myrth shouted, then to Marco alone, *"Oracle!"*

"It's Oracle," Marco explained, holding his hands up, placating the tense soldiers all around. "He's speaking to Oracle."

Myrth was quiet a moment, all eyes on him. "We always have a problem, Oracle," he said aloud. His words brought the tension down once again as the goblins realized what had happened. Myrth fell silent, listening to the seer, then he looked up at the tableau around him and muttered, "You have no idea." Oracle continued talking to Myrth through the connection they shared and after a moment, Myrth vocalized his side of the conversation, "Daemons are a problem?" he asked, confusion lifting his voice an octave. Myrth frowned and slowly stood again, assuring the goblins he was well and they could stand down. "I will do what needs to be done," he said, "Thank you as always, friend." The Earth Master closed his eyes a moment and Marco felt him smoothing the jagged forcelines pouring from him and surrounding them all.

Eyes flashing open, Myrth glared at Palo, took three long strides toward him and smacked him hard across the face. Goblin blades danced around the room as Kita and Auros-Gado leapt to stand before Myrth, their own blades trained on Palo's chest.

"You forget yourself, Master," Palo hissed.

"No, you forget yourself!" Myrth shouted, pushing past the goblins again. "I am the Earth Master! You are a mere kitten paddling in a pond!" He pulled himself up to his full height, beak to chin with Palo. He added low, "I turned you over my knee more than once when you and that scalawag," he pointed to Nepo, "were whelps running through the streets of this city."

Palo studied Myrth, his eyes taking in the goblins and Marco at the Master's back, another head-sized rock in the man's hands. He looked to Clippen and

Nepo who remained staunchly at his back, although their eyes had lost their fight. Then to DJar and the new Nura, Shi'Shou. "Let calmer heads prevail here for now," he said. He stepped out of Myrth's reach and turned his back on the room. It was an invitation to continue the fight, an enticing opening for any who dared take it. No one took it. With a deep breath, Palo returned to his seat and relaxed into the chair. He smiled languidly at the room. "What did our dear Oracle say?" he asked. "I assume his communication means he is dreaming again."

Myrth signaled for the room to be cleared and he waited for the goblins and Land-Nymphs to leave. After a moment, only his honor guard and the two dungeon guards remained. Myrth returned to his seat. He looked at DJar, leaving the others to watch him and wait for a response regarding Oracle. "I have a proposition for you, *Shuwarr*," Myrth said, not bothering to translate for the others. Nepo jumped in to do so when he realized Myrth was not.

"I will hear it," DJar answered.

"Help me, and I will release your bond." Beside him, Clippen made a strangled sound as Nepo translated the offer. Myrth refused to look at the Land-Nymph.

"Does this have something to do with Oracle's dream?" Palo asked.

DJar frowned, "What help would you ask for?"

"An army of black daemons is descending on us from the Great Southern Wilds." Several intakes of breath followed his words. "My friend, a High Time Mage, has seen it and knows it to be true."

"A High Time Mage?" DJar asked, disbelief in his voice.

Myrth nodded. "You can control them," the Earth Master pressed, "The black daemons."

DJar's eyes flared, "An army? Not in my power, Little Brother. One or two, perhaps I have some influence over them, but not an army."

Auros scoffed as Nepo translated, "I don't believe him, Master. He controlled those black daemons on the way here."

"No, not true," DJar waved a finger at Auros. "It was an influence incantation, nothing more. I am unable to control the moblings."

Myrth and DJar stared at each other.

"Take him back to the dungeon," Palo said as the silence grew.

Shi'Shou stomped her foot and brought the butt of her spear down hard on the wooden floor at the same time. "Unacceptable," she growled in Fae. Her voice was high and had a sibilant, purring quality.

"No!" Clippen returned. "He is a prisoner of war, a murderer, and kidnapper. He will go to the dungeon!" he shouted at the female Nura.

"It is not my bond you hold, Fae," she growled, changing her stance and hefting her spear.

"*Shi shi shi shi shi,*" DJar hushed. "He does hold mine, Shi'Shou."

"Only because you sent me away," she muttered, standing at ease once again.

"I will return with three conditions," DJar held up his fingers as he listed them, "A bath and daily cleaning of the cell, fresh water, and one meal a day." He added as an afterthought, "My kind are carnivores."

Clippen glared at the daemon-kin, mulling over his demands as Myrth translated. "She goes too, and doesn't leave without our knowledge." Clippen returned, pointing at Shi'Shou.

"Shi is fed also, twice a day," DJar countered. "I will share my bedding and water with her."

"You will continue to present yourself daily for questioning," Nepo added.

"Yes, of course."

"You will help me," Myrth added.

DJar frowned and shook his head, "I do not see how."

Myrth's eyes hardened to granite and he asked, "*Are* you honorable?"

DJar bowed at the waist but did not answer.

"Go with honor, *Shuwarr*, Daughter of the Sands," Myrth said, voice low, as DJar straightened. "Auros-Gado, escort them and see that they have clean clothes, bedding, water, and food."

"Yes, Master," the goblins chorused, falling into a box formation with the Land-Nymph guards, surrounding the two Nura.

The Daemon's Bargain

The four bond-holders sat quietly, studying the floor and their hands. Marco found a chair and sat as well. Myrth sighed and looked at Palo, "That was stupid," he said, "If you'd have consulted me, I would have told you it wouldn't have worked. Even if the Daughter of the Sands hadn't been here, beating him would have nullified your bond on him."

"It was worth a try," Palo said. "Besides, now we know the Daughter of the Sands is here."

"And likely has been here the whole time, it sounds like," Nepo said with his own sigh.

"That *is* a clever trick," Palo said. "How do they do that?"

"It's not Air," Myrth said. "I do not know what it is or how they do it. I do know that the strongest ones can just appear while the weaker ones must use a focus item, similar to the way Air Mages use staves and swords to draw flying discs."

Clippen chuckled, "We only use the staves and swords so that the circles are even. We don't *need* to use them."

"What about Oracle's vision?" Nepo asked.

"We need to prepare," Myrth said. He studied Palo for a long, hard minute. "I am willing to forgive you for tossing me across the room," he said.

Palo scoffed. "Thank you, Master. You are not my underling, you are free to rise against me without retribution, without ill will. The goblins that aided you, are mine. I understand they are your creature, so I forgive them." He studied the hawk man a moment and smiled. "We're still friends." For another second, his gold-green eyes flashed to Marco and his smile warmed.

"I never doubted our friendship, Grand Syra," Myrth said with his own smile.

"I doubted the integrity of the Palace," Clippen muttered. "Throwing Earth Mages tends to be a bad idea, Palo," he said with a smile. Palo ducked his head in feigned embarrassment.

"Let's talk," Palo said. "Tell us now what Oracle said, Myrth."

"There is an army of black daemons rising from the Vast Wildlands to the north. His visions show them engulfing us, overwhelming the entire peninsula. Nightmare, Hawkethorne, Sea Spray, are all first in their path. We need to prepare while we can."

"Does he know how long we have?" Nepo asked.

"No," Myrth said. "Days, cycles, maybe a season."

"That's not very long, not if it's an army," Palo said.

"Do you think DJar can help?" Nepo asked.

"I think he still knows more than he is willing to say," Myrth said. "And now he has some sway and power, with his *Aliith* revealed, his bound mage."

"Let's walk and think," Palo said, "Ramble through the city. Come back for dinner with ideas." They stood as one, but stopped when Marco planted his feet before Palo. "Marco," Palo said.

"Are we friends?" Marco asked. "Because I was ready to bury you when I saw you threatening Myrth."

Palo looked away, truly uncomfortable.

"And you two," the man continued, glaring in turn at Nepo and Clippen. They looked away as well.

"We did not anticipate that you would be here, that you would run to Myrth's aid," Nepo said. "We had hoped that Myrth would have gone along with us and simply stepped aside."

"I apologize, Marco," Palo said. "It was my idea to try to shake the daemon-kin. Myrth is right, I should have consulted him."

"I am a High Earth Mage of the Potentate, Palo." Marco said. "I am a soldier of the Academy. Both of those institutes, despite their own internal rivalry, are yours. That makes me *your* soldier. I like you. I enjoy your company. I consider you my friend. But I am Chosen of Earth and Myrth is my lifeline. I am a Mage of Man, the first since the time of the Hero Masters, and I need the training he can give me...the training ONLY he can give me. I accept your apology but I ask you, please do not EVER leave me with no choice but to kill you again." The room's slight swaying increased for a moment before stopping.

Palo recalled Marco and his fiery boulder, perfectly sized for bashing heads and bringing down the Palace. He nodded, eyes downcast. "I am truly sorry, Chosen One." He looked up at Marco, "Thank you for staying your hand." Marco nodded. "I still call you friend, I hope you see me the same. Now, walk and think too. Return for dinner, and if you see Marladon, tell him of the vision and invite him to dinner as well." With a nod, Marco fell in line behind Myrth.

The next morning, DJar and Shi'Shou were presented to Palo, Myrth, Nepo and Clippen again. Marco and Marladon had joined the four, seated to the side. DJar took note of them and saluted Marladon, "Brother," he said. "You missed our playtime yesterday."

"I did," Marladon said. "I have no claim on you and no control over these uncouth barbarians." The Fire Master smiled, silver orb eyes glittering. DJar bowed his head. Shi'Shou remained aloof, a step behind DJar, armed as she had been before.

"Good morning, DJar," Myrth began.

"The suns have blessed us once again," DJar replied. "On this day, I come before you and ask, will you release me?" Nepo translated as the Nura spoke.

"What can you tell me of the black daemon army that is to descend on us?" Myrth asked.

"Nothing. I know nothing of a black daemon army."

"If you knew," Marco interrupted, "Would you tell us?"

DJar turned slightly on his heels to face the man. "You do not hold my bond, I owe you nothing, Pale One," the Nura said.

"Would you?" Myrth asked.

DJar did not reply. He turned back to Myrth, remaining silent.

"Tell me of Tekalo," Nepo said into the silence.

"I know no more of him," DJar said.

"Does she?" Marco asked, pointing to Shi'Shou.

The bodyguard hissed, bright fangs bared. "I owe you nothing, Pale One," she said.

"Does she?" Nepo asked. She hissed again. "No, I am not asking you *Aliith*, I am asking your master. *Shuwarr* DJar. Does your *Aliith* know of Tekalo?"

"No one holds her bond, she need not answer and I will not answer for her," DJar said.

"So," Marladon mused, "she does know something." DJar and Shi'Shou both stared at him, faces schooled to stillness.

"I will not consider releasing your bond until I know of Tekalo," Nepo said.

"I will not release you this day," Myrth said, "When you are able to help me, I will consider releasing you."

"I will not release you," Clippen said. "I am owed retribution for my people."

DJar turned to Palo. "Will we play today, *Tepok-Myir*?" DJar asked. "Shi'Shou will stand down," the daemon-kin smiled.

"I am disinclined to do so, and I will not release you from your bond," Palo purred, languidly. "Return to your cell if you have nothing more to say." When he was gone, Palo leaned forward, elbows on knees, tail twitching.

"Maybe you should beat him," Nepo sighed. Palo chuckled and Myrth glared.

"Might be fun," Palo agreed, "but what would be the point? If his guard didn't slit my throat from behind, his bond would be forfeit."

Marladon spoke up. "Perhaps a wager?" Everyone looked to him. "He tried to challenge you, Myrth, once before, to become the holder of his bond, if I understand." Myrth nodded. "Could you wager his bond?" Nepo and Myrth exchanged a glance then nodded together.

Palo sat up straight. "If I win, his guard tells us what she knows. If he wins...I release his bond."

"You would release him?" Clippen asked, voice low.

"If I win, he answers our questions. Nepo and Myrth may release him. You and I would still hold his bond," Palo said. "And if I lose, I release him. We learn nothing but he is still held by three."

"We need to be careful," Myrth reminded them. "They may not honor Clippen's bond as he's Fae. For now, they don't have a reason to ignore Clippen but if he becomes the only one holding DJar, they're likely to leave."

"Ask him tomorrow," Marladon encouraged.

Palo shook his head no, "Why wait until tomorrow? Let's ask him now." Palo stood up and hurried after the Nura. The others followed in his wake. They hurried to the foyer and then through a door on the left to a study. There were several secret doors here that led deeper into the Palace. Palo pushed on a small shelf near the back of the room and a panel clicked open, letting them into a hallway. Just in front of them sat the stairs down into the dungeon. They hurried down, loud enough that when they reached the bottom, the guards were facing the doorway, swords drawn. DJar and Shi'Shou were already in the cell, DJar standing at the door, hands relaxed on the bars, Shi'Shou crouched behind him in the straw. She hissed upon seeing them.

"*Tepok-Myir*?" DJar greeted. He bowed his head.

"I've consulted the others and have a proposition for you, *Shuwarr*," Palo said. He stepped up to the door, hands on the bars above DJar's as Myrth translated. The Nura waited, eyes smoldering. "A wager."

"A wager?" DJar repeated in Fae.

"We fight. If I win, your *Aleet*, answers our questions," he smiled at the female Nura, his gold-green eyes gleaming in the torchlight.

"*Aliith*," DJar corrected. "And if I win?"

"I release your bond."

DJar pulled his hands from the cell's bars and studied the group who'd gathered behind the snow leopard man. Shi'Shou whispered to him, too low for Myrth to hear. DJar closed his eyes and the small room filled with his power. Marco had felt it before, as if boulders were slung into hammocks that were tied to his arms. Clippen snarled in response to the weight.

"Magic?" DJar asked.

"You cannot use magic or your bond is null," Palo said, shaking his head. He glanced at Myrth who nodded in agreement as he translated.

"I cannot fight or my bond is null. It seems to me," DJar said, "that the rules would be suspended for this wager."

Palo hesitated.

"No," Myrth said. "No magic, no weapons, no seconds." He glanced at Shi'Shou.

DJar closed his eyes for a moment and turned toward Shi'Shou. With a purr, she reached into a belt pouch and pulled out two white necklaces, their silver chains running through her fingers as she held them out to DJar. He stepped over to her and took the objects then returned to the door. "Do you know these?" he asked, holding them out to Palo to study.

"Molbdyn bone charms," Marladon said, voice low.

"Yes, Brother," DJar said as Palo took them.

"Bone charms?" Palo asked, holding them gingerly.

"They stop magic use," Marladon offered. "I've seen them in the Misty Lands and Black Vale. There was a wildling in the Embers when I was young who used one to find his way."

"They feel heavy, unsafe," Palo commented, looking up at DJar.

"Try one, with your friends around to save you from it," DJar said with a smile. Palo smirked as Myrth translated. "No magic, no weapons. I will still beat you, *Tepok-Myir*. You will mewl at my hands."

Palo nodded and passed the charms to Marladon. "When you feel strong enough, tell the guards. We shall see who cries."

"Your guards bring my meal when the Fiery Sisters are at their highest. Let us meet when they touch the horizon." Palo nodded his agreement.

Back in the main study, Palo sat and Marladon laid out the two bone charms in front of him. "You've seen these before?" the Grand Syra asked.

Marladon nodded. "They are rare constructs from the Molbdyns. I've never held one, or worn one."

Palo picked one up and put it on, slipping the clasp closed easily behind his head. "I don't feel any differently," he noted. Closing his eyes, he stepped into the Mage Realm. Everything looked the same, he reached out and nothing was there to grasp. With a gasp, Palo fell from the Mage Realm. He returned quickly for another look. Water and Air were there. He could see the forcelines of Earth eddying lazily around the room. He could see the pinpricks of Fire in his body as well as the others'.

Marladon was there, then, joining him. "What happened?" he asked.

Palo tried again to reach for the Miasma of Air and Water that surrounded them all, but he could not touch it. "It's gone," he whispered. "I can see the magic, but I can't touch it. When I try, it is just gone." He opened his eyes and took the bone charm off. Then he returned to the Mage Realm. Where he held the bone charm in his hand, he could see it in the Mage Realm. "It looks like ... it looks like the Nura." Palo opened his eyes and stared at the charm. He stepped back into the Mage Realm and gathered water to his will, it came easily to heel and when he opened his eyes, the globe of moisture he'd called from the miasma splashed onto the floor.

Nepo frowned at him and the water that had splashed across his legs."Are you up to wearing it?" he asked.

"Yes," Palo said, nodding. "It will definitely stop me from using magic."

"DJar wouldn't be stopped?" Nepo asked.

Palo shrugged. "I only know it works on me."

Myrth shook his head, "No, he wouldn't hamper you and risk cheating at a wager for his bond. I believe they will work on both of you." Nepo stepped into the Mage Realm and Marco realized he was sorting his Water "forcelines."

Clippen had the central courtyard cleared of benches and bonfires to make space for the brawl, and as the Fiery sisters neared the horizon, DJar and Shi'Shou were brought up into the light. Palo placed the bone charm on himself and took the other to DJar. DJar bowed at the waist and offered an open hand. Palo handed him the charm and DJar put it on. "They are ..." DJar paused, thinking of the correct Fae word, "uncomfortable," he finished with a smile. Nodding, Palo backed away a few steps, watching DJar.

The daemon-kin stripped off his shirt, the bone charm bright against his dark gray skin. He turned his back to Palo and stretched, flexing muscles across his torso and arms. DJar glanced over his shoulder at Palo. With a smile, Palo took his own top off, lazily making certain that DJar saw all his scars. Palo stretched his arms and shoulders as well. Flexing his hands, his claws sprang from his fingertips.

"Rules?" Nepo asked, joining the two in the center of the courtyard. Marco, Myrth, Marladon, and Clippen sat near the door, out of the way.

"You were an emissary to the Ruby Hills, *Tepok* Nepo?" DJar asked. Nepo nodded and translated for Palo. "Do you know the Tabar-ring Rules?" Nepo nodded again.

Nepo explained to Palo, "Tabar-ring is a famous square in the Ruby Hills kingdom. Fights happen there often enough that they have their own set rules. First blood," Nepo held up one finger, "the one bleeding can ask that the match end, and he will lose." Nepo held up a second finger, "Pinned, meaning that one cannot stand or continue to fight. The one doing the pinning wins." A third finger indicated the third rule, "Suitably bloody, meaning that I, as a bystander, fear for one's life." Palo nodded his understanding. "No weapons, no magic," Nepo restated. "Claws, bites, throws, grapples, all fair. Striking to kill, blind, or maim, no."

"I understand," Palo said with a nod.

Nepo turned to DJar, "Tabar-Ring rules, I will be the referee." DJar nodded, turned to Shi'Shou and whispered to her. She bowed her head, then approached Myrth.

"Little Brother," she greeted before closing to within arm's length of the Earth Master. "My *Shuwarr*, requests that you tend my weapon. He does not want his plaything to worry I will interfere." She spoke Fae with a purring accent that rolled her r's. She held out the spear and Myrth took it. Then she took a third bone charm from her pouch and placed it around her neck. She blew Palo a kiss and bowed to him.

With a smirk, Palo returned his attention to DJar. The daemon-kin sank into a fighting stance, lowering his center of gravity, hands up in a ready position. Palo stalked toward him, lowering his own center, shrinking in on himself to shorten his torso. They circled each other, staring intently, taking each other's measure. Nepo stood back, waiting, watching closely.

As they circled, they closed the distance between them, half a step at a time, until they were within grappling distance. Keenly fast, Palo reached out and swatted at DJar. He hadn't committed fully to the swing but his bared claws swiped hard across the Nura's face before he pulled back and took a step away from the daemon-kin.

"First" Nepo called and he jumped between them, breaking their contact, a hand out toward each of them calling for a pause.

DJar growled and hissed at Palo, looking around Nepo's taller frame. "Move Nepo," he rumbled, forgetting his manners as he wiped away the blood that was seeping from the four raking claw marks along his cheekbone.

Nepo backed away quickly letting them resume, circling so he could see Shi'Shou and Myrth without turning his back on the combatants, before saying, "I'm calling that a continue," raising his hands in a sign of placation. The witnesses nodded in agreement.

DJar's eyes blazed and he returned to his lowered stance, moving less as Palo circled him. Palo's movements, more sure now, still remained guarded and deliberate. He closed the distance again until they were within grappling reach. The Nura launched himself into the air and barreled into Palo, sinking claws into his shoulders and wrapping his legs around Palo's midriff. Palo grabbed him in reaction and they fell hard to the ground, rolling over and over again while they bit and clawed at each other. Nepo leapt away as the ball of fury rolled toward him. They came to rest with Palo pinned under the Nura, both of them screaming in rage, biting at each other's cheeks and ears, and burying their claws into each other's flesh. Palo removed one hand from DJar's side, leaving blood seeping in its wake, and reached up to punch the daemon-kin in the face, hard. He repeated the punch three times before DJar shifted his grip on the Grand Syra enough to try and stop the blows. This gave Palo some leverage but not enough to move the daemon-kin from him and rise. He twisted and rolled, freeing a leg, which he then used to drive his knee into DJar's side. The pain of the blow loosened DJar's grip on Palo's arm and Palo rolled away from the daemon-kin. Standing, breathing hard, he snarled at DJar who leapt up, facing the Grand Syra, hissing in challenge. Nepo glanced between the pair of them and nodded. There had been no prolonged pin and neither was sufficiently bloody when compared to some of the battles he'd seen in the Tabar-ring.

Without warning, DJar leapt again, riding the Semian to the ground, biting and scratching at Palo's face and neck. Palo hit back, claws digging into DJar's temples and forehead, scratching blindly at the daemon-kin. Palo rolled them again until he was on top. He grabbed DJar's hands, pinning them to his own chest. DJar dug into the flesh there, pulling a scream of pain and rage from Palo. He bit deep into DJar's ear and shook his head. DJar let go and switched to punching Palo's face and kicking his torso, trying to stop the Semian from biting. Palo had leverage and grabbed DJar around the shoulders, adding that control to his hold on DJar's head. He lifted his smaller opponent and heaved him up and away, sending DJar headfirst into the ground near him.

Palo leapt for DJar, landing on him with all his weight, driving clawed hands into DJar's ribs and ripping the skin. DJar punched up at Palo, and tried to twist and roll away, but the Semian grabbed his hands, pinning them to the ground. DJar wrapped his legs around Palo, squeezing. He screamed into Palo's face. Palo roared in reply then bit, hard, sinking his fangs into the Nura's neck. Somewhere behind them, Nepo shouted. "No Palo! Don't kill him!" Hot blood seeped into Palo's mouth and he squeezed tighter. DJar screamed, every muscle tense, squeezing as hard as he could around Palo's midriff, trying to damage the leopard man. Palo closed his jaws tighter on the Nura's neck.

Suddenly DJar's legs dropped, he stopped straining against the Grand Syra's grip, every muscle limp. Palo waited a moment, tasting flesh and blood in his mouth, feeling the daemon-kin's pulse on his tongue, his heaving chest beneath him. He let go of the Nura's neck and growled low, rubbing his muzzle against the side of DJar's face, mouth close to his undamaged ear. "You're mine," he whispered. He pulled back enough to make eye contact. DJar's eyes smoldered and he nodded his head slightly. "Say it," Palo whispered. "Make me believe it."

"I am yours, *Tepok-Myir*," DJar whispered. Nepo's panicked shouts and Shi'Shou's screaming continued somewhere behind them. For a moment, they were the only two in the world.

Then Palo straightened, still straddling the daemon-kin. "Relax Nepo," Palo purred. "Why would I kill such a hard-won prize?" He reached up and removed the bone charm, letting it drop to the ground beside them. Beneath him, DJar started to move to take his off. "No," Palo purred. He set his hand down squarely on the charm, pinning it to DJar's chest by digging his claws into the dark flesh. "You wear yours." DJar glared up at Palo, eyes flaring, and a snarl on his lips. Palo leaned in close, hissing in DJar's face. "Is that insolence I see in your eyes?" Palo asked, flexing his claws. The Nura sucked in air around clenched teeth. "The fight is over," Palo whispered, "No more rules. Don't make me call the fluid from your body and drown you in your own blood." He stared down the Nura, waiting, momentarily uncertain how much Fae the daemon-kin had understood. DJar closed his eyes and mastered his emotions. When he opened his eyes again, the fires had been banked low. "Good," Palo purred.

He released DJar and stood slowly then reached down for the Nura and helped him rise as well. Nepo was there then as was Shi'Shou, who hadn't walked over. She had moved from standing near Myrth to standing near DJar, in less than the blink of an eye. She'd lost her own bone charm and was now cradling DJar's wounds and had stepped out of the Physical Realm to work magic. Palo looked at himself and DJar, both covered in blood and bleeding from scratches, bites, and gouges in at least a half-dozen places. "We aren't sufficiently bloody?" he asked, incredulous.

Nepo studied them a moment and shook his head, "No, not for Tabar-ring rules." Palo looked at DJar who was watching him while Shi'Shou worked.

"I don't know about this one, DJar" he indicated Nepo. "I don't think he's a very good referee." Nepo scoffed and shook his head. "Genow!" Palo shouted. Then he did a double-take, "Myrth, where's Genow?"

"Genow? At a blood sport?" Myrth shook his head, "Not my Genow."

"There is a great deal of pain and suffering in the city, Palo," Clippen said. "Genow has been helping the healers."

"I'll fetch him," Marladon said, hurrying away. Palo closed his eyes, waiting, the pain of his wounds starting to flare across his skin as his adrenaline subsided. His head began to spin lazily as he stood near the others.

It was just another moment before Marladon returned with Genow. The elf was still wearing the tabard of the Healer's Guild and, as he hurried over to Palo, disdain bloomed across his face. "Unbelievable," he muttered. "There are people fighting all over the city and you two are up here carousing." He reached for Palo but the Grand Syra waved him off.

"No, DJar first."

Genow turned to the Nura. Shi'Shou hissed at him, protecting DJar from the Fae. It was the first time the elf had seen the second Nura and he hesitated, blinking in surprise. "I don't think she wants me to," Genow said with a disdainful look at Palo.

"Are you healing him," Palo snapped with a glare. "You've staunched his blood but he still bears wounds. Watch." He held out his arm to Genow. "Show her," he said. Genow frowned and closed his eyes, stepping into the Mage Realm. He passed his hands over a cut on Palo's forearm. Life magic poured across Palo's skin, knitting flesh, closing the wound.

"There is poison here," Genow whispered. His hands lingered on Palo's arm for a few more minutes.

"You're poisonous?!" Palo exclaimed, a note of delight in his voice.

DJar smiled at his delight. Genow stepped back, holding out Palo's healed arm to Shi'Shou. "Now, may I?" the elf asked.

DJar nodded and Shi'Shou took a step back, hovering and still concerned for her commander. "You won't be able to use magic on him, so long as he wears the bone charm," she said.

Genow reached for the necklace but Palo stopped him, "No, Genow." Palo turned to DJar, moving to stand just shy of touching. "I will give you your power back," Palo took hold of the bone charm, "for my service and pleasure," he whispered in DJar's good ear. Shi'Shou translated his words in a soft whisper, barely audible. DJar closed his eyes then nodded. Palo took the charm off the Nura and handed it to Shi'Shou. "Good," he said, purring low in the Nura's ear.

Genow laid his hands on the Nura's neck first and poured Life Magic into the daemon-kin. He closed his eyes while he worked.

"You did magic on DJar with the charm," Palo said, wagging a finger at Shi'Shou. "Did you just trick me?" he asked.

Shi'Shou grimaced. "I did not do magic *to* my *Shuwarr*, I did magic *about* my *Shuwarr*." Palo frowned at her but didn't ask for clarification.

"He is odd," Genow muttered. "I've never worked on a daemon-kin before. I will have to go slow."

"You've healed Sage before," Palo noted.

Genow opened his eyes and glanced at the Grand Syra, surprised. "Sage is a Land-Nymph." He shook his head and returned to working on the Nura. "It's just a visage curse."

Several minutes passed before Genow opened his eyes again. "I've done what I can to stop the bleeding. I need to save some of my strength for Palo. I can finish my work on the rest of your wounds tomorrow or I can close them completely now and leave you with scars."

Shi'Shou translated for Genow and DJar, "What care I for scars?" DJar asked, voice low, "I will lose them at my next molting." Genow looked down at the daemon-kin, realizing that tiny scales comprised the skin. "Except the ear," DJar indicated the ear Palo had chewed on and shredded. "Can that be fixed?"

"I can do it tomorrow without a scar or tonight and leave scars," Genow repeated.

"Tomorrow then," DJar said.

Genow nodded and turned to Palo, "And you, Grand Syra?"

"Leave the scars for my collection, Genow," Palo said. "It was a hard-fought battle and I want all to know how well DJar did."

Genow's scoff was echoed by Shi'Shou and they caught each other's glance. Shi'Shou muttered in Nura under her breath. DJar hung his head, sheepish.

"What'd she say?" Palo asked. "Nepo."

"I didn't hear," he lied, hiding a smile.

"What did she say?" Marco asked Myrth in his head.

"*There's not more than a brain cell apiece*," Myrth thought to his apprentice, also hiding a smile.

When Genow had finished, he excused himself for dinner and bed. Clippen had three more chairs brought and dinner was served in the courtyard to all present.

"There is just the matter of the wager," Palo said, eyes heavy on Shi'Shou as the last of the food disappeared. She glared at him as Myrth translated for Djar.

DJar sighed. "I will speak to Shi'Shou about the answers to your questions, *Tepok* Nepo, Little Brother Myrth."

"We cannot wait longer to prepare for the daemons," Myrth said. "We should all return to our homes and call up our armies." He waited for nods before continuing. "I will take my goblins to Hawkethorne."

"I have scant resources," Marladon admitted, "But I can take the dragons to the Vale."

"Oracle says you are the most at risk, Marladon," Myrth warned.

Marladon nodded, "Dragons and Vale Warriors? I like those odds."

"Home defense then?" Nepo asked, looking at Palo. "I can marshal supplies."

Palo nodded. "I will send for the full Potentate tomorrow and we will start for the Crest." He looked down the table to Marco. "Are you with me or Myrth, Marco."

"I will go with Myrth," Marco replied, confused that he'd been given a choice.

"And you," Palo pointed at DJar, "are staying with me."

"You hold my bond, *Tepok-Myir*," DJar bowed his head. "Will the others release me?" he added, looking around the table at them.

"Let us see what your *Aliith* has to say," Myrth replied. With a hmph, Shi'shou disappeared. They all blinked at the spot where she'd been sitting.

"She is not gone, *Garpok*," DJar hurriedly explained, cutting off Clippen's anger. "She has returned to our cell. I will speak to her about your answers."

Mustering

The next morning, the sound of arguing Nura met Palo's ears as he descended into the dungeon. At the bottom, he was greeted by two Star Clan Land-Nymphs, both with blue-black hair cut short. "Grand Syra," they chorused, their voices as identical as their haircuts. The two Nura ceased bickering as the Land-Nymph nearest the door bowed to Palo and continued, "We have not yet met, "I am Poliene. My blood sister is marriage sister of Timmil, who is married to the late Mara, third marriage sister to Clippen." The thoughts that had been spinning in Palo's head ceased and he stopped to take Poliene's hands in greeting.

"Poliene, welcome. I am Palo, Grand Syra of the Southern Peninsula. My lands stretch from the Great Southern Desert to the Vast Wildlands and to all the seas around us. But of all my lands, Olimidia is my favorite. When I was a boy, I played here with Clippen. He is Moon Clan, yet you are Star Clan. Timmel and Mara, inter-clan?"

"Yes, Grand Syra."

"My heart aches for the loss of our Mother." He looked deep into the ruby red eyes of the two Star Clan Land-Nymphs. Because there was no second formal greeting, he knew he'd already met the second Land-Nymph and, although he wasn't expected to remember his name, it would be rude to ask after being introduced to the first. "Thank you, for guarding these two. I know it is a great burden."

"We serve Clippen," the second Land-Nymph said. Palo set a hand on the outer shoulder of each and nodded. They then stepped aside and let him pass to the prisoners. He stopped at the door, grabbing the bars.

"Another wager, *Tepok-Myir*?" DJar asked from where he sat, seemingly in meditation.

"Open it," Palo ordered, tapping the door. Poliene leaned in with a key and undid the lock. As the door opened, DJar looked up at Palo and hastily stood. Palo grabbed him by the throat and threw him up against the far wall, holding him there by the neck. Shi'Shou hissed. DJar held up a hand to her, palm out.

Palo growled low, mouth on DJar's neck where the wound from the night before was still tender and healing. "You tasted sweet, Nura. Do you need another lesson?"

"No, *Tepok-Myir*," DJar relaxed under Palo's grip and the snow leopard man pulled away, studying the daemon-kin's eyes, where the fire banked low.

"Good," Palo said, dropping him. DJar landed lightly and straightened the linen shirt he wore. Palo waited until he had DJar's attention. "I've had an interesting conversation with Myrth this morning. Enlightening, perhaps not as informative as I wanted it to be, but it was definitely interesting." He paused then smiled, waiting for Shi'Shou to finish translating for DJar. "Let's go. Bring all your stuff," he added with a wave at Shi-Shou's spear.

Upstairs, they met once again in the tea room. The bondholders were joined by Marladon and Marco. Palo took a seat next to Myrth. When he was seated and Shi'Shou and DJar stood before him, he smiled, "I see you are well this morning, *Shuwarr* DJar, *Aliith* Shi'Shou. You are both honorable." DJar and Shi'Shou exchanged glances and then looked at Myrth who'd translated the greeting for them.

Myrth explained in Nura, "Palo has begun instruction in your ways, such as I know them." The Nura frowned, first at Myrth then at Palo, then at each other.

"It is a good day to be alive, *Tepok-Myir*," DJar began. "I come to you this day to ask, will you release me from my bond?"

"No," Clippen snapped without thought.

"I just won it," Palo said. "I'm not about to release you."

"Tell me of Tekalo," Nepo said again. DJar looked to Shi'Shou. She sighed and looked away.

"I have asked my *Aliith* what she knows. She truly does not know why Tekalo vanished. The last communiqué between her and my squad, he was still pursuing them."

"And when was that?" Nepo asked while Myrth translated. DJar looked at Shi'Shou.

"Nearly two cycles ago." she said.

"Where was he?" Nepo asked.

"In a Mortak settlement near the Embers," she replied. The Masters chewed on this information for a moment.

Marladon leaned close to Nepo. "There are only two or three possibilities aside from the Embers themselves," he said.

"I too, do not believe he has died, *Tepok* Nepo," DJar continued. "I believe he has left the Maelstrom."

"You were taking him to the Crystal Hills," Myrth added.

"I wasn't taking him anywhere, Little Brother," DJar said. "This is my *Aliith*'s knowledge. Is it enough to let loose my bond, *Tepok* Nepo?"

Nepo studied them for a long moment. "I am honorable," he said. "I release you, *Shuwarr* DJar. Go, and hold no ill will toward me or my people." DJar bowed at his words.

DJar turned to Myrth. "Can you help me?" the Earth Master asked.

"I do not possess the ability to control an army of moblings, Little Brother."

"And you?" Myrth asked, pointing to Shi'Shou.

"I owe you nothing, Semian," she hissed. Myrth bowed his head.

DJar interrupted, "I have spoken to my *Aliith*, she does not believe either of us can help." His words met a silent, contemplative Myrth.

"I cannot release your bond, but my path leads elsewhere," Myrth said after a moment. "I transfer my bond to Clippen."

DJar stood for a moment staring at the Land-Nymph. Then he bowed low at the waist. "I will honor this transfer Little Brother," he added, "Fae," with only a buried threat of disdain.

"Three bonds hold him? Or only two?" Palo asked.

"He is held by three, Clippen holds mine and his, just as before he held yours and his," Myrth explained. Palo nodded. Myrth continued in Nura, "I have spoken to Clippen. He will release you from my bond when you have proven yourself useful in our fight. It will be his discretion as to what is useful." DJar bowed his head.

"DJar, Shi'Shou," Palo said, "You will join my retainers when they arrive from Gaity. For now, you will be given rooms in the Academy across the road. I trust you to remain honorable." The two Nura exchanged glances.

"I am yours," DJar said, saluting the Grand Syra as he had saluted Marladon before.

"Good," Palo said. "I've sent a messenger to Gaity. The Potentate will be here soon."

"We should go," Myrth said. "I will contact Jay and let her know our plans before we leave. I will take my guard with me and have Sylus bring the goblins from Dragon Ridge and meet us in Hawkethorne."

"I will leave now," Marladon said. "Stay in contact, friends," the Mortak said, standing and saluting DJar. "Fare well, Brother Nura," he added before leaving.

Myrth and Marco rose. The Earth Master stopped next to DJar. The Nura met his pearl gray eyes. "You are honorable, *Shuwarr*," he said in Nura. "Gods willing, you will see the Crystal Hills again."

"We all knew the risk of hunting in the Maelstrom, Little Brother. None expected to return. *We* will be the most surprised when we do." Myrth nodded his understanding and then led Marco out.

They crossed quickly to the Academy where Auros-Gado were waiting on the front steps. "Master, we are ready to travel," Auros said. Gado handed Myrth his pack and the cushion where Jerrold had remained stitched since DJar had first unsettled the dragon fairy. Myrth pulled the pack open as he dropped the cushion to the ground.

"Come Jerrold, we are leaving the Nura here," Myrth said. He pulled out an empty glass jar and called for Jay. He waited a moment, noticing Genow approaching from the gate. He still wore the Healer's Guild tabard. "Genow?" Myrth asked.

"Master, I'd like to stay and continue to help here."

"We won't have a healer," Marco said.

"No. Still, they have need of me here and you may not even see battle in Hawkethorne."

Myrth nodded. "Stay, Genow. Tell Nepo I'm returning you, that should make him smile."

Genow smiled and nodded. "Thank you, Master." He stopped to take Marco's hand. "Be careful, Man."

"I will, Genow." he promised. Then the elf hurried back the way he'd come.

"Jay," Myrth called again into the jar. A stablehand came with four horses, while Myrth waited. He closed his eyes and stepped into the Mage Realm, traveling down his bond to Sylus, calling for the commander.

"I hear, Master," Sylus said.

"Bring my army and honor guard to Hawkethorne," Myrth directed.

"Even Sennat?"

"Yes," Myrth said with a little hesitation. "We are taking a defensive position at the mountain valley. Pack accordingly."

"I'll leave a contingent and we will see you in Olimidia."

"No, I'm leaving now. I'll meet you there."

"Very good, Master," Sylus said.

"Myrth?" Jay called from the jar, "Are you there?" Myrth dropped his connection with Sylus and answered Jay.

"We have some information for you. I need you to meet me at Hawkethorne with your mirrors," Myrth said.

"Hello to you, too. Yes, I'm doing well," she snapped, sarcasm dripping from her birdsong voice. "The summer breezes are bringing me all sorts of good weather for setting up delicately balanced constructs a cycle's journey from my current position."

"Jay," Myrth said again.

"I will be in Hawkethorne, awaiting you," she lilted.

Auros-Gado suppressed their smiles when Myrth looked up. "One too many horses," he said to the stablehand. "Thank you." Marco grabbed a light bay, as the two goblins took the matching Palace Blacks. The stablehand bowed before leading the last horse back to the stable. "Jay, Palo is going to take the Potentate to the Crest to watch and wait." There was a long silence. "Did you hear me?" Myrth asked.

"Yes, Myrth," Jay said. "Tell Palo I will leave him my jars so that we can stay in contact."

"Will he know them?"

"I'll make sure he can't miss them," she said.

They had been so long on the steps that Palo, Clippen, DJar and Shi'Shou were crossing the road toward them. "I'll tell him," Myrth said. "See you in Hawkethore." Myrth slipped the jar back into his pack before Palo's party reached them.

"I thought you'd be gone," Palo said.

"I waited to let you know that Jay is going to leave you her jars. She says you won't be able to miss them."

"You know, she should make me my own set," Palo said. "Tell her 'thank you.'"

Myrth nodded and moved aside to let the four into the Academy. "Let's move," he said. The goblins quickly secured their packs and Marco's which they'd packed for him when Myrth asked him to attend that morning's "ceremony." They mounted and Myrth followed the horses on foot as they left the Academy. Turning left, they took the main road down the central peak to the Central Plaza at its foot.

Here, a huge fountain babbled, the statuary depicting the four Hero Masters, the first to harness the elemental magic set loose on the Southern Peninsula when the first Greater Daemon broke through from the Void. None of them had a name that Marco knew, except for Syra, the elf, the first Water Mistress. The elf was joined by a goblin and a stag Semian. Standing behind them—anchoring them, Marco liked to think—was a Man. *"Which Hero Master held which power?"* Marco asked Myrth silently as they turned right and followed the road through a half-deserted market quarter toward the north road out of the crater.

"Your real question is, 'What did the Man wield?'" Myrth chided. *"Earth,"* he answered.

Beyond the crater, they continued north, retracing their path for three days, stopping at the Crossroad Inn. There, Myrth warned the innkeeper that the armies were moving north and that he and the staff should expect his goblins and then the Potentate. Despite the concern on the human proprietor's face, he didn't ask why the two armies would be passing by. After the Crossroads Inn, they continued on, stopping near the Wild Woods, before closing in on the Forest of Fear, where they spent the night.

The night was as dark in the Physical Realm as it was in the Mage Realm. The Fiery Sisters had set not long before and Rysk was yet to rise. Marco sat with his eyes closed, looking at the nearby Forest of Fear in the Mage Realm. It was covered in Shadow. He could feel the Earth there, somewhere beneath the Shadow. The land had been poisoned by Shadow centuries before when a Greater Daemon died there, its blood poisoning the soil, killing the trees and souring the water, turning it to a black sludge.

"Are you watching the Forest?" Gado asked. Marco nodded without opening his eyes. "I heard you've been there."

Marco did open his eyes then, weighing Gado, trying to decide if he was leading to a joke at Marco's expense. He saw no evidence to suggest that so he nodded. "Last year, the trolls captured me and Tekalo while we were camped ... here, I think." He added the last with a straight face, looking around with feigned nervousness. "I'm not sure whether I will be able to sleep tonight." Auros suffocated a smile as Gado joined Marco in looking around them at the dark.

"You were captured by the trolls?" Myrth asked from where he sat across from Marco. "I thought you'd rescued Temeres and Almira."

"I did," Marco confirmed, "after I'd been captured."

"How'd you get out of the warrens?" Gado asked in a whisper. "I've heard it's impossible...well, I imagine you just burrowed out with your magic."

"Tekalo led us out, actually," Marco admitted, wondering to himself why he hadn't thought to tunnel out of the warrens with his magic. "*I could probably have done so,*" he thought.

"I'm glad you escaped. I hadn't realized you were captured," Myrth said. "We should probably set a watch, just in case."

"Gado, go first," Auros said, "I'll go next." Myrth and Marco nodded.

That night and the next day passed uneventfully. As they traveled, the Forest of Fear encroached on the northern road, dead trees and poisoned soil threatening to engulf the road from the right, and the Wild Woods receded on the left. Ahead of them, the Quartz Mountain range grew. The five mountain peaks rose high above the Fanterra Plain, each a quartz rock monolith. The tallest of the peaks, Imperial, towered over the Forest of Fear at its base, little vegetation grew on the mountain and in the winter, when the snow came, it was impassable. To the east, beyond Imperial and the Forest of Fear, the Gemm hills grew into the foothills of the two smallest peaks, Majesty and Perrin, which were covered in mossy, shaggy coats of green. Ahead of the party loomed the two larger peaks, Sakwa and Owin, pink and white, respectively, and practically barren. When the suns' light hit them just right, rainbows glinted off wind-polished surfaces.

By nightfall, they were too close to the peaks to see the setting suns. Here, at Owin's base, was a large campground surrounded by palisades. When they reached it, they found it occupied by a small group of two goblins and four humans. Opposite the entrance to the campground stood the guardian statues of Hibend Trail, the fastest way to Hawkethorne Valley. The two large goblins stood when Myrth and Marco entered the campground, Myrth riding Jerrold. "Master," they intoned.

"May we join you?" Myrth asked.

"Certainly, Master, Chosen of Earth," a black-haired human said. "We are glad to have you. You are on your way home?"

"I am," Myrth confirmed, dropping from Jerrold's back and retrieving his pack and cushion from the dragon. Jerrold shrank down to lap-size and bounded over to Marco, climbing the man after he dismounted. "You?" Myrth asked.

"We carry messages from Oracle and Herdan to the Plain." He paused for a moment, "We do not have one for you." He smiled, "I am Kryn," he said, "these are my comrades. We will be on our way in the early dawn."

Myrth and Marco greeted them all, then Auros and Gado stepped forward. "We are Auros-Gado," they said in unison.

"Brothers," the new goblins held out their hands in greeting and the four shook hands and clasped arms all around.

"How is the trail?" Myrth asked Kryn.

"It is passable at the higher reaches, best in the suns' light."

"It still tends toward ice in the darker patches," one of the other humans added.

Kryn nodded. "We have eaten," he said, "but you may use our fire."

"Thank you. Shall we split the watch?" Myrth asked. There were nods all around.

The goblins and human messengers spent the night in quiet conversation with Auros-Gado while Marco and Myrth meditated and worked on the forcelines together. Up against the Quartz Mountains, Marco realized that they were a monumental store of Earth magic. "*Here,*" Myrth said in Marco's head, "*This is their forceline.*" The Master pulled a strand of magic from the cloud around them that was nearly as wide as a man is tall. "*It starts here, in the bedrock beneath Imperial and wells up to flow toward Dragon*

Ridge. As it nears the Dragon Hills, it is pulled into the current that goes to Gaity."

"Does it have its own line tied to you?" Marco asked.

Myrth shook his head no, *"It is part of the bedrock line."* Myrth was silent for a moment then suggested, *"Take the first watch, Marco."* Marco and Myrth met each other's eyes as they stepped from the Mage Realm together. The messengers around the fire were turning in and Auros and Gado were looking expectantly at them.

"I'll do first watch," Marco said. "I'll wake you in a few hours, Auros." The goblins nodded and lay down near each other, between Myrth's bed and the messengers.

After an uneventful night full of fitful sleep and troubling troll dreams, Marco woke to the sounds of the messengers breaking camp and hurrying on their way. Myrth had taken the last watch of the night and had broken camp with the messengers, packing all but the bedrolls his companions slept on. Marco quickly stored his and then looked at the two statues marking the trailhead. He knew of Hibend Trail from stories but had never climbed it. Behind him, Auros-Gado stirred as well and started to clean their beds. "Are the horses going up too?" Marco asked, patting his bay on the nose.

"Yes," Gado said. "They'll be fine. We'll have to walk them," he added when he saw Marco start to mount. With the camp cleared, they turned toward the trailhead. Myrth had strapped Jerrold's cushion to Auros' horse and the dragon fairy now perched on the other Palace Black's saddle.

Passing under the stone banner held aloft by the two human statues, the company also left behind Palo's domain. It was the end of the Fanterra Plain and the beginning of the Warlord Herdan's mountain kingdom. Marco knew from the history lectures of his youth that Herdan's kingdom was not represented by a Syra and therefore was not governed by Gaity. Herdan ruled supreme here. Myrth led the way through a maze of quartz boulders until they

neared Sakwa's base. There, the path they were following along the
ground mounted the stone monolith, carved deep into the rock's
face. The trail was wide enough for a horse and rider to pass
single-file and they did so, with Myrth leading, Auros-Gado in
between, and Marco bringing up the rear. The grade was not arduous
and they made good time. However, there was nowhere to stop for
lunch. Near midday, Myrth called a halt and Gado carefully squeezed
by his horse in order to search his saddle bags for food to share. They
were hundreds of feet from the ground now, the trail clinging to
Sakwa's side. They were nearing another switchback where the trail
dug deep into the rock in order to make a steep turn before twisting
back on itself, slightly higher than before and growing more shallow.

Marco had been doing his best to concentrate on the Earth
Cloud around him and not on the air beyond the trail and the long
drop to the plains below. Not for the first time he thought that it
looked as if there should have been a wall or hand rail in places. If
there had ever been a railing, it was gone. Gado passed food to Auros
who squeezed past his horse and handed some to Marco.

"Where do we camp?" Marco asked, chewing on the dried fish
Gado had found.

"At the top of Sakwa and Owin, there's a meadow. We'll stay
there the night and ascend to Hawkethorne tomorrow. Myrth said.

"If this is taking your breath away, just wait for Imperial's flank,"
Auros said with a smile, "and the Chasm Bridge."

"Don't fret, Marco," Myrth chided from the front. "If you are
troubled, call the Earth to your aid. *It* will obey." The Master's
emphasis implied that the goblins had not obeyed and they were
chagrined, eating quickly and signaling to Myrth when they were
ready to carry on. Marco followed them, trying not to worry about
the climb beyond the meadow at the top of Sakwa and Owin.

Near sunset, the trail changed from a sharply chiseled path in
the side of the quartz monolith to a wide, sweeping staircase cut

through a crack in the stone. At the top of the stairs, they spilled out into the meadow where it seemed that the New Seed season was just beginning to melt the snow and coax plants from the soil. With the Fiery Sisters still above the horizon, they had ample time to explore their surroundings, collect scrub brush for a fire and bed down before dusk grew across the sky and the Ghost Moon reached his zenith. Auros-Gado released their Palace Blacks to forage on the young grass and Marco did the same. Jerrold curled around Myrth's shoulders, continuing his nap.

"It feels like snow tonight, Master," Gado said.

Myrth nodded. "Marco, make us a shelter, it'll be good practice."

"Make us a castle, Marco," Auros said with a laugh. Marco smiled but a glare from Myrth changed his mind and he did not follow through. Marco closed his eyes and stepped into the Mage Realm. He grabbed the Earth Cloud and shaped it into a bowl, turning it on its side and flattening the bottom to create a cave-like hollow large enough for the horses and the four people, along with a fire. "Nice, but it's a shame there aren't any crenelations," Auros commented as Marco opened his eyes.

"*How do I make it permanent without staying in the Mage Realm,*" he asked Myrth. "*Like a ward?*"

"*In a way,*" Myrth explained. "*Whereas you tie a ward to yourself, as Earth Master you will tie it to a current.*"

"Any current?"

"*Yes, any nearby one will do.*"

Marco reached out to a nearby eddy that was bubbling up from the bedrock. He urged the forceline to coalesce around the Earth Cloud bowl he'd formed and it lazily obeyed his will. When he was certain the eddy would behave itself, he opened his eyes and stepped back to the Physical Realm. When the cavern he'd made remained intact, he started breathing again.

"Tomorrow, when we leave, you'll put that eddy back how you found it and let the Earth Cloud return to its rightful place."

"Yes, Myrth." Marco waited for the Master to turn away before reaching out to the Earth Cloud and denting the top of the cave, adding a handful of crenelations. Gado's appreciative chuckles brought them to Myrth's attention and he rolled his eyes and shook his head.

In the morning, they were glad for the shelter, waking up to an inch of new-fallen snow. "Where's Master Nepo when you need him," Auros grumbled, standing in the mouth of the cavern, stretching his full body, touching the top lip of the cave by standing on his tiptoes.

"We'll make it," Gado judged.

"The flank's path will be slippery with the snow," Myrth warned Marco, "but it's not so bad that we have to wait for the suns to melt the ice before starting."

They packed quickly and doused the fire, spreading the coals and unburnt brush around the cavern floor. Then they stood back and waited for Marco to release the Earth and return the area to its original flatness. Myrth appraised his work once the eddy had been returned to its meandering and the soil replaced the cavern. "Good," the hawk-man said. *"A bit more practice at returning the current to how you found it,"* the Master added silently. Marco bowed his head in acknowledgment.

They started across the meadow toward Owin's summit. Pointing the way, Auros explained their route. "We'll cross Owin's shoulder, avoiding his peak and head for Imperial." The slate-gray quartz mountain towered over them. Its surface was a maze of cracks and crags, some of them deep enough to allow tiny gray trees to find purchase and grow. Birds of prey circled the peak, hunting for their breakfast. "That crag there," Auros pointed to a deep crack halfway to the top of Imperial, "that's the path to Hawkethorne Valley. We take a trail up Imperial's flank to reach it, pass through, cross the Chasm Bridge, and then we're practically home."

"You're not from here," Marco breathed, eyes searching Imperial for the trail they were meant to use.

"I am," Myrth said, taking the lead from Auros. The goblin waved Marco on to follow the Master and joined Gado at the back.

They crossed the summit and climbed Owin's shoulder. The snow only reached a depth of about two inches, making the ground slippery. Imperial grew more daunting as they drew nearer until they were standing at the base of the gray quartz cliff that formed the towering peak. This close to the mountain, there would be no direct sunlight once the suns began to set. The trail appeared before them, the scraps of underbrush that found purchase on Owin's shoulder giving way to a chiseled path that traced its way up the mountain as the one up Sakwa had done before. It was smooth enough for the horses but steeper than the lower trail had been. Marco turned to look at his horse and the two Palace Blacks behind him. Catching his frown, Auros asked, "What is it?"

"Are the horses going to make it?"

"If you believe it and trust your animal then, yes," Gado said. "They were surefooted below, they will be okay here. We may want to blindfold them and lead them across the Chasm Bridge as I don't think any of them are actually from here. We should wait and see how they react to it, though."

"Your bay is a good horse, he'll be fine," Auros added.

They climbed. The trail took them around to the south and then east, gently corkscrewing around the peak rather than cutting deep switchbacks as the other trail had done. Below them, Owin's bulk was replaced by the tumbling crags of Imperial. Hundreds of feet below, the dark smudge of the Forest of Fear spread out from the mountain like a second shadow. To the east, the green summit of Majesty welcomed them. When they reached the northern side of the mountain peak, the trail sliced into a crevasse that had cleaved through that section of the peak. It led them back to the Owin side where the trail once again slowly corkscrewed upward, this time moving north until they reached the deep crag that led to Hawkethorne Valley. Two more statues greeted them.

They were stooping eagles made of stone with bronze beaks and talons. An errant breeze ran through the crag and the two statues played an eerie note, each one an octave different, sounding like a disconcerted pipe organ. Myrth stopped between the two statues, closed his eyes and took a deep breath, sighing. "The cries of Limina," Auros whispered from the path behind Marco, near his elbow, "Welcome home, Myrth." he added, loud enough for the Master to hear.

"Limina was the avian Semian who led the tribes of the valley when Herdan brought war," Myrth said, resting a hand on the right-hand eagle, looking at Marco. Through their connection, Marco saw human soldiers in black and blue armor marching through the streets, ransacking stick huts. As Myrth walked away, entering the chasm, the memories went with them.

"Herdan took over Hawkethorne during Myrth's lifetime?" he whispered to himself. The history books he'd read had made it seem as if the human warlord had always ruled here.

"Go on, Marco," Auros commanded from behind. "We can't leave you behind to gawk when you're in front." Marco shot him an animated glare that brought smiles to both goblins' faces. With his own chuckle, Marco started between the hawk statues, another breeze bringing forth a forlorn note.

The chasm he walked through rose high above him, a frigid darkness falling all around. Marco glanced up to where the sky could be seen far above. The sheer rock sides were coated in ice, water puddling across the ground, making walking through the chasm difficult. Myrth's silhouette moved slowly ahead of Marco, where more light could be seen.

At the far end of the chasm, Myrth stepped out into sunlight and then down, descending a set of steps. Marco reached the end of the crevasse and blinked in the bright light. Myrth was a few feet below him and thought, "*Steady, Marco, the footholds are slippery.*" Marco looked down at Myrth and gasped. The crevasse opened onto a set of wide steps that curved gently down into the mountainside, forming a flat, natural alcove, offering enough room for a horse and rider to stand, even change direction. Beyond the alcove and carved steps, on all sides of Marco, the mountain fell away to darkness, hundreds of feet below. From the natural alcove, a narrow footbridge spanned the chasm that he had walked out into. Marco looked up. They were inside a jagged crack in Imperial's peak. The quartz continued upwards another fifty feet or so before forming the barren top of the monolith. Across the chasm, the other half of the splintered peak dared them to defy gravity and cross.

"Easy Marco, you'll spook your horse," Myrth said aloud. Marco closed his eyes and focused on the Earth Cloud all around him. He knew he could call it to heel and it would obey at the speed of thought. He opened his eyes, taking a deep breath and releasing it before leading the horse carefully down the steps to the alcove. Here, as in the crevasse, water had puddled and turned to ice. Myrth continued, "The Chasm Bridge has been known to invite people to their death. Don't let an errant wind knock you or your horse from it," he said. "It's only a handful of steps across to the Sheltering Valley. We are nearly there."

"This is a last line of defense, isn't it?" Marco asked. "How did Herdan even get this far? How did those soldiers march through the streets?"

"They did not come this way," Myrth said with a sigh. "They came from the depths, through Gemma and the underground passages." He paused, frowning and looking around him and back up the steps and trail, "The last of the free Avians retreated to the crevasse and Summit Meadow."

"You?" Marco thought. Myrth shook his head no. In his mind, Myrth showed Marco scenes from a cozy cottage window, human soldiers marching past as avian Semians screamed and fought or ran.

"The nestlings and their mothers were passed over and avoided," Myrth said aloud. "Even the men who fought for the Valley were spared and taken alive at all costs. Herdan didn't want to harm the people living here, he simply wanted what we had and he had the forces to take it."

"And Limina?" Marco asked.

"She couldn't bear to live here with humans and led a handful of Avians away to the Southern Desert and its glittering seas." He sighed, catching Auros at the top of the steps out of the corner of a pearl-gray eye. "Imperial shelters us; Hawkethorne Valley lies just across the bridge." He stepped away from the alcove and was across the expanse in twenty steps.

"So long as your horse doesn't balk, this is a quick crossing. If your horse won't go," Auros said from behind Marco, "we can blindfold it and try a second time. If it still won't go, I'd suggest a little Sand Snake magic rather than reversing and making your way back down, around the Forest of Fear and through Gemma."

Marco rolled his eyes at the goblin and followed Myrth's example, stepping confidently from the alcove and starting across the Chasm Bridge. The horse hesitated, nickering and tossing its head, eyes wide. "Come on, baby," Marco urged. "Look, we can do it. It's safe. You're with me." He steadied the horse's head and tried to catch its eye.

Auros nodded. "Nice try. Hang on and I'll tie up its eyes." He gently draped a linen shirt over the horse's head, deftly balancing on the edge of the alcove, seemingly unperturbed by the lack of rock inches from where he worked. With the shirt secured, Marco patted the bay a moment and then started again. With a reluctant head toss, the horse gave in and followed Marco, quickly crossing the bridge to the second crevasse. Myrth followed the trail and waited for Marco to join him in the sunlight on the other side after removing the linen shirt from his horse's head. Before him, sheltered in the cleft of Imperial, sat Hawkethorne Valley.

The Sea of Dreams

At the far end of the crevasse, the land fell away once again, only this time, it rolled downward in gentle, terraced hills, covered in lush greenery. Here, a large cleft in Imperial's peak, sheltered a small city. Steep winding roads and trails dropped from the highest farms and fields, nearly equal in height to the chasm's mouth, to a crystalline pool at the bottom of the cleft. The stick cottages from Myrth's memory remained, but they'd been joined by a handful of stone and mortar buildings, the tallest of which sat halfway up the other side of the cleft.

"Herdan's castle," Myrth supplied with a nod. "Home to the Sea of Dreams."

As soon as Auros-Gado joined them, Myrth led them down the dirt path, reaching the bottom of the cleft in a few minutes. Curious onlookers waved at Myrth, some calling out to him. He returned their waves and smiles. A handful of children began to gather and follow them, their big eyes brimming with questions and curiosity. Many were Semian, mostly avian with a handful of felines and canines. The rest were humans with pale skin and dark hair and eyes. "*Vale Warriors,*" Marco thought, seemingly to himself. Looking at them and the human farmers they passed, Marco suddenly realized why so many people they met assumed D'Mique was from the Vale.

Myrth interrupted his thoughts, "*They no longer consider themselves Vale Warriors,*" he said. "*They are Herdan's people.*" After passing around the pool, they climbed again and were soon at the polished oaken door of the castle.

A small Avian Semian that could have been Myrth's relative greeted them. "Master Myrth, Herdan is at rest. Oracle bids you welcome and asks that you refresh from your journey before speaking to him. He did ask me to take any message you may have."

"And the Steward?" Myrth asked.

"She is busy but we have arranged dinner together this evening, upon Oracle's request." He paused a moment then added, "Mistress Jay arrived yesterday. She asked to see you when you are rested."

"And my companions?" Myrth asked.

"We will take your horses, there are rooms made up for you and your companions. Oracle is, as ever, accurate and an ingenious host."

"*And a show-off,*" Myrth added silently. Marco squashed his smile.

"Master, Auros-Gado," the greeter continued. "We will see you to your previous quarters. Oracle felt that you would prefer to room with your apprentice, Master." Myrth nodded and the greeter opened the door. Three young men exited and collected the horses as Marco and the goblins took their packs from their mounts. Myrth collected his belongings, Jerrold, and the pillow before following the greeter into the castle. The diminutive hawk led them to a winding staircase and motioned for Myrth and Marco to ascend. "I will send the Mistress to you in a moment," he said.

"Thank you, Tasco," Myrth said with a nod and smile. Tasco bowed and Auros-Gado followed him deeper into the castle.

The stairs spiraled upward, bare stone walls on both sides as they climbed. However, at the top, they entered into a large, lavishly decorated, round room, the stairs coming up through a trapdoor in the center of the space instead of along the wall. Half of the room's wall space held windows that looked out across the cleft to the crevasse where they'd entered. Marco didn't remember seeing tower rooms from the other side of the valley. Looking up out a nearby window, he realized that the top of the tower burrowed into Imperial's stone cliff face. Close to the windows, a settee and overstuffed chairs offered comfortable places to lounge and enjoy the view. Nearby, four wooden chairs were arranged around a brass table that bore a burdensome number of fruit, enough to rival the finest spreads in the kingdoms of the Fanterra Plain. The large bed, its brass fittings glinting in the sunlight that streamed across the room, sat against a tapestry-festooned wall, its red curtains pulled back to allow easy access. Myrth set his pack down and Jerrold leapt onto the bed, happily curled up on the pillows at the head of the bed while Myrth removed his cloak, draping it across a chair near the table. He removed his boots as well, leaving his stockings and trousers on.

Other than his arms and head, Myrth was human, strong but obviously older, growing wiry as his youth slipped away. He cocked his head when he saw Marco studying him. Embarrassed, Marco looked away and set his pack down near the settee. "Only one bed," he noted.

"Do you want to take turns between it and the settee? I can ask if there is another room for you, although...Herdan's castle is small by necessity, and there are few rooms for guests." Myrth waited for Marco to nod before continuing, "You can have the bed first."

There was a knock on the door just as Marco started to undress and he hurriedly covered up as Jay entered. "Oh, Marco," she said, startled that he was there. "I am sorry. I did not know you were here." She waved a handful of mirrors at Myrth, turning her back to the man. "I am setting these up just outside the Sea of Dreams," she said. "We will be able to scan the Blasted Lands, although not in as great detail as I can see the Broodlands from my Tower."

"Good," Myrth took one of the mirrors from her and looked through it to a volcanic plain and Mount Myrs rising in the distance. "We need to focus them on the Great Southern Wilds," Myrth said. "I suspect Tekalo has found himself there."

Jay closed her eyes, nodding, and the mirror's vision shifted, panning around to show the Great Southern Wilds in the near-distance. The shark Semian opened her eyes and studied Myrth as he looked into the mirror. "What are you hoping to see?" she asked. "He disappeared quite a while ago."

Myrth frowned and continued looking into the mirror for a moment before he sighed and shrugged his shoulders. "Perhaps we will see him coming home," he said. "It will help Nepo."

With her own frown, Jay nodded acceptance and turned to Marco. "Oh, you're still dressed. Change, Herdan wants to meet you." She smiled and left, disappearing through the floor and down the tower.

"We will call on Herdan and then find Oracle," Myrth said, rifling through a wardrobe for clean clothes for he and Marco.

Freshened from the trail, they made their way down out of the tower, Marco following a step behind Myrth. At the ground floor, they continued through lavish white halls lined with tapestries depicting battles and mountain vistas until they reached a throne room. No one sat upon the throne, but two goblins were present, one standing and one sitting, at a desk near the throne. A familiar goblin face looked up from where he leaned over a pile of papers and he smiled. "Master Myrth, Marco," Tierren greeted. He stepped forward and the she-goblin seated behind the desk stopped talking. Smiling, she waited. It had been nearly a year since Marco had met the sandstone-colored goblin soldier, Tierren, and the winter here at home had been good to him.

"Tierren," Myrth greeted. "How is Samsha?"

"She is well."

"And your brother, Rogan?" Myrth continued. Tierren nodded, his black hair had been pulled up in a top knot and it bobbed as he turned to smile at Marco, large fangs flashing in his mouth.

"How do you fare, Mage of Man?" he asked.

"I'm doing well," Marco said. "Palace life suits you," he added with a smile.

"Samsha is with child, so I've taken on domestic affairs and left the battles for the younger men." Tierren patted his thick middle with an appreciative grin.

"Steward," Myrth bowed to the seated she-goblin. "I am in advance of my goblin army. As Oracle is here, I'm sure you know the details, perhaps better than myself."

"We welcome you and your army, Master Myrth," the goblin said. She had the same black hair as Tierren and the same pointed nose and high forehead. Her skin was a mottled gray and yellow where it showed around her courtly robes. "As always, once a son of Hawkethorne Valley, always a son of Hawkethorne Valley. Yours are welcome here."

"We heard from the Wind Mistress that Herdan wanted to see us," Myrth said with a bow.

"Of course," she smiled. "You know the way?"

"Yes," Myrth bowed to both and left, moving past the table and around the throne to the private quarters. The door was guarded by a young avian Semian, covered head to toe in black feathers—a crow.

"Master Myrth," he said, opening the door for them. Myrth passed through into the warlord's private chamber. A large bed took up much of the space. There were three elfin healers milling about the room, each wearing white tabards. At the foot of the bed, a second throne sat and a papery-thin man greeted them from it. His hair, though still black was thinning and wispy. The skin on his hands, so thin that his veins could be seen within, stretched over gnarled knuckles. The yellowed fingernails that clasped a metal rod had been nicely manicured. His face lit up in warmth and happiness when Myrth closed the distance and knelt before him.

"Master Myrth," Herdan said, his voice as papery thin as his body appeared.

"Warlord Herdan," Myrth bowed his head and Herdan petted his feathers. Marco schooled his face to stillness and focused on the forcelines tied to him.

"Whom have you brought? Come closer," the warlord commanded, beckoning with his whole hand. Marco approached and bowed.

"Marco is my apprentice, Warlord," Myrth informed him.

"You're a tall one. Good Vale stock? Are you one of my people?" the warlord asked, curiosity coloring his papery voice with a lilt.

"No, Warlord," Marco replied. "I'm from The Nesting."

"The Nesting? We keep the Promise here, young man. Don't we, Myrth," Herdan snapped.

"Yes, of course," Myrth agreed.

"Despite the distance, we keep the Promise." He recited, his blue eyes gazing off into the distance, reading remembered words, *"Keep them safe, for the shining hope does dwell there."* Myrth and Marco nodded in unison. The Promise had existed for longer than written history. Fae, Semian, and Mortaks, all promising to protect the humans who lived in The Nesting, guarding them so that they would be ready when the prophecy came to pass. At one time, people may have known the exact prophecy they awaited. Or, perhaps it had already resolved and keeping the Promise for no reason was what the denizens of the Fanterra Plain did now, out of habit. No one could say.

"An apprentice, you say?" Herdan asked, leaving the former conversation behind.

"Yes," Myrth said with a beaky smile.

"You?" The warlord laughed, a breathy rasping sound. "And you? A mage? A Mage of Man?"

"Yes, Warlord," Marco said with his own smile as the old man continued chuckling. An elfin healer closed on them, and laid a hand on Herdan as he started gasping and coughing.

"We will have to ask you to leave, Master Myrth, Man," she said. "The warlord is tiring." Myrth stood, clasping the ancient hand of the warlord, bending forward to let the old man pet his head again.

Marco turned away and hurried from the room, waiting near the empty throne and Tierren for Myrth. "Samsha is pregnant?" he asked as he waited.

"Indeed."

"How is Rogan taking it?" Marco asked with a smile. He wasn't as close to the goblins as D'Mique had been but he knew the pair were blood brothers, just as Auros and Gado were.

Tierren smiled, "He's bored but supportive."

Myrth appeared, smiling at the Steward. "How is the warlord's health?" he asked.

"We do not discuss his frailty, Master. He is sanguine most days and still very interested in the goings on of the court and his valley kingdom. Yet, he tires easily and the elves are often at work on his lungs and heart."

Myrth nodded at her words. "Where might I find Oracle?"

"He is at the Sea of Dreams, Master," she said.

"Alone?"

"Yes, last I knew." With a curt bow, Myrth turned toward the door.

Marco gave a wave and a nod before following Myrth from the room, back the way they'd come to the front door of the castle. The young hawk let them out with a bow.

Cold shadows that still held the chill of winter had descended into the valley as the suns moved toward setting. Without a word or thought, Myrth led Marco down a path and into a cave near the northern wall of the castle. The cavern floor had been carved into well-used steps. Years of lamp usage had covered portions of the wall with soot. The lighted path led down into a deep quartz cavern where a gray quartz building had been constructed. Jay was here, setting up mirrors by lamplight, each one held aloft in a bubble of solidified air that could be pushed around, grabbed, and carried as needed.

"How do you find Herdan?" she asked with a quick glance up at Myrth.

"Do you know if there are succession plans?" he asked by way of response.

"I do not, but I am sure the Steward has things well in hand."

"She is a competent leader," Myrth agreed. He absently poked a mirror bubble and watched it skitter toward two more, where they bounced and rebounded off one another. "Not your Eyes, but good," he said with a smile. Marco studied a mirror near his head. The scene inside showed a large active volcano, Mount Myrs. Near the foot of the volcano, it looked like a castle wall rose from a lava lake.

"Where is this?" he asked, grabbing the bubble and spinning it to Jay and Myrth.

"The Embers?" Myrth and Jay chorused. "Marladon lived there for a time," Jay continued. "It's a dragon nursery."

"Is Oracle inside?" Myrth asked. Jay nodded and returned to her un-bubbled mirrors. Myrth signaled Marco to follow him and they continued around the round building to a discreet door. Myrth opened it and stepped into a small antechamber. He closed the door behind Marco. "The Sea of Dreams, Marco," he said, opening an inner door.

Myrth had been here before, nearly a year ago. He'd been called here by Oracle who was adamant that only the eight people he and Driselle had seen in the Sea of Dreams could win against the Greater Daemon bearing down on their world. It had proven true. Then, the nine seers had met him in almost total darkness. Now, the lights within the Sea of Dreams glowed brightly, the flames dancing in the polished surface of the giant black gemstone that made up the floor of the dome. Oracle sat across from the door, meditating on a large floor cushion. There were eight other cushions along the edge of the schorl.

Oracle opened his eyes as Myrth approached across the stone. Hesitantly, Marco followed him. "I am glad you are here, dear friend," Oracle whispered. His eyes fell on Marco. "Hello, Man Child." Marco nodded in response.

"How are your dreams, Oracle?" Myrth asked, kneeling in front of the wolf Semian.

"Troubled, full of darkness, Shadow, and destruction."

"Can you find someone?" Myrth asked.

"I can try," Oracle said, frowning, his wolf ears drooping.

"Tekalo has disappeared," Myrth said. "Nepo cannot feel him on the forcelines." Oracle frowned at him.

"I will try but if he's not on the forcelines..." the wolf Semian trailed off and closed his eyes. Myrth felt him withdraw and knew that he'd gone deeper than the Mage Realm, down into the *Hisseth,* searching.

"Whoa," Marco breathed, leaping off the Sea of Dreams as the crystal reacted to Oracle's power. Pinpricks of light danced across the blackness, some of them deep within the stone, others at its surface. Marco watched them swirl and dive. Then, one floated up out of the depths and as it hit the surface, it opened into a white sphere. Inside the sphere, Tekalo's head and shoulders were visible. Marco gasped. The sphere winked out as Oracle opened his eyes. The wolf Semian shook his head.

"I cannot see him, Myrth. Yet, I know he is there. He has not died."

"Could he have left the Southern Peninsula and you are not be able to see him?" Myrth asked.

"The Sea of Dreams is localized to the lives here, on the peninsula. If he has moved beyond it, then yes." Oracle snarled, silently bearing his teeth. "If I can't see him, it's possible he will never return." Marco's heart sank and he stared at the stone floor where he'd last seen his friend.

Myrth closed his eyes and steadied his emotions, the world around them swaying slightly at Oracle's revelation. "Let's not tell Nepo that last part," he whispered to the seer. Oracle nodded in agreement.

The next day, Myrth's goblin army arrived, streaming through the crevasse and into the valley one or two at a time. The first to arrive were a pair of advance scouts, who were greeted by the Steward and Myrth. They would find encampment in the underground tunnels, they were informed. One went on to secure their camping sites while the second returned the way they'd come, taking word to the others of their welcome. Sylus led the next group to come through the crevasse. He and Vellin found their way to Myrth and the Steward leading the remaining Honor Guard, while the soldiers continued past them to the encampment.

"Master," Sylus greeted. The diminutive elf passed his horse to a hawk Semian stablehand.

"How was your journey, Sylus? Vellin," Myrth greeted the other elf with a nod.

"Nicely uneventful, which is how I like to start a war," Vellin said. Sylus nodded in agreement.

"We had a safe journey and are all accounted for here. Counting your full Honor Guard, your force is one hundred strong," Sylus informed him.

"And Dragon Ridge?"

"There is a contingency squad of twenty," his elfin lieutenant answered. Myrth nodded. Sylus waited, biting his tongue. "There is more, Master," Sylus said. Myrth looked at him. "I want to state my disapproval of moving your entire army here simply because Oracle is dreaming again."

Myrth sighed and nodded. "Your opinion is noted and I am glad that you have shared it. Still, Oracle is rarely wrong." Sylus grimaced. Myrth continued, addressing the Honor Guard, "We have been given rooms in the castle but must sleep two to a room." Sennat looked disappointed but hefted his and Vellin's packs. He was followed up to the castle by the other elves and the goblin Chay. Sylus stayed with Myrth and Marco. "If nothing comes of this in the next three cycles, Sylus," Myrth conceded, "I will send half of the goblins home."

"Very well, Master," Sylus said with a bowed head and a squashed triumphant smile.

They spent much of the rest of the day ensuring that the goblin army was comfortably ensconced in the caverns below Hawkethorne Valley. The door to the cave system sat near the Sea of Dreams, in a different cave opening. From the surface, the tunnels snaked through the crystal monolith, eventually making their way to the other side of the Quartz Mountains and the Gemm Hills.

As night crept closer, Marco and Myrth settled in their tower room. It was Myrth's turn on the bed. He pulled out his set of jars. "Nepo?" he called, waiting. Marco lay down on the settee and turned his back on the hawk man, intent on listening in on his Master's conversation. "Nepo?" Myrth called again.

"What do you want, Myrth?" It was Palo's voice emanating from the water-filled jar.

"Is Nepo with you?" Myrth asked.

"Yes, Myrth," Nepo said.

"And DJar?" Marco perked up at the mention of the Nura.

There was hesitation before Palo responded, "Yes, he is at the Academy. If I shift slightly to the left of where I'm sitting," there was a pause, "I can see them. He and Shi'Shou are happily ensconced across the way."

"Why do you ask?" Nepo pressed.

"There's something stuck in my craw," Myrth began.

Palo snickered, "Sounds like an avian problem." Nepo chuckled.

"No, it's a Grand Syra and Magistrate Clippen problem," Myrth grumbled. "I've been thinking about something DJar said," Myrth continued. "When I left, DJar said to me that he would be the most surprised to return to the Crystal Hills from the Maelstrom."

"The most surprised of whom?" Nepo asked.

"Of them all?" Myrth answered with his own question. "That's what has me thinking." He paused, listening to the silence, trying to figure out how to put to words the thoughts that had been spinning in the back of his mind. "It's not Tabar Row, but the Gray's of the Crystal Hills do enjoy their wagers."

"He was here on a bet?" Palo asked after a long silence.

"I do not know. But, if they were sent here, they would have to bring something back to prove they were here, rather than just camping out in the Vast Wildlands for a season."

"The Land-Nymphs," Palo breathed through the jar.

"Trophies or prisoners," Myrth whispered back.

"Do you think Tekalo is a prisoner?" Nepo asked. He scoffed at his own question, "I just can't see that."

"No, I don't believe he is," Myrth said, "However, he may find himself in the Crystal Hills if he chases DJar's squad all the way home."

"Do we ask DJar about this tomorrow?" Nepo asked.

"Or, do we assume that we will see Tekalo reappear soon," Palo suggested. They were all silent for several long minutes. "Goodbye, Myrth," Palo said. "I'm going to finish my wine now. Tell Marco his princess will be there soon. Herdan recalled her and Temeres." Myrth looked over and caught Marco's eye, passing him a fleeting smile.

"I'll let your drinking buddy know that he missed out on a quiet night," Myrth replied. Marco rolled his eyes before rolling back over to sleep.

Two days later, Marco's breakfast was interrupted by Morn, another diminutive hawk-man doorman. "Chosen One, I was told by Master Myrth to let you know that the Mage Princess has returned. She is crossing the valley now." Marco stood quickly, knocking into the table and sloshing water from his and Myrth's goblets. Myrth chuckled as Marco hurried from the room.

Marco rushed through the castle to the front door and let himself out. Staring up at the crevasse where they'd so recently watched the goblin army stream through, Marco caught two people in black leading two Palace Blacks down the side of the cleft. He knew them, even from so far away, Almira and her bodyguard Temeres. He rushed to meet her, flying along the trail as it led down to the pool and then up the other side of the valley to her.

Almira saw him coming and called out a greeting just before her bodyguard blocked Marco's path. Marco nearly barreled into the Protector before skidding to a halt. Temeres' bright blue eyes seemed cut from glacial ice for a moment as he weighed Marco. Marco had first met the Vale Warrior in the mud trolls' dungeon after being captured and taken to their warrens under the Forest of Fear. There, he'd rescued the man and helped him find his way to safety. Now, returned to health, Marco realized just how much had been taken from the Protector last year. Healthy Temeres suddenly reminded him of a set bear trap—barbed wire, tight springs, iron jaws with bone-breaking teeth, and a hair trigger. His whip-thin build probably fooled some into mistaking him as non-threatening. Marco knew better. "Temeres," Marco breathed.

"This is the Mage Princess of Hawkethorne Valley," Temeres said, his baritone voice even and bone-numbing cold. "These are her people you have rushed past, even pushed aside. You will show her the proper respect and you will not touch her in public."

Marco's heart skipped a beat and he looked behind him. Avian Semians lined the path he'd hurried up. *"Did I push them?"* he wondered.

"Make way for the Princess," Temeres warned.

Marco looked back at the Vale Warrior, dressed all in black with three white feathers in his cap, and his eyes rested on Temeres' hands. One on his belt and the other on the hilt of his rapier.

"Honestly, Temeres," Almira admonished from behind, her beauty hidden by a black veil held in place by silver chains attached to her own, two-red-feathered, black cap. In the abstract, the Mage Princess having a bodyguard, a Protector from the Vale no less, was absurd. As a Fire Mage, Almira could handle herself and woe to anyone who touched her without her approval.

Swallowing hard, Marco took a step back and moved aside. "No, he's right. I will follow you back to the castle." Marco winked at her and she chuckled under her breath, a heady, deep sound that started his heart racing. Temeres glared at him, waiting for Marco to school his face to "solemnly admonished" before the Protector continued down the path. Almira shook her head as she passed by and Marco joined them from behind, admiring the Princess as they crossed over to the castle.

There, Morn met them at the door. "Temeres, Princess Almira, welcome home."

"Hello Morn," Temeres said. "We will take our leave and refresh from the road," Temeres ordered.

"And then breakfast," Almira added. Once the door had closed behind them, Marco had taken her hand and kissed it through her glove. Temeres studied Marco when he noticed them holding hands, but said nothing and didn't kill him, either. "How is Herdan?" Almira asked.

"He is well, still asleep, I believe," the young hawk-man answered. "The Steward is about, if you would like to talk to her."

"No, no," she said. "I will see you at breakfast, my love," she added, taking her hand from Marco and lacing an arm through Temeres' offered elbow. Temeres led her deeper into the castle, toward the throne room. With a happy sigh, Marco nodded, returning slowly to finish his breakfast with Myrth.

When Marco re-entered the dining hall, Myrth had been joined by Oracle. "Good morning, Seer Oracle," Marco greeted, returning to his plate of fruit. Oracle nodded toward him, chewing noisily. Wolf features did not lend themselves to polite table manners.

"Your princess is here, good," Oracle said after he'd swallowed his food.

"She'll be along shortly," Marco added. Oracle nodded and for the first time Marco wondered how much the seer already knew. *"Is it impolite to ask?"* Marco thought toward Myrth.

Oracle smiled, and shook his head.

"No, it's not impolite," Myrth thought in return.

"I am a High Time Mage," Oracle said. "The world happens in my head before it happens before my eyes, but only by the briefest of moments. The gap is ever so slight. "I am, however, also bound to Myrth. Therefore, I can hear your thoughts when you converse with him in my presence."

"And Sylus too?" Marco asked. Myrth nodded. "Oh," Marco frowned, trying to remember if he'd ever thought something awful in the elf's presence. Oracle smiled.

"You would have known if you'd said something untoward and Sylus heard," Myrth assured him aloud, a chuckle in his voice. They lapsed into companionable silence, eating. Marco finished his plate, sipping water while he waited for Almira and Temeres.

The door opened a moment later and Temeres led the way. He'd changed into a clean Potentate uniform, his three-white-feathered cap left behind. His pale skin looked freshly washed, but his feathery blond hair still held dust from the road. Almira had also changed, leaving her Potentate uniform behind. She'd dressed in an emerald green gown that glowed against her coffee-colored skin. The veil she wore with her Potentate uniform that hid her face in its entirety, had been exchanged for a lace blusher veil. Her smile beamed at Marco through the veil. "Hello, love," she said. Marco stood and crossed to her, ignoring Temeres' glare.

"Oracle!" Myrth shouted as the table rattled behind Marco. Marco spun quickly, Oracle had gone stiff, convulsing, claws gouging into the wooden tabletop. His eyes, open, did not see them.

"He's having a fit," Temeres said, pushing past Marco to gain the wolf-man's other side, opposite Myrth. Almira glanced around the room, searching for any other threat. Marco pulled her close. As quickly as it had started, it ended and Oracle slumped, hitting his head hard on the table, knocking plates and glass goblets to the floor. Myrth reached out to him as Temeres checked for signs of life.

"He's closed off," Myrth said. "He lives." They righted the wolf, waiting for him to return.

Another minute passed before Oracle stirred. He gasped, glanced quickly between Myrth and Temeres, before focusing on Myrth. "The Sea of Dreams, now!" he whispered. "All of you," he added. Myrth helped him stand and they made a small parade out of the castle and down the path to the cave where the Sea of Dreams lay.

Jay's mirror-bubbles now bounced around the area and four of Myrth's goblins patrolled them, looking for daemons and Land-Nymphs. The seer and Master Myrth pushed through the bubbles, ignoring the goblin soldiers, and entered the round room where the schorl lay buried. At the Sea, Myrth motioned for Marco, Temeres, and Almira to stop while Oracle continued across. Where he walked, the stone glowed purple, wolf paw prints that skittered across the polished stone. On the other side, Oracle fell to his knees on his cushion and turned back toward the door where everyone else had stopped. With a snarl, he smacked the stone. Where his paw touched the Sea of Dreams, the vision erupted across its surface.

A deep darkness engulfed the land. Oracle felt the fear and death looming over him and drew inward, crouching protectively. Sparks appeared around him, dancing in the thick inky blackness. They coalesced into red-hot embers and the darkness pulled back to show a banked fire surrounded by bones. Guttural goblin filled his ears, although Oracle couldn't see the speaker. "His fire burns eternal," *the voice said,* "but the bones will save him." *Oracle stood and looked around. The voices remained incorporeal. He studied the ground he stood upon. There was darkness everywhere. The rocks beneath his paws were black obsidian and basalt. A light flashed across the stones and rainbows glinted off their surface. Like the beacon of a lighthouse, the light drew Oracle's attention to the center. Oracle looked up toward the light and there she sat, D'Mique, hunted, crouched low in the darkness as the shadows covered the light's source and plunged her again into the inky nothingness. Oracle turned his head back toward the bones and the fire, the only thing to see. Three figures stood there, silent. Marco, Temeres, and Almira.*

Marco felt a numbness bloom across him as he looked down into the Sea of Dreams at his own face, flat in the darkness next to Temeres and Almira.

"D'Mique?" Myrth asked. When no one answered him, he muttered, "She was with Tekalo."

"That bone altar," Temeres breathed. "I know it, it's in the Vale."

"What did the goblins say?" Marco asked.

"'His fire burns eternal but the bones will save him,'" Almira translated.

"Who?" Marco asked. He looked to Oracle but the wolf was still in his trance, sharing the vision across the Sea of Dreams. It began again, the inky complete darkness filling with dancing embers that coalesced into the flame and the bone altar. "That looks like Shadow Magic," Marco said. "How it looks in the Mage Realm." The goblin voices echoed around the room once more, drawing a shiver from Marco. As the vision finished again, Oracle awoke and withdrew from the schorl. The vision slowly faded, Temeres' face the last thing to disappear into the unlit surface of the giant gemstone.

"I do not know this place," Oracle said. "But you three must go there. You will find D'Mique there."

"D'Mique was with Tekalo," Myrth repeated. He studied Marco, the world around them swaying slightly. Myrth started pacing in the small space he had, walking back and forth between the antechamber and the Sea of Dreams' edge. Rumbling grew around them but not so great that Marco felt the urge to start building a shield above them. Instead, he reached out to the forcelines and started smoothing them. Marco frowned as Myrth called out to Sylus, "*Sylus, send a soldier to find Jay. Tell her I need her to turn her bubble Eyes to the Black Vale.*"

"*Yes, Master,*" Sylus acknowledged. The swaying and rumbling subsided and Myrth stopped. He closed his eyes and stepped into the Mage Realm. Marco felt the forcelines smooth and the Earth Cloud settle around them.

Myrth returned and sighed, "Thank you, Marco," he started. Marco ducked his head in reply. "You need to go," the hawk-man said, looking at the three of them. "To the Black Vale."

"We were recalled here," Almira said. "I'd be leaving my people." She shook her head no, "I cannot."

"D'Mique was last with Tekalo, who is missing," Myrth said. "If she is in the Black Vale, she is in the daemon's path. She knows where Tekalo is. We have to find her."

"Almira," Marco said, taking her hand. "D'Mique is my friend, Tekalo my best friend. Please, for me."

"You cannot ask me to choose between you and my people, Marco," she whispered. "You will lose." He frowned and pulled her close. She hesitated before returning the hug.

"We will not ask you to leave your home and your people," Oracle said. "Time is fickle, and so are visions. You should go but you are free to take your own path and Time will flow, inevitable."

"My Princess," Temeres whispered. "I ask leave to go." All eyes fell on him. "I know where the bone altar is. Marco will not find it. If D'Mique is there and the daemon army is going there, I need to return...for *my* people."

"I will keep your princess safe," Myrth said with a slow nod. "You and Marco need to go." Temeres studied the Earth Master, blue eyes hard. "She is my princess too, Temeres. When Herdan passes away, who will take the Valley but Almira? She's Limina's line." Eyes softening, Temeres nodded at the Master's words before turning to face Almira.

"I release you, Temeres," Almira said, frowning, her voice hitching slightly. "Stay safe, keep my love safe, and return to me, both of you."

"Myrth?" Jay called from the doorway. "The mirrors have moved."

They waited for Oracle to stand and join them before meeting Jay at the door into the Sea of Dreams. Beyond the dome, she'd lined up all the bubbles and their mirrors so that they could be viewed from the path. The goblin soldiers were still patrolling them, looking at each one. Sylus had joined the effort, along with the other members of Myrth's Honor Guard.

"This one," Sylus called from near the entrance. The diminutive elf waved them over. They hurried past bubbles that showed various images of a deep round valley made of black, volcanic rocks. Some views lay closer than others and each mirror was at a slightly different angle and magnitude. The one Sylus had called them to looked away from the Black Vale toward the Great Southern Wilds. In the far distance, a river gleamed. Between the river and the dark forest that formed the northern border of the Great Southern Peninsula, darkness covered the land. "I thought it was rock when I first looked," Sylus said.

"It's moving," Almira whispered. "Are those...?"

"Black daemons," Myrth said. The horde covered the distant shore. "Jay—"

"Give me a moment, they don't move as quickly as the Eyes," she said, anticipating the Earth Master's request. She closed her eyes and stepped into the Mage Realm. All around them, mirrors spun lazily in their bubbles and as they did so, the images inside them changed. They focused on the river instead of the Vale.

"Oh," Sylus breathed. The mirror near his elbow focused on the port of T'Mok. Pyres had been built and the dead were being burned. For a moment, they watched the Mortaks work, rebuilding and clearing the area. In the first mirror Sylus had noticed, the angle and magnification had changed and they could now see the black daemons clearly. The creatures had piled up against the large river, uninterested in crossing the deep channel of water. Yet, as they milled about along the shore, they were slowly moving downriver. "There must be thousands," Sylus whispered.

"The darkness is coming," Oracle said behind him. "When they reach the coast, they'll be able to cross the river at Freeport."

"We need to go, Marco," Temeres said. "If D'Mique is at the bone altar, we need to get there before the horde does."

He nodded and turned to Almira, hesitant.

"Just go and be safe," she said into the silence he left. "Return to me." He pulled her close and threw up her veil, kissing her. Holding her close, he breathed in her scent. Then, setting his jaw, he took a step back and nodded.

"I will see you soon, my love." He turned and left. Temeres bowed and followed him out. Almira turned away from them, her eyes falling on another vision of the horde. From above, she could see that it covered the land.

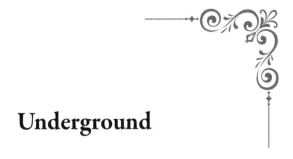

Underground

Marco walked slowly until Temeres pulled even with him. "Let's hurry," the Vale Warrior said. "Get your stuff, pack light. How's your horse?"

"He's been good so far, sturdy, strong, unafraid."

Temeres nodded at the words. "Good, we'll take him."

"How is yours?" Marco asked with a smile. Temeres stopped long enough to study Marco, meeting his brown eyes. Temeres' cold ice eyes didn't blink and Marco looked away. "I'll be ready in three," he said as Temeres pushed past him and broke into a lope up the trail to the castle. Inside, Marco stopped Tasco and asked him to help ready the bay horse he'd come on. He and Temeres were leaving. Tasco agreed and Marco hurried to the tower room to pack. He threw his uniform into the pack along with his Potentate cap. He grabbed a small dagger from the table. It was little more than a hunting knife but it might prove useful. Checking his pack, he noted that he still had a few days' worth of rations and a small bag of grain for his horse as well.

Myrth's thoughts interrupted his packing, *"Be careful, Marco,"* the hawk-man began, *"Temeres is expendable and he will give his life to save you. He will guard you while you work."* Buried in that reminder was the veiled threat to keep his secret safe, to not work outside of the Mage Realm.

"Yes, Myrth," Marco replied.

"*I'll contact Marladon and let him know that you and Temeres are on your way. Take the underground tunnels to Gemma then out to the Black Hills and on to Nightmare before turning north to the Vale.*" The path traced through his mind, as if Myrth was looking at a map, drawing the route with a pen.

"Yes, Myrth," Marco said aloud, thinking it too. He grabbed his packs and hurried down the stairs. "We are leaving now," he added. Temeres was standing with Tasco and Morn. "Ready?" he asked.

With a single nod, Temeres led the way. Their horses stood ready, just outside the castle door. Temeres' Palace Black had been replaced by a dapple-gray that stood next to Marco's bay. They grabbed the reins and Temeres led them back down toward the pool. "Myrth says to go underground to Gemma, then to Nightmare," Marco said. "He's going to let Marladon know we are on our way."

Temeres glanced back at him in acknowledgment and led the way to the tunnel opening. Myrth's goblins were camped here. When they noticed Marco, they came to attention or bowed. Some called out, "Chosen One," and waved as he passed. The camp seemed upbeat. Being goblins, none of them seemed to mind being underground, away from the sun. The air inside the cave was close but not stifling, the light provided by oil lamps that created overlapping golden pools.

Temeres hurried them along the path to a large stone door that was closed and barred, guarded by two large humans and an eagle-woman Semian. The three stood unmoving as they approached, and when they'd closed the distance, the dark-haired man greeted them. "Temeres, I heard that you'd arrived with the Princess. Leaving?" Blue eyes fell on Marco, weighing his presence.

"The Princess is safe, the Earth Master guards her now. The Chosen One and I are heading to the Vale."

"War rises," the eagle Semian said. Temeres nodded agreement.

"Travel quickly," the first man said, "and then return." The three of them lifted the bar and swung the stone away revealing a dim trail through the mountain. Near the door, several torches waited in racks along the wall. Temeres grabbed a string of them, pulling four away that were all tied together with a leather thong. He held one out to Marco, the rest dangling between them.

When Marco went to take it, Temeres pulled it away, "No, light it," he explained.

Sheepishly, Marco did as he was told. Stepping into the Mage Realm, he pulled Fire from his hands and fed it into the pitch coating the end of the torch. It burned a cheery red-orange, almost the natural color of flame. With the torch lit, Temeres handed it to Marco, untied it from the leather thong and stowed the other three on his horse's saddle. "Four is enough?" Marco asked.

"No," Temeres said, "it's just a convenient amount to carry. We can pick up more in a few hours." Temeres paused. "You've never been down here?" he asked. Marco shook his head no. "It can be disconcerting for Earth Mages, I hear." Temeres studied him for a moment. "Tell me if you need to rest," he said. "We..." Temeres stopped, pursing his lips. "I've stood against you in the past but I know you are a good man. I would not allow you to be with my Princess otherwise." Marco studied the Vale Warrior a moment, wondering what to say until Temeres continued. "I remember you saving me."

"I was happy to," Marco said. "I couldn't leave you there."

Temeres smiled at the obviousness of the statement. "We don't know what we are going to find. That horde was close to the Vale. We need to go there. I don't want our safety to be compromised because you're trying to prove yourself to me or impress me for some reason. I don't want you to be afraid of asking me for help. It's not weakness, it is strength to rely on a comrade."

Marco started to deny that he'd ever do such a thing but stopped and nodded. "I will let you know if I need a break." With a nod, Temeres turned around and started down the tunnel, leading his horse. Marco followed him with the torch, pulling his own horse behind.

Within, the world narrowed to the light that the torch threw across well-worn cavern walls. The darkness above them felt heavy, the layers of granite and quartz dozens of feet thick weighing on them. For Temeres, the path before them lay dim, obscured by his horse's shadow as they walked. He knew this path well, had taken it in both directions on several occasions. It was the most convenient route in and out of Hawkethorne Valley, if not the quickest. Almira did enjoy taking her time to return to Herdan's side when he called. The path quickly sloped downward, winding its way through Imperial.

For Marco, the world did not dim. As the stone door closed behind them, the Earth Cloud engulfed him. He hesitated, but Temeres did not. The Vale Warrior started down through the tunnel and Marco had his light source. Marco followed him, trying to focus on the dappled-gray horse in front of him. *"Any tips?"* Marco thought toward Myrth. It took a moment for Myrth to answer.

"Take breaks and close your eyes; meditate to remain focused and centered," Myrth answered.

The golden Earth Cloud was everywhere, above him, below him, in front and behind. There were no walls and no path, only the golden cloud. Marco could only see where he was going by watching the horse. Even the torch's light bled into the Earth Cloud. Then, only a few yards from the door, the forcelines appeared. "Wait," Marco said, stopping Temeres. The Vale Warrior was suddenly in front of him, studying him. Marco looked through him at the giant, slow-moving currents that eddied and swirled in front of them. Marco closed his eyes and started slow, deep breaths. He felt the forcelines pulling his soul toward them. Up and down and around in sluggish whirlpools, he went. Marco opened his eyes again and focused on Temeres' blue eyes. Flame lit his face, golden like the Earth Cloud all around them and the forcelines that surged through everything. Vertigo set in and Marco closed his eyes again, taking deep, slow breaths to stop himself from vomiting.

Temeres nodded. "Take a moment, Marco," he said. "The stronger the mage, the worse it is."

Marco felt Myrth then, steadying the forcelines around him. Marco focused on his breathing, trying to stay centered in his body instead of carried away with the strong Quartz Mountain currents that welled up from the bedrock. When he opened his eyes again, Temeres was still there. "I'm ready," Marco said. "I can't see the path, but I can see you and your horse."

"Follow us, then, Chosen One," Temeres said. He turned and started down the path again, moving slow enough that Marco could easily focus on him and the horse.

One by one, they burned through the torches until the last one grew low. Temeres stopped and waited for Marco to come close. "We're here, at the Chasm." He handed his horse to Marco and opened a wooden door before them. Beyond, they stepped into a narrow rock crevasse. Hundreds of feet above them, blue sky could be seen. Where they were, at the bottom of the crevasse, there was no sunshine. Water, ice and snow filled the area although there were several feet of dry ground near the door. Marco took a deep breath as he left the encasing earth behind. He studied the snow and water around him, enjoying seeing anything other than the golden Earth Cloud.

"This is the Chasm?" Marco asked a moment later. Temeres nodded. "The same as the Chasm Bridge?" Marco pointed up to the jagged slice of sky they could see. Temeres nodded again.

"We wound our way down to ground level inside Imperial," the Vale Warrior explained. "From here, the path is basically flat. We are going to follow a river through Majesty's base to the Cut and then join the Root Elf tunnels and make our way to Gemma." He paused for a moment. "It is my understanding that the rest of the way is not as difficult. There's something about Imperial." Marco closed his eyes and studied the Earth Cloud and forcelines from the Mage Realm. It was true. Imperial, all around them, was a wellspring of Earth. Marco pulled back, away from his body and the Chasm. He could see that Majesty, although still coated in the Earth Cloud, did not have the same overwhelming forcelines that Imperial did. Nor did any of the surrounding lands. He returned to the Physical Realm and nodded. "We'll rest a while, have some food." Temeres instructed. "There are camps along the route from here on, in the caverns, of course."

Temeres released his horse and Marco followed suit. The beasts drank and then pondered munching on a few scraggly bushes that were attempting to bud here at the bottom of the dark crevasse. Unable to eat, Marco closed his eyes and dozed until he heard Temeres stir beside him. "Come, Chosen One," Temeres said. "We can rest in camp at the Cut." With a nod, Marco stood. Temeres grabbed his horse by the reins and moved down the crevasse, following the snowmelt downhill to another door like the one they had used to enter the crevasse. He opened it and pulled another four torches from a rack that looked well-supplied. Pausing, he waited for Marco to light one. This time, Marco took the time to change the flame's color to a bright white. Temeres nodded his approval and led the way.

Underground, the Earth Cloud engulfed Marco again. Temeres waited for him to center himself before starting down the path. They were still within Imperial, although the forcelines were not as overwhelming here and did not leave his head and stomach spinning. He followed the dappled horse for a few miles. As they walked, the runoff from the Chasm joined with other rivulets and ran along the edge of the path. A dull roar started encroaching on Marco's senses. Then, they came to a juncture. The slate-gray Imperial spliced with a gray-white rock wall. Here, the tunnel had been gouged by water and chisels, allowing both the small river and their current path to meld with a large underground river that tunneled through the white-quartz underbelly of Majesty.

"Is this the Cut?" Marco asked, raising his voice over the echoing river that burbled beside the path.

Temeres frowned and shook his head, "We are moving to Majesty. There is a large mine ahead, that's the Cut. It's abandoned now," he added.

They kept to the river, working through their torches once again. As they left Imperial, the Forceline eddies calmed and soon grew tame enough that Marco felt more at ease. As the third torch burned the last of its pitch coating, the tunnel opened out into a wide, underground thoroughfare. Both Marco and Temeres paused as they entered, surprised to see a large company of elves. They were camped in the center, round leather tents set close together. The river that Marco and Temeres had been following continued across the thoroughfare, the tents giving way to it, and dove back into the white quartz on the other side. Temeres stepped away from the wall and stopped a passing elf. "Who commands here?" he asked.

"Vale Warrior?" The elf hesitated, caught off-guard by being stopped. "Lendra commands," he pointed toward a white tent with a red banner atop its peaked roof before hurrying on. He, like the other visible elves, wore gray on gray uniforms. Marco had seen the livery before—these elves were from Gemma. Temeres led them to the central tent where a handful of elves stood in conference around a table. Scattered papers decorated the otherwise empty tabletop. The elves looked up as Temeres stopped at the open wall of the tent.

"Vale Warrior, welcome," a thick-boned female elf greeted. Like the other four, her hair was cut short and out of her way. Her black orb eyes reflected the torchlight that lit the room.

"Captain Lendra?" Temeres asked. The elf nodded in acknowledgment. "We are on our way to the Vale. How go the roads?"

"Take the Cut to the surface and the mining route to Nightmare. That is a safe route and you will avoid the gatherings in Gemma."

"Arlan is staging his armies?" Lendra did not answer his question, simply weighed him with her eyes. "Thank you for your advice. I am inclined to follow it."

"Are you outfitted for the road?" she asked.

"Yes, enough to get to Nightmare and join the Fire Master. We would ask for a bed this evening."

Lendra nodded. "There is space at the outskirts of the camp." Temeres and Marco bowed and hurried in the direction she had pointed.

"Has our plan changed?" Marco asked as they wound their way through the encampment. Temeres nodded. As they reached the last tent, Temeres waved a silent greeting to a pair of elves that sat drinking near their tent on the edge of the encampment. He stopped, and settled his horse near a rivulet of water and a large boulder. With a bit of work, he was able to secure his horse to the rock. Marco sighed.

"Our plan is the same. It takes the same amount of time to reach Nightmare along the mining route as going through Gemma and across the foothills," he answered at last. "The road is less hospitable, but if Arlan is staging his armies in Gemma, it will be easier to avoid the area." Marco nodded in understanding.

———— ⟋⟍⟍ ————

The next day they started north along the wide thoroughfare. The way had been lit by the elfin army and soldiers with horses and on foot kept them company as they traveled. No one stopped them or questioned their passage and near dark, they reached the mine's entrance. A large portcullis had been closed over the opening, finally barring their progress. Temeres stopped and sighed. "We'll stay here tonight, take advantage of the soldiers' presence. Tomorrow, at dawn, we'll leave." They found an alcove near the door but far enough away from the soldiers that they wouldn't disturb them, then bedded down, tying their horses once again to nearby boulders.

"Vale Warriors?" an elf said, approaching.

"Aye," Temeres said. "I am of the Vale. Do you have news, friend Elf?"

"We were on patrol out into the Blasted Lands and heard rumors of a great force." The soldier sat down near Temeres. He was lithe, armed with a crossbow at his hip. His white hair had been braided into a series of cornrows and then pulled into a topknot. His round face had once been jovial but was now careworn, dusty from the road. "Seer N'Ktoa brought word to us that the rumors we were hearing were true. A monstrous horde of black daemons would be attacking the Black Lands. She bid us flee to the Quartz Mountains and Gemma, or to Nightmare."

"N'Ktoa is not known for her strength of vision, but she is a doomseer," Temeres acknowledged. The elf smiled, hinting at his penchant for laughter in better times.

"The Vale is in their path, we hear," he said.

"We go now to defend it," Temeres lied, indicating himself and Marco.

For the first time, the elf took notice of Marco and his black orb-eyes widened. "You are the Chosen of Earth," he whispered, ducking his head quickly. "Arlan and all his lands honor you."

"Thank you," Marco whispered. "We are hoping to pass quickly from here and so would prefer no ceremony on my part."

"As you wish, Chosen One." The elf studied them, thinking. "Do you go then, to Nightmare? Master Marladon is riding north with his dragon army before Mid Summer begins."

"By my calculations, we will be in the Vale on the last day of High Spring," Temeres admitted. "We intend to pass through Nightmare but will not be waiting for the Fire Master."

"You know your will and your strength, Vale Warrior and, with the Chosen of Earth, you will succeed, no doubt."

"And if you were us?" Marco asked after letting the elf's words sink in.

"I would join the dragon army, if I were the one marching north into the waiting horde," the elf whispered. He ducked his head, embarrassed by his honesty and the temerity of speaking so to the Chosen of Earth.

The dawn brought sights unseen before. From their vantage point on the highest crag, three pairs of glowing fiery eyes surveyed the land below. Far to the north, along the coast, lay the Mortak city of Freeport. Refugees had been streaming south all night, most of them fleeing with no personal possessions or supplies. Some had been bloody, many crying for lost loved ones. When the first Mortaks had reached the Misty Lands, their tales had seemed unbelievable. "Black daemons attacking *en masse,* in daylight, their daemon-spawn eyes a misty gold." It had reminded many of the year before when a Greater Daemon had breached the world and holed up in the Fire Master's domain to the south, controlling daemon-spawn and others across the land. Now, looking down at the Blasted Lands between the Misty Mountains and Freeport, the three satyr-like creatures—Goraths—could just make out the front line of the horde. The black daemons advanced slowly over the broken desert, traveling faster along the coast where the road offered better passage. Somewhere along that route, refugees were falling to the daemons, almost escaping, dying as their hope for rescue died.

The largest Gorath scratched his ram chin in thought, sharp nails brushing through short red fur. His ram horns curled down close to his eyes, invading his peripheral vision enough that he had to turn his head slightly to catch the eye of his mentor, Savli, the elder Gorath.

"Do we defend?" Savli asked in a gruff whisper. He looked at his red-gold-furred charge. His own chin boasted a long scraggly goatee and his horns had grown so long with age they'd had to be filed to allow him sufficient range of vision for hunting. He banded them in iron now. Savli's own fur had grown more mottled and peppered as he'd aged, where once he'd been a bright gold, the color of burnt cream rather than the fire of Harvest leaves that his charge Puko sported. The red-furred Puko looked again at the daemon horde. Seer N'Ktoa had called to their own seer, warning them to flee to Nightmare and the Fire Master, to fall back before the darkness that was coming. Savli had convinced Puko to send the tribe south, but Puko could not go to the Fire Master, so he bid his mother to take the tribe to the Vale.

The third Gorath turned away from the morning scene and studied the Misty Lands behind them. "If we defend, we die with honor," Rayn said. "I would die for this home." Puko rolled his eyes at his squire's poetic declaration. He turned as well, his cloven hooves clicking on the craggy rocks of their look-out point.

"What is there to defend?" Puko asked. "We have sent the tribe south. Mother will carry them onward. If the Vale is in danger, she will seek the Fire Master. He will be happy to have them." Puko studied the land around them. The Misty Mountains held forests and swamps full of life, a bastion in the wastelands of Mount Myrs' lava plain. The Gorath tribes called this land home, along with the

Sun Goblins and Bog Elves. "From what the seer said, there is no saving this place for now. But we can return to it." He pinned Rayn with a hard glare, his daemon-fire flaring. "Would you die for empty swamps and ruined trees?"

"No master," Rayn admitted, ducking his head low. His own spiraling ram horns had barely begun to turn toward the ground. He had a lot to learn and decades to go before he would wear iron bands. When Puko said no more, Rayn stood, wrapping his light, linen cloak around his shoulders, covering the pinto fur of his upper body, leaving his black-furred goat-legs bare. "Do we follow the tribes, then, Master?"

Puko nodded. "Yes, we will fall back to the Vale."

"And is *it* worth defending?" Savli asked, picking up his stave from near his hooves. Its bones and feathers rattled as he moved, starting down the craggy rocks. "A Man Child home?"

"A defensible basin will offer us more protection than the swamps will," Puko admitted as he followed his mentor and Rayn took up the rear. "The Black Vale's cliffs will slow the horde that N'Ktoa warned us about and that our Little Brothers flee." The three Goraths made their way down the mountain, disappearing into the mists. Behind them, the black daemon horde pressed forward, ever-seeking their prey.

Worth Defending

For three days, Marco and Temeres followed the mining route from Majesty's base along Perrin's foothills. The eastern peaks of the Quartz Mountains were less barren than those to the west of Imperial. Here, green finery clung to the cliffs, shoulders, and flanks of Perrin and Majesty. From the south, approaching the mountains meant skirting the Forest of Fear. However, on the north side, the Blasted Plains ran right up to the Quartz Mountains. There were no forests, only scraggly brush stands and low scrub tree copses. The mining route lay still-visible, following a rill that ran parallel to Perrin's base. Where mining carts and metal merchants had once taken this road toward the Black Lands, today, they went through Gemma. Arlan found the wealth that trade generated more important than keeping outsiders away from his underground elfin city.

Along the way, a variety of soldiers joined Marco and Temeres. Goblins and humans in mix-and-match sets of found and hastily made armor comprised the majority of those traveling toward the Fire Master's fortress. These soldiers were on their way to join Marladon, answering his call for volunteers to join his dragon army. As Marco and Temeres drew closer to the Black Lands, Mortak farmers started to appear on the road. Some pulled carts of possessions, while others carried what they could on their backs. They'd been warned of the coming horde and were hurrying to the safest places they knew. Marco stopped the occasional group of farmers and asked where they were going. As one, they'd answer, "The Gemm Hills," seeking safety by moving beyond the Quartz Mountains to the Fire Masters' domain.

The mining route soon took the pair of travelers away from the Quartz Mountains and into the Black Hills. Climbing through the hills, Marco and Temeres reached the bowl that held the Fire Master's Fortress as the Fiery Sisters set on the third day. Marladon had been busy since leaving Olimidia. The farmland surrounding his Fortress had turned into a massive army camp. His dragon army milled about in the dying light, large black beasts patrolling between the tan tents and yurts that covered the land.

Temeres sighed as Marco pulled up next to him. "Let's press on before the light fades," Marco said. "We can eat and sleep at the Fortress." Nodding, Temeres motioned for Marco to lead the way. The road dropped into the valley and fell straight across the plain, creating a direct route to Fortress Nightmare.

Near the tents, a pair of Mortak soldiers stopped them. They wore Marladon's red and black livery. Their swords looked new and unused. Their dark hair had been cut short enough not to be visible under their helmets. "Friends," the first greeted.

"I am Marco, Chosen of Earth," Marco announced. "I've come to speak to the Fire Master." Visibly shaken by Marco's introduction, they stepped aside quickly and motioned for him to continue onward. When they'd left the guards behind, Temeres chuckled. It was the first time Marco remembered hearing anything close to mirth from the Vale Warrior.

They weren't stopped again until they reached the drawbridge that led into the Fortress. Marco stopped at the lip of the fog-filled moat. He'd been here before, about a year ago. Then, he'd sneaked into the kitchen through the midden, led by Marladon, on a bid to regain the Fire Master's throne by killing the Greater Daemon. In his mind's eye, Marco remembered the giant stone snake that had proven more than capable of taking down a Greater Daemon, Marco's

strength in Earth ripping the forcelines from Myrth, breaking him, body and soul, and nearly killing the Earth Master.

Two Mortak guards approached them. Unlike the ones guarding the camp, they were seasoned, their weapons worn with use. Marco and Temeres dismounted and waited for the guards to draw close enough for a conversation. "I am here to speak to Marladon," Marco said. "Or Kryoso, if the Master is busy."

They studied him and Temeres. "I know this one, Temeres. Where is your Princess?" the second guard asked.

"She remains with her people in Hawkethrone. She has released me to return to my home in this time of war. We wish warmth and safety for the night before starting to the Vale," Temeres answered.

"And you?" the first guard asked.

"I am Chosen of Earth, Marco of Trinik." His reply brought only a studious, cautious raising of the eyebrows.

"Master Marladon did not mention your arrival, Chosen One, I will summon his steward. Wait here," the first one said. He disappeared through the postern, leaving Marco and Temeres with the second seasoned soldier for several minutes. They passed the time staring at one another, the jangling of the horses' tack the only sound.

Then the Portcullis opened and Kryoso appeared. The Mortak steward hadn't changed much since Marco had last seen him. His physique was enough to make some jealous, sculpted muscular perfection and bronze skin, where most Mortaks were pale. Despite this strength, Marco had never seen Kryoso wield a weapon and he had none now. The Fire Master's steward was a Shadow Mage—a secret only known by a handful of people. "Marco," Kryoso greeted in a high tenor voice. "We weren't expecting you."

"Myrth didn't tell you we were coming?" Marco asked. Kryoso stopped mid-step, thinking.

"Marladon didn't say. I suppose it's possible that Myrth did contact him and Marladon let it slip." Kryoso shrugged. "Come, I will find you food and a bed." He waved to the guard who had fetched him, "T'Lon said you were merely passing, not joining our force."

"We need to hurry on to the Vale," Temeres supplied, falling in line with Marco as Kryoso led them into the fortress.

"We are for the Vale as well," Kryoso said. "They leave in four days' time."

Temeres shook his head. "All the same, we will be in the Vale in five days. I cannot wait for your force to be ready for travel."

"Can we sit with Marladon?" Marco asked.

Kryoso hesitated, pursing his lips. "I will show you to a dining hall and have food brought. I will ask Marladon if he wants to join you."

"And you?" Marco asked.

Kryoso smiled. "I will join you, Man Child," he said with a chuckle. "It has been many seasons since we sat and talked. I hear stories of your growth from Marladon."

They followed the steward into the Fortress. Up the front steps, they entered a large great hall. Roughly half the passages of the obsidian fortress were large enough for the great dragons that made up Marladon's army. There were other, human-sized corridors secreted away in the walls, for servants and soldiers to use. It had been these secret corridors that Myrth's Honor Guard had used to breach the throne room when the Greater Daemon had taken control of the area a year ago. Walking into the throne room now, Marco had to catch his breath as the daemon interrupted his thoughts. There were six large black dragons in the room, holding court with the Fire Master. Marladon sat slumped in his throne at the center of the room.

He smiled when he saw Marco. "Oh! You're here already," he said.

Kryoso rolled his eyes and scoffed, catching Marco's eye. "You didn't mention them, Marladon," he accused.

"Didn't I?" Marladon sat up straight. He reached for the nearest dragon. "You remember Marco, Gideon King?" he asked the dragon. The dragon's narrow jaws parted and it hissed in greeting, its forked tongue tasting the air. The other dragons moved closer, black scales hissing across the stone as their tails moved, their claws clicking and clacking on the stone. A sudden disquiet crept over Marco and his smile faded as he came to a stop nearly five yards from the throne. The space between him and the Fire Master had filled with the menace of the large black dragons. The last time Marco had met these dragons, their eyes had been milky white, their actions and thoughts controlled by the Greater Daemon. Now, their black eyes reflected the light from a dozen lamps that lit the room.

Nonplussed, Kryoso continued past the dragons and sank to a knee at Marladon's feet. "As good hosts, I was going to feed them and have rooms made up. Marco asked if you would be joining us, my Master."

"Gideon remembers you, Marco," Marladon said, seemingly oblivious to the question Kryoso had relayed. He scratched the dragon king's chin before looking back down at Kryoso, finally addressing the question. "Yes, I will join you." He looked up at Marco and Temeres and weighed them. "You'll want to freshen up from the journey. Did you come by Gemma? Arlan has been keeping me updated as to his progress."

"We took the mining route," Temeres informed him. "We'll see our rooms first and then return for dinner. It is my plan to leave early tomorrow. We cannot wait to press on to the Vale."

Marladon nodded once. "As you wish, Temeres. We will follow you, so know that if the forces are too great, fall back and wait for us."

Marco returned the nod. "We will," he promised. Temeres reluctantly agreed.

"Good. Kryoso, show them to their rooms and have supper brought for the four of us," he ordered. Kryoso ducked his head and hurried out. He wasn't gone long, leaving Marco and Temeres to shuffle their feet surrounded by five curious dragons, each roughly the size of a small whale, with a neck and tail the same length as their body. Marladon steepled his fingers and watched the two humans at the foot of the steps that led to his throne. He seemed unaware of the discomfort his dragons were causing. "I must apologize. I lost track of the days and didn't realize how quickly you would travel. I should have at least had the rooms prepared."

"Your army is significant, Master," Temeres said, trying his best to ignore a dragon's tongue as it flicked in and out a handbreadth from his face. The dragon's head was, Marco realized, as big as their own, the jaws full of fangs.

"Yes," Marladon agreed. "But they're all farmers, green. I don't know how many will turn and flee when they see the horde." With a chuckle, Marladon seemed to realize how close his dragons had crowded to the two visitors. "Enough, back off, all of you," he barked. "I am sorry, I wasn't paying attention to them. They are mirroring my curiosity. I have been wondering how the two of you are here. I know you are going to the Vale. Myrth asked me if I thought I could press north to aid you, and I will. But how is it you two? Myrth, as usual, didn't explain."

"He is often thinking of two or three things at once and communicates in the moments between his thoughts," Marco said, defending his Master.

"Annoying," Marladon added. The dragons had backed away, returning to the sides of the room, fanning around the central throne once again. "Over dinner, then," Marladon said as Kryoso reappeared and beckoned to the two of them. Grateful to be away from the dragon coterie, Marco and Temeres hurried after him.

They left through a side door, opposite the one they'd entered the year before to kill the Greater Daemon. The hall beyond was human-sized. The walls and floor, formed from gleaming obsidian like the rest of the fortress, were relieved from black monotony by portraits and the occasional weapon rack. Being internal walls, there were no tapestries to keep the cold at bay.

"Here we are," Kryoso directed, pointing to two iron-bound doors. "We will take supper in the library down the hall," pointing away from the throne room. "We are trying to conserve, so it isn't a sumptuous feast, but warm food and good wine is more than many can hope for." He smiled and bid them enter.

Inside, the room was functional, undecorated, but the bed looked warm and inviting after the evenings of sleeping on cavern floors and rough trails. Not for the first time, Marco was grateful for his village upbringing, where he had always had a warm bed to sleep in and food to eat. There was warm water in a basin near the bed and Marco undressed and washed the dirt from his arms, neck, and face. There was a small wardrobe with a handful of robes and tunics that would fit him. He dressed in his spare Potent uniform instead, leaving his cap behind. He heard Temeres leave before he was done dressing and knew he'd be last to dinner.

When Marco joined the others, they were just settling into their meal. They all stood to welcome him and Kryoso poured out some wine from a jug as they all sat again. "Thank you, Master," Marco said.

Marladon shook his head and waved Marco away. "Call me Marladon, please," he said. "I'm away from my charges and it's just us." He smiled, thin-lipped. Marco nodded and raised his glass in salute. Temeres started on his roasted vegetables as Marladon asked, "So, how is it you two?"

Marco was left to answer, chewing between sentences and eating slowly. "Oracle saw us in the Vale. It was a dream of fire and darkness. We are looking for D'Mique."

"Oracle," Marladon rolled his eyes. "Myrth gives him too much credit, if you want my advice."

"Myrth has known him for ages. They are bound together," Marco said.

"Do not misunderstand me, Marco, I do not intend to attack your master. I would never want to put you in a position of needing to defend him. That wouldn't be fair of me. I will fight my own battles with the Earth Master." He smiled. "It is simply my opinion that Oracle's visions should be taken with a grain of salt and scrutinized, not leapt upon."

"Where the Vale is concerned," Temeres said, giving Marco a chance to eat, "I choose to leap. The vision showed the Vale engulfed." He paused. "My family is there," he added, his blue eyes turning to hardened steel.

Marladon held his hands up in surrender. "The great Temeres," was all he said. He said it without emotion making it impossible to tell if there was any sarcasm or deference carried by the phrase.

Marco jumped into the sudden silence, "What are your plans, Marladon? You are leaving soon?"

"Yes," Marladon said. "When we sent out a call, we said to be here before the end of High Spring but we can't wait that long. Scouts returning from the north say the horde is coming, moving quickly. Jay has been in touch and can see them with her makeshift Eyes. The horde is moving south and there hasn't been any significant resistance. The Misty Lands, the Vale, they are the most likely to stand against the daemons but the forces there, despite their skill, are not big enough. My dragons can help even those odds. I can help."

"*Marladon could help*," Marco thought. He remembered Marladon's fireballs flaring through the darkened throne room, harrying the Greater Daemon as the goblins and Land-Nymphs attacked its armored lower body. He nodded to himself.

Early the next morning, Kryoso met the two men at the front gate with their horses. He'd had their packs filled with grain, rations and first aid items. Kryoso stopped Marco before he could mount, and let Temeres start through the gate before he spoke. "Be careful, Marco," he said. "Temeres is a great warrior but he isn't going to choose you over his family. You'll need to look after yourself, even while working with the forcelines." Marco frowned at him a moment before nodding. He and Kryoso each held the other's secret; Marco knew Kryoso's affinity and Kryoso knew enough to suspect Marco's true strength. "Safe travels, Marco," the steward added.

Marco replied, mounting, "We will see you again in a few days."

"No, I am to remain here. Marladon will be behind you shortly. May you be successful." Marco frowned at the news but nudged his horse into a trot without another word and hurried after Temeres.

Marco drew even with Temeres as they followed the road northeast away from the fortress. The neat tents of Marladon's army continued to line the road, slowly giving way to farmlands, some bereft of life while others were full of greenery and chickens. "The steward is a good friend," Temeres said. Marco nodded noncommittally. "He warned you about me?"

Taken aback, Marco frowned without answering.

"That's fair. I can be single-minded. But you are the love of my Princess. Losing you would devastate her, so..." he trailed off, leaving unsaid the conclusion. Marco would be protected, even when others would not because Almira loved him and Temeres lived for Almira.

The road they followed was lonely and they saw no fellow travelers all that day or the next. Midday of their third day on the road, the refugees appeared. The first few groups had the same look: staring eyes, tear-stained faces, and vacant minds. Many were wounded and in various states of undress. Some wounds were ghastly, inflamed and infected. Some people Marco and Temeres passed had broken bones, a few, missing limbs. They had traveled as best they could, their families and friends bearing their burden. There were more than Mortaks in the groups. Humans, Semians, and elves were intermingled with the Mortaks. They were city-dwellers, merchants and shopkeepers, as well as farmers from the volcanic valleys of the Blasted Lands.

They did not look up at Marco and Temeres as they passed. Fear and desperation pushed out every other emotion. They were going to Fortress Nightmare and that was the only thought they could hold on to. As the Fiery Sisters set, Temeres pulled to the side of the road and Marco followed him. "I want to see if we can find a camping group of refugees so we can get some information," the Vale Warrior explained. "Are you able to press on?" Marco contemplated the sky. Rysk would not rise until the early morning hours, perhaps three hours before the Fiery Sisters returned. That meant they'd be traveling in the dark for an unknown amount of time. Perhaps another five hours, he estimated, before they'd have to sleep, whether they found a group of refugees to question or not. With a reluctant sigh, he nodded.

They met no refugees well enough to stop and set up camp that first night, and eventually Temeres called a halt. They bedded down quickly beside the road, far enough afield that their horses and supplies would not tempt would-be thieves. The last thing either of them wanted to do was fight a desperate refugee over food. Marco retreated to the Mage Realm to check the forcelines before drifting off to sleep. Pulling up, away from the Earth Cloud and lazy currents around him, he climbed higher until he could see the rising Shadow to the north. There, along the coast, the Shadow magic that marked the daemon horde dripped down along the shoreline. Marco opened his eyes and stared up at the stars above. He sighed, trying to remain calm, looking at the forcelines that attached to his chest. With deep breathing, he was able to smooth them. The calmness pressed out with them and spread from him to the eddies and whorls around him, soothing the agitated Earth Cloud.

The crowds of refugees grew as they pressed on the next day. Some, Marco noted in the afternoon, whispered about the Vale Warriors. At last, when the suns were near setting, Temeres bade a young father stop. The man had three children and a wife in tow, all of them piled on a pony cart that he was pulling as best he could. "Do you know of the Vale?" Temeres asked, dismounting.

"We've heard tales from those coming fast behind us, Warrior. The Vale stands and vows to fight. but not alone. The Misty Realm was overrun and some took shelter in the Vale: Bog Elves, Sun Goblins and even the Gorath tribes. Some men, without families," he hastily added, "have joined the stand. The seer warned all not to stay, but it was Doomseer N'Ktoa, who brought word." He paused, his eyes hardening, "I chose to save my family. When they are safe at Nightmare, I will return."

"Do not," Marco said. "Your son needs his father, not stories of bravado." The father glared up at him.

"Chosen of Earth speaks true, if rudely," Temeres said, stepping into the tension that suddenly boiled from the man. "You are a farmer, not a warrior. Stay safe in the fortress and take choice land for your children and grandchildren when the war is over."

The father hadn't quite recovered from the realization that Marco was Chosen of Earth—and that he'd been moments away from yelling at one of the most powerful mages in the land—when Temeres remounted. The pair of riders nodded their appreciation and moved on.

Marco stepped into the Mage Realm as they rode, trusting his horse to keep to the track. Rising above them, he could see the progress of the daemon horde. Frowning, he realized he wasn't knowledgeable regarding the cities beyond the Nesting, Dragon

Ridge, and Olimidia. He knew roughly where other cities of the southern half of the peninsula could be found...roughly. Yet, he had not even the faintest glimmer of understanding about ports and trade routes or centers of power at the north end of the peninsula, so far from his home. The Shadow along the coast was growing closer to them. There was a horseshoe shaped basin in the distance that remained Shadow free while all around it, the inky dark puddle of daemonic magic rippled. "Is the Black Vale a horseshoe shaped valley?" he asked.

"Why do you ask?" Temeres returned.

"It stands alone, untouched by the Shadow along the coast."

"And the mountains to its north?" Temeres asked.

"They are covered in Shadow," Marco said, opening his eyes and returning to the Physical Realm to look at Temeres. The Vale Warrior turned away, eyes ahead of him on the trail. "I estimate we'll meet the black daemons tomorrow," Marco whispered.

Temeres pulled his horse to a stop. "Are you prepared?" he whispered, eyes as unbending as the steel blade that rode his hip. Marco looked away, back north to where he imagined the Shadow magic lay in wait. This moment had never occurred to Marco.

"Do we have a plan?" Marco asked.

"Fight our way to the Vale, join the forces that are keeping it free." He watched Marco for a moment, then added, "There are families there, women and children, farmers, elderly, refugees who could not make the journey to Nightmare. They need us. Focus on that, Marco, not on the fear."

"I am Chosen of Earth," he whispered. "I am Chosen of Earth."

"A stronger Earth Mage, I have not seen," Temeres added. "Master Myrth has a deadlier affinity, summoning quakes, but your subtle skill requires a greater strength." Temeres beckoned Marco to lean in close. "Do you know how long until we reach the Shadow? Without interruption, we would reach the Vale tomorrow midday."

With that information, Marco closed his eyes and flew upward again, surveying the land before them. "If we stop here, about four hours."

"Then we stop here. They will move at night. We can meet them well-rested and ready tomorrow morning. We will ride quickly through their ranks, fighting only when we have to." He turned off the road, motioning for Marco to follow. "When we meet them, drive onward to the Vale. If we are separated, we will meet there, not before."

Marco nodded, throat suddenly dry. They bedded down for the night, once again several feet from the road, hoping that no one would notice them. Their sleep was fitful at best and early the next morning they were awakened by a herd of deer stampeding down the road. Temeres dressed quickly and mounted, drawing his sword. "Stay close, Marco," he breathed. "They're about." They rode quickly, quietly, north, avoiding the road but following it. As the Fiery Sisters rose, voices rose ahead of them.

An unease filled the air, creeping along Marco's skin as they pressed forward. Then they broke through a line of trees and found a campsite overrun with black daemons. The refugees had tried to hold them off and paid the price. The daemons were killing the men, striving for the women who had cowered or run off into the woods and down the road. Marco pulled the Earth Cloud to heel, forming balls the size of apples and endowing them with Fire. Temeres charged forward, his silent attack bringing him within striking distance of a large black daemon before it realized he was there. A sweep of his blade and the black daemon toppled heavily to the ground. Marco's explosive rocks plowed into the other daemons, scattering them as Fire burst around them, eating at their Life force. Daemon screams mingled with those of the women and men.

A hurried examination proved that the camp was suddenly clear of daemons. Men and women cried, huddled together on the edges of the encampment. "Hush," Temeres ordered. "Run, silent and fast, run south until you can't run anymore," he ordered. His words hurried them out of the camp, three women and a handful of children, followed by two wounded men, bleeding heavily. Temeres turned his horse north and motioned for Marco to follow quickly and they returned to the trees, hurrying through the growing sense of unease.

Marco stepped into the Mage Realm as they rode, ducking over his horse's neck, closing his eyes and forcing himself to be calm and centered. In the Mage Realm, he could see the approaching black pools of Shadow. "There's a wall of them to the northwest," he shouted, returning to the physical world. Temeres veered eastward. "Closer to the coast," Marco returned, checking their heading again. The Vale Warrior turned further east. Marco checked a third time. Soon it would be impossible to avoid the black daemons, but for now, if they kept this heading, they would skirt between two large groups. "Steady on, Temeres," Marco said, opening his eyes again.

Looking to the left and right, Marco could see the black daemons as they scuttled through the pine forest that had grown up along the road, covering the harsh, rocky land in greenery. None of the daemon-spawn creatures veered toward them as they infiltrated the front. Then the creatures were before them. Temeres drew his sword again, readying himself for the crash as his horse met the daemons.

Marco reached for the Earth Cloud and pulled together a dozen orbs, endowing them with Fire and flinging them into the waiting monsters. Where the flames found Life, they exploded. Crashing and exploding into the line, black daemons screamed, veering away from the heat and flames, ignoring colleagues as they fell beside them. With a scream, three of the creatures turned and fell on Temeres. Marco pulled the Earth Cloud into a snake and sent it dancing through the daemons. It bowled them over, knocking blade-like legs out from under the bristle-haired human torsos and thick round bodies that reminded Marco of a spider's thorax.

Iron blades fell from the sky around him as the daemons attacked. His horse veered away screaming. Marco threw the Earth Cloud into a shield above him, a disk of stone that deflected the blades. His snake had disappeared, the earth that made it melting away when his will was gone. He threw his shield at a large armored black daemon that was closing on Temeres. The rock disc bashed into the back of its head, knocking it over just shy of Temeres' horse. Temeres pressed through the other daemons' defenses and then streaked onward, not bothering to stay and fight. Marco followed his lead, throwing the Earth Cloud up in a wall behind him to stop any black-daemons from following them. He grabbed another snake of sand and brought it alongside the horse. It undulated next to him, flowing over the ground and around the trees as if sentient, a hound on a lead racing after the prey.

The next attack felled Temeres' horse as a black daemon armed with a poleaxe swept the horse's legs, toppling it. Temeres flew from the dappled horse's back, rolling and landing on his feet, sword up to defend himself from another daemon with a mace. Marco threw his snake toward the mace-wielder, diverting its blow, knocking it off guard. Temeres sliced for its throat, moving forward the moment the blood spurt from the goat-like face. His horse had regained its feet and was running south, away from the battle.

"Go Marco!" the Warrior shouted. Marco pulled the horse to a stop and helped Temeres aboard. "Fool!" the other man hissed.

"Then I'm a fool," Marco retorted. He flung the Earth Cloud up around them, encasing them in stone as he'd seen Myrth do before. There was a hole at the top for air. Otherwise, they were entombed. The daemon's wasted no time on the rock and quickly moved past it, bleating and calling to each other.

"Did you notice their eyes?" Marco asked, breathing heavily, forcing part of his mind to remain focused on the rock wall around them.

"No," Temeres said after shaking his head in disbelief at the question. "I was busy killing them."

"They're not flames. They're golden, but not on fire."

Temeres took a steadying breath. "We can't stay here. Your horse can't carry both of us." Marco closed his eyes and stepped into the Mage Realm. Beyond his tomb, the daemon horde surrounded them. Black Shadow magic flowed in all directions. He opened his eyes and slid from the bay's back.

"Take the horse, Temeres." As the Warrior protested, Marco pulled his snake from the Earth Cloud once again. He touched it and it felt solid beneath his hand, even though it was made of sand. Marco closed his eyes, studying the Shadow as it flowed around them. "Get ready, there's a break in the horde coming that we can use to leave."

"How are you leaving? Afoot?" Temeres asked.

"Just go, Temeres," Marco said. His Earth snake undulated and slithered around Marco's feet, lengthening and widening, growing more substantive. "It's nearly here." Marco's snake rose between his legs and he sat back into the sand. It held him.

Temeres gaped at him for just a moment. "Oh, this isn't good," he whispered. "I'll stay beside you and protect you, Chosen." Marco hesitated, wanting to tell him there was no need, but he nodded instead.

"Now," Marco said and the encasing stone fell away to the north. There was about twenty yards between them and the oncoming daemons when they ran from the tomb. Temeres raised his sword and charged forward, the Earth snake and Marco slithering behind.

Rayn stood, sucking air through his teeth. "End of the line," he said. Savli stood as well, glancing to where Rayn indicated. He could hear the black daemons bleating in battle and see how the forces had slowed. There, in the trees, someone was putting up a fight instead of simply fleeing or dying. The three Goraths had stepped away from the Vale's mouth for a break, letting a cadre of Vale Warriors take their place. Puko remained seated, meditating, trying to gather strength for their next turn defending the Vale from the seemingly endless stream of black daemons. Savli looked down onto the forest below. The cliff they stood upon dropped away before them, tumbling straight down for nearly fifty feet before ending in glass-like shards of rock. It mirrored the cliffs behind them, making climbing to where the Goraths rested nearly impossible from any direction. Behind them, jagged obsidian cliffs formed a near-complete circle, protecting the Black Vale. The entrance to the Vale was a mere twenty feet across, a split in the cliffs that had been smoothed over time to allow easy passage in and out of the area. Now, the Vale Warriors, a company of Elves, a handful of Sun Goblins and the Gorath tribes took turns defending it from the black daemons that decided to try their luck at entering. No daemon left the defensive choke point alive and none of the guards of the Vale would venture out across the Blasted Plains. When the occasional refugee party appeared, they needed to make it all the way to the entrance before anyone would pull them in and save them.

At first, there had been time for refugees to make it into the Vale. Now, more often than not, they died shy of the walls and the Goraths had taken to watching them from the clifftops. "Aren't they coming from the wrong direction?" Savli asked. Below them, the streaming horde of black daemons had formed a frothing eddy where the battle raged, south of the Vale.

His comment pulled Puko from meditation and the red Gorath stood, joining them at the edge of the cliff. He squinted at the eddy in the horde. "Looks like two humans," he muttered. "One on a horse, the other on a...," he paused a moment before ending, "dragon."

"Vale Warriors to be certain," Savli said with a nod, "Otherwise, there'd be no reason for any battle that lasted long enough for an eddy to form in this stream of daemon-spawn."

Rayn chuckled, "What will you give, Puko, if they last five minutes?" he asked.

Puko smiled, rubbing his red-furred chin thoughtfully. After a moment he nodded, "You can loot the bodies, Rayn. Take what you will." Rayn beamed at the generous offer.

"And if they last longer?" Savli asked. Rayn scoffed at the idea and spat cud at the elder's feet. Savli glared but turned to Puko instead. "Puko?" he asked.

Puko watched the Warriors fighting through the daemons for a handful of seconds before replying. "If they last ten minutes, we'll go help them," he said. Rayn chuckled and Savli nodded.

"A bet then, from the mark. If they last five minutes, Rayn loots the bodies when the horde passes. If they last ten minutes, we join them against the horde," Savli summarized. The others nodded their understanding and Savli continued, "And...mark!" They started counting.

As the two Warriors pressed forward, the eddy in the ranks of the black daemons morphed. Some daemons, realizing there was a battle to be had, joined the others swarming through the trees, while others fell before the Valian blades. Rayn began to cheer quietly when the eddy pushed in smaller as the two humans appeared on the brink of being overwhelmed. Savli continued counting, purposely paying no heed to the battle so that his count would be as true as possible. Puko crouched, watching and waiting, observing the humans through the trees as they ducked and dodged and reappeared in the midst of the spindle-legged black daemons. Rayn's cheers grew more fervent as Savli ticked off the seconds and minutes. When he reached five minutes, Puko shrugged. "Better luck next time, squire. It was a good bet, but they are Vale Warriors, the finest humans on the peninsula, I hear tell." The red Gorath's joking tone wasn't lost on his fellows and they all chuckled.

Savli continued the count and Rayn squatted near Puko, enamored of his master's intensity. He'd lost interest in the battle itself and focused completely on Puko, Savli's count a cadence in the background, a rhythm echoing a heartbeat. "Nine and twenty-four. Nine and twenty-five. Nine and twenty-six." Puko frowned and stood. He eyed Savli, trying to judge how serious his mentor was and if he would hold them to the bet. "Nine and forty. Nine and forty-one." Savli continued. He returned the glare and nodded. Puko looked back toward the warriors and their eddy of daemons. He crouched and, as Savli neared the end of the ten minute count, he started playing with the bone charm around his neck, its beads and bones tinkling softly. "Ten," Savli finished. He smiled and bowed low, horns nearly touching his furry haunches. "By your leave, my Prince," he said reverently. Puko removed the bone charm and held it out for Rayn who took it wordlessly then retreated a few steps, although there was no such thing as a "safe distance."

Puko stood, eyes closed. The Fire sparks within him began to grow and consume his Life energy. What the Flame took, it returned, and soon a closed system of energy exchange churned through him. Puko opened his eyes. The daemon-fire there blended with the Fire that was spreading across his skin. In less than a minute, Flames engulfed the Gorath. Clothed in fire, Puko started down the cliffside toward the eddy, his cloven hooves finding purchase on the slick glass-like rock. Savli and Rayn followed him.

At the bottom, Rayn drew his swords, spinning them expertly, and Savli called Air to his will. Black daemons streamed past them, intently marching southward. Puko charged into them, barreling several of them over. Where his skin touched them, the flames leapt to the daemon-spawn, gobbling up the new Life force it found. Daemons began screaming, running from the burning effigy in their midst. Rayn and Savli joined the prince, catching the daemons that tried to flank him.

Nearing where he judged the eddy to begin, Puko called the Fire from his body and flung his arms outward, spinning the Fire into a ball. Savli's Air joined it, stretching the ball into a tornado. Given life, the fire tornado danced away from the pair, out of control, sweeping up daemons and trees alike in its maw.

Marco flagged and the Earth snake crumbled beneath him. They'd cut a line through the horde together and could see the obsidian cliffs of the Black Vale rising above the trees to their northeast. *"No,"* he thought. *"We're so close!"* Beside him, Temeres had fallen back to defend him, the bay offering the Earth Mage as much shelter and defense as possible. But the daemons were closing on all sides. Most had continued to stream past, unperturbed by their fellows. Yet enough stayed to join and battle that the fight had been nearly unending since leaving the first tomb. Twice before, Marco had resorted to encasing them in the Earth snake and calling up a new one after catching his breath. But not this time. His concentration had shattered and he could no longer hold the Earth together.

Through the fight, Temeres had said little. Now, he screamed in defiance, a rage-filled shriek that crescendoed into an ululation. His sword flashed around them, driving the black daemons back, deflecting their iron blades. Marco saw no other escape, he clambered up onto the back of the bay, trying to cling to the saddle instead of Temeres. The Vale Warrior stood in the stirrups to reach the daemons before their blades could land, leaving the bay to decide which direction to face. Marco felt the horse kick out behind and the buck nearly knocked him from his precarious perch.

Then, with a roar of heat and light, the world exploded. Flame engulfed them, hellfire raining down around them, the daemons bursting into flame. Instinctively, Marco reached for the Earth again and everything went black.

Following in the tornado's path, the flames pushing the black daemons away from their intended path, the Goraths crossed to the sight of the battle. Burnt earth and burnt flesh had been churned together by the fire tornado and the hellfire rain that had followed it. Puko, still aflame, left fiery hoof prints in his wake. Then, they reached the horse. It looked none the worse for wear, all considered. Puko frowned. It had no riders. He held out a hand and Rayn returned his bone-charm. Puko draped it over his head, clasping it in the front before slinging the tiny hook to the back. As he worked, the charm suppressed the flames that had engulfed him. When they were gone, his red fur returned, seemingly untouched by the Fire.

"There," Savli said, pointing with his staff. In a rend of earth, a black-clothed figure moved.

With a nod, Puko hurried to the figure and helped him to stand. Startled, he dropped the man roughly to the ground. "Ho! Temeres," Puko said. He noticed the second figure and pulled it from the rend as well. "But, surely this isn't your princess." Puko held Marco up by the arm so that he could look into the man's bleary face for a moment before dropping him the two feet to the ground as well. Marco landed heavy, with a groan, and slumped forward, head down to the earth.

Temeres pulled his senses together and regained his feet. He took note of the horse, the fires, the dead daemons and the three Goraths in turn. "Puko," he breathed.

Savli closed in on Temeres, his daemon-fire eyes burning in a mask of grizzled fur. "Well, no wonder you lasted so long," he said in the cultured drawl of the Goraths. His ram features broke into a smile that showed large white teeth. The satyr daemon-kin sat back on his haunches, his bone staff tinkling as he moved.

"I am grateful for your assistance," Temeres added with a nod.

"Savli won the bet," Puko said with a noncommittal shrug.

Rayn reached down and pulled Marco to his feet, studying him. "This isn't a Vale Warrior, is it?" he asked. "He looks nothing like your fellows, Temeres."

"That's Marco, Chosen of Earth. He's from the southern farming villages."

"A Mage of Man?" Savli said as Rayn dropped him and Marco fell heavy again.

"Chosen of Earth?" Puko mused. He picked Marco up again and this time waited for the man to find his footing before releasing him.

Wide-eyed, Marco glanced from one Gorath to the next. He'd heard tales of the daemons but thought they only lived in myths and stories. At eight feet tall, they towered over him and would have loomed over even Nepo. Their spiraling horns made their bodies top-heavy and even more intimidating. The brown furred one had shorter horns and seemed younger, while the one with the staff was obviously elderly. The red-furred one, who'd picked him up and steadied him, continued studying him, sitting back on his haunches, his furry satyr legs wide-spread to balance the weight of his large ram horns. Covered in fur, he was unclothed save for a bone charm...the same Molbdyn bone charm that Palo and DJar had worn cycles before.

"I am Marco of Trinik, Chosen of Earth," he started, addressing the red Gorath before him.

The Gorath bowed his head, "I am Prince Puko of the Kairra. My mentor and uncle, Savli, my squire, Rayn."

"That was you? You're a Fire Mage," Marco asked and answered. He indicated the bone-charm. Puko nodded once.

"You are aiding the Vale?" Temeres asked.

"We are, as are others. Most of the refugees continued south to Nightmare but...," he trailed off. Leaving his sentence unfinished, he moved on. "There are a number of infirm there and the Kairra and other tribes. We hold the Vale at the Gate."

"Come," Savli said. "The flames will only hold the horde back for so long." He stood and started along the burn trail back toward the black cliffs of the Vale. Temeres followed him. Marco hurriedly grabbed the bay's reins and pulled the reluctant horse after them.

Puko walked beside Marco, scratching his chin. "Wasn't there a dragon?" he asked.

Marco studied the daemon-kin, trying unsuccessfully to read the Gorath's emotions around his fiery eyes. Giving up, he smiled. "No, no dragon. Chosen of Earth," he said with a sly wink. "I'll show you once I'm rested."

Puko smiled, his wide flat teeth barely visible between his furry lips. "Then let's hurry." He picked up the pace, walking normally, his long legs carrying him quickly back toward the Vale.

The Waiting Horde

D'Mique sipped the tea Kryoso had placed before her. Once she'd entered the Fortress, he'd insisted she stay a moment, eat, drink, and rest while a horse and supplies were prepared. The story he'd woven hardly seemed believable.

"Second-hand knowledge relayed to him by Marladon, susceptible to exaggeration and misunderstanding," she reminded herself. Yet, there were facts she could focus on. Oracle had sent Marco and Temeres to the Vale. She'd missed them by mere days. Marladon marched north to save them, to head off the black daemons and save as many people as he could. She'd missed him by even fewer days. The fastest way to get her message to Myrth was to ride back into the horde. It was tempting to travel to Hawkethorne instead. Five days by horse, running away from the daemons, would bring her to Myrth. While she didn't know the way, she was fairly certain the roads leading west out of the black lands would take her where she wanted to go. *"Or, ride north for two days back toward the advancing horde, press hard, and catch up to Marladon."*

Kryoso sat across from her, watching her and sipping his tea. He set the cup down and waited for her to stir. "I shouldn't tarry," she said after digesting his story. "The sooner I report to Myrth, the better." She hadn't offered her own tale to the steward apart from saying she had been separated from the others, left for dead, and made her way back as best she could. Kryoso nodded slowly.

"Your horse is ready, I'm sure, packed for a week's travel." He stood and she followed him. He'd provided a reasonable set of armor, padded breastplate and tassets along with leather greaves and vambraces. It was mismatched but functional, and, more importantly, her size. She'd taken longer to find a sword that felt balanced in her hand and it now ro0de her hip, a long-lost weight that she now realized she relished. The sword had been joined on her belt by a small leather pouch with some coin, just in case, and a hunting knife.

At the fortress' door, an elderly guard greeted her and handed her the reins of a Palace Black. She patted its nose. The horse would be war-trained, she realized, perfect for running headlong into an army. She mounted as Kryoso wished her a safe journey. Outside the Fortress, she followed the road north. She could see the army that she followed, their passing written in the dirt and mud along the road and the trampled grass to either side of the track. Mixed in with the horses and wagons, the boots and paws, she saw large draglines and clawed feet, like a large bird's, marking the passing of dragons. She nudged the black horse to a canter, eating up the ground.

For the rest of the day, she hurried north, meeting no one on the road. As the suns set, she came across a group of refugees huddled around a small fire. They studied her furtively, noting the Palace Black and her sword and armor, and said nothing as she passed. The night would be dark, she realized, the Ghost Moon rising a few hours before dawn. She stopped to look around and considered returning to the refugee's fire. With a grimace, she turned around and found the refugees once more. "Apologies," she started. A large man rose to greet her. "The night is dark, I have a long ride tomorrow."

"You are joining the Fire Master?" he asked. She nodded. "He isn't far ahead, maybe a day or two since we met them and they gave us supplies."

"You are nearly to Fortress Nightmare. I was there this morning. Another day or two with little legs," she added, noting the young children hiding near their mother. She smiled.

"Join us, Lady," the man offered. "Stay here through the dark night." He held the horse while she dismounted.

"I am with the Earth Master," D'Mique offered. "Not a mage," she added when the man's eyes grew wide. "Simply a retainer from the Academy."

"We are originally from Freeport. I worked as a barber for the sailors and merchants that docked there." D'Mique had foggy memories of the port city. She nodded in understanding. "This is my wife and her sister, our children." Heads nodded in greeting. One of the women made to offer D'Mique some of their food but she waved it away.

"I have stores, thank you. Save yours for the children and yourselves." The woman gratefully returned the food to the pot near the fire with a nod. D'Mique pulled rations from her saddlebag before returning to sit with the refugees. "I am grateful for the company and the fire," she said as she sat. She ate quietly as the women made beds for the children and helped them to fall asleep. "If you trust me to, I will take the first watch, good barber," she offered. The refugees tossed a glance back and forth then agreed that they would let her stand over them. "I'll wake you in a few hours," she said as she finished her food and stood.

Through her watch, she saw no cause for alarm. She could hear animals passing in the darkness, but none of them veered toward the fire. When she tired, she shook the barber awake and lay down near the fire and the Palace Black, dozing until the Ghost Moon rode high in the sky. The barber was collecting his family and gathering their supplies into bags and packs. "We are breaking early, Lady," he said.

She nodded in reply, stood and cleaned her stuff quickly. "Thank you again," she said as they prepared to leave the site, "for the fire

and the company." The barber waved her on and then hurried south
with the rest of the family in tow. D'Mique turned north, continuing
along the road. With a frown, she realized there would be other
refugees ahead, not all of them as well-off as the family she'd spent
the night with. She wondered how many had been swept up with the
advancing dragon army, becoming camp followers in hope of safety,
food, and rest.

She hurried, urging the horse onward by the blue light of Rysk.
Near dawn, she passed a few more camps that were gathered close.
Together, all of them would be too formidable for typical black
daemons to attack. Humans, Semians, and Mortaks formed the
refugee groups and most were women and children. D'Mique
realized that the men likely joined Marladon in his march north,
leaving their families to flee for Nightmare. Two days passed this way,
D'Mique joining groups of refugees near sunset and leaving as Rysk
rose. The second day of Mid Summer saw her on the road again.
From the refugees she'd spent the night with, she knew she'd catch
Marladon this morning.

Only a few hours passed and the Fiery Sisters rode the
mid-morning sky when D'Mique reached the outriders and camp
followers. A pine forest had grown up along the road, spreading
outward toward the blasted lands of Mount Myrs' volcanic plain as
she rode. Now, older men, wagons full of supplies, and a number of
women and children kept to the road and the barren patches beneath
the pines. D'Mique hurried past them and no one stopped her. A
human warrior on a Palace Black was certainly on their side.

Then she could see the dragons. They formed a phalanx in the
center of the army. Horses and foot soldiers accompanied the great
black beasts. She rushed to them and shouted for Marladon as she
reached the rear line. Dragon tails whipped and snake-like heads
swiveled to follow her progress. "Marladon!" she shouted again,

starting to push past them, hoping Marladon was at the head of the phalanx.

"To the front, Lady, with the king," another soldier called from where he walked next to a dragon. She waved at him in acknowledgment and kicked the horse to a gallop. Word of her approach flew forward and soon the army had halted. Marladon appeared, his silver-orb eyes wide at her appearance.

"D'Mique?" he said. "What are you doing here?" He'd been riding on one of the black dragons and slid to the ground as word of her reached him. She pulled the horse to a halt and leapt from the saddle, breaking into a run across the last few yards between them. Seeing him, even more so than seeing Kryoso, flooded her system with relief.

"Do you have your jars? I need to talk to Myrth," she called. He caught her as she ran toward him and practically fell into his arms, her legs collapsing beneath her. He helped her kneel so she'd be safe, and knelt down beside her.

"Yes, I have my jars," he said, pushing his own questions aside with a mental shove. He signaled for a nearby horse and rummaged through the packs. D'Mique shivered, cold despite the clothes she was wearing and the warmth of the sunshine. Tremors ran through her arms. He pulled out a silk-wrapped jar full of pebbles and held it out to her, steadying it as she reached for it. "Myrth," he called.

"Myrth!" D'Mique shouted into the jar.

A long minute passed and then Myrth replied, "D'Mique?"

"She's here with me, Myrth," Marladon interrupted.

"At the Vale?"

Marladon rolled his eyes, "No we're on our way. She's come from Nightmare, given she's riding my Black."

"Myrth!" D'Mique interrupted. "There's no time. The daemon army...the tree daemons..." she started hyperventilating.

"Calm, Lady," Marladon commanded. "Breathe first." She closed her eyes and started taking slow, deep breaths.

"D'Mique?" Myrth asked, voice calm. "You've come from Nightmare. Alone?"

"Yes," she answered, trying to continue breathing slowly, swallowing around the waves of emotion that were overwhelming her. *I've made it, I've found them,* she repeated to herself.

"You left Olimidia with others," Myrth continued, feeding her facts to help her focus. "Some took the Nura prisoner back to Sea Spray. You continued with Tekalo and Trillip, and Burl. You went to rescue a baby."

"We followed the tree daemons into the Vast Southern Wilds. They turned on us, made a deal. Trillip and Tekalo exchanged themselves for T'Pani," she started. Tears welled in her eyes. "Then," she caught a sob in her throat, "the tree daemon double-crossed us and sent the black daemons after me, trying to get the baby. I lost her!"

"You lost T'Pani? The baby?" Marladon asked for clarification. D'Mique nodded, trying to focus on her breathing. "How are you here?" he asked.

"They left me for dead. When I woke, the baby was gone, the daemons had attacked the town and were moving downriver. A goblin merchant took me aboard and dropped me off at Ebony Bay. I've been trying to catch up to you to report in," she told the Fire Master.

"Does that make sense?" Marladon asked the jar. "She's in a state," he added, resting a hand on D'Mique's shoulder. Not too long ago, she would have flinched away from the Master, fearing his power. Now, she found strength in a familiar face. He smiled tight-lipped and waited for Myrth's response.

"Tekalo and Trillip are with the Nura," Myrth restated. "And they have the baby as well?"

"I think so," D"Mique said. "But I don't know."

"Don't wait for my reply," Myrth said from the jar and then he was gone.

Marladon grimaced. He stood, rewrapped the jar and returned it to the horse's pack. The Palace Black D'Mique had brought nuzzled his shoulder before he helped D'Mique stand. She continued shivering. "Are you well?" he asked, noticing her reaction.

"I..." she started. Then it hit her. "Daemons," she said. Marladon took a split-second to realize what she meant. He stepped into the Mage Realm and returned a moment later.

"They're close, some are nearing our front lines, but the main body is still a day ahead, near the Vale."

"Master Marladon!" a soldier called from before them. "Daemons!"

"Can you ride?" Marladon asked D'Mique. She nodded and he helped her up onto his Palace Black. "Keep her safe," he whispered to the horse before turning and disappearing into the rank of dragons.

Myrth stared at the Fire jar then closed his eyes for a long moment. He'd spent several hours through the last days tending the forcelines as Marco's power distorted them. For the last two days, he'd been able to rest, watching as Marco worked to keep his lines smooth and those around him calm as well. He reached out along their bond, "*Marco,*" he called. "*D'Mique is with Marladon, they will be there soon.*"

"*There will be a lot of fire here when they arrive,*" Marco replied.

Myrth broke the connection and reached for Jay's jar. He stopped. "*What do you mean?*" he asked. Oracle's vision of darkness and fire played through his mind. The bone altar in the Vale, D'Mique at the Vale, and flames.

"*The Goraths are here. One of them's a Fire Master.*"

"*No,*" Myrth breathed. He reached for Marladon's jar again and called to him, "Marladon!" When there was no answer, he grabbed Jay's jar. "Palo!" he called.

Palo sat near the fire, watching the rising suns and the waking camp before him. The Potentate had set camp three days before. It hadn't taken them long to find Jay's jars floating in what appeared to be a shining glass box. Palo had easily dismantled the spell, saddened a bit by having to break one of the Wind Mistress' ingenious creations. Beside him, his Nura charges sat, seemingly in meditation. Having spent a cycle with them, he was convinced the *Aliith* didn't actually meditate. Instead, she used the time for spying on the others.

"Palo!" Myrth called from the jar full of rocks. Palo studied it a moment, trying to decide how agitated the Earth Master was by the tone of his voice. "Clippen!" Myrth shouted. Palo whistled, his sharp call pulling several eyes toward him. He signaled Clippen. DJar had opened his eyes at Myrth's shout for Palo and he and Shi'Shou stood, moving aside to make room for Clippen to sit beside Palo at the front of his camp tent.

"We're here," Palo said, touching the jar with Earth to complete the connection and answer Myrth.

"D'Mique is with Marladon," the Earth Master said. "Alone."

"Nepo!" Palo shouted. Myrth stopped and waited for the Water Master.

"Myrth," Nepo greeted as he joined the group near the communication jar. "What did you say?"

"I didn't realize you were there," Myrth started.

"Resting before starting back to Sea Spray," he explained. The lion-man picked up the jar. "What did you say?" he repeated, fear and anger edging the Water Master's voice.

"D'Mique has reported in. She's alone, with Marladon, just outside the Vale. She says the Nura have Tekalo and Trillip prisoner." Three sets of eyes swung in unison to glare at DJar. The daemon-fire in the Nura's eyes flared in response and he tensed, ready for anything. Shi'Shou hissed and stepped forward, spear ready. "She says they may have the baby. They'd made a bargain, Trillip and Tekalo for the infant, but then they reneged and sent this black daemon army after D'Mique."

"I am here, Little Brother," DJar added in Nura, addressing Myrth through the jar as the glares continued.

"DJar," Myrth paused for a moment then provided a quick translation of his previous comments ending with, "How much do you know about this?"

"None," DJar snapped. He frowned and closed his eyes gathering his thoughts and controlling his emotions. "My second has not followed my orders," he returned. Nepo translated quickly. "I would go to him and demand an explanation," DJar requested. Nepo shook his head even as he translated the request for Palo and Clippen.

"No," Palo said. "That sounds too convenient."

It was DJar's turn to glare, "Do you doubt my honor?" he hissed. No one answered him.

The tense silence grew and then Shi'Shou spoke, "I will go," she said. "I will find Ordvyn. I am not bound to the brethren nor the fae but only to you, my *Ti'er.*" Nepo translated for the others as Shi'Shou bent close to Palo, nose to nose and hissed in fae, "You will not abuse the *Shuwarr* in my absence."

"Go, my *Aliith*, deliver my message to Ordvyn and find out what he has done." Nepo translated for Palo and Clippen. In the blink of an eye, Shi'Shou was gone. Her disappearance took a second longer to register on those gathered around the Earth Master's jar.

Palo sat for a moment before asking, "How long will it take her to return?"

DJar thought a moment and shook his head. "She need not return. Give her a cycle to find my second. She will report back through our bond."

"Did you hear that, Myrth?" Palo asked.

"I did," the hawk-man said. "I will let Marladon know that he has to hold off the horde for a cycle. I will send my goblins to help, and Arlan's elves are ready as well."

Myrth's jar went silent. Palo scratched his forearm, studying DJar in the morning light.

Clippen hissed and stood. "Tell it," Clippen said to Nepo, "That all the Land-Nymphs better be unharmed." Nepo waited for Clippen to storm off before relaying the message. Nodding, DJar closed his eyes.

Myrth tried Marladon's jar again. "Marladon!" A minute later, without an answer, he turned his attention to Sylus. *"Sylus, ready our army."*

"Yes, Master," his elfin lieutenant said. Myrth sat staring at the jars.

While he sat there, Jay joined him in the tower room. "Do you have an update? I heard you shouting for Marladon," she said.

"I do, of sorts. D'Mique is with him."

"D'Mique? Oh good!"

"Some good, some not," he said with a sigh. "Puko is at the Vale," he added with a snap of his beak.

Jay giggled. "Well, that does explain why the horde hasn't overrun it."

"Marladon cannot go there."

"He should feel the pull on the forcelines before he gets too close to the Wildling Prince."

"He should feel the pull on the forcelines before he gets too close to the Wildling Prince."

"Yes, but not before endangering himself and his army needlessly."

Jay's smile faltered. "Maybe he's ignoring you," she offered, "Let me try." She pulled the jar to her and called Marladon's name. Several minutes passed without an answer. She frowned and sat quiet for a minute. "The horde is bearing down on Marladon's army. The Vale is his best chance and they need his reinforcements, even with Puko there." Myrth nodded.

"Masters," Sylus said, appearing at the staircase into the room. "Where are we going? Do we leave now or in the morning?"

"We are going to the Vale, to bolster the armies there. We'll leave a guard of twenty here." Myrth informed him. "We'll leave in the morning." Sylus nodded and retreated.

"Marco?" Jay asked. "He made it to the Vale and let you know about Puko."

"Yes," Myrth closed his eyes and reached out to Marco. "*Puko and Marladon cannot be near each other, Marco.*" he said. "*Puko has no control over his power, he's a Wildling. He will rip the Forcelines from Marladon and the element will become uncontrolled.*"

"*He's wearing a bone-charm, like the ones Palo and DJar wore when they were fighting,*" Marco replied.

Myrth thought about this new information. "*Admirable, but we can't chance the Forcelines jumping to the Gorath. Marladon needs to know that he can't go to the Vale.*" Myrth sent his thoughts to Marco along with his memories of Oracle's vision. "*You, Temeres, Almira, D'Mique, all at the Vale. 'His fire burns eternal but the bones will save him'...that has to be Puko.*"

"*I'll go,*" Marco replied. "*I'll find Marladon and warn him away, and then bring D'Mique here.*"

"*Give me the day to rest, Apprentice,*" Myrth said with a sigh. "*You're decimating the Forcelines.*" Aloud, he added, "We'll keep trying to reach Marladon and warn him as well."

Chagrined, Marco replied, "*Tomorrow then, Master.*"

Ensconced in the center of the dragon phalanx, D'Mique heard the outriders meet the daemon horde without seeing it. Shouting, bleating, screaming, all joined with cries of fear and rage and the clatter of weapons. D'Mique frowned and stayed beside Marladon, where he'd commanded her to ride. She'd started to join the soldiers up front when the fighting began, but Marladon's command had brought not only her but the horse to a halt. She'd tried to reason with him, that she wasn't his retainer but Myrth's, and that she would fight as long as she was able. "You're a soldier of the Academy," he had reminded her, "and I am a ranking officer. You're still a cadet, Daemon Slayer or not. Now sit there."

D'Mique seethed as the battle continued. Marladon had halted the advance of the army so that they could form defensive ranks as the main body of the daemon horde approached.

Commands passed through the lines, to hold and brace and stand. A lull in the sound of fighting covered the area in an eerie silence for a ten-count before the bleating and screaming began again. This time, the sound of fire could be heard as a group of dragons joined the battle. From what Marladon had said, D'Mique believed that ten of them had established a shield, protecting the heart of the army with claws, bites, and dragon flames. She could just see them from her position. Looking up at Marladon, where he sat just behind the head of the dragon king, she could tell the battle wasn't going as well as he liked. "*He needs better foot soldiers,*" she thought.

"Stay steady," Marladon shouted down to one of his runners. The young Mortak sprinted for the front lines with the message. The Fire Master's eyes fell on D'Mique and he grimaced. "The horde has been fought to a standstill," he said.

"They'll start flanking us!" she shouted in reply.

Marladon nodded and motioned for two more runners to carry word to the flanks. "Set wards and shields," he said to them. "We camp here." He turned to a fourth runner, "The outliers need to come in to the dragon phalanx," he said. "Hurry!" The boys took off running, shouting their orders as they went.

"Daemons are no match for dragons, even when there are thousands?" D'Mique asked.

"No match for *organized* dragons," Marladon corrected her with a smile. "We can't rest, but we'll be safe here for the night."

His dismissiveness worried her. "*Safe?*" she thought. "The daemons will gain strength at night," she said. Marladon frowned and sat up tall to survey the battlefield. She realized he had also stepped into the Mage Realm and was whispering to himself. The dragon king hissed and nodded. Marladon returned and looked at her, contemplative.

"We agree, they will gain strength, but we can hold the line, nonetheless."

"And tomorrow?" she asked.

"Tomorrow will come." He clicked his tongue in the dragon king's ear, and the dragon lowered his head to let Marladon down. He pulled his pack horse close and both of them heard Myrth call his name from the stored jars. Marladon grimaced. "He sounds agitated, doesn't he?" Marladon asked. He pulled the jar from his pack and unwrapped it. "Myrth," he replied. "You've caught me at a bad time. There are daemons swarming us."

"Marladon, you cannot go to the Vale," Myrth said. "Puko is there." D'Mique watched the Fire Master grow even paler.

"Noted," he breathed.

"Marco will help D'Mique get there," Myrth continued.

"Why?" Marladon asked, frowning up at her atop the Palace Black. "She's safe here with me."

"She needs to be with Puko, Marco, and Temeres."

"According to whom? Oracle?" Marladon scoffed.

"Yes!" Myrth shouted from the jar. "Have you ever known him to be wrong?"

D'Mique had the impression that Marladon rolled his eyes, which was impossible with silver orbs and no pupils.

"Send your apprentice then," he said after pressing his fingers to his temples for a moment. "I will let D'Mique decide where she goes."

They both waited for anything further from Myrth but the jar remained silent. Marladon sighed, shrugged, and rewrapped the jar, returning it to the horse's pack. He looked up at D'Mique, studying her.

"Who's Puko?" she asked.

"The mage who killed the last Fire Master," he said. He watched fear and incredulity stumble across her features. "He didn't mean to, he's a Wildling and...so very strong," he breathed, closing his eyes and stepping into the Mage Realm. He was gone for three very long minutes before he reopened his eyes. "His presence is there in the Forcelines but it's muffled, muted." He thought for a moment more, as if weighing options. "If I am too close to him, he will rip the Forcelines from me as he did Cinder." D'Mique dismounted to stand next to the Fire Master. "And this time, there wouldn't be another Fire Master to pass the Forcelines to. They would stay Puko's."

"I thought there couldn't be a Wildling Fire Mage. If they don't learn to control their power, they die," D'Mique said.

"Puko is tricky," Marladon said with a dry laugh. "He likes to burn." He pulled out some rations. "I'm going to eat and sleep now.

Keep watch and wake me if the lines don't hold. Do NOT leave the phalanx," he warned. "I'll relieve you before the Ghost Moon rises."

"I should hope so," she muttered as he crawled under the dragon king, disappearing into a tangle of dragon limbs and tails.

It made her nervous sitting beside the dragon king through the day. The black daemons had been brought to a standstill by the dragons and their fellow soldiers. Yet, they simply held their position and it seemed to D'Mique that they'd fallen into a stalemate. The sounds of battle grew sporadic as the afternoon wore on. With the setting suns, Marladon reappeared and bid D'Mique to rest through the night. He assured her that he would keep her safe and—after consulting Gideon—that they hadn't lost any ground to the daemons.

With nightfall, the daemons did grow in strength and they pressed inward from the east and west, causing several troops to rally to either side, making the frontline vulnerable. D'Mique slept fitfully, dozing and waking when the battle grew loud around her. In the morning, wounded soldiers began to appear near the Fire Master's central encampment. Most were not gravely wounded. However, a small pile of the dead also began to form. Marladon went to examine them, leaving D'Mique to eat some of her rations alone.

Mid-morning, Gideon's mewling hiss brought Marladon running and he quickly mounted the dragon, who lifted him high above the army. In the distance, between them and the black cliffs of the Vale, a commotion stirred the daemon horde, forcing them to turn away from the dragons and defend their rear and flank. "Vale Warriors," he muttered at first, then remembered, "No, Marco. Pack your bags, D'Mique. Marco will be here in just a moment. Take my Black," he added.

As the commotion closed on the dragon's frontline, Marladon passed word that the approaching fight was Vale Warriors making their way to the central encampment. Then, a burst of wind lashed across the plain, bending and cracking trees as it spread outward. A tornado formed, bouncing through daemons, sending black bodies spinning through the air to crash somewhere in the distance. Marladon's heart skipped a beat. He knew only one mage who birthed tornadoes and sent them barreling outward indiscriminately. "Not Vale Warriors," he hissed as he retreated to the Mage Realm.

There he fell deep into the Fire pinpricks that rode his and the dragon's skin. The only person he knew who made tornadoes as a weapon was Savli, the Kairra's co-leader. "*And where Savli roamed, Puko wasn't far behind.*" As he followed the Fire down, he found the Forcelines. Unlike those of Earth, Fire Forcelines dwelt in the depths of the body, connecting to others across the planet through a diffuse cloud of heat. Marladon was alone at the seat of his power. No one shared a bond with him, and few Fire mages had the strength to reach so far down into the Flames. Concentrating, he could feel the strong Earth Mages around him—Fire and Earth being intimately entwined. He could feel Marco closing the distance between them and the power that echoed through him to Myrth, Sylus, and the goblins scattered about in his army. He could feel the strange muted power of Puko, still far enough away that Marladon felt safe. "*Savli left him in the Vale, good,*" Marladon thought.

"Are you ready D'Mique?" he asked, returning to the Physical Realm. "Marco is riding with the Gorath Savli. They won't be able to stay long."

D'Mique paused in stowing her rations and looked up at Marladon, shielding her eyes from the Fiery Sisters so that she could see his face. "Did you say Gorath?" she asked, incredulity lacing her words. She caught herself wanting to protest that the great daemons were myths but she bit her tongue and frowned as he nodded down at her. "*Are there ANY real myths?*" she wondered as she mounted the Palace Black.

Marco followed the path of the tornado as it breached the no-man's land that had formed between the daemon horde and the dragon phalanx. Terrified soldiers turned and ran from the small, devastating storm just as it reached their line and suddenly dissipated, blowing through the phalanx as a strong gust of wind. Once clear of the daemons, Marco rode his Sand Snake past the nearest soldiers and dragons of Marladon's army. Behind him, the daemons were slow to close in on the Earth construct and the Gorath that followed it.

Marladon watched, wide-eyed as Marco's construct mount vanished in a hiss of sand, falling back to the earth and disappearing, leaving Marco to walk the last few feet to where he sat astride Gideon. The large golden-furred Gorath behind him slid to a halt, not at all winded, despite running from the Vale.

"Marladon!" the Gorath beamed, seeming genuinely pleased to see the Fire Master. His wide, outstretched arms invited the Fire Master down for an embrace. D'Mique blinked at the creature that had haunted more than one childhood nightmare. He was well over seven feet tall, a giant, grizzled, satyr just like in the stories. Where she'd expect curling ram horns, his had been filed down and capped in iron. Her gaze stopped at his long staff, where, true to her nightmares, bones—some human—clattered as he moved.

"Savli," Marladon greeted from where he remained astride Gideon. "That tornado was close to my own." With feigned surprise, the Gorath turned and studied the path he and Marco had made, now walled over by the army. "I offer greetings to you Savli, Prince of the Kairra," Marladon continued with a shake of his head, scowling at Marco while following the formalities Savli's presence demanded. Movement caught his eye and Marladon glanced up. As the daemons recovered from the Wind attack, they started forward, determined to cause pain, and the dragon phalanx soldiers were beginning an advance to try and gain ground. Marladon glared down at Marco. "And you! Marco! Does Myrth know you're doing that?!" Marladon made a swimming motion with one hand to indicate the Sand Snake.

Marco thought for a moment, frowning. "Well, yes," he said, not sounding very certain before changing the subject. "We've come for D'Mique."

"And I bring word from dear Prince Puko," Savli began. The Gorath had a long, drawn-out accent, as if the vowels of the words comprised their own syllables. "He apologizes for not being able to come in person. He wishes you well and bade me say, 'I was first,'" Savli shooed Marladon away; "Move along," he ended with a wide smile full of white, flat teeth.

Marladon snickered, cutting it off quickly. "We are able to fight the daemons to a standstill, Savli." I think if it's all the same to you and Puko, we will remain here." He waited for Savli to bow in acknowledgment. "How fares the Vale?" he asked.

"We hold the Vale. There are many infirm, but we have elfin healers. The daemons have not cut off the sea, so we have fresh fish and fresh water." He paused before adding, "But the horde is odd. They do not attack the Vale, merely stray toward it occasionally."

"This is the Lady Warrior," Marladon introduced. "You will escort her to the Vale?"

"I will," Savli crooned. He closed the distance to D'Mique and bowed low, making a flourish with his bone-rattle staff. His head, with its horns, was nearly twice as wide as her body.

She swallowed hard, and tried not to show the fear she felt coursing through her. There was definitely a human skull on Savli's staff. *"Just because it's there, doesn't mean he killed them,"* she tried to convince herself.

"D'Mique," Marco added, "We were worried about you."

"We?" she asked.

He nodded without elaborating. "Come. Savli will make us another path through the daemons and we'll be safe in the Vale soon. Temeres is waiting for you, too."

She held up a hand to stop him. "Why am I going to the Vale?"

"Myrth has ordered you there," Marco said. "Oracle had a vision of you, me, and Temeres in the Vale."

D'Mique gazed at Marladon steadily. *"Does Myrth take this too seriously?"* she wondered.

"You must go, you were ordered to go," Marladon said. "Myrth's retainer outweighs my command."

"I'm ready," she said with a sigh as her frown furrowed her forehead.

"Go quickly, Marco," Marladon cautioned. "Myrth may know what you are doing but you'll weigh heavy on him and sap his strength." Marco nodded and started away from the dragons.

With a bleat, Savli started back north toward the cliffs of the Vale, running easily, his shaggy furred legs eating the ground. Marco pulled a snake made of sand out of the ground around him and followed Savli. Reluctantly, D'Mique urged the horse to follow in their wake.

At the front line, the daemons were attacking, pulled across the no-man's land by Savli and Marco's first passage. Now, seemingly incensed, they threw themselves against the dragons and foot soldiers that stood there. "Make way!" Marco cried.

As the soldiers fell back, Savli's wind shoved the daemons away, a strong gust throwing spindle-legged black bodies up into the air. With a path cleared, the tornado reappeared. It churned the earth as it pressed north, ripping plants, trees, and black daemons from the ground and flinging them outward and away. Into the void it made, Marco flew, followed by the Palace Black, which had broken into a gallop to keep pace with the Gorath. The tornado that Savli had loosed veered westward, bowling into the main body of the daemon horde. As it did so, black daemons screamed and rushed toward the three travelers. Savli paused, stepping into the Mage Realm to form a new tornado that he sent raging northward, aiming roughly for the Black Vale. They moved on, following the tornado, movement keeping them from bogging down in a battle with the horde. The tornado, once again, veered westward before reaching the cliffs. Savli bleated, stopped, and threw a third tornado out ahead of them, clearing their way. It held true and they sprinted after it, Savli setting the pace. This tornado fell into the previous storm path, trekking northeastward on a true path toward the Vale.

Another half-hour's running brought them to the clearing at the base of the obsidian cliffs of the Vale. Where the cliffs split, a huge iron portcullis had been set. When the defenders saw Savli approach, his tornado dissipating before him, they worked to raise the gate. The horde was just behind the galloping horse. "Go!" Marco shouted, falling back and leaping off his Sand Snake. He sent the Earth out to smash into the advancing, frenzied daemons. Bodies crunched against the suddenly solid sand. Savli slid under the gate before it was raised high enough to let the horse in. Marco guarded their rear until the horse could enter. Then the Vale Warriors signaled him and he fell back, waiting as long as he could before turning and running, skidding under the bars as the portcullis fell. Archers and Fire Mages shot through the iron bars, driving the daemons back.

D'Mique slid from the Palace Black and an elderly soldier took the horse away. She looked around. There were tents everywhere, housing pallets and beds and hammocks. Refugees had been piled on top of one another, making room for any who made it to the gate. All around her, steep black obsidian cliffs rose about fifty feet. Above them, on the top of the cliffs, Goraths stood, their horned silhouettes stark against the bright sky.

"You made it without any blood," a cultured, Gorath voice said above and behind her, echoing that same long, drawn-out voweled accent of the other. D'Mique turned. The red-furred Gorath's eyes blazed with daemon-fire and he smiled wide. Her skin crawled. He wore nothing except an intricate charm necklace that looked made of bones and beads. It was strung around his thick neck with a gold chain. Savli joined the red-furred Gorath. "Rayn keeps losing these bets, Savli," the red-furred one said.

"What did you win, My Prince?" Savli asked.

"Nothing I can say in polite company," Puko leered. Savli returned the smile, and his own fiery eyes stayed on D'Mique too long.

D'Mique felt her breath catch in her throat and a shiver crawl through her stomach and up her spine.

"I thank you, Savli," Temeres said, coming to D'Mique's rescue. "Rayn lost because he thinks you are old," the Vale Warrior added. A handful of nearby warriors chuckled and whistled. "Lady, this way. I'll take you to where you can rest."

"Thank you," she said, following him. It took a mighty act of will to turn her back on the Goraths.

To Make Amends

With a slice from a blade of light, the tree daemons who'd taken the Land-Nymphs captive had rent the Physical Realm, creating a rift into a world of swirling sands and Shadow Magic. They'd taken their three prisoners to a fortress not unlike the Fire Master's, but made of Shadow instead of obsidian. The days blended into one another as the Land-Nymphs sat in the strange Shadow fortress. They'd been brought to this sepulchral world so long ago, that even Tekalo had lost count of the passing time. Grudgingly, he'd admitted to himself that with no suns it was impossible to tell one day from the next. The Nura who'd brought them here took turns keeping nonchalant eyes on the three prisoners, although the only one they really seemed concerned with was Tekalo. Ordvyn, the leader, along with the one the Land-Nymphs had nicknamed Mage, took turns keeping Tekalo bound, unable to use magic, although he could still access the Mage Realm.

Stepping from the Shadowy world to the Mage Realm had been simple enough for Tekalo. In the Mage Realm, the stone walls of the fortress could be seen, but the inky darkness of Shadow magic covered them. Returning his consciousness to his physical body, Tekalo found himself in the strange, dark world again instead of the Physical Realm. At any given time, returning from the Mage Realm would bring on a beating from the Nura holding the binding that kept him from using magic. It wasn't every time, and it wasn't only

Mage or only Ordvyn who would rush to his side and start kicking him. This time no one appeared and Tekalo let go of the breath he'd gathered anticipating a blow from a tree daemon.

Tekalo studied the other two prisoners. His fellow Moon Clan Land-Nymph Trillip sat dozing, slumped over, his bound wrists tucked in close to his chest, his face hidden by bright candy pink curls. Despite the lack of magic ability and the warning that leaving the fortress would kill him, Trillip had taken every opportunity to attack any tree daemon short-sighted enough to be within arm's length. Even tied, he had managed to kick and bite, wounding several of them. Orska, T'Pani's Star Clan nurse, had been held prisoner longer than either Trillip or Tekalo. She had proven to herself that there was no way to get away from this group of tree daemons. She was waiting, biding her time she said, waiting for an opportunity to escape. Her black hair had been pulled back in a ponytail and her blue eyes gleamed in the half-light when Tekalo met her gaze. She was not bound; the tree daemons thought she was broken. There had been times over the last few days that he'd wondered if she was playing or if she really had resigned herself to this fate.

Most of the Nura sat nearby, while two or three of them were patrolling the walls of the fortress. They formed a half-circle around a large fire several strides away from their prisoners. Earlier, they'd made a stew and shared it out to their company as well as the Land-Nymphs. Now, with the food gone, they were talking in their guttural, sibilant language as they prepared for bed. Ordvyn, as always, was the center of attention, although his own thoughts most often lingered on Tekalo and the magic bonds. Since arriving in the fortress, Tekalo had made a careful count of them and had concluded that there were ten of them in total. It was hard to be certain, as they all looked alike, but some had weapon preferences that were different from the others, some were bigger, others thinner. Orska had given them all nicknames to keep track of them, Paper Boy, Mountain,

Hands, Mage and Boss Man were the ones most often present in the fortress. Boss Man—Ordvyn—had taken over for the Captain once Tekalo had captured him, Orska had said. Before that, all the others had fawned over the Captain every chance they could, like they now fawned over Ordvyn.

Tekalo sat watching them watch him.

Within the blink of an eye, she appeared, startling the entire company. Tekalo gasped a moment after she'd appeared, bringing Orska's attention to the newcomer. Tree daemons suddenly appearing had become normal over the last several days. Until now, however, they had announced their appearance with a sickly green rift in the air near the fire. This time, however, there had been no warning. The newcomer had simply popped into existence in the middle of the circle around the fire.

The newcomer wore the same gray uniform as the others but where their heads were bald, the newcomer had long, white dreadlocks. Beads and trinkets woven through her dreadlocks spun in a grand arch as the newcomer turned swiftly toward Ordvyn. The spear, expertly wielded, cleared the area around the fire sending Nura diving for cover as it traced an arch, following in the wake of the newcomer's hair and baubles. Ordvyn rose hastily as the newcomer took two leaping steps toward him and punched him squarely in the jaw. He dropped heavily to his backside, still conscious.

Trillip giggled under his breath—a half-mad sound that worried Tekalo—and sat up. The newcomer was shouting at Ordvyn, animated, waving the spear dangerously near any who came too close or moved too slowly. The others picked themselves up from the ground and backed away, rather than hurrying to Ordvyn's side.

"Who's that?" Tekalo asked Orska, as Ordvyn regained his feet.

The nurse frowned, bright cerulean blue eyes wide in surprise. "I don't know. I've never seen her."

"Maybe his wife," Trillip suggested with another laugh, this one loud enough to bring some tree daemon eyes to focus on them. He raised his chin defiantly, green eyes as sharp as glass, little fangs bared in a death grin. Trillip's laughter had ended the newcomer's tirade and she looked around the fortress. She turned back to Ordvyn, then to Mountain and Mage. She seemed to be asking questions that the others answered in short bursts.

Then her fiery daemon-eyes fell on the Land-Nymphs and she crossed to them, spear up, ready to defend herself if necessary. There was no point trying to escape so the three Land-Nymphs simply sat, ready for the fight she was bringing their way.

"Tekalo?" she asked. Her voice was cultured, purring and sibilant. The three Land-Nymphs looked at one another and then glared at the newcomer in reply. "One of you is Tekalo? Your Master is worried about you."

"Nepo?" Tekalo asked. He grimaced, knowing his response had singled him out as the Chosen One.

The newcomer nodded. "And the baby?" she asked.

Choking on a sob, Trillip spat at her, "She's gone!"

Frowning, the newcomer looked at Ordvyn and shouted back at him. He hissed a reply. She turned to face the three prisoners again. "Are you well? Cared for? Abused?" she asked, switching languages seamlessly.

Scoffing, Tekalo pulled his now-dirty shirt up to show off the green and purple bruising that blossomed across his midriff, ribs, and stomach. She shouted at Ordvyn who replied in the same tone. In response, the newcomer sank to the ground and appeared to step into the Mage Realm. She was close enough to the Land-Nymphs that they could have wrested her weapon away and overpowered her. Instead, the three sat and watched her, shocked into inaction.

Hundreds of miles south, DJar held up a hand to signal for Palo's silence. They sat together in the front reception area of Palo's tent, the open door catching the late night breeze. Palo had been reading through a list of supplies brought by Nepo, adding side comments that DJar could not decipher. DJar closed his eyes and stepped away, falling silent and motionless as he talked to Shi'Shou. Palo's voice trailed off and DJar could feel the *Tepok-Myir's* curiosity and irritation ride the air between them. The Nura was gone long enough that Nepo and Clippen approached. It'd been nearly seven days since Shi'Shou had disappeared from the camp. As he listened to his *Aliith*, DJar's frown deepened. Then, with a sigh, he opened his eyes. Smoldering daemon-fire met the eyes of those around him in turn, beginning and ending with Palo. Clippen glared, arms folded across his chest as if anticipating bad news.

"My *Aliith* has found my second," DJar began, speaking slowly in Fae. "They have Tekalo and two more, the one with flower hair and the nurse. They are going to the Crystal Hills." He hesitated. Then, with a defiant grimace, continued speaking directly to Clippen. "They do not have the baby."

With a primal scream, Clippen leapt on the Nura, bowling him over in a flash of gold and white. "Clippen!" Nepo shouted but neither he nor Palo moved to intervene. Clippen pummeled DJar, who screamed and fought to defend himself, as claws raked at his face and the Land-Nymph's teeth sank into his blocking arm.

"*Tepok-Myir!* Please!" DJar cried. He shouted in his language but Nepo didn't try to translate or understand. "I am yours, please!" DJar said, finding the words in Fae. "I can heal!" He screamed again as Clippen doubled his effort to reach the Nura's neck and face. DJar shouted in his language, pleading once more and this time, his words caught Nepo's attention.

Nepo hurried over and grabbed Clippen, pulling him bodily from the Nura. "Palo, he says he can help, he says he knows what happened," Nepo shouted, struggling to drag Clippen away from DJar. Palo moved then, stepping between the two, glaring down at the Nura who'd remained prone, covered in blood from a series of shallow bites and gashes, before turning to help Nepo with Clippen. Palo held the Land-Nymph close and waited for his friend to begin seething, shaking with rage but back in control of his emotions. When Palo was certain Clippen would not attack DJar a second time, he released him to Nepo and turned back to DJar.

Palo grabbed the Nura by the arm and lifted him, standing him up. Instead, the Nura crumpled to his knees at Palo's feet, breathing heavily, avoiding eye contact. "You can help?" the Grand Syra asked, emphasizing the word in Fae, realizing that DJar had misspoke before. DJar nodded. "But, let me guess, not with finding the baby," Palo concluded. DJar remained motionless and said nothing. "Clippen deserves your death, DJar." Clippen sobbed behind Palo as Nepo held him. "Talk," Palo ordered, "Quick now, you're on borrowed time." DJar glanced up to Nepo, who translated Palo's words.

"My second is no longer following my orders," DJar said and Nepo translated, speaking low as he held Clippen. "He has set a spell, as the jar explained," he indicated Myrth's jar, "calling up the mobling horde, but he has mistaken it. It is unresolved."

Nepo motioned for him to stop and added, "I don't think I have the correct words, Palo. The spell was made wrong, misspoken, broken," he clarified.

Palo reached down and grabbed DJar by the chin, pulling the daemon's eyes up to meet his green-gold ones. "How does that help?" he asked.

"The moblings are chasing the two targets and will continue chasing them until they are both brought to my second," DJar continued. "The only way to truly stop the moblings is to resolve the spell. Otherwise, even *if* you kill every black daemon in the

Maelstrom, they will continue streaming from the Vast Wildlands, forever, searching for the retainer and the baby." Palo released his chin and straightened after Nepo's translation sank in. Clippen had quieted in Nepo's arms, but his pink eyes were ruby-hard and still ready to kill the daemon-kin.

"And the help?" Nepo asked.

DJar hesitated, studying the three standing above him. "I will take the retainer to my second," he said, meeting Palo's eyes, his daemon-fire banked to embers. "We can Walk the Sands. I am not as strong in my faith as my *Aliith*, and cannot Walk as long as she, but it will keep the retainer safe from the moblings and we will make good time." Nepo's face grew puzzled as he slowly translated and he was frowning by the time DJar stopped speaking.

Clippen held up a hand, and DJar flinched away from the sudden movement. "With the Lady Warrior taken to your second, that part of the spell is resolved?" he waited for DJar to nod after the translation. "So long as she is there, the horde will then only seek T'Pani?" he clarified. DJar nodded slowly, keeping his eyes steady on the Land-Nymph.

"Alive or dead?" Palo added. "If T'Pani is dead, will they still look for her?"

"I do not know," DJar admitted. Nepo translated again, "Yet, the mistakes my second made in the incantation are from bad wording. It is likely they would search for a dead target as well as a living one."

Nepo paused in his translation, "Sorry, I don't know the exact words he used, but I think 'bad wording' is close to what he means."

"Convenient," Palo said with a frown. "The way you help is by taking more prisoners north, leaving us to deal with the daemon horde, free of us."

"I am honor bound, *Tepok-Myir*, to aid you and to remain a prisoner until my bonds are resolved. Leaving the Maelstrom does not change that." His eyes flared a moment and he looked up at them all, grimly calm as he waited for Nepo to translate. "I would ask that the Avian Little Brother's bond be considered released once I complete this mission. Resolving half the spell that is driving the daemons *would* be helpful."

"You will release the other Land-Nymph prisoners," Clippen hissed, "now."

"I cannot release them now," DJar said with a shake of his head. "I am not commanding my company. My second is. I will have to retake the company to release them. I will send Tekalo back once I am there."

"You will send all the prisoners back," Palo said.

"No, we need to keep the nurse for when the infant is returned to my second and the spell is resolved." DJar met their harsh glares in turn, unblinking, daemon-fire banked, leaving his eyes soft and black.

"If we let him go," Clippen said to Palo after a moment, "We will never see him again, you know that." Palo nodded and started scratching his forearm.

The Grand Syra moved away from the group, grabbing Myrth's jar as he left. He stopped several yards from his tent, staring out at the canvas shelters around him where his mage army slept. *"If we could resolve this with minimal bloodshed..."* he thought. With a sigh he called, "Myrth," bringing the jar to life with a touch of Water magic. A moment passed and the hawk Semian replied, sounding half asleep.

"Shi'Shou reported in. Tekalo is being held by the Nura hunting party but in order to release him and Trillip, DJar needs to return to them. He wants to take D'Mique with him. The black daemon horde was caused by a botched incantation, and D'Mique is their target."

"D'Mique is at the Black Vale with Puko, Marco, and Temeres," Myrth said after a long, silent, minute. Palo thought about that for a moment. He frowned at the jar.

"If we let him go, will DJar return?" Palo asked.

Myrth sighed. "Such work on his part is helpful to our war effort. I will let Clippen decide if it is helpful enough to release him from my bond. You and Clippen will still hold his prisoner bonds, even with mine gone. He will return, for he is honorable."

Palo looked from the jar to DJar. "Are you honorable?" he asked himself.

Myrth answered him, "Honor is all they have, Palo. It holds their society together. He will return."

Palo studied DJar for a moment then ended his conversation with Myrth, closing the connection without a goodbye. Jar in hand, he returned to the group at the entrance to his tent, the firelight glinting across the scales on DJar's bare arms and dancing dangerously in Clippen's eyes. Nepo had released the Land-Nymph and thus far, DJar was still alive. "Are you honorable?" Palo asked again, this time loud enough for DJar to hear.

"I am yours, *Tepok-Myir*, I will return," DJar answered in Fae.

Palo scratched his arm, studying the Nura, thinking. "Nepo," he said quietly. "There's something...troubling me." He leaned forward, studying DJar closely. "Be certain of these words as you translate." Nepo nodded once. "How many bonds hold you here, *Shuwarr*." Nepo meticulously translated the question.

DJar's face went unreadable and his eyes began to burn. "Three," he said.

Nepo added, "Yours, Clippen's, and Myrth's," for Palo's benefit.

Palo paused in his scratching. "And, how many bonds are on you?"

DJar closed his eyes and after a moment opened them, answering, "Seven."

"And who holds those bonds?"

DJar frowned at him but answered, "The Fae, yourself, the avian Little Brother, my *Aliith,* the Gray Syden, and my second, Ordvyn."

Palo knelt down on one knee next to DJar. Grabbing him by the neck, he pulled the Nura close and studied him nose to nose, sniffing. He smiled, fangs large. "That's six. You like to slice the truth thin, Nura." DJar went pliant in the Grand Syra's hand. He smiled and his eyes flared for a moment before they returned to low, smoldering embers.

"Who holds two bonds?" Nepo blinked in surprise then translated the Grand Syra's question.

"You, *Tepok-Myir,*" DJar whispered. "I am yours."

Palo released him and looked up at Nepo, questioning. Nepo shrugged. "Explain," Palo ordered the Nura.

"My life is yours, as it is Syden's. Until you and Syden work out how to share that Claim, or until one of you releases the Claim on my life, I will divide my time equally between you. However, the prison bond you hold takes precedence over the Claim Bond."

"A Claim bond," Nepo repeated in a whisper. Palo looked between the two of them, standing again. Nepo studied DJar for a long, hard moment, then said, "He will be back, Palo. A Claim bond is like the bond between two goblin blood brothers. It's immutable. You didn't even know about it, yet, he was honoring it anyway."

Palo studied the Nura, digesting what Nepo had just said. "I will send you to the Black Vale to pick up D'Mique. You will take her to your second and resolve that part of the spell." He sat down again in his padded wooden chair near the entrance to his tent. "Clippen?" he asked.

"When Tekalo is returned and T'Pani is found, Myrth's bond will be released," he said. "Mine will not be. He will never be rid of my bond but he can work on Myrth's and, perhaps, return our child to us."

DJar turned to face Clippen on his knees and bowed, touching his head to the ground. "I accept this condition," he said. He straightened, waiting.

Palo stood and surveyed the others. He scratched his arm in thought. "Sleep now," Palo ordered, "Tomorrow DJar, I will sketch you a path to the Black Vale. I take it, you'll be able to find your second after collecting D'Mique."

DJar nodded, bowed again, then stood and retreated to his tent.

"Where did the Claim bond come from?" Palo asked. Nepo closed his eyes in thought.

"'I am yours,'" Nepo said. "When did he start saying that? After your brawl?" Palo thought a moment, then nodded in agreement. "That's when," Nepo concluded.

The newcomer opened her eyes, flames of daemon-fire burning brightly in the half light of the Shadow fortress. She focused on Tekalo. "My *Ti'er* is coming. You will be released when he reaches us. We are to wait here until his arrival. Provided you wait patiently and behave yourself, no further abuse will come to you." She stood in one motion and stepped away from them before turning back to Ordvyn and snapping at him in their language. Ordvyn snarled but made no move to counter her. He returned to his seat beside the fire, moping.

The three Land-Nymphs exchanged glances but said nothing and returned to watching the tree daemons, waiting.

Of Daemon Slayer and Daemon-Kin

The Black Vale was once a colony of the North, like the Embers in the west," Temeres said. Marco, D'Mique and he stood in an underground cavern. Behind them, the path led up to the easternmost cliff of the Black Vale. To their right, a path led down to an underground spring and the ocean. The spring provided fresh water that ran downhill through a carved obsidian channel before joining a brackish pool. Vale Warriors trudged past from time to time, fishing or collecting clean water for cooking, drinking, and caring for the wounded.

Here, to the left, was a large altar made of bones, tied together with leather. Large leg bones formed the legs of the structure, while carefully spaced rib bones had been tied tightly together to form the flat top. Bowls holding spices, incense and berries, dominated the offerings. Beeswax candles were scattered about, two or three of them lit, burning fitfully in the dark. The light from the candles illuminated the bat-winged, deer-headed bone monstrosity that loomed over the altar's top. The path to the altar had been hidden, a break in the mirrored-surface of the obsidian that seemed solid, even as Temeres stepped through it and disappeared around the corner.

"The god worshipped here is Abhig," Temeres continued. "He is Chaos. The offerings are meant to placate him so that there will be no chaos."

D'Mique scoffed. There'd been a great deal of chaos for the last few days. Once Marco and Savli had re-entered the Black Vale, the daemon horde had suddenly focused on it. Goraths, goblins, and elves from the Misty Realms had taken up positions atop the cliffs and at the gate, pelting the horde with Air and Fire to keep them at bay. The red Gorath Puko had unleashed his power early this morning as well, standing along the cliff above the Gate and, with Savli's help, sending huge fiery tornadoes out across the plains. The horde had been slow to rebuild and return from the destruction wrought by Savli's and Puko's infernal storms.

"Who worships here?" Marco asked.

"The Goraths, some of the bog elves," Temeres answered. "Not many humans although Abhig is rumored to be a god of the Pale Ones.

"Vale Warriors are descended from humans in the North," Marco started. "The Pale Ones?" Temeres studied him a moment before nodding. "DJar referred to me once as one," Marco added.

"We inherited the altar and allow Abhig's worshipers to visit. When the Masters took control of the area, the governors of the North lost interest in the Vale, and we've been left to our own devices since. When the northerners stopped coming, there were fewer worshipers."

"This was the altar in Oracle's vision?" D'Mique asked. Marco and Temeres nodded. Long, slow, echoing clip-clop footsteps reverberated through the obsidian cavern. The three humans turned to greet the approaching Goraths. D'Mique's heart fell when she saw that it was Puko and his two cronies. Over the last couple of days, she'd come to know several of the great creatures. While they all made her skin crawl and seemed overly jovial and familiar, only Puko and Savli made her afraid to turn her back on them. Marco and Temeres didn't seem to have this same reaction to any of them.

"Pardon us," Puko said when they noticed the three humans standing before the altar.

"Savli, please," Temeres said, bowing and stepping aside to make room for the elder Gorath. Savli thanked him and shook his bone staff in two lazy loops above his head as he approached the bones and knelt in prayer. D'Mique and Marco followed Temeres a few steps away. Puko and Rayn sat back on their haunches next to the humans to watch and wait.

"Do you also worship Abhig, Temeres?" Puko asked quietly.

"No," he said with a dismissive shake of his head. "Vale Warriors do not worship gods."

"You?" Puko asked Marco, he spared a curious glance for D'Mique as well.

"No," D'Mique said as Marco shook his head. "We don't worship gods. My people worship our ancestors."

"Ah." Puko smiled at her.

"Do you also worship this god?" she asked him.

Puko grimaced and shook his head, no. "What use do I have for gods of Chaos?"

"You are chaos," Marco said with a half-laugh.

Puko flashed a too-wide smile, "As are you, Mage of Man," he said.

"Temeres says the prayers are to *end* chaos," D'Mique noted.

Puko smiled and leaned in, his daemon-fire eyes close enough to lick her cheeks with orange light, "What use do I have for gods of Chaos?" he asked again. One large fire-eye closed in a conspiratorial wink. D'Mique pulled back and stepped away, moving to a safer distance. *"Still within arm's reach, though,"* she thought, realizing that the Gorath's arms were nearly twice hers in length. Her skin crawled and her stomach churned. Temeres stepped up close to her, lending her strength with his sure, calm, presence. *"How does he know?"* she wondered to herself.

"We will leave Savli to his prayers," he said and offered D'Mique his arm. She took it and he turned her around. Marco stepped between her and Puko, following them out.

Away from the Goraths, D'Mique took a calming breath. Temeres dropped her arm and stopped to study her. "They don't mean you harm," he said. "They're daemon-kin, but the Kairra are well-known to us and to the Masters. They are valuable allies."

D'Mique frowned and nodded, but thought, *"Say what you want, allies or not, they're creepy."*

For another three days, D'Mique spent as much time as possible avoiding Puko and his two companions. The other Goraths in the Vale were better company, she decided. It hadn't taken her long to discover that the women were camped above the Vale in four separate groups, one for each tribe. Where the male Gorath's had huge, spiraling ram horns, the women had slender horns that didn't quite curl. The women branded them with runes and pictures that told significant tales of their lives instead. The elder and more important the woman, the greater the scarring upon her horns.

"Human Female," a red-furred female Gorath greeted D'Mique that third evening. Her voice was nearly identical to Puko's, lending her a dusky tone. "We watched our Savli bring you in from the Dragon Master's camp."

"Yes," D'Mique said, stopping and shielding her eyes from the light of the Fiery Sisters. The red-furred Gorath wore no clothes but her shoulders were adorned by a mass of chains, beads, and ribbons that none of the other Goraths wore. She bowed her head, presenting her horns. They were wreathed in branded flames. Among the flame motifs stories of hunting and leadership danced. One of the other women of the tribe was using a hot iron to add herringbone hatching lines to each horn to signify the start of a new tale.

"Please, sit with us. I am Kairra," the red Gorath added.

"My name is D'Mique," she introduced, joining the pair of Goraths on the ground near a small cooking fire. "Do you have the same name as your tribe or are you of a different tribe?"

Kairra smiled, wide and inviting, her damon-fire eyes ablaze, "I am the leader of the tribe. Therefore, the tribe takes my name."

"Oh!" D'Mique bowed her head. "I am sorry, I had no—" the Gorath's laughter brought her to a halt. She smiled and waited for the laughter to die. "Puko is your son then?"

"Yes, mine and Dinar's. Savli and Dinar were brothers."

"I am Rayn's mother, one of Savli's mates" the second Gorath added, "Corrah." She bowed her head in such a way that she presented her horns for perusal. D'Mique saw stories of hunting and leading the tribe as well. A single flame motif surrounded one of the stick-figure Goraths that danced along the middle of her delicate horns.

"You must be very proud of your sons," D'Mique added, trying not to show any visible signs of the discomfort Puko caused her. *"Rayn doesn't come across as creepy though,"* she acknowledged to herself.

"Yes," the pair chorused. Kairra continued, "We would rather have daughters, but our sons are strong and brave and bring us joy." Corrah giggled at her words, and looked away from D'Mique. "You are a warrior," Kairra said, pointing to D'Mique's sword. "Do you lead a tribe?"

"No," D'Mique said with a shake of her head, resting a hand on the hilt of her sword.

"Not yet," Corrah added. "One day, perhaps. You are still young." The pair nodded, smiling at D'Mique.

"Join us for the evening meal," Kairra invited. "You have no horns, but you have a story to tell."

D'Mique smiled and agreed to return after the Fiery Sisters had set.

That was where Marco found her two hours later. She was sitting with eight female Goraths and their children, sharing food from a huge, black pot that hung bubbling over the central Kairra Tribe fire. Marco caught her eye and that of the leader. He waited for an invitation from one of the females before approaching.

"D'Mique," he said, joining her on the ground. "I've heard from Myrth." She waited, setting her spoon down in a bowl full of rice and leaves. "He is on his way here from Nightmare and will be bolstering Marladon's forces with elves from Gemma and goblins from Dragon Ridge."

"Good," she said with a nod. "Will we be joining him then?"

Marco's smile faltered. "I will," he said.

"But not me?" she asked, concern and disdain blooming across her face. Marco recognized her defenses rising.

"You're going elsewhere."

"Home?!" she snapped. "I don't need saving, Marco!" she continued.

"No. Not home." He paused long enough that her anger cooled from hot to brooding. "Do you remember DJar?"

D'Mique's green eyes searched his face before her eyebrows raised. "The tree daemon prisoner that Palo is keeping in Olimidia?"

Marco nodded. "Myrth is ordering you to accompany him north."

D'Mique blinked at him, taken aback. "Myrth is ordering me north...with the...tree daemon?" Marco nodded again. "Did you hit your head?" she asked.

"No," Marco smiled sympathetically. "I'm not entirely clear about what is going on," he said. "Myrth said he will tell you when he arrives tomorrow."

"He told you instead of waiting to tell me?" she asked.

Marco hesitated. He felt as if there was a trap laid before him, but he wasn't sure what to say to avoid it. "I..." He shut his mouth and shrugged. D'Mique pursed her lips tight enough to make them pale, then turned back to the fire and food, making a show of ignoring him and rejoining the conversation. Marco sighed, stood, and took his leave.

DJar woke with the suns the next morning. He packed a bag with two changes of clothes and donned his gray uniform. Stepping from his tent, he glanced around at the army of mages surrounding him. They wore the same black uniform as the *Tepok-Myir*, all of them with two or three red feathers in their hats. He'd deduced they stood for the rank of the soldier, although it wasn't an army rank as the *Tepok-Myir* also had three. *Tepok* Nepo approached with a small cloth bag. "I've brought you rations," he said. His grasp of the Noble Tongue was rudimentary, but he was easily understandable and DJar appreciated the Semian's efforts. DJar bowed, appreciative. "Are you ready?" he asked.

"I cannot Walk the Sands without a focus," DJar admitted. It was the last obstacle to leaving. If they wouldn't trust him with a blade, he wouldn't be able to Rend. "I require a blade." Nepo studied him, honey eyes narrowing with suspicion.

"A blade focus? It must be a blade? How about a stick?" Nepo asked, pointing toward a nearby pile of firewood.

DJar shook his head no and bowed. "My apologies, *Tepok* Nepo. It must be a blade. As I said, I am not as strong in my faith as my *Aliith*."

Nepo bade him wait and he went to consult Palo. DJar listened to them rumble at each other and then Palo poured from the tent. DJar could feel his anger and sank to his knees, bowing, hoping to placate the great cat and avoid any claws or fangs.

"Why do you need a blade as a focus?" Nepo asked, translating Palo's Fae words to the Noble Tongue.

"To Rend," DJar said. He kept it as simple a reply as possible. Palo frowned and returned to his tent. When he came back, he held a stiletto. He presented it hilt first to DJar, and motioned for the Nura to take it. DJar did so with a frown. It was not a weapon he was used to wielding for Rending or otherwise, and would have preferred a glaive or falchion.

"Show us," Nepo said.

"I must be conditionally released from my bonds, *Tepok-Myir*. I will Walk the Sands for you. I wield my power for you. When my task is complete and I have returned, I will once again set aside my powers." Palo nodded in agreement at the translated words.

DJar closed his eyes and stepped away, reaching into the darkness that flickered at the center of his being and pulled power to his hand. He coaxed it across the blade. Pulling Stasis from the Nether, he wrapped it around the endowment making the blade doubly endowed. Then he returned to the Physical Realm. The blade looked ordinary in this realm, which Nura knew as the Dream, but with a flick of Shadow and a slice through the air, DJar rent reality. Palo and Nepo both stepped back, away from the sickly green light that marked the edge of the tear in space DJar had created. Within, beyond the border held open by DJar's will, a swirling vortex of purple and gray sand danced.

"Walk the Sands," Palo whispered. DJar released the Rend and purposefully undid the two endowments on the blade before making eye contact with Palo. He forced himself to be calm, the fire in his eyes that had blazed forth at his use of power subsided. He would not be seen to challenge the *Tepok-Myir* if he could help it. Palo spoke and Nepo translated, "Your *Aliith* does that without a blade? She just closes her eyes and steps in there?"

DJar considered for a moment, then nodded slowly.

"Was that Shadow?" Palo asked.

"I am daemon-kin, *Tepok-Myir*. I am Shadow, I use Shadow."

"The blade will work?" Nepo asked. DJar bowed and signaled his grudging approval.

"Do that again," Palo purred. DJar studied him a moment, trying to decide if the *Tepok-Myir* was excited about the power DJar wielded or if it was simple, feral curiosity. Then, closing his eyes, he stepped away, first reaching into his soul, then into the Nether. He endowed the blade with his internal flame once again then formed the second endowment from Stasis. He could feel Palo watching him work, although he knew from his time in the Maelstrom that the *Tepok-Myir* —and any other mages here—would not be able to see his working, only the final product. The myth from his childhood about Maelstrom-born monsters not being able to Touch the Nether had proven true. With the two endowments in place, DJar opened his eyes and sliced the air, Rending reality and opening a door once more. Eyes ablaze, he waited, holding the Rend open while Nepo and Palo both studied it.

"No!" he snapped as Palo made to step through. "You cannot." Palo glared at him. "The air is poison, you must walk with Stasis." He waited wide-eyed as Nepo translated.

"Stasis?" Palo asked, looking between DJar and Nepo, who shrugged in response.

DJar gave them a look, uncertain how to explain such a fundamental aspect of reality. "Yes," he said, allowing the Rend to close. He left the blade endowed and slipped it into his belt. "I am prepared to leave, *Tepok-Myir*," he continued, dismissing their curiosity. "I do not know where to find the female retainer."

Nepo translated as Palo spoke. "The Black Vale is along the east coast, almost straight east from here," Palo began. "Follow the Crest to the peaks and along them." He pointed toward the towering peaks near their camp. "As you leave the peaks behind, you will come to the lava plains of the Black Lands. Continue east until you come to a large trade route. Follow that road north."

Nepo added, "You should meet Marladon and his dragon army as you travel the trade route. He can help you find D'Mique."

DJar nodded then shouldered his pack. "In your name, *Tepok-Myir*," he said, saluting Palo before pulling the knife from his belt and Rending reality once more. With a quick check, he bowed then stepped through the rift, closing the hole in reality behind him and disappearing from the Physical Realm.

It took him a moment to get his bearings after returning to the Realm of Sands from his extended stay in the Dream—the Physical Realm—with the Semians and the Fae. The purple and gray sands swirled around DJar as he studied them and waited for his eyes to adjust and the Nether formations to become visible. The five peaks at the heart of the Maelstrom existed in the Dream and the Realm of Sands. Here, they teemed with Light and Stasis. Down deep, far below the surface, a Shadowy maw led to the Void. DJar took a deep breath, renewing his faith in Shi'Dowana. *"Protect my steps, Mistress of the Sands,"* he thought. He judged it would take him about three days to reach the end of the Maelstrom peaks. Around him, the sands carried the faint traces of movement from the Dream. If he concentrated, he could find Palo. The feline Semian was standing next to him, nearly on top of him, scratching at his forearm. *"You have quite the tell, Master of Mine,"* DJar thought.

He moved on. His passage through the ghostly suggestions of tents and mages would leave them none the wiser. If any of the Fae or Semians understood how to Touch the Nether, they might have set a ward or trap to warn them of his passing. However, true to all the tales, the Maelstrom-born did not know of the Nether or the Realm of Sands and he Walked unnoticed among them.

DJar passed quickly from the Crest to the foothills. Most of this land was barren in both the Dream and the Sands. However, as he traveled nearer the Maelstrom Peaks, trees started to appear. Here in the Sands, they were fonts of Stasis and Air. Resting near them could prolong the time spent Walking the Sands for those of lesser faith. DJar gravitated toward the trees, using the Air and Stasis to buoy him to further distances.

After a few hours, DJar removed the stiletto from his belt and Rent the Sands, stepping back to the Dream. Training and discipline kept him from changing his breathing pattern, although there was always a hitch that burned deep in the lungs when stepping from one plane to another. Time and Space distorted in the Sands and he was nearly a full day's journey from the encampment on the clifftops.

DJar had stepped back into the Physical Realm in a glade near a stream. He cast an eye upward to judge the suns and time of day—still shy of midday. Then he reached out to the Nether and cast a Light Ward, binding it in Stasis, which would hold it without his will. The Nura sighed, taking a deep breath. He smiled. *"It's been a long time since I was truly alone and free,"* he thought. He looked around, judging how close he'd come to the Maelstrom Peaks. *"Rest now,"* he told himself, *"the Peaks will be havoc."* From previous experience, he knew that Walking the Sands was exhausting near the Maelstrom Peaks and he contemplated swinging wide out onto the volcanic plains to avoid the Stasis eddies the mountains caused. *"It won't add much to my travel time,"* he thought, *"and caution is often wiser."* With a decision made, he sat, cross-legged, and drifted first into meditation, then into sleep.

He dozed, his Light ward hiding his presence, until midday. With the suns high above, he woke. Before standing, he reached out to Shi'Shou through their bond. *"I come,"* he told her.

"I wait, my Ti'er," she replied. *"Ordvyn is angered rather than recalcitrant,"* she added.

DJar frowned at her information. *"I will be a cycle in coming. Perhaps his mood will change."* She did not reply, but he felt her doubt echo along their bond. With a sigh and a glance around the clearing, DJar stood, undid the Stasis hold on his Light ward and then Rent reality and stepped into the Sands. As he passed from the Dream to the Sands, the Light ward dropped. Anyone looking wouldn't have seen any change in the glade.

Within the Sands, DJar waited again for his eyes to adjust. The Maelstrom Peaks loomed closer than he remembered them being when he left the Sands earlier in the day. He turned his steps northeast, starting down, out of the foothills, away from the Peaks and out onto the volcanic plains. There were Formations out in the desert that he could try to reach for the night. At least, they existed according to legend. His company had only spent a few days looking for them and Shi'Shou had criss-crossed the plains since without finding anything. *"Still,"* he thought, *"Perhaps we just weren't far enough east. If there were any reason to build a Formation in the Maelstrom, it would be to escape the peaks' havoc."*

He set off through the Sands. The trees, with their Stasis and Air, dwindled and then vanished as he traveled. He walked for the remainder of the day, stepping from the Sands back to the Dream every couple hours to rest and take his bearings. While he walked, he could feel the twin suns moving through the sky, although they couldn't be seen from the Sands. When he felt them nearing the horizon, he paused and concentrated on the Dream. Seeing no evidence of life around him, he stepped from the Sands and quickly built a Light Ward around himself, holding it in place with Stasis once again. *"I've had no luck with Formations on the plains,"* he thought with a self-deprecating smile. Then he pulled the bedroll from his pack and settled in for the night, doing his best to find a comfortable position on the rough ground. He realized, lying there, that it'd been quite a few cycles since last he slept rough. "Even the palace dungeon had provided more comfort than I have now," he whispered.

It was late afternoon, the next day, far out in the Blasted Plains, that DJar saw the walls of the Formation. They loomed out of the sand, pushing the swirling storm of purple and gray away to make room for the blocky Shadow structure. It bled Shadow magic into the sandstorm around it. As DJar approached, he could see that it was only the size of a large hut. He made his way around the inky stones to the door on the north wall. Stasis leapt from him to the walls as he passed across the threshold and the Sands departed. He breathed deep and relaxed. So long as a Nura occupied a Formation, the Stasis barrier would function and he could rest without expending energy to stay within the Realm of Sands.

Looking out over the southern walls of the Formation, DJar could see the tops of the Maelstrom Peaks. He was approximately two-thirds past them. Even with swinging wide to find a Formation and avoid the Maelstrom's whirling energy, he was making good time. Likely, he'd be to the eastern coast in two more days, provided the ancient maps he'd memorized before leaving the Crystal Hills were correct. He contemplated the stone ground for a moment before reluctantly pulling out his bedroll.

There were no trees on the volcanic plains where he Walked. After leaving the Formation behind, DJar continued east, Walking the Sands as long as possible but exiting more often to rest than he had with trees present. Mid-morning, he sat in meditation in the Dream. He'd pushed away worries about the long walks ahead of him, as he balanced his time between Syden and Palo, his growing distrust of Ordvyn and his actions, and a gnawing fear that he would be imprisoned forever in the Maelstrom if he failed. *"Just breathe,"* he'd told himself as he turned inward to contemplate the black flame of Shadow burning at his center.

The suns had moved quite a bit before he opened his eyes and glanced around him. His gray uniform matched the volcanic plains, he noticed with a smile, camouflaging him to any passing eye. Standing, he started east again, Rending the air as he walked and ducking into the Sands before the rift closed. As the day wore on, he turned further south once more to rejoin the path Palo had traced for him. The next time he stepped from the Sands to rest, he had left the Peaks behind. Ahead of him, forested hills of basalt were growing from the volcanic plains. He thought for a moment and nodded to himself. *"I've reached the coastal area."*

Remaining in the Physical Realm, DJar continued up the hill to the first trees, where he paused. Although their Stasis and Air didn't show here in the Dream, he could still draw Stasis from them to replenish himself. He reached into them, tapping their wells and pulling power inward toward the dark flame at his center. Taking too much would wither the tree but sipping from a small grove didn't hurt them. DJar closed his eyes and reached out to his *Aliith.* *"Shi'Shou,"* he called.

"We wait, my Ti'er," she replied. *"There has been no change in our circumstances."*

"My arrival time remains unchanged." he informed her.

"Very well, my Ti'er." He bowed to her mentally and withdrew. With a sigh, he ran a hand across his head, annoyed that his hair was growing so long and it would be several more days before he could shave.

He climbed to the top of the hill and looked out across a rolling landscape. With a grimace, he Rent the air and stepped into the Sands to survey the land ahead. Here, once his eyes adjusted, he could see that the hills had been replaced by a flat rocky plain, broken and jagged in a few places. Passage would be significantly quicker here in the Sands, and he started off. The trees remained, growing around jagged outcrops and breaks in the stone plain. DJar moved from one copse to another as he traveled east toward the coast.

Stepping into the Dream, DJar paused to rest near the end of the day, the Fiery Sisters sat low in the sky, not quite touching the horizon. He had passed through the rolling hills and now found himself in a dry pine forest. Contemplating the sky, the trees around him and the mental maps in his head, he struck off northeast through the trees. *"I should reach the trade route soon,"* he thought. Walking in the Dream was slower but he feared passing the road if he Walked the Sands. *"There'll be no way-markers in the Maelstrom,"* he thought. Setting a steady pace through the trees, he siphoned Stasis from them as they brushed against him and their branches caught his skin.

In the growing dusk, he climbed over a pair of hills and then looked down at a well-traveled road. Ahead of him, between the hills and the road, a large encampment held several Pale Ones. DJar pulled Light around him, setting a ward to hide within. He waited to make certain none of the people had noticed him in the trees. When they didn't react to his presence, he dared breathe again. Watching them for a moment, he relaxed. They weren't soldiers or trained in the martial arts. Farmers or shopkeepers seemed to form the majority of the company. Many were young. He watched the edges of the encampment for a time, looking for patrols or outliers on watch. There didn't seem to be any far from the camp. Rending the Air in front of him, he stepped into the Sands. As he left the Physical Realm, his Light Ward dropped away.

DJar started down the hill and through the center of the encampment. He Walked through the Sands for several yards, turning north as the trees dropped away around him, assuming he'd reached the road beyond the camp. He walked north along the barren path for several minutes, then joined a group of trees. Stealing himself to be discovered when he stepped into the Dream, DJar Rent the world before him. He cloaked himself in a Light Ward as he exited and furtively looked around in all directions. The Rift closed behind him. There'd been no screaming, no sudden shouts. He waited, but nothing approached. He had overshot the north road by only a few yards and could still see it, now on his left, through the pines.

After resting a moment, he studied the lay of the road. It appeared to travel straight on, no hills interfering with its chosen direction. *"Straight on until I see the moblings, then,"* he thought to himself. Returning to the Sands, he continued onward.

As the last daylight faded from the sky, DJar stopped. Ahead of him, the Shadowy ink-black moblings could be seen through the swirling Sands. Red wisps of Fire Magic danced before him as well. *"This is them,"* he thought. He closed the distance between himself and the Fire Magic wisps. Then cautiously, he drew the stiletto and Rent reality. Shouts accompanied the opening in the air and swords flew from scabbards to point at him as DJar stepped from the Sands and into the Dream. The Fire wisps had marked Marladon's dragon army, but he had inadvertently stepped from the Sands into an encampment full of Fae. All around him, Fae clambered. DJar held out his hands, showing himself harmless...despite the stiletto. Dragons were turning to see where the commotion came from as the soldiers decided whether to attack the creature who had appeared out of nowhere or simply defend against it.

"DJar!" Myrth called, hurrying over. "He's with us," the Earth Master shouted as he ran. Reaching the elves, he pressed through the forest of blades, pushing them aside until he reached DJar, hands out to hold the elves at bay. Slowly, the elfin soldiers lowered their weapons and stepped back.

DJar bowed to Myrth after sheathing the stiletto. "As I was instructed, I have come," he said.

Myrth studied him a moment with an assessing eye, before speaking, "We need to reach the Vale, past the black daemons," the Earth Master said, motioning toward the towering black cliffs that could be seen above the nearby pines.

"I am released from my bond to use my powers in the *Tepok-Myir's* name. We can Walk the Sands and pass by the moblings unmolested," DJar informed the Semian.

Myrth nodded. "Let me tell Marco so that we do not startle the Vale Warriors as you did these elves."

DJar's eyes flared and he smiled, looking around at the nervous soldiers. One, approaching, he recognized. "Brother," DJar said with a salute to Marladon.

"You startled everyone," Marladon responded.

DJar bowed, but it was with a flourish rather than chagrin. The Fire Master scoffed and shook his head. As Myrth closed his eyes and entered the Mage Realm to speak with Marco, Marladon continued. "You made good time."

"Walking the Sands allows one to pass quickly through the Dream," he explained, choosing the Fae words carefully. "I will be able to reach my second within the cycle."

"They are ready," Myrth said, interrupting the pair as he returned from the Mage Realm. They nodded at his words.

"Safe travels, DJar," Marladon said with a final salute.

"Fight well, Brother," DJar said. He pulled the stiletto from his belt and Rent the air, drawing a wide, smooth line that fell back to create a hole into the Realm of Sand. Gasps and murmurs echoed around the clearing. DJar stepped away and reached out quickly with his mind. He used a simple To-Fro pattern to throw his natural Stasis ability over Myrth. The barrier spell remained visible as it settled over the Semian's shoulders. "Stay within the barrier, Little Brother," he warned as he led Myrth into the Sands. "The air here is poisonous to your kind."

They moved quickly through the blowing, swirling world. The trees of the surrounding forest allowed DJar to trace a winding path between groups of black daemons while remaining in the Sands. The Shadow density grew as they neared the Vale, showing where the moblings were congregating. As the darkness surrounded them, DJar used the stiletto to prick at pools of Shadow, moving the black daemons by making them uncomfortable where they were standing, keeping Myrth free from the Shadow Magic. Near the Vale, DJar stopped. Ahead of him, the cliffs resolved into a large blocky Nether Formation. "There?" he asked. Myrth nodded.

The obsidian cliffs of the Black Vale loomed over the Sands, Shadow drifting off them into the swirling air. The pools of Shadow that marked the black daemons fell back, away from the Formation, and DJar was able to pass quickly from the edge of the mobling army to the gaping maw that opened into the Black Vale. As they entered, the Stasis field that engulfed Myrth leapt to the walls, providing breathable air and the ability to rest to all within. DJar motioned for Myrth to stand still and he continued around, studying the walls. Unlike the one he'd found near the Maelstrom Peaks, this Formation looked like one of the Starfield Forts he knew from home. He looked at Myrth. "Do you know the history of this place?" he asked. "Was it built by the Hills Kingdoms?"

"Yes," Myrth confirmed. "Ages ago. The Vale Warriors who live here are descendants of the Pale Ones."

"Ah," DJar said with a dawning understanding.

"I've warned them that we would appear from a rift. We shouldn't surprise them. Cut where you will," Myrth said.

"Step close, Little Brother and I will Rend here," DJar said. He sliced the air around them and they stepped through as Myrth closed the distance. Once free of the Sands, DJar hurriedly stowed his blade and held up his hands.

As before, their appearance startled nearby warriors. However, no one drew on them, having been warned that they would appear out of thin air. Marco rushed to Myrth, calling for him. DJar turned to greet the apprentice with a bow, but he was interrupted by a voice behind him. "What a clever trick!" The voice came from above him and DJar turned to look up at a red-furred Gorath.

"Gorath?" DJar gasped, eyes flaring brightly. "How are you here?" he asked.

It was the Gorath's turn to look at him startled. "You speak my grand dam's language." The Gorath chortled in the Noble Tongue, wide white teeth flashing and his own fiery eyes blazing.

"There are Goraths in the Maelstrom?" DJar asked Myrth, incredulous.

Myrth nodded, greeting Puko with a nod of his head. Puko returned the bow, drawing out Myrth's name to two syllables. Myrth glanced up at the clifftops where more Gorath stood. "Yes, there are a few tribes," he answered DJar, feeling like he was stating the obvious.

"I am Prince Puko of the Kairra," Puko introduced. "I haven't heard the Noble Tongue since my grand dam died several long years ago."

"How are you here?" DJar asked again, looking from Myrth to Puko.

Myrth answered, "The Goraths have always lived in the Misty Realm just shy of the Great Southern Wilds."

"Well, perhaps not always," Puko admitted. "My grand dam and grand sire moved south through the Great Southern Wilds as young calves."

"And you were born here? How can you..." DJar started, then he trailed off, noticing for the first time the bone charm that Puko wore. "Ah," he said, pointing to the charm, "I see. A Molbdyn Bone Charm." He paused and Puko fingered his charm necklace. "That explains much."

"I gather that Puko is able to control his power with it," Myrth said. "You did not have it the last time we met," he added, studying Puko.

"For the sake of all, I chain myself," Puko admitted, dropping the charm to his wide chest.

"Your power is uncontrolled?" DJar asked. Puko nodded. With a frown, DJar stepped away, closing his eyes. He was gone for almost a full minute before returning. "Little Brother, there is something wrong. I cannot sense the Gorath in the Nether."

Myrth contemplated him, "What does that mean?" he asked.

"I don't know," DJar said.

Frowning in confusion, Myrth stepped into the Mage Realm. He could see the Gorath as he'd always been able to see him. He returned to the Physical Realm and studied the Nura.

DJar returned the frown and shrugged. He turned back to Puko, "May I see your power?"

"We have better things to do," Myrth muttered, glaring at the Nura. He turned to Marco, who'd been standing wordlessly beside him, waiting for the three to speak in a language he understood. "Fetch D'Mique," Myrth instructed, and Marco nodded before turning back the way he'd come.

Puko removed his bone charm, dropping it at the Nura's feet. The Gorath's fur sparked and began to sizzle. Fire grew and spread across his arms and legs before covering his torso, chest and finally, his head. As a flaming beast, he smiled. The daemon-fire of his eyes was lost in the conflagration that raged across his skin, the flames driving back the settling night within the Vale. He did not burn out and the power of his Fire felt heavy on the forcelines around them. Puko danced in a slow circle so that DJar could see his entire body engulfed in flame. Then he stooped and retrieved the bone charm, replacing it. Where the charm touched him, the Fire died away and he was soon his normal self. He bowed, as if catching fire and extinguishing his flames had been a grand show on a stage.

As he finished his spin, Marco returned with Temeres and D'Mique in tow.

"It is a shame he cannot control his Fire," Myrth said half to himself but in the Noble Tongue. "Puko is a valuable ally, but one we cannot afford to allow south of the Quartz Mountains."

"No," DJar said. "He controls his Fire. It's his Chaos that is uncontrolled."

Myrth studied the Nura for a long minute while DJar frowned at the Gorath, a frown deepening across his face. "Chaos?" he asked at last.

"What do you mean?" Puko asked.

A light suddenly dawned on DJar, "You are Maelstrom-born," DJar motioned to all around him, "You do not know of Chaos or Stasis." He continued, "The Nura are creatures of Stasis. The Goraths are creatures of Chaos. Just as the moblings are creatures of Shadow. You...You *can* see Shadow?" he asked for confirmation, frowning suddenly. Myrth and Puko nodded.

They stared at one another for a long minute, DJar's daemon-fire eyes aglow. The Nura turned to Puko, "You should come with me. You should go to the Bone Cities, to the Chaos Masters who rule there. They can teach you to control the Chaos and free you from the charm prison."

"I can't leave my tribe here without my protection," Puko said. "The black daemons are intent on breaching the Vale."

"When the retainer leaves," DJar motioned to D'Mique, "The moblings will follow her." All three of them studied the lady warrior who waited nearby.

D'Mique glared at the tree daemon, unsure why he'd pointed at her. "D'Mique," Myrth started. He sighed. "You are going north with DJar. According to DJar's *Aliith*, the Nura who sent the black daemon horde after you botched the incantation." Myrth stopped and interjected something to the tree daemon in its language. He then translated as DJar explained again. "The spell wasn't closed properly. As it is worded the black daemons are to secure you and T'Pani and bring you to his second—the one who spoke the spell. Even though you were brought once before, you have to remain with him until T'Pani is also brought before the spell will resolve."

"They don't have T'Pani?" D'Mique breathed, hearing this for the first time. Myrth stopped, snapping his beak shut, and he shook his head. D'Mique closed her eyes and held up a hand for a moment, requesting silence. She bent forward, seeming ill and stayed that way for some time. "Why can't the second come here, then?" she asked without looking up. She straightened, her green eyes sharp and nearly aglow themselves. "I don't think going north with it is a good idea, Myrth," she said, jabbing a finger at DJar. "They double-crossed Trillip and Tekalo, took them prisoner, and then sent the black daemons for T'Pani as well. They can't be trusted."

"The second was in control then and is in charge now," Myrth explained. "He won't follow DJar's commands and the company won't return to DJar's control until he is back with them. DJar is honorable." D'Mique raised her eyebrows at that. "He remains our prisoner and is only allowed to work magic in service to the goal of taking you north and keeping you with his second until T'Pani is found."

She scoffed. "And how does that work?" she asked.

"When you reach the company, the black daemons will only hunt T'Pani. We'll be able to find her by following them."

"That's your plan?" she asked.

"That's the plan," Myrth muttered, frowning.

She closed her eyes in thought, trying to see how this all fit together. She felt there were parts missing. *"Did I miss so much sailing home?"* Opening her eyes, she studied DJar. *"What twists and turns brought us here?"*

After a moment, she sighed. "I am a soldier in your army, Master Myrth, and your retainer. Against my better judgment, I will go. But," she glared at the Earth Master and her eyes seemed alight with their own green fire, "I am not going alone with it," she said, pointing at DJar once more for emphasis.

Puko chuckled. DJar waited for a translation from Myrth, then frowned at her.

"No," Myrth said, "you shouldn't go with just him." D'Mique returned the tree daemon's frown. Myrth looked around, eyes lingering on Marco as he contemplated Oracle's vision.

"I will go, Master Myrth," Puko said. "I am intrigued by this stranger's offer. If it is true that the Vale will no longer be harassed once the Lady Warrior leaves, I am free to follow."

"Should I go, Myrth?" Marco asked. "He's honorable," Marco added, gesturing toward DJar. "I remember Oracle's vision too. The deal is that they will let Tekalo go when D'Mique gets there, correct?" He waited for Myrth translate and then nod before finishing, "I'll return with Tekalo."

"And leave me there with these two?" D'Mique asked, flabbergasted, motioning to the two daemon-kin.

"I will go with her," Temeres said, stepping forward. "I, too, was in Oracle's vision. Even when Marco returns, you will not be alone," he added.

Puko held up a hand, "Master Myrth, I will look after your retainer as if she were my own." He smiled and D'Mique's skin crawled.

The Earth Master sighed. At the back of his mind, he remembered Oracle's vision. He spoke to DJar, who frowned, then translated for the others, "DJar, take Temeres, D'Mique, and Marco with you. Send Marco and Tekalo back. Free Trillip. Orska and D'Mique will wait for T'Pani and the spell to resolve. Temeres will wait with them." DJar bowed his head. "Afterward," Myrth added in the Noble Tongue, "you and Puko may do as you please. You will be free of my bond when D'Mique and T'Pani are both returned to Olimidia."

"I will comply." He bowed deeply. "I go at the *Tepok-Myir*'s behest and will return to serve my remaining bonds." Myrth's pearl gray eyes hardened before he bowed as well, ending the discussion.

"Collect your things," Myrth said to Marco and D'Mique. He pulled Marco aside, thinking only to him, "*Once you are within the Great Southern Wilds, I do not know if you will be able to contact me. Please try.*" Marco pressed his lips together, then nodded slightly and hurried to find his pack.

Walking the Sands

P acks ready, the group gathered in the middle of the Vale. DJar and Puko were talking, animated as they pointed to the humans. Myrth stood between them and his retainers, frowning and interjecting from time to time. "We are ready," he said as DJar's words died away. He turned to the humans. "DJar is not very strong in Stasis, the magic that allows him to shield others as they Walk the Sands. He will need to stop and rest often while shielding the four of you. When you are Walking the Sands, the black daemons will lose sense of D'Mique and turn toward T'Pani. When DJar rests, the black daemons will be drawn toward D'Mique. Before you reach the Southern Wilds, you will have quite some time to rest without worrying about them." He waited for Marco and Temeres to acknowledge their understanding. "When you reach the Vast Southern Wilds, you will have to defend him and D'Mique from the daemons while he rests. Once you reach his second, you will not have to worry about guarding D'Mique."

"I have already said, Master Myrth," Puko added, "I will protect your retainer as if she were my own. You need not fear."

"Good," Myrth said. He looked at Marco and Temeres.

"I understand the risks," Temeres said, and Marco nodded.

Puko turned to Rayn and Savli. He took a sword, scabbard and all, from Rayn, and saluted his squire with it. Then he rose from his haunches, strapped the sword around his waist, bounced a few times on his hooves and roared. His eyes flared. DJar bowed to Myrth again before drawing his stiletto and Rending the air in a half-circle large enough for Puko to duck through. He stepped away and threw his barrier over the four charges, then opened his eyes and walked through the Rend into the Sands.

D'Mique watched the visible white barrier spell fall across her shoulders. It looked made of smoke and she reached up to brush at it. Marco grabbed her arm, "No, don't. It looks delicate," he said. Her cheeks flushed and she turned to follow the Gorath and Temeres into the glowing hole in reality the tree daemon had made. Once she and Marco were in, the tear disappeared. She looked around.

They stood in the center of the Black Vale cliffs, the obsidian rocks replaced by Shadow-laced blocks. Before her, down the path to the underground altar, a red glow drew her attention. "Do not stare too long at the altar of Chaos," Puko translated for DJar. All around them, the Vale was empty. No Goraths, humans, or elves could be seen or felt.

"Are we still in the Vale?" she asked.

"Where are we?" Marco asked at the same time. "This looks sort of like the Mage Realm but our physical bodies are here." Puko asked the two questions of DJar and translated for the humans.

"We are still in the Vale, *Aliith-el*," he said. "Although, it is more appropriate to call it a Nether Formation, built to harness Stasis and Hold any travelers who Walk the Sands." He nodded to Marco, "This is the Realm of Sands. It is the truth beyond the Dream that we believe to be reality." Puko and Marco both looked at him, frowning. DJar returned their frown but said no more. After a moment, the Nura turned and motioned for them to follow him to the gateway out of the Vale. At the gaping maw between the cliffs, visible through the sand, pools of Shadow marked the black daemons as they hovered near the Formation's walls. "I am not taxed within the Formations. I want to wait here and see if the moblings begin to move on when they cannot sense the *Aliith-el*," he explained, nodding as Puko translated.

For a moment, DJar stood watching the black daemons Then he sat, just within the blocks of the Formation. Realizing that the Nura wasn't going to rise any time soon, the others soon joined him. Sitting at the gate, watching the blobs of Shadow as they milled about, they waited.

"Can you hear me Myrth?" Marco thought. There was no answer.

Hours passed and the pools of Shadow did appear to be less organized to D'Mique's eye. "The suns weigh heavy," DJar said in Fae. He turned to look at the four behind him where they sat, waiting. The *Aliith-el*'s green eyes bored into him. He remembered the first time he'd ambushed her, nearly killing her beside the fountain in the Fae city. She'd been saved only because he'd misjudged her reflexes. He suspected she knew he was the one who'd missed her that night.

"Are we staying the night here?" Temeres asked and Puko translated. "Should we bed down?"

"If we do, we will prolong our travels. However, the moblings will, perhaps, move on," DJar replied.

"They don't seem to be intently running off toward T'Pani," D'Mique noted angrily.

DJar nodded, "Yes. However, there are too many unknowns to assume that the Fae's plan will *not* work. It is my understanding that they did not always focus on you either, *Aliith-el*."

"It may be," Puko added after translating DJar's words, "That one of the hive mind must sense the Land-Nymph Child before the rest of them know where to find it." He repeated himself to DJar, in the Noble Tongue.

"Just so," DJar agreed. "Bed down. We will wait here for the blue sun to set. There is no day or night in the Sands, only the weight of the suns as found in the Dream."

D'Mique tried to sleep and dozed fitfully. When her eyes were open, she found herself staring up at the swirling purple and gray sands that filled the world beyond the Formation's walls. *"How did I end up here?"* she found herself thinking, *"The kidnapper and murderer is now saving us?"* Suspicion gnawed at her. *"How can Myrth trust him? We can't trust them,"* she concluded. Noticing that Marco was awake, she turned to him. "Do you trust him?" she asked, looking briefly at DJar.

Marco thought a long time, "He stayed in Sea Spray and Olimidia when he didn't have to. He had a bodyguard with him the entire time who could have killed all of us, but he didn't allow her to." Marco shrugged one shoulder and met D'Mique's eyes. "I don't know, maybe you had to have been there. Maybe you had to have seen how he behaved. He may not know this Stasis magic very well, but he's powerful. He didn't have to stay and he still doesn't have to. Yet, here we are and here he is."

D'Mique chewed on his answer. "What is your priority?" she asked him, voice hard.

Marco blinked at her. He didn't answer for a long minute. "Tekalo," he said, "He's my best friend."

"Your safety, Lady Warrior, is my priority," Temeres whispered from where he lay on her other side. "I never trust anyone, if it helps you feel better." She could hear the smile in his voice. D'Mique closed her eyes.

"Aren't you going to ask mine?" Puko drawled.

"Do you have one?" she asked, leaning up to glare at the Gorath who knelt between them and DJar.

"I will see you safely to the second, as Master Myrth has asked," Puko replied.

D'Mique studied him for a long moment. She looked past him to the tree daemon. "How much of our language does he understand?" she asked.

"Some," Marco and Puko said together.

"Enough to know if you translated wrong?" she asked.

Puko chuckled, sending shivers up and down D'Mique's arms. "Yes," he said. "Although, I do like the way you think, Lady."

At his laugh, DJar had turned to look at them, eyes aglow.

"Try to see it from his perspective, D'Mique," Marco whispered, pulling her attention back to him. "He was captured, dragged to Sea Spray by creatures he considered one step above beasts. His sense of honor and duty require him to act a prisoner despite that, until he hears from his master. But his master isn't going to send for him because he's lost in the wilderness and as far as anyone knows, he's dead. He had a bodyguard he sent away and now he's trapped by that same sense of honor and duty, sitting in this alternate plane, outnumbered by the beasts who are holding him prisoner."

D'Mique glared at Marco. "He killed people, he tried more than once to kill me. Remember that."

"Like myself," Puko interjected, "the Nura is daemon-kin. We are, above all, practical. It serves his purpose now to aid you, Lady, even though it once served his purpose to kill you."

"So, I'm safe until his purpose changes?" she asked.

Puko grinned. "Yes."

"From both of you?" she wondered to herself.

"Time to go," DJar called in Fae, rising. He stretched, waiting for them to join him at the gate. "We must exit slowly, to regain our Stasis barriers as we leave. I will be the last one out," Puko translated for them. He left the Formation with a slow, even gait and the others fell in line behind him. Once DJar was outside, the Formation turned off. The blocks became less visible and the sand closed in around them. D'Mique fought against a sudden urge to flee. Instead, she focused on Temeres and Marco, falling in line between them as they followed DJar, and Puko brought up the rear.

As they walked and her eyes adjusted, D'Mique noticed hints of structures in the surrounding sand. Ahead of them, in between the pools of Shadow that marked the black daemons, delicate, jagged branches of white and yellow were growing from the bedrock beneath their feet. DJar was leading them in that direction. When they reached the first of these, D'Mique gasped. *"They're trees,"* she realized. The faint white outlines were made of the same white smokey magic that formed the barrier draped over her shoulders and surrounding her. Glittering light played along the strands of smoke that delineated the plants. DJar waited a moment, resting a hand on the tree. He surveyed the possible paths before them.

Pausing, Marco closed his eyes and was surprised to see that he could step into the Mage Realm. Its familiar muted purples and grays surrounded him. All around, the pools of Shadow marked the black daemons. Drifting upward, he could see that there were no clear paths between where they stood now and the Vast Southern Wilds ahead of them. He opened his eyes and returned to the Sands. "There are no clear paths, DJar," he said. Puko translated but DJar seemed to understand and nodded.

"We can push through them," DJar said. "My concern is that they will sense the *Aliith-el* and trail us, making it difficult for me to rest."

"How far can you travel?" Puko asked in the Noble Tongue.

"With trees, further," DJar said. "But I need to rest soon. Short rests and bursts of travel will be better than long travel and long rests, I think."

"Especially when we pop out in the middle of this horde," Puko added, surveying the pools of Shadow. Puko turned to the humans and relayed in Fae. "Our guide thinks it best if we do short bursts of travel followed by short breaks so that he can often rest instead of resting for a long period of time."

"How far can you go?" D'Mique asked and waited for the translation.

"If I rest for twenty minutes, I can travel twice that length of time. It is short, but it means that we need not tarry for a long time in the Dream. The longer we are in the Dream, the more energy your guardians will have to expend and the more tired they will become."

"Can we rest in another Formation?" Temeres asked as Puko finished talking.

DJar thought a moment before answering, "I do not know of any others. The ancient maps I studied of the peninsula before the Maelstrom did not show any and the texts from the same period only suggested that they may have existed. We found none in all our time criss-crossing the plains between the Peaks and the Wildlands."

"Then let's think a minute about how we rest," Marco said.

"How fast can you make a dome, Marco?" D'Mique asked. "I know Myrth has used them to shield encampments and buy us time. He can build them in a matter of moments."

"I cannot make it from here," Marco said after a brief moment in which he tried to reach the Earth Cloud. "I think, like Myrth, a matter of moments."

"In the time it takes for them to be startled by our appearance and react?" Temeres asked. Marco studied him, thinking and frowning. He shrugged.

"Would it be nearly completed?" Puko asked. "If I am unleashed before we step through and we startle them with a fireball, you can follow me and build the dome around the tear in reality before the Nura even exits."

Marco nodded. "Let's try it," he said. "Here? Now?" he asked. Puko spoke to DJar, explaining the plan. The tree daemon nodded. He drew the stiletto and waited, poised to Rend the air near Puko. Marco looked around at the Shadows. They were everywhere, dozens of black daemons on all sides. Where the party stood, a pocket of space gave them their best hope of building the dome without trapping a black daemon inside it. Puko took off his charm and passed it to D'Mique as flames began to eat across his flesh. Once he was fully engulfed in flame, he nodded to DJar.

The Nura drew a half-moon tear with the dagger, large enough to let Puko duck through, and opened a doorway into the Physical Realm. The fiery Gorath charged through, gathering Fire from his body as he did so and throwing it outward in an arch around the tear. Marco followed the Gorath, drawing the Earth Cloud to heel as he exited the Sands. His wall was shoulder-high before the black daemons around them started recovering from the sudden firestorm that had erupted in their midst. Before they could bleat in anger or surprise, the wall grew to ten feet and the dome sealed shut. Marco held the wall as D'Mique, Temeres, and DJar stepped through the Rend in space. The dome's interior was lit by the flames that ate Puko's body, orange-yellow light filling the space. Marco checked his forcelines and smoothed them as best he could. Working near Puko, he noticed, it was nearly impossible to smooth the Earth lines while the flames burned.

"Rest, DJar," Temeres ordered. "The black daemons are trying to enter the wall. They can sense the Lady."

"Marco," D'Mique said, "I saw Myrth build one of these before. He could maintain it despite a horde of scalawags trying to get in. Can you do that?"

Marco closed his eyes and stepped into the Mage Realm. He studied the structure of the wall and watched the black daemons worrying it. He returned and nodded. "Yes, I think I can. They are gouging it with swords and axes but none of them have strong blades that will quickly cut through the stone. I will rebuild it as needed to keep it strong."

"Every moment is borrowed," Puko said to DJar in the Noble Tongue. "Rest while the Earth Mage keeps the dome."

With a nod, DJar sank to the ground and retreated into his now-familiar meditation.

Puko held out a large, flaming hand to D'Mique. It took her a moment to realize he was waiting for his bone charm. She returned it, dropping it gingerly into the flames. When it touched him, the flames died. He draped it across his shoulders and did the clasp. By the time he'd settled it in place, his flames were gone. He smiled wide at D'Mique, then sat back on his haunches. He closed his eyes. With his eyes closed and his flames snuffed out, the dome plunged into darkness. D'Mique frowned. She could sense Marco and Temeres next to her but she couldn't see them.

With a sigh, she sat down and closed her eyes. Beyond the stone wall of the dome, D'Mique could hear the bleating and screams of the black daemons. Scrabbling and scratching along the wall traveled back and forth around and around, high and low, as the daemons searched for weak points in the barrier.

Twenty minutes passed too quickly and DJar stirred. "How is our mage?" he asked Puko, glancing at Marco. His daemon-fire eyes cast weak light around the dome. Puko translated for Marco.

Marco fell out of the Mage Realm when he heard his name. His brown eyes focused on the dim form of the Gorath before sighing. "I can hold the wall longer. Although, it will be nice to rest."

DJar nodded, standing. He took his dagger and Rent the air. The others stood and he draped a Stasis barrier over all before leading them into the Sands. Marco was the last to leave the dome and he stepped through the Rend, letting the wall fall down as the rift closed behind him. Howls of frustration chased him through the hole in reality, their echoes lost to the swirling sand.

DJar set a brisk pace, spending the rest of the hour marching north through the blobs of Shadow. He stopped at the top of a ridge and they looked down into a shallow bowl-shaped valley. DJar leaned against a shaggy tree at the edge of the ridge. He closed his eyes for a moment. D'Mique and Temeres stood beside him, Marco and Puko on D'Mique's left, Temeres between her and DJar. Halfway down the slope, the Shadow blobs parted and there was a large enough clearing that Marco could form a wall.

"Do you know how to work Earth?" Marco asked Puko. With a soft laugh, Puko shook his head no. "Do you?" Marco asked DJar.

"Work?"

"Earth," Marco repeated. Puko translated for the Nura. D'Mique and Temeres eyed the three of them in turn.

DJar shook his head. "No," he said. "I cannot. I do not know of this Earth magic."

Puko cocked his head and looked at Marco. "Our brother," Puko indicated DJar, "has powers we do not know of and it seems we have powers he does not know of." Marco thought for a second and then nodded.

"I am ready to hold a wall once again," Marco said, changing the subject. DJar and Puko nodded. "When we get to that clear spot," Marco finished. He started down the easy slope, DJar following close behind. Puko, Temeres and D'Mique brought up the rear.

At the clearing, Puko removed his charm once again and handed it to D'Mique. She took it gingerly as flames bloomed across his chest and head. Then, as before, he charged through the tear in reality followed closely by Marco and Temeres, Marco building a wall in the seconds between Puko's fiery appearance and the black daemons reacting to being attacked by once invisible forces. Temeres' blade caught one that leapt over the young wall and landed inside.

A flurry of blades clattering sent echoes ringing through the closing dome. D'Mique drew her sword, ready to aid Temeres, but he dealt swiftly with the infiltrator. The golden light that lit its eyes faded as its blood pooled under its fallen black body, spindle legs askew. The dead daemon took up fully half the space within the dome. Puko, still aflame, grumbled at Marco, "Make a hole." Then he touched the black daemon. Flames leapt from Puko to its bristle-hair and the thing was soon alight, filling the space with the stench of roasted flesh and burnt fur.

Puko didn't appear fazed by the stench he'd created but the others found themselves huddled together as far from the burning daemon as they could go, shielding their noses and eyes as best they could. "Why, Puko?" Marco muttered, breathing through his mouth and starting to cough.

"They are a hive mind," Puko said, turning to face the others and seeming surprised to find them all standing against the far wall. "The ones beyond the wall will think twice about attacking, even though they know the Lady is here. The next time we appear, the ones near us will remember that jumping into the wall leads to death and fire." He smiled wide, flames licking out between his flat teeth. Then, he held out a hand to D'Mique, approaching the others. She handed him the bone charm, and soon the dancing firelight that lit the domed chamber came from the daemon's corpse instead of the Gorath.

DJar dropped to the ground where he was and closed his eyes, retreating into meditation and rest. "We are nearly free of the black daemon horde," Marco supplied as he joined D'Mique and Temeres, all three also sitting down against Marco's wall.

D'Mique glanced past Temeres to Marco and then beyond him to DJar. "It's midday, isn't it?" she asked.

"It feels like midday," Temeres said, eyes traveling to the top of the rock dome. The smoke hole Marco had created as Puko lit the black daemon's corpse let sunlight into the haze-filled chamber. "What do you think, Puko? You see the sky more than we do."

Puko looked up at the hole then down at the humans. "Hmm," he thought for a moment. "The Ghost Moon is young," he said, "recently risen. Yes, it's midday."

"Are we going to do this all day and night?" D'Mique asked.

Marco frowned. "I can't do this all day and night."

"You say we are nearly free of the horde?" Temeres asked. Puko nodded with Marco. "How much longer?"

"I think one more time traveling with DJar in the sandy world," Marco guessed.

Puko called to DJar, speaking in the Noble Tongue. DJar stirred, fiery eyes leaping to his traveling companions and then to Puko. "Two," the Nura said to them, holding up his fingers to illustrate the number, "or one long."

"I asked him how many more times we would Walk the Sands before resting for the night," Puko explained. "I would prefer one long, myself."

"Let's rest long enough to press on once more," D'Mique said. The others nodded and Puko informed DJar of their decision. DJar nodded in agreement and returned to his meditation and rest.

The five rested for some time. Beyond the wall, the black daemons had overcome their fear of the creatures within and they milled about, poking at the stone occasionally to test its strength. From the Mage Realm, Marco could see the black Shadow beings tracing the outline of the Earth Cloud that he'd piled high to create the dome. He could hold the Earth easily, he'd discovered, without having to refill gashes or knicks from the black daemons and their blades.

As they sat and waited for DJar to rest, Marco explored his new companions. While DJar remained a wispy smoky shell in the Mage Realm, Puko was strangely present. Fire normally appeared as pinpricks of light within items that generated heat. Flames in the Mage Realm were amassed pinpricks, as if someone had gathered all the pinpricks into a ball or sheet. Puko, in the Mage Realm, looked *made* of flames. Rather than being formed of Fire pinpricks, his body appeared to be a glass vessel filled with writhing flames that swirled and churned like magma.

DJar stirred. "We go," he said, standing. Marco opened his eyes and returned from the Mage Realm. They regained their feet and Marco, D'Mique, and Temeres fell in line, following the two daemon-kin into the Sands as they'd done before. Marco released the Earth Cloud as he stepped through the tear. He watched as the wall fell and the tear closed. Surprised black daemons hesitated to close on the rift in reality, caught unmoving as the tear closed.

An hour later, Marco stepped into the Mage Realm and noted the passing of the horde. DJar stopped. They stood a hundred yards from the last of the black daemons. "We watch, we wait," the Nura said. Puko sat back on his haunches near Temeres and D'Mique.

Marco told them what he was seeing. "The black daemons are just milling about. Not following us. But they also don't seem to be going anywhere else."

DJar sighed and Puko translated for him. "I am tiring but let's press on, out of their line of sight and out of the wind." DJar said, "Then we will stop for the night."

"Out of the wind?" Temeres asked. "Do you mean downwind?" he asked Puko.

Puko considered. "So they cannot smell us," he clarified.

They walked on across the plains for another hour. As they walked, Puko asked Marco, "What wards can you set? Can you set a daemon trap?"

"A daemon trap?" Marco repeated. "I..." he paused, thinking, *"Oh, he means the daemon wards that elves set."* He replied, "no, but I can build a shelter that will keep us safe through the night."

DJar stopped at the top of a rise and looked behind them. He could no longer see the moblings. There were also no trees and he had reached the limits of his strength. He Rent the world without waiting for the others to catch up with him or prepare. Yet, when they saw the tear open, they hurried out into the Dream and he followed them. The Fiery Sisters were touching the horizon, and the Ghost Moon was well on his way across the sky. There were no black daemons here.

They stood at the top of a rise, surrounded by scrappy brush and tufts of grass holding on to life at the edge of a volcanic plain. To their southwest, the peaks of the Quartz Mountains could still be seen, lower than they'd been before. Marco studied them for a moment. He stepped into the Mage Realm and floated upward, looking around. They were not yet north enough to see the Vast Southern Wilds from the Physical Realm, although he could see the looming Shadow that covered them from his vantage point. He opened his eyes again and looked around. They'd left the daemon horde behind. Out of the corner of his eye, he realized that the others were all looking at him, expectantly.

He closed his eyes again and stepped into the Mage Realm. Below him, beneath the Earth Cloud, he found a large, steady Earth Forceline. Tapping into it, he used the power to build a large dome. With it completed, he tied the structure to the Forceline below them. Then he opened his eyes. Concealed, the others visibly relaxed and DJar wilted to the ground. Puko looked on while Marco hurried to him. "DJar," he said, reaching out to the Nura. DJar's eyes flared and he looked up at Marco, his face pained. "Are you...?" DJar pulled away from him with a hiss. Marco pulled back, raising his hands.

They sat that way until Temeres interrupted, "I have an oil lamp, if you could light a fire, Chosen One." Marco stood and turned away from the Nura, crossing the space to Temeres and D'Mique.

"What are you doing?" D'Mique hissed at him as he cupped his hands around the wick of the oil lamp and lit it by pulling warmth from his body.

"I thought he was hurt," Marco said, rubbing his hands together to regain warmth.

"And if he was?"

"We need him, D'Mique," Marco said. She grimaced but pursed her lips instead of replying.

"He tried to kill me, more than once," she whispered, turning away from them. Avoiding the others left her staring at Temeres. The thin-faced Vale Warrior's pale blue eyes met hers and he blinked slowly, studying her. She had the sudden impression that he was memorizing her mannerisms, her gestures, and the moods that accompanied them.

"We can all sleep tonight," Marco said. "The wall will hold."

"Did you set a ward?" Puko asked.

"No, I can't set a Shadow ward. That's an elf's skill."

Puko called to DJar and asked him something, presumably if he could set wards.

DJar nodded and stepped away. Marco felt him gather his power but didn't notice any working. Then DJar returned and spoke briefly to Puko.

"He set a ward, though not a Shadow one either. He set," Puko interrupted himself to clarify what DJar had said before continuing. "He set a sunlight ward..." Puko shrugged.

Marco stepped into the Mage Realm and studied the rise. His wall, made of Earth, remained strongly tied to the Forceline beneath them. As he studied the Mage Realm, he noticed that the Earth current was slightly discolored, but there was no hint of the Nura's working. He returned. "I don't see anything," he admitted, "Except the Earth's discolored."

"That discoloration was what we were using to track them," D'Mique informed him. "I think Tekalo said it had something to do with how they worked magic."

Marco sat in thought, studying DJar. "If Teek didn't know, I'm not going to figure it out," he muttered to himself. D'Mique shrugged. With a half-chuckle, Marco laid down and turned away from them, back to the oil lamp's light, facing the wall. Puko curled up as well, still on his haunches but his chin resting on his chest. D'Mique realized it'd be impossible for him to lie on his side with his horns on the sides of his head. His blazing eyes opened once to greet her and he smiled when she looked away. Reluctantly, D'Mique lay down near the lamp, back to the wall. It took her a long time to fall asleep.

The next morning, DJar shook them awake, startling D'Mique. He bowed his head to her. "Time to go," he said. She nodded and waited for him to move on to wake Marco. Temeres was stretching, working knots out of his shoulders. She watched as he dropped to the ground and started doing push-ups. Puko stirred near her as she stood and stretched herself. Marco was the last to wake. He stood and stretched. There was little to clean up and they were ready to move on soon after waking.

Before leaving, Marco released the dome from the Earth current and smoothed the surrounding forcelines as much as possible. Puko, even though he hadn't worked any magic for some time, still managed to cause waves and eddies in the surrounding magic. "Are there many Gorath mages?" he asked the large daemon-kin as they prepared to leave.

"There are some Air and Earth among the tribes. I am the only Flame." He paused a moment, contemplating Marco. "When I was young, my grand dam told tales of Pale Ones who held magic in their bones but it is few and far between."

Marco nodded in response. "Do you affect the other Gorath mages as you do the Fire Master?" he asked.

"Only the Flame Mages," Puko said with a smile and a wink. Marco blinked at the Gorath as Puko turned and followed DJar through the tear in reality. Temeres and D'Mique fell in line behind the Gorath. Marco stepped into the Mage Realm for a moment. The black daemons were far behind them, but the Shadow pools that showed the daemons' positions were heading their way. Marco hurried through the Rend and DJar closed it.

Their trek across the Blasted Plains continued. The volcano, Mount Myrs, grew closer and the Quartz Mountains further away. After four days, the Shadow pools marking the black daemons started creeping south from the Vast Wildlands that lay before them. When Marco mentioned it, Puko explained that they were homing in on D'Mique. For five days, the daemons did not harass them. In the middle of the fifth, however, they reached the northern front of the horde that was hunting the Lady Warrior.

They were in the Sands, staring uphill at the Shadowy pools that could be seen through the purple-gray swirling sand ahead of them. Beyond the horde's border, large trees beckoned to them. DJar longed for the respite the glowing structures afforded him.

He turned to Puko, "We are nearly to the Southern Star Formation, our destination," he said. "We must Walk through the moblings now. One more rest here," he added, readying his stiletto.

Puko nodded and handed his bone charm to D'Mique as he translated DJar's words. Marco signaled he was ready and joined Puko as the Gorath charged through the tear that DJar created. Black daemons broke into a run when they saw the Gorath appear. Bleating and screaming, they tried to close the distance before Marco's wall formed. Yet again, the stones grew together at Marco's call and the daemons crashed impotently against the barrier. Blades and hooves scrabbled across the dark surface as they tried to dig through. Marco stood still, eyes closed, using the Earth Cloud to fill the holes as quickly as they formed. After the initial charge, Shadow pooled around the structure. The black daemons continued worrying the stone.

"Myrth?" Marco thought. He waited for the Avian Semian to return the thought.

"Marco," Myrth breathed through his mind. The Earth Master's relief danced through Marco's head, and he smiled in the dark. *"Where are you?"*

"We are at the edge of the Southern Wilds. DJar says we are two days from where they are holding Tekalo."

"Make careful note of where it is," he urged.

"I will," Marco promised.

As Marco stood guard, rebuilding the wall as the daemons' iron blades and blade-hooves dug into it, the others slept. DJar was the first to stir with the rising of the Fiery Sisters. His eyes flared in the dark, landing on Marco. "The moblings," DJar began, "are busy?"

"No," Marco shook his head. They'd stopped trying to dig into the wall once the Ghost Moon had set near midnight. "I think they're sleeping."

"Have you slept?" DJar asked. Marco shook his head no.

"I've dozed. I can travel today and tomorrow." Marco paused, hoping that DJar's silence meant he understood. "We won't need to protect the Formation?" he asked.

"No," DJar said. "No more moblings when we join Ordvyn."

"Ordvyn is your—"

"My second," DJar finished with a nod.

Their conversation woke the others and when Puko joined them, DJar switched to speaking in his language with the Gorath. Puko nodded and translated for the others. "We are two days from the Formation. Once there, the Lady will be with Ordvyn and her part of the spell will resolve."

D'Mique interrupted, "Why didn't he just keep me with him before? He left me for dead." Puko asked her question.

DJar frowned before answering, "He didn't realize he'd botched the spell." Puko paused, "I'd like to add, Lady, even if he knew, why would he care?"

D"Mique glared at him. "Why do you care?" she asked, motioning to DJar. Puko translated.

"I don't," DJar said. "I am honor-bound to aid *Tepok* Myrth and the *Tepok-Myir*. They care." Puko chuckled as he translated. D'Mique's glower deepened and the Gorath's smile broadened.

"Will we have to fight your company?" Temeres asked, interrupting.

"No," DJar said. "I will deal with Ordvyn as honor demands. The others will fall in line once I return."

"Shi'Shou is already there," Marco noted. "Do they all know you're coming?"

"Yes," DJar said, "even Ordvyn," he added when Marco tried to continue. Silence stretched out between them all. "We go," DJar ordered and he Rent the air, stepping into the Sands. He waited just inside the gateway to cast his Stasis barrier over the others as they joined him, D'Mique and Temeres, then Puko, and Marco last. Marco undid the Earth Cloud and let the wall return to soil as he disappeared into the rift.

Here in the Sands, they had to push through pools of Shadow. There was no skirting around the edges or avoiding large groups of black daemons. Each time they did so, Marco felt the daemons turn to look at them, as if the black daemons could sense their passage. They'd only traveled for twenty minutes before he realized that the pools of Shadow trailed after them, following D'Mique.

"They're following us," Marco said. His words caught Temeres' attention and the Vale Warrior drew his sword. Neither he nor D'Mique could see the Shadow magic. For them, the Sands remained gray and purple swirls beyond their Stasis barrier.

Puko chuckled. "They can't reach us, even if they can sense us," the Gorath said, urging Temeres to put away his sword. D'Mique felt eyes upon her, as the daemons followed her, matching her steps as she trudged through the Sands. She slowed. "Keep up the pace, Lady," Puko whispered to her, his clopping footsteps moving slowly beside her as she passed through the Shadow magic. "We still have to make the trek, best not to dally." D'Mique glanced up at Puko who looked down at her over her shoulder. His expression, daemon fire eyes burning bright in the half-light, was indecipherable. She hurried to keep up with Marco and DJar, Puko simply lengthening his strides without quickening his pace to keep up with them.

An hour on, they reached the first of the large trees that formed the Great Southern Wilds. DJar stopped, resting a hand on the tree, drawing strength from it. D'Mique joined the group close to the tree daemon as Puko hunkered down a few strides away. DJar took deep, cleansing breaths, eyes closed. His demeanor touched off a memory. "You take strength from the trees?" she asked. DJar's eyes opened and he looked at her. He threw a glance at Puko who translated her question. DJar nodded in reply. "Like an elf," D'Mique said, turning to Marco and Temeres. "I've seen Sylus do that. Elves can replenish their magic by taking strength from plants."

"So he *is* a tree daemon?" Marco asked. Temeres and D'Mique laughed under their breath.

DJar spoke then and Puko interrupted them. "We need to go," the Gorath said. "DJar can only Walk a bit further before he rests. We will need to leave the Sands." Marco felt his own shoulders slump and he nodded. They followed as DJar pushed himself away from the tree, leaving it reluctantly.

He moved from tree to tree as they went and another half hour passed. He'd now traveled in the Sands over twice as long as his normal stint. "We leave now," DJar said, squeezing his eyes shut.

Marco stepped into the Mage Realm and looked around, Shadow lay all around. "We are going to exit in the middle of them," he warned.

Puko nodded and removed his bone charm, dropping it into D'Mique's outstretched hand. "I will send out a wall of fire, they will light instantly."

"Fire will confuse the others," Temeres added, drawing his sword. "I will watch your flank, Prince," he said.

"I'll build the wall as I have before," Marco said.

"Make the wall between us and the flames," Temeres added derisively, casting a leery eye at Puko. Marco scoffed. Puko paused in his bounding and glared at them, looking sidewise through the curve of his flaming horn.

Puko signaled to DJar and D'Mique drew her sword as the tree daemon sliced the air in front of the Gorath. Puko leapt from the Sands and charged into the midst of a throng of black daemons. Where he touched them, they burst into flame, the magic Fire that ate at Puko leaping to the black bodies, hungrily eating away at the Life energy, consuming them. Black daemons screamed and gibbered. Puko's second attack was a wall of flame that arched from his out-flung hand starting at his right and forming a semi-circle before them. Temeres followed the Gorath, rushing to defend him from a pair of black daemons to his left. D'Mique followed Marco from the tear, sword ready. A third black daemon joined the attack on Temeres. Blades and hooves flashed through the firelight and Temeres blocked two swift attacks. A third caught his thigh before the Vale Warrior could parry.

D'Mique ran to join him, sword raised to greet the black daemon. Behind her, DJar shouted. Marco's wall grew slowly around them this time as he tried to keep the black daemons out and the burning ones away. The wall lifted from the soil just behind D'Mique as she reached the black daemon and blocked its next blow. Two more swords swung into view and she ducked and dodged out of their way. Bladed legs pawed at her, trying to gore her. Somewhere at the back of her mind she remembered daydreaming about single-handedly taking out entire hordes of the creatures. That was before she'd actually fought one. Now, she realized that each black daemon was the equivalent of a seated rider on a trained warhorse. She strained to stop the sword blades that quested for her and dodged the flailing legs as best she could. Temeres, beside her, forced the attack, taking advantage of the defense she'd added.

"The wall!" DJar shouted behind them. Out of the corner of her eye, D'Mique could see that Marco's undulating wall had reached thigh-height. Much taller, and it'd be difficult to climb back over. DJar had exited the tear in reality and dropped the barrier spell around them. He closed his eyes and D'Mique realized he was working with magic a second before a great gust of wind ripped between her and Temeres and bowled over the three black daemons they'd been holding off.

"Go!" Temeres shouted and he and D'Mique broke away, turning and running to the wall. Fire flashed by behind them, alighting the daemons that were still trying to pick themselves up off the ground. D'Mique followed Temeres over the wall, diving head-first without thought as to how they would land on the other side. Prone, D'Mique watched the wall grow quickly and finish in a protective dome. There were no daemons within, and all were accounted for. Marco tied the wall to a lazy Earth current he found far below them.

He closed his eyes and watched the black daemons swarming the wall. They'd learned to be cautious, he decided, and were hesitant to do much more than surround it.

"That was foolish," DJar grumbled at D'Mique.

She blinked at him a moment, then scoffed. "I thought you didn't care."

"I don't," he said with a glare. "I am honor-bound to complete my mission."

D'Mique stood and checked her sword, deciding to ignore the tree daemon. Black daemon blood coated the blade, proving that she'd done some good. She grabbed some dirt and used it to scrub the blood off the blade so it wouldn't etch the metal. Temeres did the same, working carefully until his blades were clean. He had two large cuts, one on his shoulder and another on his thigh. He bound the wounds with linen bandages from his pack. With a frown, D'Mique realized she had no such thing in her pack. Traveling with an elfin healer had spoiled her.

Puko approached. "Where did you drop my charm?" he asked. For a moment, D'Mique's heart fluttered into her throat and she looked back toward where the gateway had been. DJar sat, seemingly in meditation nearby, but he held out the bone charm. "Ah," Puko bowed and crossed to the tree daemon to collect it. DJar spared a long look for D'Mique but said no more. She looked away.

"I appreciated the assist, Lady," Temeres said with a wink as he caught her eye. She sighed and nodded a thanks before dropping to the ground again, this time to rest.

As they rested, the black daemons continued to circle them, occasionally testing the wall. Marco dozed, confident the wall would hold while DJar meditated and slept.

Temeres woke D'Mique, nudging her hard enough to startle her. "Time passes," he said. The chamber was lit by the feeble lamp beside him.

"It's night," D'Mique said, feeling as if darkness lay all around them, beyond the stone wall. Temeres nodded but said no more.

"We should Walk the Sands once more, then rest before reaching the Formation," Puko translated for DJar.

Marco stood, stretching and yawning, "We can do that. How long should we walk?"

DJar frowned and stepped away. When he returned he said, "We are half a day from the Southern Star Formation. Let's walk another hour now."

"Are you well enough?" Marco asked, eyeing the Nura.

DJar studied him then nodded. "I could ask the same of you. When we reach the Formation, we will be able to rest while the others find the child. I will send my *Aliith* to talk to Myrth."

"One more hour, one more night," D'Mique summarized. Temeres and Puko nodded. "Let's go," she said. She looked expectantly at DJar and he obliged by Rending the air near him and stepping through into the Sands. As the others joined him, he passed the Stasis barrier to them. Marco released the wall before the rift closed behind him. As the wall fell, he watched the pools of Shadow close in on D'Mique. As before, they could sense her, even though they couldn't see her.

D'Mique waited for DJar to start north and then fell in step behind him. He led them from one copse of trees to the next. As they moved, Shadow pools followed them. After several minutes, DJar motioned for Puko and Marco to join him. "Do you see?" he asked, pointing ahead of them. Everyone looked to where he pointed. D'Mique saw only the swirling purple and gray sand that danced beyond the Stasis barrier spell that lay about them all. Beside her, Marco frowned and nodded.

"There's a clearing ahead, no black daemons there," he supplied for Temeres and D'Mique. "It's still quite a long way ahead," he noted to DJar.

"We should try to outpace the black daemons," Puko noted. "That will allow us to make camp without fighting them for space." He smiled, eyes smoldering. DJar nodded and started off again, his pace quickening. Still leading them from copse to copse through the Great Southern Wilds, DJar hurried north.

D'Mique was starting to breathe hard when he finally stopped and nodded to Marco and Puko. With a flash of steel, he Rent the world and they poured out into the darkness of the Vast Wildlands. D'Mique had only a brief glimpse of trees before Marco's wall grew around them. Her heart fluttered. The mighty pines that she'd last seen over a season ago, as she lay half-dead beneath them, brought back memories of chasing daemons and being chased by the black daemons. She sat down hard as Marco and Temeres lit his lantern, and had to fight back a sudden wave of anguish. *"Saisin, Gera, Burl!"* Marco and Temeres dropped next to her.

"Lady?" Temeres asked.

"The rest of them," she whispered. "They didn't make it, did they?" Confusion met her words. "Burl," she said.

Understanding dawned on Marco, "You're the only one we've heard from. But that doesn't mean they didn't make it. Only that you were the first to report back."

Puko translated for DJar when the Nura asked about their conversation. DJar studied D'Mique for a moment. "We can ask my second if he saw any more of them, *Aliith-el,*" the tree daemon offered, his voice oddly soft, his gaze weighty.

She nodded after Puko's translation, but all of their words did nothing to erase the certainty she felt in her heart. *"The others are gone."*

The company spread out to rest in their dome. They had one more day's journey before they reached the Formation and the black daemons would stop following D'Mique. DJar sat down near D'Mique and sighed, closing his eyes. She studied him from where she lay. He'd never voluntarily sat near her before. His gray uniform wore well on the road and seemed as fresh as the day he'd donned it. The last time she'd been this close to him, he'd been bald. Now, his hair was growing back, forming a black shadow across his once-bald pate. Patches of skin, she noticed for the first time, were covered in scales that caught the lamplight and reflected it back toward her, leaving the impression that golden glitter could be found on the tree daemon's arms and chest. All the tree daemons had seemed similar to her...except...DJar nagged at her and left her with a strange unease in her stomach. "Do you speak my language?" she asked.

"Some," he answered without opening his eyes.

"You tried to kill me," she said.

DJar opened his eyes and chuckled, the flames dancing with his mirth, "You dodge well, *Aliith-el.*" He smiled at her and she realized it held no animosity. "I misjudged you that night by the fountain." He stopped smiling, "Even before with the moblings," he pointed to Temeres, "two wounds. You? No wounds."

"You killed my friend," she said.

DJar's merriment switched off. "I did not," he said, "I led, I am not a Fae hunter." She glared and he held up a hand. Motioning to Puko for translation before he continued. "I take responsibility for the actions of all in the company. I am responsible for the actions of the Fae hunter and will bear that burden. But I, *Shuwarr* DJar, did not kill your friend."

Puko added, "If he missed you, human, he can't be good enough with a blade to hunt Fae."

Temeres' chuckle added to their conversation. DJar looked between them and smiled. With a shrug, he closed his eyes again.

"Will you tell me who killed my friend?" D'Mique asked him.

"Of my company, there were three Fae hunters. I will say no more."

"And if I guess which one, when we get there tomorrow?"

"No," Djar said with a glare. "That is not a game to play. I will say no more."

She watched him settle in for the night and noticed for the first time that he held his hands in his lap, fingers entwined. As his meditation deepened, so did his breath, and the tree daemon was soon asleep.

D'Mique watched him sleep. "*He didn't kill any Land-Nymphs, but will accept that burden,*" she thought. "*So we'll never know who actually killed anyone,*" she decided. Frowning, she closed her eyes and tried to sleep.

"*Aliith-el,*" DJar said. D'Mique startled awake. For a moment, looking up into the fiery daemon-eyes gave her vertigo. The daemon studied her as she sat up. "I spoke to my *Aliith* and she asked my second. He did not see any of the bodies of your comrades before setting the horde on you." D'Mique sighed and nodded, trying to hold in the sob she felt building in her throat. DJar studied her. "*You* commanded?"

His question threw her for a moment and she started to deny it. "*I didn't command us, Tekalo did.*" She paused, *"Didn't he?"* She shook her head, thinking about how the others had looked to her for direction throughout the hunt for T'Pani and the tree daemons. "It was a group, we all worked together. There wasn't a commander."

DJar pursed his lips and sighed. Then he stood in one smooth motion. "We go now." His movement brought the others out of their dozes and they quickly packed, ready for the final push.

They walked silently through the Sands, making their way from tree to tree. The pools of Shadow had closed on D'Mique and continued to track her. However, they had not yet formed into a new horde. Nor had the original horde reached them. Stopping near a large glowing tree, Marco and DJar pondered the black daemons' behavior. "Perhaps they know she's near your second," Marco posited.

DJar shrugged his shoulders. "We will rest once more before the Formation." he said. They surveyed the surrounding Shadow pools.

"It looks like we will be able to find space for a rest if we keep to the right," Marco said, indicating a clearer swath of forest to the northeast. DJar acknowledged with a nod and they started in that direction.

Reaching a clearing, DJar sliced open a gateway and Puko strode out, bone charm still in place. There were, according to Marco, black daemons moving closer, but he had sufficient time to exit the Sands and build a wall without Puko's surprise attack. Marco grabbed the Earth Cloud and threw up the domed wall around them, completing it before Temeres, D'Mique, and DJar exited. Temeres' lantern's light danced along the stone walls as he and D'Mique sat down beside it to rest. Not for the first time, Marco considered how dark the dome must be for someone who could not see the Earth Cloud's golden light all around.

"There will be no fight when we reach the Formation?" Puko asked.

DJar frowned and spoke quickly to Puko who translated for the others. "There will be one fight. Ordvyn disobeyed my orders. When he was left in charge, he was bound to follow my original directives. He did not. He must pay with blood for this failure."

"And no one will side with him?" Temeres probed.

DJar shook his head no. "My *Aliith* has assured me that they will not. When she delivered my initial displeasure, none stood by him and they agreed to wait for their proper commander to return."

"Will we be sneaking in?" D'Mique asked.

DJar shook his head once more. "We will simply enter. I must rush Ordvyn to gain the advantage, he is a strong hunter."

"Did *he* kill my friend," D'Mique asked, catching the title DJar had used. The tree daemon paused, growing distant and cold, eyes blazing. He stood silent for a long, uncomfortable minute, but did not answer her question.

"If we sliced our way into the Formation, that would give you a greater advantage over your second," Puko noted, translating.

DJar turned his attention to the Gorath. He tilted his head in thought and closed his eyes. "It has merit," he said in the Noble Tongue after thinking for a moment.

"But we cannot walk to the Formation in the physical plane," Temeres noted. "Too many black daemons, right?" Marco confirmed his suspicion with a nod.

"We will Walk the Sands until we can see the Formation," DJar said. "Then exit and rush to the center, where we will reenter the Sands."

"And the poison air part?" Marco asked. "The barrier you cast when we enter the Sands keeps us from breathing the poisonous air. If we are entering the Sands at a run so that you can ambush your second in command, how will we breathe?" he asked.

DJar shook his head no and motioned for patience while he thought. Then he answered, "You will be entering the Sands inside the Formation. You will not need my barrier because the walls will already hold one." The party lapsed into silence when Puko finished talking as they turned the plan over in their minds. "Rest," DJar said, following his own advice and dropping smoothly to the ground.

D'Mique frowned as she followed his directions. *"If he kills his second, that's one less to worry about,"* she decided.

Marco woke them a short while later. "We need to go, there are black daemons closing in on us." They woke and packed quickly in a now-familiar routine, and DJar soon led them through the Sands, from one copse of trees to the next.

"If he's not a great hunter and he's not as strong magically as others, why is he the leader?" D'Mique whispered, watching the tree daemon, but not expecting an answer.

"You're following him," Puko murmured, dipping low to speak near her ear. He loomed over her shoulder, giant spiral horns invading her peripheral vision. She swallowed and stepped away from the Gorath. He smiled at her reaction. "Leadership isn't about physical or magical strength, Lady," he continued. "It's about charisma. Brother DJar is likable, confident, sure of his step, his plan, and himself. That is what makes him a leader. If one leads well, one need not fight well, for there will always be someone skilled in a deadly art ready to devote their lives to a great leader." D'Mique studied the Gorath's blazing eyes for a moment, his lips pulling back in a wide grin that showed off his flat teeth.

She looked again at the tree daemon and frowned. *If he had deadly, devoted followers, why did they leave him a captive? Why did his second betray him? Maybe he's not really much of a leader after all.* She kept her thoughts to herself and walked faster, trying to distance herself from Puko.

Soon, DJar stopped and he waited for them to gather around. "There," he whispered, pointing. Ahead of them, the trees parted and a large stone fortress grew from the forest floor. It looked almost like Fortress Nightmare, D'Mique realized. "There are no moblings between us and the Formation. We slip into the Dream here, follow me as quickly as you can. I will Rend the air after passing through the barrier and we will leap back into the Sands beyond the wall, there."

"What will we find inside?" Temeres asked. DJar explained and Puko translated quietly.

"It is an empty fortress. There is a walkway along the top of the wall for a look-out. There are ladders to climb up and down in each corner. I think there is a barrack, but I cannot be sure. Some Star Formations have them, whereas some do not.

"You need not fight, but I ask that you do not leap for your imprisoned friends. If you do so, the others may think that it is indeed an ambush and they will defend themselves and the prisoners. After I have dealt with Ordvyn, I will fulfill my promises." The others nodded in understanding and agreement.

"You three go first," Puko said to Temeres and Marco. "If I barrel out right after DJar, there is a greater likelihood for misunderstandings." DJar Rent the air and they stepped from the Sands and into the Physical Realm, nodding in agreement with the Gorath.

Where the fortress had been before, there was a large clearing. Nothing else delineated the presence of the Formation in the Sands. DJar broke into a trot and Marco followed on his heels. D'Mique and Temeres chased after him. All three humans had longer legs than the Nura and easily kept pace with him through the remaining trees and into the clearing. Puko ate the distance between them with great, ground-shaking strides. Despite giving them a head start, he was towering over them as they reached the middle of the clearing. DJar suddenly pivoted, skidding in the leaf litter that covered the ground, as if sensing a presence to his left. He screamed and Rent the air in front of him, diving back into the Sands. Marco, D'Mique, and Temeres leapt through the opening just as Puko rammed through.

DJar had not waited for them. Through the tear in reality, D'Mique stumbled to a halt, running into Marco as Temeres sandwiched her from behind, all three humans nearly toppling over. They'd emerged, as DJar said, in the middle of a fortress. In front of them, a large fire burned. D'Mique gasped as nearly a dozen tree daemons leapt to their feet, grabbing for weapons. Not far from the fire, Tekalo, Trillip and Orska huddled. When the Land-Nymph's saw the humans, they also leapt to their feet, startled cries echoing off the obsidian stone walls. Into this confusion, Puko barreled, having to stop almost instantly to avoid stumbling over the three humans and toppling to the ground.

DJar's momentum drove him to Ordvyn, who was also rising, reaching for his glaive too late to save himself. With another death-dealing shriek, DJar plowed into the other Nura, driving him to the ground. All around them, the companions stopped in mid-reach, realizing they were not, personally, under attack. They backed hastily away, dropping to their knees a safe distance from the two commanders, who were now tussling on the ground just shy of the fire. Two Nura, instead, rushed for the three Land-Nymphs, drawing swords as they moved to secure their prisoners.

"Last words, Ordvyn," DJar hissed in his second's face, fangs bared, hand squeezing his second's throat. Ordvyn struggled against the *Shuwarr*'s grasp, kicking and flailing. "Insubordination is punishable by death," DJar whispered. "I send you now to the Sands, brother."

"Jeriko," Ordvyn gasped, his voice a breathy, struggling whisper. DJar dropped him, as if his second had suddenly burst into flame, a twin of the untrained Gorath. Belly to belly, DJar's eyes flared and then banked low. Ordvyn, gasping and coughing, turned onto his stomach, disengaging from the fight with his *Shuwarr*, and crawling away from the fire, fighting to refill his lungs as DJar knelt, unmoving, behind him. Shock coursed through DJar, numbing his limbs for a long minute.

Then DJar stood slowly, covering his face with his hands, hunching his shoulders as if closing in on himself. He froze for a ten-count. He knew what he had to do. He knew what it would look like. Then, with a despair-filled scream he pulled all his power into a projectile, spun, and threw the Air at Marco. The power hit the human full force and sent him flying across the center courtyard. DJar's sudden attack triggered the other Nura who flew into action.

They swarmed over Trillip and Tekalo as the two Land-Nymphs shouted incoherently and started to rush toward Marco.

Temeres and D'Mique drew their blades as their own shouts answered the echoing screams around them. Temeres started toward DJar while D'Mique moved to check on Marco. A sudden crunching blow from Puko felled the Vale Warrior before he'd taken two steps. Shi'Shou, spear in hand, met D'Mique before she'd taken a second step. The blade at the end of her polearm looked deadly pointing directly at D'Mique's chest. D'Mique froze. Another step would have impaled her on the weapon. The sound of Temeres hitting the ground behind her forced her to take a split second glance away from the spear and to the fallen warrior at Puko's feet. "NO!" she screamed. "*No!*" She screamed in her head, *"I knew it! I knew it!"* She spun to check all sides, knowing she was out-numbered. Marco hadn't stirred. Tekalo and Trillip had been forced back to their knees, tree daemons surrounding them. Orska knelt nearby, hands up and out, empty; a gesture of surrender.

The tree daemon whom DJar had attacked now stood beside him. D'Mique recognized him as the one who'd broken the bargain once before. He and DJar whispered together and each tossed a glance in D'Mique's direction as her anger grew hotter. Tight lipped, DJar nodded and approached her where she stood between her fallen protectors. He gestured toward the tree daemon with the deadly spear trained on D'Mique's chest, and the long-haired daemon frowned but did not lower the spear or change her stance.

DJar looked at Puko and they spoke for a moment in the guttural tree daemon language. D'Mique worked to control her breathing. *"Again! How did we fall for this again!"* DJar then signaled to Puko and the pair moved past D'Mique to stand in front of Tekalo. D'Mique fought the urge to attack them from behind but the female tree daemon with the spear glared at her and she subsided, settling for exchanging venomous glares with the female tree daemon instead.

Puko translated for DJar when they reached the Land-Nymphs. "Tekalo," DJar greeted. Tekalo didn't respond. The irony of their juxtaposition was not lost on either of them and DJar found himself savoring the unpleasant look on the Land-Nymph's face. "Your freedom in exchange for mine. You may go." He gestured, "Take Marco with you. Tell Myrth," DJar paused. "Tell Myrth, I am honorable. Tell Palo, I will return." Then, to Orska, "You need to stay for the infant." He didn't bother explaining this, and Orska glared at him but said nothing and remained kneeling. DJar then contemplated Trillip. "I have been instructed to free you. Yet, I should take you back to Shirk's mate. She'd like to carve you up slowly, no doubt." He waited for Trillip to hiss at him as Puko translated the words. "Go with Tekalo, stay with the *Aliith-el*," he said, motioning to D'Mique, "as you choose."

"Where is T'Pani, D'Mique?" Trillip asked, catching her eye around the daemon-kin.

She shook her head, "I don't know, Trillip. No one knows. They were hoping to find her once I got here. But..." D'Mique motioned to Marco and Temeres.

"As I understand the plan, Land-Nymph," Puko said, "Once the child is found, she must be brought to him to fulfill the spell he botched," Puko pointed to Ordvyn.

"Hmph," Trillip smiled and it wasn't pretty. "Not so good at spells, Boss Man?" he asked the tree daemon. The second-in-command snarled at Trillip.

"Decide now," Puko translated for Trillip. DJar nodded at the Land-Nymphs, picked up the dagger from where he'd dropped it in his flight toward Ordvyn, and Rent the air. "The moblings will not enter the Sands," he said. Puko translated hastily as the *Shuwarr* spoke. "Leave before the Stasis field falters. It will fade quickly once we depart the Formation. This Rift will last only a few minutes without my magic to keep it open." He whistled sharply and the tree daemons flew into action, dousing the fire, collecting weapons and supplies and falling in—a company ready to march. Ordvyn used his glaive to make a second Rend in the air at the far corner of the Formation and they started to disappear through it. One of the larger Nura collected Orska as he went past and they fell in with the others.

Puko returned to D'Mique. "Come willingly, or I'll knock you out and carry you." The Gorath smiled wide, eyes flaring.

D'Mique looked around, frantic. She closed her eyes, screaming silently in her head. "I don't understand what has happened!" she snapped. "They're still bringing T'Pani here? But we're not staying here?" *"If I'm with Ordvyn, they can find T'Pani. He was supposed to stay here...Gods, what is going on?!"* She closed her eyes, shaking in anger. Then she opened her eyes and her gaze fell on Trillip.

The candy-haired Land-Nymph was angry, lost, uncertain. Tekalo was free but T'Pani would be coming back to the tree daemons. "If I go with them," D'Mique said, "the others can find T'Pani, and bring her to us." She swallowed around all the fear and anger she was feeling. She focused on that truth. "I do not want to be alone with the daemons." She held up a hand to Puko as he shifted toward her, "But I will go," she finished and sheathed her sword. Head bowed, she turned to fall in line with the others.

Indecision danced through Trillip for another moment as the Gorath followed D'Mique and the line of tree daemons. Trillip grasped Tekalo's hand and pulled him into a fierce hug. "If I go, I can reunite with T'Pani once she's here, I can help D'Mique," he whispered. "If I stay, I can help find T'Pani."

"We'll find T'Pani," Tekalo said. "I do not know what is going on but there's some sort of plan." He grasped Trillip by the shoulder.

"I promise you, we will find her. Come, we need to get Marco and Temeres through the tear."

Trillip shook his head, "No. I will see you again," he whispered, parting from Tekalo with a soft kiss on his cousin's cheek.

"What?" Tekalo gasped, startled.

Trillip turned to hurry after D'Mique before she disappeared through the Rend, leaving Tekalo alone with Marco and Temeres, who were just beginning to stir. He hurried to lift them and toss them out of the gateway, heaving Temeres out just as the Rend closed. There they lay in the center of a clearing, alone in the Vast Wildlands.

Epilogue

J eriko.

Oracle startled awake and knew he was still dreaming as he sat up in the Hisseth. "It's not possible to dream in the *Hisseth,*" he *thought. He sat a moment, contemplating what had awakened him and how he had come to be here.* "There'd been a voice," he *remembered.* "Voices did not happen in the *Hisseth.*" *He swallowed and looked around slowly. At the edge of his nerves he could feel it: that creeping unsettled sensation that started as a knot in his stomach and spread out to raise the hackles on his neck and back. He was being watched.* "Watching does not happen in the *Hisseth,*" *he chided himself.*

The Braiding Snakes slithered past him, the lines of people's lives traveling in small braids and large braids, clumped together as they touched the lives of others, always from the beginning of time to the end of time. As they moved, they hissed. "Hissed, but never spoke," *Oracle decided. He looked to the right, toward the setting suns and the end of time. It looked as it always did. The Braiding Snakes traveled onward into the darkness and unknowable futures. Out of habit, he glanced to the left, to the beginning of time. His heart leapt. There, just at the edge of his peripheral vision, he'd seen someone.*

Gasping, Oracle sat up in bed. His heart raced in his chest. There'd been someone else there! He closed his eyes, drifting. Forcing himself back to the dream to remember it as he'd done countless times before. But it was gone. The figure that he'd caught at the edge of his vision remained a fading ghostly suggestion. "And there'd been a voice, but what had it said?" he whispered to himself. Oracle opened his eyes and frowned in the dark. "I can't remember."

The End

About Sherrie A Bakelar

Once there was a little girl who loved stories. She loved to listen to them and she loved to tell them. She loved stories in all forms: art, games, written words, movies, television shows, music, and theater. Imagine her joy when she found out that it was possible for a person to grow up and spend their whole lives sharing stories! Sherrie lives in the Intermountain West with her family and friends, and a small menagerie of furry and scaly children.

Connect with Sherrie A Bakelar

Follow Sherrie A Bakelar on Twitter[1]
Find Sherrie A Bakelar on Facebook[2]
Your next read is waiting at Books2Read[3]!
A World Bible can be found on World Anvil[4]!

If you've enjoyed this book, or even if you haven't, please consider returning to the site where you purchased it and leaving a review. Reviews are the lifeblood of independent authors!

---

1. https://twitter.com/SBakelar

2. https://www.facebook.com/SherrieABakelar

3. https://books2read.com/ap/nOOKkO/Sherrie-Bakelar

4. https://www.worldanvil.com/w/the-lady-warrior-saga-sbakelar

Other Titles By Sherrie A Bakelar

G reat Danes Don't Hunt Werewolves
    Life is confusing enough when you're a teen in a new town and a new school. A person can find themselves lost and alone, navigating an alien world full of unusual customs and strange rituals, even when they're human. Being a werewolf? That makes everything so much harder. Now, finding yourself in love with a human? Well, that just takes the cake! Yet, life has a way of tripping you up. Sometimes love is the start of an unexpected adventure and you just know it will last forever and change your life for the better...and sometimes it's the beginning of the end and you'll never be the same again.

In My Time of Dying

When you're Called to help another, death can't stand in the way. Eloise Fontaine was always running off to save someone or something, and, with her death, Eloise' twin sister, Ebony Fontaine, inherited more than a pile of belongings, she inherited her sister's final mission. Reluctantly, Ebony agrees to see it through, before she too passes away.

Sneak Peek: Great Danes Don't Hunt Werewolves

It may come as a surprise to you but I was never a normal teenager. Well, not normal in the sense of the word that you are thinking of—being a werewolf puts a bit of a kibosh on the whole "normal" thing. Sometimes I'd watch the other teenage girls around me and try to mimic them, hoping that I could learn to be normal, just as I learned to read and write, but it never seemed to work. Their laughter twittered easily, while mine was forced. It seemed to me that they were always trying to be noticed. I tried my best to remain unnoticed.

Unnoticed was how you survived in my world, the one with teeth and claws and moonlight. In that world, being noticed by anyone was the last thing I wanted. Of course, being seen as some sort of macabre hero by the local human media was definitely not normal, and it definitely guaranteed I'd never go unnoticed again. Being the girl whose boyfriend had been killed, being the girl who'd tracked down a Monster, these facts made it impossible for me to blend into the background.

I'm getting ahead of myself. This story actually begins in an old farmhouse in the middle of nowhere.

The building had seen better days. Once a proud farmer owned all the land as far as you could see. After drilling into the Ogallala aquifer he planted acre after acre of wheat and, with his first year's profit, he built the two-story farmhouse. Then he sent for his wife and children. Together the family continued to farm the land, right through the twentieth century. However as the 1900s progressed, the world changed, leaving the farmer and his wheat fields behind. His children grew up and moved away to the cities, scattered in the prairie wind as sure as any other seed. As the shadows of age closed in around the farmer working the farm became too much. With only a few golden years remaining to he and his wife, the farmer sold the land surrounding his handmade house and went to Florida. Mechanized farm equipment owned by a faceless agribusiness continued to work the fields, but the house remained untouched, and unkempt, for nearly a decade.

That was how Mike and Andrea found it one October night in the early seventies. It was perfect—miles from any road, surrounded by fields. They did not care that the windows had long fallen out or that the roof leaked. Andrea pondered the crumpled lean-to for a moment, but Mike assured her that the main support structures of the house were still sound. Someone had used more than wood and nails to build it. They had added love. Andrea replied that corny lines like that were why she loved him.

Milia entered the world shortly after Mike and Andrea took up residence in the old farmhouse. For fifteen years the farmhouse was their home and it was perfect. There was no fear, no need to hide, even on the night of the full moon, when the Mistress called all her children to her. On those nights, the isolation of the farmhouse was perfection.

Most importantly, the farmhouse was home; it smelled of grass, wind, and old wood. Milia reveled in rolling around on the old floorboards, layering the smell of home over her black fur, legs flailing in the air above her. In the farmhouse, her mother laughed often—a big wolf grin and lolling tongue—while her father hunted field mice and other rodents, returning from the surrounding prairie empty-handed as often as not. The farmhouse, built with love, knew love once again.

Whenever Milia looked back on those halcyon days, grief welled up in her throat. She knew the beautiful days of childhood, aglow in nostalgia, always ended. "We have to go," her father whispered in her ear, holding tight to his wife as the three of them looked out through a broken window at the strange, foul-smelling objects that had suddenly appeared in front of the farmhouse. "Sunset," he croaked, fighting to keep his tears in check. A deep, drowning sadness roiled around her parents, coating the air with an acrid scent almost as gut wrenching as that wafting from the intrusive objects. Milia had never caught this scent from her parents before. There had been moments of disappointment, a cloying tang on the air. Usually it appeared on the fourth or fifth consecutive night with no food to eat, but sometimes that tangy sadness came tinged with something deeper, a longing more intense, that brought with it the smell of trees in the night. It was that last mingling scent that Milia learned early on to associate with the Pack. Her mother missed them. This deep level of despair was new to Milia, somewhere in the emotion that drifted through the air, she thought she caught a whiff of the Pack, but it was fleeting and overpowered by the sickening sadness her parents felt at the loss of their perfect farmhouse.

Don't miss out!

Visit the website below and you can sign up to receive emails whenever Sherrie A Bakelar publishes a new book. There's no charge and no obligation.

https://books2read.com/r/B-A-WJFX-JCHGC

BOOKS 2 READ

Connecting independent readers to independent writers.

Did you love *Honor Bound*? Then you should read *In My Time of Dying*[1] by Sherrie A Bakelar!

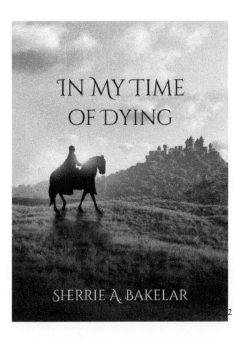

When Eloise Fontaine passed away from a heart attack, she left behind a pile of her belongings, a horse and her unfinished business. It now falls to her twin sister, Ebony, to fulfill Eloise' final Calling, Find the Farm Boy and save the kingdom, before Ebony passes away herself. Goaded on by her sister's ghost, Ebony sets out from her humble cottage to find the Farm Boy and help in his quest to regain his kingdom, usurped decades before by the Wizard King.

Read more at https://artist.sbakelar.com/.

---

1. https://books2read.com/u/3LV5B1

2. https://books2read.com/u/3LV5B1

Milton Keynes UK
Ingram Content Group UK Ltd.
UKHW011820131023
430526UK00001B/51